JANICE MAYNARD

SLOW BURN

HARLEQUIN

DESIRE

This book is dedicated to my wonderful readers.

2020 hasn't been the year we all envisioned for ourselves.
In the midst of uncertainty and change, I am so grateful for your
love of books, and I'm thankful that we take this journey together!

Special thanks and acknowledgment are given to
Janice Maynard for her contribution to the
Dynasties: Seven Sins miniseries.

HARLEQUIN®
DESIRE™

Recycling programs
for this product may
not exist in your area.

ISBN-13: 978-1-335-20945-0

Slow Burn

Copyright © 2020 by Harlequin Books S.A.

This edition published by arrangement with Harlequin Books S.A.

For questions and comments about the quality of this book,
please contact us at CustomerService@Harlequin.com.

Harlequin Enterprises ULC
22 Adelaide St. West, 40th Floor
Toronto, Ontario M5H 4E3, Canada
www.Harlequin.com

Printed in U.S.A.

Dear Reader,

I'm a sucker for stories where the hero and heroine knew each other as teenagers and then meet up again later. Sharing a past, whether painful or idyllic, gives a couple common ground, no matter how far their lives have drifted apart.

In the Seven Sins series, we have seen how one huge, painful event can be a turning point that leaves ripples in the lives of a wide circle of people.

We're all defined by our pasts to one degree or another. Some of us had great childhoods, some not so much. I hope you, like every Harlequin Desire heroine, will recognize your strengths and chase your dreams, no matter what!

Keep on keeping on!

Janice Maynard

Books by Janice Maynard

Harlequin Desire

Southern Secrets

Blame It on Christmas
A Contract Seduction
Bombshell for the Black Sheep

Dynasties: Seven Sins

Slow Burn

The Men of Stone River

After Hours Seduction
Upstairs Downstairs Temptation
Secrets of a Playboy

One

Jake Lowell had circumnavigated the globe more than once in the last fifteen years. He'd traveled everywhere and seen everything. Well, except for Antarctica. That continent was still on his bucket list. But of all the cities and countries he'd visited and/or put down temporary roots, the one place he *absolutely* thought he'd never return to again was Falling Brook, New Jersey.

The town's name was idyllic. Jake's memories weren't.

He'd left his birthplace at twenty-two, in the midst of scandal and tragedy. And he'd never returned. Until today. Under duress.

When his stomach growled for the third time, he pulled into a gas station and topped off his tank. The credit-card machine on the pump was out of paper, so he wandered inside for his receipt and to grab a very late lunch. In the end, he decided a candy bar would do for now. He'd always had a sweet tooth.

As he paid for his purchases, the stack of newspapers near the checkout stand caught his eye. The usual suspects were there. *New York Times. Wall Street Journal.* But it was the small-town paper that gave him heartburn. The headline screamed, "Vernon Lowell Lives! Black Crescent Fugitive Located in Remote Caribbean Location."

Jake's stomach churned. The story had broken over a week ago, but the local news outlets were milking it daily. He'd had time to get used to the incredibly upsetting news, but he was still in shock. For a decade and a half, he had known his father was gone. Probably living it up in the bowels of hell. Now the dead had come to life.

When the cashier handed Jake his receipt, she gave him a curious look. Too late for him to realize he should have paid cash. Would the woman see the name on his card and put two and two together? Was she part of the always speedy Falling Brook grapevine?

The name *Lowell* wasn't all that unusual, but here in Falling Brook it was radioactive. Fifteen years ago, Jake's father, Vernon Lowell, had absconded with an enormous sum of money—the assets belonging to some of Falling Brook's most high-profile citizens. A dozen or more elite clients had entrusted Black Crescent Hedge Fund with their fortunes and their futures. Vernon, along with his CFO and best friend, Everett Reardon, were financial wizards who founded Black Crescent and made piles of cash for everyone involved.

But, inexplicably, something went very wrong. The money evaporated. Everett Reardon was killed in a car crash while fleeing police. And Jake's father disappeared from the face of the earth, presumably dead.

The living were left to clean up the mess. And what a mess it was.

Jake drove aimlessly, tormented by the memories even now.

Falling Brook was a small enclave, still not much more than two thousand residents. Jake had done his due diligence before returning home. He'd waded through enough online research to know that not much had changed. This town with the rarefied air and high-dollar real estate still protected the famous from the outside world.

For a few moments, Jake parked across the street from Nikki Reardon's old house—a mansion, really—letting the engine idle. Nikki's world, like Jake's, had been destroyed by her father's misdeeds. Fifteen years ago she'd fled town with her mother, their lives also in ruins.

When Jake allowed himself to remember Nikki, he experienced the strangest mix of yearning and uneasiness. Because his father and Nikki's had been business partners and best friends, it was inevitable that the two families spent a considerable amount of time together while Jake was growing up. But what he remembered most about Nikki was his one wild night with her in Atlantic City five years ago.

Though she was four years younger than he was, she had always been mature for her age. Eons ago, she had been his first real girlfriend. Despite all that, the alluring woman he'd hooked up with in a brief, unexpected, passionate reunion in a casino hotel was far different from the redheaded, pale-skinned beauty he had known as a very young man.

That new Nikki had dazzled him. And scared him.

Muttering under his breath, Jake made himself set the car in motion. Nikki's ghost might still wander the halls of that glamorous house, but she was long gone.

His immediate destination was a small boutique hotel known for its discreetness and luxury. Jake needed the first and would enjoy the second. Though he possessed the skills to live off the land, these days he much preferred a comfortable bed at the end of the day.

Once he checked into his spacious, beautifully appointed room, he sat on the edge of the mattress and stared at his phone. He needed to let Joshua know he had arrived. Joshua Lowell. Jake's brother, his twin. The only characteristics they shared were dirty blond hair, their six-foot-two-inch height and eyes that were a mix of hazel and green.

When Josh had called to say their father had been found, Josh asked Jake to come back to Falling Brook, and had invited him to stay in his home. But the invitation was obviously issued out of duty. The brothers hadn't been face-to-face in fifteen years. Other than the occasional stilted text or email on birthdays and Christmases, or the very recent phone call, they might as well have been strangers.

Over the years, Jake had made himself hard to track down. On purpose. He had cut ties with his siblings, and now he knew little of their personal lives. When he was twenty-two, he hadn't fully understood that family was family, no matter what. He also hadn't realized that being a footloose, rolling stone would eventually lose its appeal.

Now that he was a seasoned man of thirty-seven, he was hoping to mend fences, especially since Joshua wanted Jake's input on the CEO search at Black Crescent. It felt good to be consulted.

Joshua had agreed to meet in the hotel restaurant at seven. The entire place was dark and intimate, but even so, Jake offered the hostess a fifty to seat him and his prospective dinner date at an inconspicuous table. If anyone saw two of the three Lowell brothers together again, tongues would wag.

Jake hated the paparazzi. In the aftermath of his father's disappearance, reporters had hounded every member of the Lowell and Reardon families. In fact, *any* family connected to the scandal was targeted. Jake, a newly minted university grad at the time, had already been planning to backpack around Europe, so he simply moved up his timetable and fled.

Josh—good old dependable Josh—had been left to clean up the mess. The guilt from that one decision hounded Jake to this day. His brother had rebuilt Black Crescent bit by agonizing bit. Joshua had stayed the course, faced the accusers and cooperated with the police. Despite having incredible artistic talent, he had put his dreams on hold and tried to make up for their father's despicable deeds.

Jake had done nothing but pursue a selfish agenda.

Sometimes, the truth sucked.

When Joshua arrived, Jake leaped to his feet and hugged his brother awkwardly, feeling a tsunami of emotional baggage threaten to pull him under. "Long time no see." He winced inwardly at what must have sounded like a flippant comment at best.

The two men sat, and a hovering sommelier poured two glasses of a rare burgundy that Jake remembered his brother enjoying. Although, who knew? Fifteen years was a long time. Tastes changed.

Josh downed half the glass, leaned back in his chair and managed a small smile. It seemed genuine enough. "You look good, Jake."

"So do you."

A few seconds of silence ticked by.

"This is weird." Joshua raked a hand through his hair. He wore an expensive sport coat, dress pants and a crimson necktie. Jake, in jeans and a rugby shirt, felt scruffy in comparison. But that had always been the difference between them. Josh dressed the part of a wealthy man. Jake preferred to be unfettered by society's dictates.

He straightened his spine as tension tightened his jaw. "Here's the thing," he said abruptly. "I might as well get this off my chest. I'm sorry, Josh. I'm sorry Dad screwed us over, and I'm sorry I let you do the heavy lifting. I abandoned you. But I'm here now. For what it's worth."

His brother's smile was strained. Born first by three minutes, Josh had often taken the role of "older" brother seriously. He sighed, the sound a mix of resignation and something else. "I quit being mad at you a long time ago, Jake. We all choose our own path in life. Nobody made me stay and sort through Dad's screwups."

"But we both thought he was dead." It was true. Their mother, Eve, had hired private detectives fifteen years ago. The feds had searched for months. No sign of Vernon Lowell anywhere.

Joshua's gaze was bleak. "It would have been easier if he *was* dead, wouldn't it?"

The harsh truth hung between them. Jake's stomach clenched. Authorities had recently located Vernon Lowell on a remote Bahamian island and extradited him to the United States. Currently, the patriarch was languishing in federal custody. And he wanted to see his two oldest sons.

Oliver, their younger brother, had made the pilgrimage recently. It hadn't gone well.

"We have to go, don't we?" Jake said.

Josh shrugged. "He can't make us."

"On the other hand, telling him to go to hell might give us closure."

His brother's lips twitched. "You have a valid point."

"I guess these last six months haven't been easy for you after that damn reporter wrote an anniversary piece about the Black Crescent debacle. I didn't see it until recently."

Joshua's smile broadened. "Actually, I have no complaints. I'm now *engaged* to that damn reporter."

Jake's jaw dropped. "Seriously? Why didn't you tell me that when you called?"

"You and I hadn't spoken in forever. I wanted to give you the news in person. We're planning a wedding very soon. Sophie is great. You'll like her. And you might as well know, she's the one who encouraged me to resurrect my art career. That's why I'm giving up the helm of Black Crescent."

"That explains the CEO search. I was wondering why now." If anybody deserved to follow his dreams, it was Josh. "I'm happy for you. What will happen to the company, though?"

Joshua didn't answer immediately, because a waiter dropped off their appetizers. A few moments later, Josh drummed his fingers on the table, his unease palpable. "You've played the part of a dilettante well over the years. No one realized you were a financial wunderkind." Joshua's smile was wry.

Jake tried not to squirm. "Why would you say that?"

"I've been doing some digging, baby brother. You're an uncannily successful day trader. Probably richer than I am. At the risk of insulting you, I'd say you've inherited some of Dad's business savvy. But not his morals," Josh said hastily.

Jake told himself not to overreact. "I've had some

success," he said mildly. "And I'm *not* your baby brother."

Joshua stared at him, gaze clear, jaw firm. "I want you to take over Black Crescent."

What? "Oh, no," Jake said. "Oh, *hell* no." His hand fisted on the table. "Surely, you have other possibilities."

"We do, actually. I've been interviewing candidates for some time now. But I don't know that any of them are exactly right."

"Well, you're dead *wrong* if you think I'm the man."

"Maybe." Joshua's expression was hard to read.

"What about Oliver? I'm guessing he doesn't want to give up his photography?" The youngest Lowell brother had been affected deeply by their father's betrayal, perhaps even more than Josh and Jake. His anger and despair had led him into addiction. Fortunately, he'd been clean for a very long time now.

"Oliver is finally in a good place. Finding out Dad is alive has been hard for him. He's dealing with a lot of the old anger. But he's handling it well."

Eventually, the meal came to an end and Joshua insisted on picking up the tab. A nice gesture, but unnecessary. Awkwardness returned.

Joshua frowned as he slid his credit card back into his billfold. "I need to talk to you about something important," he said. "Something I didn't want to say over the phone. But not here."

"More important than the fact our father has returned from the dead?"

Jake expected at least a smile for his snarky question. But Joshua was serious. "Perhaps. How 'bout we walk while we talk?"

With his mind spinning, Jake followed his brother through the restaurant and outside onto the sidewalk. The air was crisp, though not unpleasant. It was early November. A few businesses had already begun to decorate for the holidays, getting a jump on the busiest season of the year.

For fifteen Decembers, Christmas had been a painful season for Jake, presumably for the rest of his family, too. It was a reminder of all he had lost. The memories of happy times with the Lowell family of five gathered around the tree had faded beyond repair. In the golden years of Jake's childhood, there had been spectacular gifts: ponies, guitars, racing bikes. Everything a kid could want.

And then it was all gone. Even worse, other families, innocent families, had been hurt. Jake and his siblings and his mother had been innocent, too, but no one had wanted to believe that. They were vilified, scorned. Hated.

Jake hunched his shoulders in his jacket and matched his brother's stride as they set off down the street. He didn't want to think about the bad times, but the memories clung to him like cobwebs. There was no peace to be had in Falling Brook.

Even so, it felt good to get some exercise. For three blocks, Joshua didn't say a word. Jake tried to wait him out, but his patience evaporated quickly. "Why are you being so mysterious?"

Joshua halted suddenly, beneath the soft illumination of a streetlight. "I don't know how to tell you this."

"What? Am I dying?"

"This isn't funny."

"How am I supposed to know that? You haven't said anything yet."

Josh leaned against the light pole, his features betraying tension and exhaustion. For a man in love, he didn't look all that carefree.

He shrugged. "When that article came out back in the spring, the story omitted one very big bombshell."

"Oh?" Jake shoved his hands in his pockets, trying not to react to the gravity in his brother's voice.

"Sophie had DNA evidence proving that I had fathered a child."

"Hell, Joshua. Why didn't you tell me?"

"At first, she wouldn't reveal her source, but when she and I got closer, she finally admitted that Zane Patterson had given her the DNA analysis."

Jake was more than shocked—he was suspicious. "Zane Patterson from prep school? He was a year behind Oliver, right? What would he have to do with any of this?"

"Zane received the report from an anonymous source. He was still angry about everything his family lost when Dad disappeared with the money. So Zane saw this as a chance to stick it to me and Black Crescent. Only Sophie decided not to include Zane's info in the article."

"But surely, you've had time to prove it's a hoax. That's been, what? Six months ago? It's bogus, right?"

Joshua shook his head slowly, his jaw tight. "The report wasn't fabricated. It was the real deal. Somewhere out there is a four-year-old girl who shares my DNA. So I discreetly began investigating any woman from my past who might have matched the timing of this pregnancy. The list wasn't that big. I came up with nothing."

"So it *is* a fake report then." Jake was starting to feel as if he had walked into an alternate universe. Joshua wasn't making sense.

His twin straightened, giving Jake a look that made his stomach clench and his skin crawl with an atavistic recognition of danger.

Joshua's expression finally softened, revealing the oddest mix of sympathy and determination. "The report is legit, Jake. But I'm not the kid's father. You are."

Nikki Reardon glanced at her watch. In half an hour she would have to pick up her daughter, Emma, from Mom's Day Out at a local church in their tiny town of Poplar Ridge, New Jersey. Emma loved her twice-a-week preschool and had made several sweet friends.

The classes had also given Nikki some valuable alone time. Between her job as assistant manager at the diner four days a week, caring for her daughter and dealing with her mother's needs, it was hard not to feel stretched thin. When Nikki worked the overnight shift, her mother came and stayed.

It wasn't the best arrangement in the world, but it sufficed for now. Sometimes Nikki felt guilty about using her mother for a babysitter so much of the time, but she also believed that being with Emma gave her mom a healthy focus in a life that was empty.

Nikki's attention returned to her iPad, where she was reading a story that brought up too many bad memories. A few days ago she'd discovered that Vernon Lowell wasn't dead. Today's front-page article claimed he'd been found hiding out in the Bahamas. After a speedy extradition, Vernon now waited in federal custody for his trial.

She wanted to talk to him. He was the only person who knew the truth. Vernon and her father, Everett, had been best friends and business partners. But her father was dead. She had seen the body, suffered through the funeral. The world thought Vernon was dead, as well. But now he was back.

Thinking about the Black Crescent scandal inevitably made her think of Jake. Beautiful, stubborn, wandering Jake. Her first boyfriend. She understood why he left. Reporters had made his life miserable. She had only seen him once in the intervening years.

It had been both the best and worst night of her life.

A loud knock at the door demanded her attention. Sometimes the UPS guy did that. But this knock sounded more peremptory than a package delivery.

Cautiously, she peered through a crack in the inexpensive drapes. *Dear God.* It was Jake. In the flesh.

Why was he here? His family still lived in Falling Brook, but that was over an hour away. Why had he come? Her secret threatened to choke her with anxiety.

She opened the door slowly, trying to project mild curiosity even though her heart nearly beat out of her chest. "Jake," she said. "What a surprise."

His greenish-hazel eyes bored into her. "Is it true?"

Her brain processed a million reasons why he might be on her doorstep. "Is what true? Why don't you come in and have something to drink?"

As she stepped back and opened the door wider, Jake entered her small living room and paced, his furious gaze cataloging and dismissing the contents of her modest home. "I want to know why you sent Zane Patterson anonymous information claiming Joshua was the father of your baby."

All the blood drained from her head, and she forgot about offering Jake a cup of coffee. She sat down hard on the sofa. "My baby?" She hated the quavering tone in her voice. She had done nothing wrong.

"Don't give me that." Jake shook his head, scowling. "I know it's true. What did you hope to gain by blackmailing my brother?"

Nikki straightened her spine and glared. "If you want to sit down and discuss this civilly, I'll listen. But you're way off base. I've never had any contact with your brother or Zane, not since we were teenagers. I don't know what you're talking about."

At last, Jake plopped down in a chair and drummed his fingers on the arms. His whole body radiated strong emotion. As she tried to catch her breath, she absorbed the look of him. He was a beautiful man. Always had been. Today he wore a scuffed leather bomber jacket and jeans so old and faded they molded to his legs, and other parts, as if they had been made just for him. His soft cotton button-down shirt was pale green, the color of vintage glass bottles. Deck shoes with no socks exposed his tanned ankles.

He was tanned all over, in fact. The man had spent his life outdoors. Or much of it. His streaky blond hair needed a cut. In the summers when they were kids, the sun would bleach Jake's hair gold. Now it was more subdued.

She glanced at her watch, trying not to panic. Did he know the truth about Emma, or was he fishing? She wouldn't lie about her daughter, but she wasn't going to volunteer any unnecessary information at this point. "I have an errand to run," she said calmly. "This will have to wait."

His jaw tightened. "Then I'm coming with you."

Her stomach clenched. Having him close made her senses go haywire. Why was it so hard to be sensible when Jake Lowell was around? "It won't take me long. I could meet you for dinner later."

"I'm not letting you out of my sight, Nikki Reardon." His gaze was grim. Implacable. As if he was the hunter, and she was the prey.

"Fine," she said. She stood and retrieved her purse and keys. She had no idea what he would think when he saw Emma, but she would put one foot in front of the other until she figured it out. Her mother had pressed her to contact Jake and ask for child support, but Nikki had been too proud to beg. When Jake walked away from her five years ago without a word, she had known he was still running from his past. And that he was never going to be the man she needed him to be.

Outside, she grimaced when she saw his fancy black sports car, a rental no doubt, parked at the curb. The sleek vehicle looked wildly out of place on this middle-class street. Her own mode of transportation was a fifteen-year-old compact model with a car seat in the back.

She unlocked her car and watched as Jake folded his body into the passenger seat. He was a couple of inches over six feet, so he was not going to be entirely comfortable.

Good.

"Where are we going?" he asked.

"I have to pick up Emma from preschool."

"Emma?" The word sounded strangled.

She shot him a sideways glance, noting his sudden pallor.

"Yes. Emma. My daughter."

Two

Jake watched through the windshield as the gorgeous redhead and the bouncy little girl walked toward the car. He felt queasy. A host of other emotions swirled in his chest.

The brief ride from Nikki's house to this pleasantly ordinary brick building had been silent. Nikki's knuckles were white as she gripped the steering wheel.

Now he tried to study her dispassionately. In the midst of his clinical visual survey, the memories hit him hard and fast. Nikki naked. Sprawled across his hotel bed. Smiling. Warm and sated from their love-making. Her pale, pale skin like porcelain.

It had been one night. One extraordinary night almost five years ago. And now he was a father? Why hadn't Nikki told him? Or was this all just a misunderstanding? Even as he tried to rationalize her behavior, he couldn't get past the anonymous emails that were eventually passed on to his brother.

Despite Joshua's insistence that a baby existed with Lowell blood, Jake was by nature a suspicious man. Being betrayed by his father had taught him not to trust easily.

The rear car door opened, and Nikki helped the child into her car seat. Though Emma had been chattering excitedly, she fell silent when she spotted the stranger up front. Her eyes were green. That meant nothing. The color could have been from her mother as easily as from Jake's DNA. But the girl's blond hair was nothing like her mother's.

Jake wanted to say hello. The word stuck in his throat. Instead, he gave the kid a quick nod and turned back toward the front. He wanted to stare at Emma. To examine her from head to toe. To see if there was anything of him in her. But he didn't want to make the child uncomfortable. No point in both of them feeling weird.

Back at Nikki's house, Nikki lowered her voice as she parked the car. "I usually give her a snack, and then she'll go play in her room for half an hour or so. You and I can talk then."

Jake nodded brusquely, not entirely sure what he wanted to say. Crazy revelations were popping up in his life like rodents in an upsetting game of whack-a-mole. His father was alive. Nikki had a kid. The child was Jake's? It was too much to process.

He shoved his hands in his pockets as the unlikely

threesome walked across the lawn into the house. Once inside, Jake escaped into the small living room with a muttered excuse. Even at this distance, he could hear mother and daughter in the kitchen debriefing Emma's day at school. When Nikki finally returned, she looked tired, but resigned.

She took a chair across from him and gracefully curled her legs beneath her. Her steady green-eyed gaze and long, wavy red hair made him clench his fists as an unwelcome wave of desire swept through him. He remembered burying his face in that hair. Inhaling the scent of her shampoo. Feeling for a brief moment in time as if everything in his world had finally popped into sharp focus.

In his early twenties, he had loved her with a ferocity that was equal parts lust and devotion. He'd been waiting for her to grow up. His nightly fantasies had featured Nikki, and no one else. But just when his desire had almost come to fruition, both of their worlds had been torn apart.

Running into each other in Atlantic City a decade later had been a shock to his system. The very best kind of shock. Even now, his hands tingled with the need to touch her. But, in the end, he had been wary of the new Nikki, unable to handle how *together* she was, how grown up. She hadn't been a frightened teenager anymore. She had moved on. And she knew exactly who she was.

The new Nikki had been even more appealing than the girl he remembered. But the changes spooked him, as did the depth of his feelings, so he ran. The same way he had so many times before.

He cleared his throat. "I'll ask you again. Is it true? Is Emma my daughter?"

Nikki paled, making her skin almost translucent. "You weren't making sense earlier. I don't know why you're here. What does your brother have to do with this?"

"Don't be coy, Nikki. You sent Zane DNA results and notes that threatened Joshua. But Josh eventually concluded that he couldn't possibly have fathered a four-year-old child. So that left me. His twin. Why did you try to blackmail my brother and not me?"

As he watched, Nikki's lower lip trembled, and her eyes glistened with tears. "I have no clue what you're talking about, and I don't appreciate your accusations. If that's all you have to say, Jake Lowell, you can get the hell out of my house."

A tiny voice intruded. "You told me not to say that word, Mommy."

Both adults jumped. Emma stood in the doorway, visibly distressed.

Nikki swiped a hand across her face, drying her eyes. "You're right, baby. Mommy goofed. I'm sorry."

Jake left his seat and crouched beside Nikki's daughter. "Hi, Emma. I'm Jake…a friend of your mother's."

Emma stared at him solemnly, her gaze filled with suspicion. "Then why did she tell you to leave?"

The irony didn't escape Jake. Were all four-year-old kids this aware of social cues? He cleared his throat. "We were having an argu—"

Nikki stood abruptly, halting his explanation with a chopping motion of her hand. She ruffled her daughter's hair. "Em, would you like to watch a *Peppa Pig* episode on my phone?" Nikki gave him an exasperated look. "I don't allow her much screen time, but it would give us a chance to finish this conversation."

Emma's face lit up. She smiled at Jake, distracted by the promised treat. "They're called 'Peppasodes.' Get it?"

Jake grinned for the first time, his mood lifting despite the situation. The child's charm and obvious intelligence delighted him. "I get it, munchkin."

He stood and gave Nikki a measured glance, trying not to notice the way her soft, fuzzy sweater delineated her breasts. He wanted to hold her, to relearn the contours of her body. The sexual awareness threatened his focus. "I have another idea. If you can get a babysitter on such short notice, I'll take you to dinner."

Now Nikki's face showed no emotion at all. Her gaze was level, and her arms wrapped around her waist in a defensive posture. After a couple of heartbeats, she took her phone from her pocket, tapped a few icons and handed it to Emma. "You may take it to your room, sweetheart. Fifteen minutes. No more. I set the timer."

When Emma was gone, Nikki sighed. "The truth is, Jake, I can't afford a babysitter right now. The holidays are coming, and I'm saving every penny for Emma's gifts from me and from Santa. Can't we just wrap this up? I honestly have no clue what you're talking about. I've never been in contact with your brother about *anything*."

Jake pulled a sheet of paper from his pocket. Earlier, Joshua had printed out one of the incriminating emails. "So you deny sending this?"

Their fingers brushed when Nikki took the note. She glanced down, read the contents and moaned. If she had been pale before, she was ashen now. "Oh, my God."

Her obvious distress convinced Jake she was telling the truth. But that only deepened the mystery. "Let me pay for a sitter," he said urgently. "We need to clear the air." He pulled a business card from his wallet and gave it to her. "This is my cell number. I'll grab coffee somewhere and return a few phone calls. Let me know when you work it out. I can pick you up at seven."

She shook her head vehemently. "No. If we do this, I want to be back home to do the bed-and-bath routine with Emma. We would have to eat early. Five thirty."

He blinked. "Ah. Okay. Call me."

That beautiful bottom lip trembled again. "I'll see what I can do," she whispered.

He was incredulous to realize that he was aroused, hard and ready. It had been five years since he had made love to her, but it might as well have been yesterday. It was difficult to cast Nikki as the villain when he wanted her even now. Was he so besotted that he could ignore her lies?

Her anguish touched him despite the turmoil she had caused his family. He brushed her soft cheek with a single fingertip. "It's not the end of the world, Nik. But I do want answers. Don't try an end run. I'm not leaving town until you and I get a few things straight."

Once Jake said goodbye, Nikki made the necessary phone call and fretted. She knew a threat when she heard one. Even if it *was* couched in seeming cordiality. Jake was not a man who bluffed.

She remembered watching him play poker with other guys in high school—*after* class mostly, but whenever they could elude faculty detection. All the parties involved had been highly privileged teenagers with virtually unlimited resources.

Jake had taken bragging rights as top dog, and he loved it. People *thought* he bluffed…and would bet against him time and again. But his lazy, chilled attitude concealed an amazing skill with numbers.

Was that why he had been in Atlantic City? To gamble? If so, he would have won. She knew that much.

But gambling had been the last thing on his mind the night the two of them had gone up to his hotel room. When a hot shiver worked its way down her spine, she knew she was in trouble.

Reluctantly, she dragged her attention back to the present. Emma was bouncing with glee that her favorite babysitter was coming over. Nella was a college-aged woman who lived just down the street. She had five brothers and sisters and was no stranger to caring for little ones. Nella adored Emma and the feeling was mutual, so Nikki was free to have dinner with Jake.

Despite the gravity of the situation, she couldn't squelch a little flutter of anticipation. As she showered and changed, she vacillated between fear and excitement.

She had known this day would come eventually. But not like this.

Since giving birth four years ago, her social life had been mostly nonexistent. The only remotely suitable outfit she owned for having dinner with Jake Lowell was a sophisticated black pantsuit that she paired with an emerald silk chemise and spiky black heels. She left her hair down and added a spritz of her favorite perfume. She probably shouldn't be dressing up at all, but maybe deep down inside she wanted Jake to see what he was missing.

The scent was for *her* benefit, not his. She needed a confidence boost.

He arrived at five thirty on the dot. Nikki didn't give him a chance to come inside. She hurried out to the car, almost tripping on the sidewalk in her haste to keep him from seeing Emma again. She would protect her baby girl at all costs.

Jake hopped out and opened the passenger door of the sinfully luxurious roadster he was driving while in New Jersey. When he helped Nikki in with a hand under her elbow, she was wrapped in the smells of soft leather and warm male.

She was glad when Jake closed the door and went around to the driver's side, though it wasn't much of a reprieve. The car's interior was intimate. With every breath, she inhaled him. Not that his aftershave was overpowering. In fact, she wasn't sure he wore any. She might only be smelling soap on his skin.

Either way, she was susceptible to his considerable appeal.

"Why did you change clothes?" she asked. He now wore a conservative dark suit, though most restaurants seldom enforced any kind of dress code these days.

He shot her a cautious grin. "Because I knew you would look nice. You always did enjoy sprucing up for an evening out."

What could she say? He was right about the old Nicole Reardon. That teenager had owned two closets full of designer clothes. Nikki had lived in a pampered world that seemed a lifetime away.

Intentionally, she drew his attention to the night that had gone so well and ended so badly. "Things are different now. In Atlantic City I was wearing a cocktail waitress uniform when I ran in to you. Not exactly haute couture."

He shrugged, his sideways glance filled with dark male interest. "I can't say that I noticed. I was more interested in getting you out of *whatever* you were wearing."

That shut her up. He was right. They had both been intent on one thing. The results had been spectacular.

Tonight, Jake had made reservations at an upscale seafood restaurant with white linen tablecloths and plenty of candlelight. The ambiance made Nikki the slightest bit uncomfortable. She and Jake weren't a typical couple. And they certainly weren't celebrating anything.

Once they were seated at a table overlooking a small manmade lake, Jake gave her his undivided attention. But his face was hard to read. "Thank you for coming. I know this was last-minute."

"My sitter was available. It worked out."

"Good."

The conversation was painfully stilted. Memories of the last time they had been together swirled beneath the words. "Do you think about Atlantic City?" she asked quietly.

His jaw tightened. "Don't be coy, Nik. Of course I do. We hadn't seen each other in a decade, and there you were. Wearing one of those provocative outfits. Your legs were about a million miles long."

The flash of heat in his eyes told her he remembered *everything*. She hadn't been sure until right now. For her, the night had been a watershed moment, the culmination of all her girlish fantasies. But Jake was a man of the world. She had assumed their tryst was another notch on his bedpost.

"It seemed to embarrass you," she said hesitantly. "That I was working as a waitress in a casino. You acted very odd at first."

He nodded slowly. "I was startled. I'll admit it. I went to Atlantic City for some fun. Just a quick flight in and out. Seeing you was a punch to the gut. The girl I used to date was wealthy and pampered. I was aware that you and your mom lost everything. But witnessing the personal cost of your father's deceit stunned me. I didn't know what to do with that information or how to relate to you."

Nikki shrugged and snagged a fat boiled shrimp from the appetizer plate. "You don't have to feel sorry for me, Jake. No one *wants* to be poor, but the rapid fall in my social position taught me a lot."

"Like what?"

He seemed genuinely interested.

"Well…" She paused, thinking back. "I learned there are many very nice people in the world. And a few jerks, of course. I learned how hard a person has to work to earn five hundred dollars a week after taxes. I learned how scary it is not to have a safety net."

His gaze darkened. "Those are some damn serious lessons."

"Maybe. But I also learned my own resilience. I discovered that although I had been a pampered princess, it felt good to be responsible for myself… To know I was stronger than I knew."

Their meals arrived, momentarily interrupting her self-analysis. Despite the gravity of this encounter with Jake, she spared a moment to appreciate the quality of the food. Her scallops were plump and perfectly grilled. She enjoyed every bite. Jake would probably be astounded if he knew how many nights she shared boxed macaroni and cheese with her daughter.

Over coffee and dessert, Jake pressed for more. "When I showed you that email, you were clearly shocked. No one is that good an actress. So, if you didn't send it, who did?"

Nikki's cheeks heated with embarrassment. "Possibly my mother."

"Why?"

"About a year ago I lost my job. I was unemployed for almost ten weeks. Money was tight. Mom kept pressing me to ask for child support from Emma's father. I put her off and put her off, but she wouldn't let it go. Finally, after she had badgered me incessantly, I told her that Joshua was the father. Your brother. That he and I weren't ever a couple, but we had been intimate for a brief period. I said he didn't know about the baby. I thought that would be the end of it."

"But it wasn't."

"Obviously not."

"Why would you lie to her?"

"Because I didn't want her to know the truth."

"And that was?"

Nikki inhaled sharply. "That *you* are Emma's father."

Jake had heard the truth from his own brother. He'd had a little time to get used to the idea. But in this moment, he realized it had all seemed like a remarkable fiction until Nikki told him straight out. He felt sick and angry and everything in between.

"Damn you, Nikki. How could you not tell me I had a child?"

If he'd been expecting her to look guilty, he was way off base.

His dinner companion stared at him with cool hauteur reminiscent of the old society princess she'd been. "A little while ago you told me you still remember our night in Atlantic City. If you'll recall, you disappeared afterward. I woke up in your hotel room *alone*. The only thing missing from that scenario was a stack of hundreds on the nightstand to make me feel like a hooker you hired for the evening."

"I had a very early flight," he muttered, guilt making him ashamed. He'd acknowledged to himself at the time that he was behaving badly, but he hadn't known how to deal with the all-grown-up Nikki, so he had left her sleeping, her vibrant red hair spread across his pillow. The provocative image had almost been enough to make him stay and miss his flight.

But he had left her, anyway.

Nikki shrugged. "It doesn't matter. That night was a long time ago. I've moved on, believe me."

Something struck him. "We used protection," he said, feeling suspicion creep back in. How could he trust her? Did he know her at all after fifteen years? If he was really the father, why the secrecy?

"Not every time." She stared him down. "It doesn't matter if you believe me or not. Emma is the result of our reckless reunion. You and I were both curious, weren't we? And blindsided by sexual attraction. A decade before that night in the casino, we had been on the verge of a physical relationship. But then your father and mine destroyed everything. I suppose Atlantic City was closure, in a way. We came full circle."

They finished their meal in silence, the mountain

of regrets and what-ifs too tall to climb. Jake was achingly aware of Nikki's beauty, her poise, her intense femininity.

When Nikki was almost eighteen, Jake had fled Falling Brook never to return. Even then, he had understood what he was giving up, but his father's actions had made staying impossible. The closest Jake had come to Falling Brook in the intervening years was a visit to Atlantic City five years ago. Running into Nikki had knocked him off balance. The long-ago feelings, the yearning and the need for her, had come roaring back to life.

He and Nikki had reminisced. When Nikki finished her shift, she went to his room at his invitation. They had showered together, tumbled into bed and screwed each other until dawn. Even now, the memories made him hard.

He cleared his throat. "I'm sorry I left without saying goodbye."

She grimaced. "You're forgiven." Her gaze was filled with something he couldn't decipher. "It would have been a very awkward morning after if you had stayed," she said.

"And then you found out you were pregnant. That must have been a shock."

Her face flushed. She nodded slowly. "You have no idea. Telling my mother was hard. After Daddy died in the car crash, she imploded emotionally. Our roles reversed. She has helped me enormously with Emma, of course, but Mom leans on me."

"It makes sense. She lost her whole world and way

of life. Except for her daughter." He paused, swallowing hard. "You and I didn't do much talking that night in Atlantic City. What happened to you after you left Falling Brook? Before I met up with you again?"

"Nothing earth-shattering. I made it through four years at a state school. Got my degree. Mom and I worked multiple jobs to cover tuition and to handle our living expenses."

He had a gut feeling there was more to the story. So he pushed.

"And after you finished school? I count at least five or six missing years until I ran into you in Atlantic City."

"I got married."

"Married?" He parroted the word, feeling like somebody had punched him in the belly. "Married?" So Emma did have a dad after all. Anger returned, mixed with an emotion he didn't want to examine too closely. "I'm surprised your husband is so open-minded. Letting you go out to dinner with another man…"

His sarcasm didn't even make her blink. Nikki Reardon was a cool customer. "The marriage didn't last long," she said. "Two years. He resented my privileged past. Had a chip on his shoulder about my upbringing. I realized I had said 'I do' because I was lonely. Our relationship was doomed from the start."

"I'm sorry," Jake said stiffly. He was still coping with the fact that he was *jealous*. Jealous of a faceless man who had slept with Nikki. Since when did

Jake get jealous about *any* woman? He was a love-'em-and-leave-'em kind of guy.

She cocked her head. "And what about you, Jake? All I know is that you travel the world. I'm not sure how that's a full-time occupation, but it sounds like fun."

The note of criticism stung. "I'm lucky," he said lightly. "I learned about day-trading early in my life. And I have a knack for it. In among my many adventures, I made a few bucks here and there. Enough to eat and hit the road whenever the mood strikes me."

Nikki's smile mocked his statement. "You're wearing a limited-edition Rolex. I may not have money anymore, but I haven't lost the ability to recognize luxury when I see it."

"Being comfortable isn't a crime. I like to think I'm generous with my money. I don't maintain a huge house. So I wander. I value experiences. Learning my way around the planet has changed me and made me a better person. At least I hope so."

The way Nikki stared at him made him itchy and uncomfortable. It was as if she could see through to his soul. When was the last time he had ever articulated so honestly what he wanted from life? Never?

"You're fortunate," she said slowly. "And I don't blame you a bit. You're still a young man. Healthy. Wealthy. Unattached. Why not enjoy what the world has to offer?"

Something about her response bothered him, but he couldn't pinpoint his unease.

"We need to make some plans," he said.

Nikki lowered her fork, her expression wary. "Plans?"

"Plans for integrating my life with Emma's. I've missed four years. I won't miss any more. She's a part of me."

Every bit of color leached from Nikki's porcelain complexion. Now he could almost count the smattering of freckles on the bridge of her nose. "Absolutely not," she said, her tone fierce. "I won't have you playing at fatherhood and then walking away. Emma is happy and well-adjusted. She doesn't need you, Jake."

Perhaps Nikki realized her rejection was harsh. She circled back to the beginning. "You're a good man, but you're not father material. Emma is better off having *no* father than one who flits in and out whenever the wind blows."

He ground his jaw, trying to control his temper. "You're making a lot of assumptions about me, Nik."

"It's been fifteen years since you walked away from Falling Brook. From your family. From me. You've never been back. Not once. You juggle demons, Jake."

He felt raw. Only someone who had known him so well would dare to diagnose his behavior. "At least I don't keep secrets," he muttered.

She stood abruptly and gathered her coat and clutch purse. "Take me home, please. I want to go now."

Three

Nikki was angry. And scared. Once upon a time Jake had held her entire heart in his hands. She had adored him. They had been friends forever, and then, just as she began to grow into her feelings for him in a very adult way, their fathers had ruined everything. Jake fled, and Nikki and her mom had fled, too.

But not in the same direction.

As they walked outside, Nikki barely felt the cold. At least not on her face, hands or feet. Her chest felt frozen from the inside out. How dare he blame her? Didn't he know how many times she had cried herself to sleep, wondering again and again if she had made the right choice for her daughter? For the absent Jake...

Jake started the car but left it in Park. He reached

for her wrist, not letting go even when she jerked backward. "I don't want to fight with you, Nikki." He rubbed his thumb over the back of her hand with a mesmerizing stroke. "The past is the past. We can't change any of it."

In the dimly lit interior, his face was hard to read. "But your father is back," she said quietly. "That's why you're here. In New Jersey, I mean. To see him?"

Jake shrugged, his posture and expression moody. "Joshua and I are being summoned to the prison tomorrow. But to be clear, I came back because Josh asked, not for my rat bastard of a father."

His palpable misery twisted her heart and dissolved some of her animosity. She flipped her hand over and twined her fingers with his. "I'm sorry you have to see him. But maybe it will help. For closure, I mean."

"He won't answer our questions. We'll never know why he did it or what happened to the money. I can tell you that right now. My father never let us boys talk back to him…ever. He was always king. Arrogant. Proud. The worst part is, he turned his back on our mother, and for that alone, I'll never forgive him."

Nikki cupped his cheek with her free hand, feeling the late-day stubble. "Forever is a long time. Bitterness and anger poison your soul. I want you to be happy, Jake."

It was true. Despite everything that had happened, Nikki didn't want Jake Lowell to suffer. She could have found him when she turned up pregnant after their night in Atlantic City. Possibly. And told him he was a father. But he had hurt her so badly once in her life, she had been reluctant to trust him with the truth. Instinctively, she had known he could hurt her again. And she knew it now.

Jake sucked in a sharp breath. Audible. Ragged. "You're right. It's time to take you home." He released her, so she was no longer touching him.

Something shimmered in the air between them. Was it sexual chemistry that refused to die? Nostalgia, grief and hormones were a dangerous combination.

Nikki cleared her throat. "Sure," she said.

Jake put the car in motion. Traffic was only now beginning to taper off as commuters found their way home. Nikki stared out the window, searching for answers. Was she wrong to keep Jake away from his daughter?

When he parked in front of her house, she bit her lip and stayed put. "I'll have to think about it," she said. "You and Emma. I need time. Please."

"Okay." His voice was quiet. "I don't blame you for not telling me earlier. But I know *now*, and we'll start from here."

The following morning, after a sleepless night, Nikki drove to Falling Brook. The small community where she and her mother lived was about an hour's drive away. Her mother was with Emma at the moment. Nikki's shift at the diner didn't start until eight tonight, and it was a short one. She felt the tiniest bit guilty about leaving her daughter. But this errand was important.

At ten to nine, she pulled up in front of Black Crescent headquarters. The building had been a source of conflict over the years for the way its modern architecture stuck out jarringly in the midst of Falling Brook's mostly traditional landscape.

Nevertheless, it was an impressive structure.

Nikki had dressed in the same black pantsuit from last night. But she had exchanged the sexy stiletto heels for espadrilles, and her sleeveless blouse underneath the jacket was simple white cotton.

There would be two obstacles between her and her destination. The first was a young receptionist at the front desk.

Nikki gave the barely twentysomething kid a confident smile. "I have an appointment with Mr. Lowell at nine. Is it okay if I go on up?"

The smile faltered. "His assistant will have to okay you."

"No worries. They're expecting me."

It was only partly a lie. She *had* called Joshua to tell him she needed fifteen minutes of his time. If he wasn't in, his assistant would surely have listened to his messages. So either way, Nikki wouldn't be a total surprise.

She climbed the stairs to the second floor. The executive assistant at the desk outside Joshua's office was familiar. Nikki smiled. "Haley Shaw? You're still here?"

Haley was only a couple of years older than Nikki. She had been working at Black Crescent as a college intern when Vernon and Nikki's dad, Everett Reardon, had disappeared. Well, Nikki's dad had *tried* to disappear. He'd fatally crashed his car into a tree while fleeing the police.

Nikki hadn't been inside Black Crescent headquarters since she was a senior in high school. Nothing much had changed. Her father's old office was at the opposite end of the hallway. She didn't look in that direction. Her heart was already beating too rapidly. Being inside this building brought up painful memories.

Haley had a puzzled frown between her eyebrows. "I'm sorry, I—"

"It's me. Nikki Reardon. I'm here to see Joshua. Very briefly."

The other woman's face lightened. "Nikki, of course. How nice to see you again." Her gaze went to the computer screen at her elbow. "I don't have you on his calendar…"

The door behind the desk opened, and Joshua Lowell poked out his head. "Thanks, Haley. Please hold my calls. Nikki, it's good to see you after all these years."

Nikki entered Joshua's office and waited as he closed the door. "I won't take much of your time, Josh," she said quietly, conscious of the gatekeeper just outside the door.

Joshua waved her to a comfortable seat in front of his massive desk. "No worries. Let me have your coat. What can I do for you?"

She shrugged out of her thigh-length parka, handed it to him and sat down. Joshua was Jake's twin. By all accounts, she should be feeling the tug of sexual attraction. But despite the fact that both men shared an unmistakable physical similarity, they projected a different vibe.

Josh was very handsome, confident and appealing. But he projected authority and a no-nonsense air of being all business. Where Jake was funny, and at times outrageous, Joshua was more reserved.

Nikki folded her shaky hands in her lap. "I'm sure Jake has already talked to you since last night. I owe you an apology," she said bluntly. "He showed me one of the emails my mother sent. I knew nothing about them, and I am so very sorry. I'm going to speak to her firmly and warn her never to do anything like this again. She was trying to help me, but it was wrong. I hope you can forgive me."

Joshua leaned back in his chair and smiled wearily. "I think you and I both know that parents don't always make good choices."

"Touché."

"How did my brother react when you told him he's the father? He wasn't forthcoming about that part of the evening."

Nikki tried not to fidget. Joshua Lowell was a powerful man. "Well, you had already given him a heads-up. I suppose me telling him wasn't news. He says he wants to be part of Emma's life."

"And?"

"And I'm not sure. You know your brother, Josh. What your father did—what my father did—sent Jake running fifteen years ago. As far as I can tell, the only reason he's back at the moment is because you asked him to go with you to see Vernon. I don't think he's father material."

"You could give the guy a chance."

The suggestion was couched in mild tones, but Nikki felt the unspoken edge of criticism. Her defenses went up. "I have to protect Emma. She's my first priority."

"I understand."

"May I ask you a personal question?" she said, taking a deep breath.

His eyes widened fractionally, but he nodded. "Yes."

"Is it true that you're giving up your position here at Black Crescent? That you've been interviewing potential replacement candidates?"

Joshua nodded slowly. His gaze narrowed. "Yes. I have."

Nikki leaned forward, feeling an urgency that was perhaps not hers to feel. "Have you thought about asking Jake to replace you? I know he likes to pretend he has no depth, but he's whip-smart. Especially with finances. He could do this job and do it well. Maybe the challenge would be enough to make him stay. To put down roots."

Jake's twin sighed, and his expression filled with sympathy. "I get where you're coming from, Nikki. And, yes. That would be a great plan. But I already offered him the helm of Black Crescent, and he turned me down flat."

"Oh." The bottom fell out of her stomach. Suddenly, she realized she had been naive. She knew it was stupid to think she and Jake could have a relationship after all this time, but her need for him continued to sabotage good sense. Clearly, Jake only wanted to leave. Again.

She stood abruptly, near tears. Her sleepless night was catching up with her. "I should go. Thank you for your time."

Before Nikki could move, the door burst open and Jake strode into the room. He pulled up short when he saw her, his gaze narrowing. "What are you doing here?" The question was just short of rude.

Nikki hitched her purse on her shoulder. "I wanted to talk to Joshua. Don't worry—we're done. I'm leaving—"

Josh interrupted before Jake could speak. "It's my turn to ask *you* something, Nikki. Jake is here now, because he and I are headed into the city to see our father. It occurs to me that you might want to ask a few questions, too. Since your own father can't answer them. My dad owes you that much."

Jake's face had frozen in stone. "I don't think that's appropriate. Vernon asked to see us. No one else."

Nikki flushed, mortified. "Thank you, Josh, but Jake is right. This will be a family moment. I don't want to intrude." She scooted toward the door.

Josh snorted. "We're going to see the worthless son of a bitch who for a decade and a half let his own wife and kids think he was dead. I doubt we'll share any Hallmark moments today. You're welcome to come."

Nikki was torn. She did have questions. A million of them. Why did the two partners steal from their clients? Why did they run? Why did Vernon never come home? Why did he and Everett think it was okay to destroy dozens of lives? And for what?

Jake sighed. "Come if you want. I doubt he'll talk, anyway. He won't want to incriminate himself."

The cynicism in Jake's voice didn't entirely conceal a son's pain. Vernon Lowell had betrayed his own flesh and blood. How could he have been so selfishly cruel?

"My mother is with Emma. Let me see if she can stay." Nikki stepped out into the hallway and called her mom's cell. It wasn't hard to fabricate an excuse. Besides, Roberta loved spending time with her granddaughter. Not to mention the fact that Nikki partially supported her mother. Other than a small government retirement check, Roberta had no income. The woman who had once been a society maven and influencer now shopped for groceries at a discount store and drove a ten-year-old car.

Nikki liked to think her mother had adapted to their new reality, but the truth was, Roberta never gave up hope that one day she might reclaim what she considered to be her rightful place in the social scene.

When Nikki returned to Josh's office, the two brothers had their heads together and were talking in low tones. They both jerked upright with identical guilty expressions on their faces.

"Am I interrupting?" she asked wryly.

"Of course not." Jake gave nothing away. "We're ready to head out. You okay with the plan?"

He didn't mention Emma's name. The oblique question was odd. "I'm good," she said.

Downstairs in the employee parking garage, Joshua motioned to a large black SUV. "We're taking mine. Jake is leaving his car here. He spoke to our security guard and asked him to feed your parking meter. I hope that's okay."

"I appreciate it." She wasn't going to jockey for shotgun position. Before either man could say a word, she climbed into the back seat. The interior was nice. It reminded her of a Secret Service vehicle. Nothing wrong with that.

Falling Brook was an hour from New York City, depending on traffic and the destination. Once Joshua put the SUV in motion, Nikki fell dead asleep…

She roused as the car slowed and turned a corner. Up ahead, she saw a sign for the correctional facility.

Jake shot her a glance over his shoulder. "You okay back there?"

She nodded, rubbing her eyes and smoothing her hair. "Yes. I can't help thinking about all the times my mother and I came to the city for a play. Or shopping. Those days seem like another lifetime, another person. I was spoiled and naive."

He frowned. "Don't beat yourself up. You were the only child of wealthy parents. Of course they gave you the best of everything."

Until they didn't.

This prison, among others, made the news now and again for overcrowding and poor treatment of inmates. Nikki shivered. Her own father could have landed here before his certain conviction. Maybe death had been a kinder sentence.

When the three of them exited the parking garage a short time later, Nikki huddled into her coat. The wind whistled through the streets between tall buildings. The sun was out, but it shone hazily behind a thin veil of clouds.

Once inside they had to go through a security checkpoint with a metal detector. She began to wish she hadn't come, but it was too late to back out now.

Joshua signed a visitor log for the three of them, and then they sat in a waiting room. About fifteen minutes later, a uniformed security officer appeared in the doorway and called Joshua's name. Jake and Nikki stood, too. Her stomach fell to her feet.

Without overthinking it, she slid her hand into Jake's. He was about to see his father for the first time in a decade and a half. What was he thinking? His fingers gripped hers tightly.

The officer's face was stoic. "Mr. Lowell has changed his mind. He doesn't want visitors today."

After a moment of silence, Josh cursed beneath his breath. He and Jake had both gone pale. Joshua straightened his shoulders. "Perhaps you misunderstood. My father *asked* us to come today. We're here as a courtesy to him."

The man shrugged. "I don't know what to tell you. Mr. Lowell was perfectly clear. He's in his cell, and he doesn't want to be disturbed."

Nikki could feel the tension in Jake's body. "Well,"

he said, his tone gruff. "I guess that's it." He turned on his heel, dragging Nikki in his wake.

Joshua followed them out onto the street. They all stood on the sidewalk, stunned. Nikki let go of Jake's hand, self-conscious now that Joshua might notice.

Jake exhaled and stared at the ground. "I'm not sure why we're surprised. The old man is a class-A bastard. We've done our duty. Now we're off the hook."

Joshua shook his head slowly. "I can't believe it. Why would he ask us to come and then refuse to see us?"

"Maybe he's ashamed," Nikki said. She tried to put herself in Vernon's shoes, but couldn't imagine it. What kind of parent abandoned his family?

Jake made a face that could have meant anything. "It's freezing out here, and I'm starving." He gave Nikki a quick glance. "You up for walking a couple of blocks?"

"Of course."

They ended up at a little hole-in-the-wall place the Lowell brothers remembered from their teen years. Jake actually smiled when they entered. "We used to come here on the weekends and eat pizza and play pool. We felt like such rebels."

"Why was that?" she asked.

"Because it was a million miles from Falling Brook," Josh answered. He looked around the crowded, dimly lit room with a grin. The booths were covered in faux green leather. The wooden floor was scarred. The dartboards on the far back wall might have been relics from the Second World War.

There was an awkward moment as they were being seated. A booth for three meant that two people were cozy. In this case, Jake and Nikki. She squeezed toward the wall and tried to pretend she wasn't freaked out by the fact that his leg touched hers.

He helped her take off her coat.

Though Joshua seemed oblivious to any undercurrents, Jake's gaze, intense and warm, held Nikki's for long moments. Thankfully, the waitress came, and Nikki was able to catch her breath.

It occurred to her that the three of them had been frozen in time. Jake and Nikki had left Falling Brook fifteen years ago, headed in opposite directions. Joshua had stayed behind, the dutiful son, though Nikki had to wonder if his sacrifice had been worth it.

And now, here was Nikki, pressed up against the man who made her quiver with awareness and need. She'd had a taste of intimacy with Jake…in Atlantic City. Though she didn't want to admit weakness— even to herself—the truth was, she wanted more, even if her brain was shouting *danger, danger, danger.*

"This is a weird reunion, isn't it?" she said, clearing her throat. They had finished ordering, and now her stomach growled as they waited for their meal.

Joshua nodded. He gazed at his brother. "Weird, but satisfying. I'm sorry it's taken us this long to reconnect."

Nikki hesitated and then decided to indulge her curiosity. "Tell me, Josh. How have the finances at

Black Crescent recovered? I felt so guilty for years that those families lost everything."

Jake slid an arm around her shoulders, resting it on the back of the booth. "My saint of a brother has been able to repay a lot of the money."

Her eyes widened. "Really?"

Joshua grimaced. "Well, not at first. Although I wasn't implicated in the crime, the feds were all over me for several years."

Jake nodded. "Everything was liquidated, including your home, as you know, Nikki. Our cars, yachts, vacation properties. Oliver's remaining tuition for Harvard was canceled. Luckily for our mother, our home was in her name, since it had been in her family for generations. There were some Black Crescent assets liquidated, too, but not enough to cripple the company. It was in everyone's best interest to keep things afloat so Josh could start rebuilding."

"I'm glad to know that you were able to make at least *some* reparations," she said.

The food arrived, and serious talk was sidelined in favor of hot pizza.

Eventually, Joshua picked up the earlier thread. "Because of the nature of the crime, Black Crescent has been bound by some pretty stringent rules. Thankfully, I've been able to pay all the people our father cheated at least eighty or eighty-five cents on the dollar. It's not everything, but our clients signed off on the agreement. They were thrilled, actually, to know that they would recoup most of their investments over the long haul."

Jake's expression darkened. "I still want to know what happened to the money."

"Living off the grid for fifteen years isn't cheap," Nikki said.

"But he took millions." Jake shook his head slowly. "I doubt we'll ever know."

A silence fell, rife with unspoken emotions. Nikki wondered what Jake was thinking. Perhaps he was deciding how soon he could get back to his travels. Suddenly, her throat was tight. "I hate to break up the party, but I need to get back to Emma."

"Of course." Joshua raised his hand for the check, and then pinned Nikki with a determined gaze. "I was glad you turned up in my office today. I'd been planning to talk to you, anyway. Now that I have finally fulfilled all the company's legal obligations, Black Crescent will begin paying you and your mother a monthly stipend. You were victims, too."

She opened her mouth, stunned. "Oh, no. My father was one of the perpetrators. Mom and I are fine. Don't be ridiculous. We don't need the money."

Jake's eyes snapped with displeasure. "You're working in a diner, and you can't afford a babysitter. You are definitely *not* fine. My brother is doing the right thing."

Nikki straightened her spine, her cheeks burning with humiliation. "My life may not look like much to you, Jake Lowell, but I'm proud of what I've accomplished. The good things in life aren't always measured by dollars and cents."

Both Lowell twins were formidable when they put

their minds to it. Joshua wouldn't be moved. "What you do with the money is up to you, Nikki. Put it away for Emma's college, if you want. But you deserve to regain what you lost."

Four

Nikki didn't sleep on the way back home, but this time, she sat quietly, listening to the two brothers' conversation. It had been a strange and unsettling day. She wanted to spend time with Jake, but she was confused and worried. If she let him come around to see his daughter, Nikki might be tempted to sleep with him again.

Joshua had offered his brother a permanent, full-time, challenging opportunity, but Jake had turned him down. Wanderlust. That's what it was. Jake didn't know how to stay in one place, and he was far too old to learn new tricks now.

In the parking garage at Black Crescent, Joshua said a quick goodbye and ran upstairs. He was late for a meeting. That left Jake and Nikki standing awkwardly.

"Let me take you to dinner tonight," Jake said. "We still have plenty to talk about. And I've missed you, Nikki."

The raw honesty in his words seduced her more than anything. "I'm sorry," she said. "I have to work."

He scowled. "Are you blowing me off?"

She lifted her chin. "I'll spend a couple of hours with Emma, and then I have to go straight to the diner."

"I see."

"How soon will you be leaving?"

His face reflected shock. "What do you mean?"

"You came home to see your father. That didn't work out. I assumed you'll be heading out again soon."

"No." He leaned back against a concrete pillar. "Are you trying to get rid of me, Nik? Is that what this is about? Are you afraid of what I make you feel?"

"I'm not afraid of you," she said, the lie sticking in her throat.

He stared at her so long she began to get fidgety. "I'm staying for my brother's wedding and my father's trial. Both of those are soon. In the meantime, maybe you and I could reconnect."

"Reconnect?" She parsed the word for meaning.

He straightened and took the few steps that separated them. "I want to touch you. Kiss you. Get to know you again. Atlantic City was only a start."

When his lips settled on hers, warm and firm, her

legs threatened to buckle. Just like five years ago, this sexy, desirable man knew how to cut the ground from under her feet.

She pulled away, wiping her mouth with the back of her hand. Words came tumbling out. Words she should have censored but didn't. "I missed you so much, Jake. I fantasized about you. Wanted you. But you left me twice. Once fifteen years ago, and again in Atlantic City. Only a foolish woman would place a bet on a man who flits around the globe."

He shoved his hands in his pockets, his expression stormy. "I couldn't save you, Nikki. I couldn't save *us* back then, so I ran. I couldn't bear to stay in Falling Brook one more day. Everywhere I turned, there was another damn reporter. Digging. Poking. Prodding. Wanting every detail of our bleeding lives."

"And yet you abandoned me to the wolves."

He blinked. "Ouch. The old Nikki I knew wasn't so harsh."

"The old Nikki was a child, Jake. I had to grow up fast. It wasn't fun, and it wasn't easy. I survived, though."

"Yes, you did. You're an extraordinary woman."

Something pulsed between them. Awareness. Need. He looked so sexy she wanted to climb him like a tree and never let go. If it had been only her, perhaps she would have rolled the dice. Taken a walk on the wild side.

The kind of selfish pleasure she had embraced in Atlantic City was not a choice now. She had her mother to look out for, and she had Emma to raise. Nikki's wants and needs had to come in dead last.

"I should go," she muttered, looking at her watch. "I'm sorry your father wouldn't see you today."

"Like I said, I'm not surprised." He reached for her hand and squeezed her fingers.

"Think about it, Nikki. Not just me and Emma, but you and me. I want to spend time with both of you."

"Because you're bored and at loose ends?"

His eyes flashed. "Because she's my daughter, and you're my past."

Nikki played Barbies with Emma, started dinner and then dashed to work, leaving her mother in charge. Roberta Reardon wasn't incompetent. She was merely fragile. As Nikki poured coffee and took orders—because one of her best waitresses was out— she chatted with regulars. Half of her brain was occupied, trying to cope with the ramifications of the email she had seen on her phone just before she left the house.

It was from Black Crescent Hedge Fund—from Joshua Lowell, in particular. As he had promised, the attachment to the email was a very official-looking document. Beginning January first, Nikki and her mother would both be receiving checks for ten thousand dollars a month for a period of ten years.

The math was staggering. In the first twelve months alone, the two women together would have just shy of a quarter of a million dollars. There would be money for her mom to have almost anything she wanted, within reason. Nikki would be able to quit her job and spend these last precious months before kindergarten with Emma.

They would have financial freedom.

Why did the prospect seem so threatening? Perhaps because Nikki knew what it felt like to lose everything. She was superstitious about this extraordinary windfall. It was great that Black Crescent had recovered enough to restore much of what was lost. But Nikki's father had participated in the con, the scam.

She felt guilty.

It was late when Nikki got home, so her mom was sleeping over. That was often their pattern. Even though Roberta spent a lot of time with Emma, it was healthier for the two grown women to maintain separate residences. That hadn't always been possible in the beginning. Back when their lives had fallen apart, and Nikki had barely been an adult, they had needed to save every penny.

Eventually, things had changed.

And now, they were about to change again.

Nikki wanted desperately to go to bed, but she knew she would toss and turn if she didn't tell her mother what was about to happen. "Mom," she said. "Can I talk to you for a minute?"

Her mother raised an eyebrow. "So serious, sweetheart. What's up?"

"I had lunch with Joshua and Jake Lowell today."

Her mother paled. "Oh?"

"I found out about the emails. Your emails. And I apologized to Joshua."

Roberta Reardon went on the attack. "Well, I *won't* apologize for wanting to protect my daughter and granddaughter. Joshua Lowell is a scoundrel. He should be supporting his baby girl."

"Mom..." Nikki rubbed her temple, where a sledgehammer pounded. "Joshua is not Emma's father."

"Of course he is. Don't try to cover for him. You told me the truth."

"I lied."

Roberta Reardon stared at her daughter. "I don't understand."

"You kept badgering me when I lost my job. Trying to get me to ask Emma's father for child support. I didn't want you to know the truth, so I finally told you what you wanted to hear. I never dreamed you would try to blackmail him."

Her mother was visibly offended. "It wasn't blackmail. I never *asked* for money. I just wanted him to know he had a child."

"But he didn't."

"So, who *is* the father?"

Nikki felt her face heat. She was a grown woman, but this wasn't an easy topic to talk about with her mother. "Jake," she said quietly. "*Jake* Lowell. Not Joshua."

Roberta put her hands to her cheeks. "Well, that makes a lot more sense. You always did love that boy. He left Falling Brook, though. He's never been back. Right?"

"That's true. But about five years ago I ran into

him when I was working at the casino in Atlantic City."

Her mother looked shocked. "A one-night stand? Oh, Nikki."

"I couldn't resist him, Mom. I made a mistake. But trust me, Jake hasn't changed. He's still the proverbial rolling stone. I can't risk being with a man like that."

She was strong. She could let Jake come over, let him spend time with Emma, but Nikki wouldn't risk her heart. She wouldn't give in to sexual attraction. Not this time. The stakes were too high.

Her mother's gaze judged her. "Emma deserves a father. Even one who's not around much. He's her blood kin. What did he say when you told him?"

"Not much. I only confirmed what Jake had already heard from his brother. But Jake is only here for the trial. Then he'll be gone again."

"Life is never easy, is it?" Her mother's eyes were filled with resignation.

"It felt easy when I was a kid. You and Daddy gave me a perfect childhood."

"Nothing is perfect, Nikki. I thought I had a perfect marriage, but look how that turned out. It's hard to know what's inside a person's heart."

"I'm sorry, Mom. You deserved better."

"And so do you, my dearest girl. So do you."

Jake was answering emails in his hotel room when his phone dinged. It had been twenty-four hours since he had seen Nikki. Now she was texting him.

If you don't have plans, you're welcome to come over for dinner. Maybe even read Emma a bedtime story. As a friend.

Jake shook his head wryly. He did have plans, but he would cancel them. Nikki had made an overture. He wouldn't miss this chance.

When he showed up at her house at five o'clock, he saw neighborhood kids playing outside. The weather had shifted, and the late-afternoon temps were in the upper fifties. He reached into the back seat and grabbed a shopping bag. He had bought Emma a treat for just such an occasion.

Nikki opened the door before he could ring the bell. Her face was flushed, her fiery red hair pulled up in a ponytail. Wispy curls escaped around her forehead and cheeks. Those emerald eyes searched his soul.

"Hi," she said, giving him a wary look.

Emotion gut-punched him. This woman. What was it about this woman? She was dangerous to him, to his emotions, his good sense, his need for self-preservation.

As Nikki stepped back to let him in, he saw Emma, half hiding behind her mother's leg. He squatted, greeting her at eye level. "Hey, there," he said. "I'm Jake."

Her eyes were big, her gaze solemn. "I remember. Is my mommy gonna be mad at you again?"

Jake glanced up at Nikki. "I hope not."

Nikki shook her head ruefully. "I have to finish dinner. Why don't you two get acquainted?"

Jake rattled the shopping bag. "Would it be okay if we played outside? I hate to miss this weather. And I brought Emma a ring-toss game."

Emma's face lit up. "It *is* okay." She took his hand. "We have to go to the backyard, 'cause there's a fence."

"Presents, Jake?" Nikki's expression said she disapproved.

"Relax. It was less than fifteen bucks. I have a few friends with kids. They always tell me simple toys are the best."

Nikki spied unashamedly out the window over the sink. Emma didn't always warm up to strangers, but perhaps Jake's thoughtful gift had lowered her defenses. Nikki wouldn't be so easily convinced. Jake was a loner, a man who deliberately stayed away from any kind of home base, any kind of tie. She wouldn't let him hurt her or her daughter.

Even so, Nikki had to admit he was good with the little girl. Patient. Kind. Time and again, he showed her how to position the ring horizontally and how to hold her hand sideways to fling it. Emma got closer and closer. When she finally landed the first one, father and daughter did a spontaneous victory dance.

Moments later the duo came inside, their body language relaxed. Nikki was bemused by the way her daughter had taken to Jake. Did Emma feel some mystical bond? Did she recognize her father on some visceral level?

Nikki tried to swallow her misgivings. "Wash up, please. This will be ready soon."

Jake gave her an odd glance. "Emma wants to show me the butterflies in her room. We won't take long."

Nikki followed them, unable to squash her anxiety about seeing Jake inside her house. Emma loved butterflies. Always had, even as a toddler. On her fourth birthday, Nikki had let Emma redo her room. Bedspread, posters, mobiles hanging from the ceiling.

Jake whistled long and low. "This is amazing, Em."

Nikki waited for Emma to correct him. No one shortened her daughter's name. But Emma simply beamed. "I can name fifteen different species on flash cards," she said, "and I'm working on the others. Some of the words are hard."

Jake seemed surprised. "You're reading already?"

Emma gave him the kind of eye-rolling look that precocious kids have been giving parents since the beginning of time. "I started reading when I was three. It's easy, Jake. Don't you love books?"

He nodded. "I do, at that. And I'm glad you do, too." He stared around the room, taking in every bit of it. "Emma," he said, "I have something to show you." He sat in the rocking chair, the one Nikki had bought at a thrift store when Emma was an infant. He lifted Emma onto his lap.

She squirmed and got comfortable. "What is it?"

He pulled his phone out of his pocket. "You know the monarchs, right?"

"Of course. They're the easiest ones."

"Last year, just about this time, I was in Mexico." He pointed to the large map on her wall. "It's that pink country under the United States."

"I know," she said. "There's a kid at my preschool named Matias. He and his mom moved here from Mexico when he was a baby."

"Ah. So you know geography, too." The expression on his face when he glanced over at Nikki made her shrug and grin. Emma was very bright. And endlessly curious.

"What's jog-raphy?" Emma asked, perplexed.

"Never mind, kiddo. Here. Look at this." He cued up a video and Emma zeroed in.

"Wow," she said.

"It's part of the monarch-butterfly migration. People come from all over the world to see it."

Emma's intense absorption tugged at Nikki's conscience. Travel was something she hadn't been able to afford. At least not anywhere out of state.

Her daughter looked up at Jake, wonder in her eyes. "Do they really fill up the whole sky?"

"It seems that way. It's so beautiful, your heart wants to dance."

"And maybe you wished you could be a butterfly, too?"

His voice got all low and gravelly. "Maybe I did."

Nikki tried to swallow the lump in her throat.

"Will you help her wash her hands? I've put pasta in the pot. We'll eat in five."

In the kitchen, she concentrated on her task, but her brain raced like a hamster in a wheel. Jake had so much world experience to share with his daughter. Nikki had traveled as a teenager, but taking trips had ground to a halt when she and her mother had been sent away from the only home Nikki had ever known.

Her father had cleaned almost everything out of the checking and savings accounts. Her mother had been forced, by necessity, to sell most of her jewelry that first year so she and Nikki wouldn't starve.

When Nikki's two dinner companions returned to the kitchen, they were discussing the merits of brownies versus cupcakes.

Emma took her usual seat at one end of the table. "Mommy makes both of them good. You'll see."

"No pressure," Nikki muttered. Her daughter wouldn't understand that a man like Jake had dined on the world's finest cuisine in dozens of the most cosmopolitan cities.

But Jake was unfazed. "Comfort food is the best," he said, digging into his spaghetti as soon as Nikki was seated. "This is amazing, Nikki."

"I'm glad you like it." She had set the table so that Emma was between her two parents. Maybe Emma didn't feel the weight of the moment, but Nikki definitely did. Judging by the look on Jake's face, he did, too.

During the entire meal, he watched Emma with a combination of pride and wonder that would have been adorably macho if Nikki hadn't been so torn about the future.

When the meal was over, Nikki put on her stern-mommy look. "Into the shower with you, ladybug. And don't forget to brush your teeth."

When Emma disappeared, Jake raised an eyebrow. "Isn't she a little young for that?"

Nikki picked up the plates while Jake gathered the silverware. "Three months ago, she informed me that baths were for babies. She's trying her best to grow up as fast as she can, and I'm trying my best to slow her down."

Jake watched Nikki put the dishes in the sink, then he dropped the silverware and pulled her close, tucking a stray strand of hair behind her ear. "You've done a great job with her, Nikki. She's smart and funny."

"I'm glad you think so." Nikki backed away. She was supposed to be focusing on her daughter, but with Jake this close, all she could feel were her wobbly knees and sweaty palms. After fifteen years, she should have developed some kind of immunity, but whatever pheromones he'd been blessed with made her crazy.

They weren't touching. Not really. Not anymore. But the eight inches of air between them vibrated with deep emotion. She wanted him.

Did he feel the same urgency?

"I need to check on Emma," she croaked. "Don't worry about the kitchen. Make yourself comfortable in the living room. I have basic cable."

His lips twitched. "Go, little mama. Look after your chick."

The whole time Nikki supervised Emma's drying off and choosing clean pajamas and picking a bedtime book, her skin quivered. Jake was in the next room. Waiting. He was staying to talk about Emma. She knew that.

Maybe Nikki was the only one in this house acting immature.

When Emma was completely ready for bed, Nikki kissed the top of her head. "Would you like Mr. Jake to read your bedtime story tonight?"

The little girl's face brightened. "Sure. But I need to get a different book."

Nikki glanced at the picture book in her daughter's hands. It was a Caldecott Medal winner about Irish fairies and sliding down rainbows—one of Emma's favorites.

"I don't understand, sweetie. You love this book."

"Yeah, Mommy. But it's kind of *girly*. Mr. Jake is a boy, and he's real smart. I've got other books he'll like better." Before Nikki could stop her, Emma was tearing through her bookcase, moving and tossing and stacking until she found what she wanted. "Here it is."

Nikki frowned. "I thought we agreed that book was a little too hard for you to read right now. Maybe next year, Emma." It was a thick, several-hundred-page volume about the solar system.

"But I'm *not* reading it, Mommy. Mr. Jake is."

"It's far too long, baby."

"He can do just a few pages."

Nikki knew when she was beaten. She followed her daughter to the front part of the house where Jake was sprawled on the sofa resembling the dangerous male animal he was. He hadn't bothered turning on the TV. Instead, he was staring at his cell screen.

When they walked into the room, he immediately dropped the phone. "Hey, there."

Emma walked right up to him and handed over the book. "Will you read me a story? I picked this one for you," she said, beaming. "Because you told me you liked zubzertories."

Nikki shot Jake a puzzled glance.

He smiled. "Observatories. And I'd love to read this to Emma."

"Ah. Well, twenty minutes, no more, please." Nikki needed to get Jake out of her house before her resolve cracked.

Even when she left the room, Jake's low, masculine voice carried in the small house. It was impossible to ignore him, impossible to pretend she didn't react to him strongly.

Fifteen minutes later, Nikki returned to her daughter's room. "Time for bed, Emma."

"Just one more chapter, please, Mommy."

Nikki had played this game far too many times. "Now means now. Tell Mr. Jake thank you."

Emma slid off Jake's lap. "Thank you, Mr. Jake," she said, her expression doleful. The sad-little-girl act sometimes won her five extra minutes, but Nikki held firm this time.

Nikki managed a smile for Jake, though she was

nervous and jittery. "There's beer and wine in the fridge. Help yourself."

He gave her a slow, sleepy smile. "I'm good. Take your time."

Emma yawned. "Can Mr. Jake tuck me in?"

Nikki froze. She was pretty sure Jake did, too. It was one thing for a visitor to read a book. Tucking in was for family members. "Um, no, sweetheart. That's for mommies and little girls." She picked up her *baby*, who was getting almost too heavy to carry like this. "I'll be back, Jake."

Five

Jake stood and paced. Suddenly, this small house felt stifling. The home-cooked meal. The cute kid. The beautiful mother. All the things he had managed to avoid in his life.

In Atlantic City five years ago, Nikki had appeared as a sexy woman from his past. A chance to indulge in some hot and heavy no-strings sex. But now, Nikki had changed. She had moved on. She had grown up and matured. Or maybe she had already changed five years ago, and he hadn't seen it.

Though Jake admired her for the life she had created despite her father's deeds, he was wary. He'd been on the run for far too long to be seriously tempted by the idea of *settling down*. It would be unfair to let Nikki think that he might. Better to keep his distance and fight the sexual hunger that consumed him.

Maybe Nikki was right. He had no business playing "Daddy" unless he was ready to go all in. And he wasn't.

Returning to Falling Brook had been hard enough.

This little blue-collar town where Nikki lived, Poplar Ridge, was less than an hour away from where she had grown up, but by every other measure, it might as well have been on a different planet. Jake had hung his hat in all kinds of communities over the years. He'd enjoyed luxury, and he had found meaning in testing himself with deprivation. But all the while, he had known he had a safety net. He always had money.

Even when he fled Falling Brook and the reporters that were hounding him, he'd had secret money saved from playing poker. Jake had used his skills in daytrading and gradually built his fortune.

But Nikki and her mother had been left with virtually nothing.

Roberta Reardon had come from a social background and a generation where trophy spouses entertained and visited the spa but weren't employed. Nikki had been seventeen, almost eighteen, when her father disappeared. Not a child, but certainly not a full-grown adult. In the midst of grief, her whole world had imploded. At the time, Jake had insisted she was partly to blame. Even now, he regretted that.

He had lashed out at his teenage girlfriend, because the truth was too much to bear. Vernon and Everett had embezzled money and left their families behind. In search of what? If Everett Reardon hadn't been killed, if he had joined his partner in the Bahamas, what were the two men hoping to accomplish?

That unanswered question had shaped Jake's life. Bitterness and angry regret kept him on the run. Or maybe it was the memory of the woman he had lost that locked him in a lonely cage of his own making.

Thinking about the past was never fruitful. Jake shoved aside the baggage and sprawled in a chair, his focus returning to the present. What would Nikki and Roberta do with their windfall from Black Crescent? Jake had thought about asking if Joshua could add Nikki and her mom to the list of people Black Crescent was repaying, but Josh had beaten him to the punch.

Would Nikki and Roberta want to return to Falling Brook?

His turbulent thoughts were eventually interrupted when Nikki appeared in the doorway. Her ponytail was mussed from being in bed with her daughter.

"Is she asleep?" he asked.

"Close," Nikki said. "She played hard today."

Jake patted the sofa beside him. "Come sit with me."

Nikki hesitated, but did as he asked. It didn't escape his notice that she left a good four feet between them.

Didn't matter. He felt connected to her and drunk with wanting her. He didn't know what to do about that.

"Emma is delightful," he said gruffly.

"Thank you." Nikki's response was subdued. In fact, she seemed to be having trouble looking at him.

He sighed. "You're right about me. I don't know that I'm father material. I'd still like to hang out with her now and then while I'm here. But I won't cross any boundaries, I swear. I would never tell her she's mine. That would be cruel."

Finally, Nikki lifted her head. "I don't know if you saw it, but what happened between you two tonight was extraordinary. She's usually shy with strangers, especially men. But with you, she was happy. Excited. How can I *not* tell her the truth?"

Now the roles were reversed. Nikki wanted full disclosure, and Jake was uncertain about the future. "Let's give ourselves time," he said, feeling some unseen noose tighten around his neck.

"So, what? You'll just stay away until we figure it out?"

"Do you have a better idea? If our goal is not to hurt our daughter, we both have some thinking to do."

She nodded thoughtfully. "I suppose you're right."

"But let me be clear about one thing."

Her eyes widened. "Oh?"

He reached for her hand, stroking the back of it with his thumb. "I don't think I can stay away from *you*. I'm feeling the same things I felt five years ago. Seeing you face-to-face destroys me. Everything inside me says, 'Hell yeah!' I want to make love to you, Nikki. Rather desperately, in fact."

Her eyes flashed with anger. "Those feelings in

Atlantic City didn't last 'til morning, Jake. You're a flight risk."

"What does that have to do with me wanting you? Besides, I don't think this attraction is one-sided… is it?"

Tears sheened her eyes. Her chin wobbled. Her fingers curled around his. "No. But at what cost?"

"It will be our little secret. Just the two of us."

"We both know that secrets can tear a family apart." Her gaze clung to his, begging for assurance.

"Not this one. I give you my word. Come here, Nik. Let me show you."

They met in the middle of the sofa, a ragged curse from him, a low moan from her. He wrapped his arms around her and pulled her close, kissing her recklessly, telling himself there was no danger. Sex was good. Sex was healthy.

Her body was soft, pliant. Her scent tantalizing.

She was perfection in his arms. That one night in Atlantic City had haunted his dreams. He told himself he had embellished the memories…the way their bodies seemed to recognize each other. But something had been different that night, and it was different still.

He wanted Nikki to be his teenage sweetheart, but she was not the same woman now. She had made a life for herself. What had Jake ever done but run?

Despite his unease, he couldn't walk away. Touching her, kissing her, needing her. It was as simple and perfect as falling asleep in a feather bed. But the dark edge of lust was something more. Dangerous. Powerful. He was a man who respected women, yet in this fraught moment, he felt capable of behavior that frightened him.

Why, after so many years, did Nikki still have the power to push him beyond all reasonable boundaries?

When she put a hand to his chest and shoved, he was almost relieved.

"Wait, Jake. Please."

He released her instantly, still recognizing the beast inside him. "You changed your mind." His tone was low and flat, his mood mercurial.

She met his stormy eyes bravely. "I want you every bit as much as you want me. But I don't have the same freedom you do. Every choice I make, every road I take, affects at least two other people. My life is inextricably tied to my mother's and to Emma's. I don't have the luxury of spontaneity or reckless pleasure. As much as I wish things were different, I have to face the truth."

"So you *won't* make love to me?" He was frustrated now and trying to pretend this conflict wasn't proof of all his misgivings.

"I don't know," she said, the words taut with misery.

"That's no answer, Nik."

"Then how about this? Not now. It's too risky."

"Does Emma wake up during the night? Is that it?"

"Not usually. But it feels wrong with her in the next room."

"How can it be wrong if our being together created that perfect little girl?" Nikki was pale, obviously distressed. It was all he could do to keep his distance.

"Jake," she said quietly. "This thing between us is like sitting in front of a fireplace on a cold night. Even though we scattered the logs years ago, and the blaze went out, somehow, a couple of small embers stayed close enough to create danger. I can't explain it. We're a weird paradox. Virtual strangers who somehow know each other very well."

"You don't feel like a stranger to me." It was the God's honest truth. One encounter in fifteen years? They should be awkward together. Instead, touching her was the easiest thing he had ever done. He wanted to drown in her.

"Maybe we need to back up. Spend some time talking. Getting reacquainted."

"Talking?" He clenched his fists. "What will that accomplish?"

She lifted her chin. "You think you know me, but you don't, Jake. We can't pick up where we left off fifteen years ago. And not even where we were in Atlantic City. Time changes people. I've changed."

His body vibrated with sexual tension. He was hard and desperate—a toxic combination. There was the tiniest possibility she was right. Only in Jake's case, he had dealt with the tragedy in his past by moving slowly through the years. He'd made plenty of money. But he lived from day to day. Alone. Sometimes in the midst of a sea of people, but alone.

Now he was back in New Jersey. What was his next step?

Emma complicated the outcome. Enormously.

Maybe Jake could be a lover, but not a dad. It was painful to admit.

He exhaled and told himself no man ever died from unfulfilled lust. "What do you want to talk about?"

"Would popcorn make you feel better?"

His nose twitched, already imagining the scent. "With real butter?"

"Sure."

He followed her into the kitchen. Nikki's body language was wary, as if she knew he was on a short fuse. As he watched, she pulled out an old-fashioned aluminum popper. She added oil, seasoning and kernels, then put a chunk of butter in a tiny pan and set it to low.

Her small dinette chair was barely big enough to support his weight. He sat, anyway, his knee bouncing under the table with nervous energy.

When there was nothing to do but wait, she joined him, her body language guarded.

Jake plowed ahead. "What shall we talk about?"

Nikki shrugged. "You first."

"Will your mom want to go back to Falling Brook now that money won't be an issue?"

"Honestly? I don't know."

"I guess she's made friends here."

"Not really. We've moved around a lot, at least we did before Emma was born. For years, we used my mother's maiden name. A dozen different apartments. A dozen not-so-legal leases. She was terrified that someone would recognize her from the news."

"That's understandable." Wasn't that why Jake, himself, had fled?

The sound of the first pops ricocheted in the small room.

Nikki jumped to her feet. "You want wine?"

"Coke goes with popcorn. If you have any…"

She cocked her head. "Jake Lowell is asking for a sugary soft drink?"

He crossed his arms over his chest. "It's been a stressful week. I think I'm entitled."

"That's an understatement, for sure. Here you go." She got a can and handed it to him, then reached up into the cabinet for bowls. "I'll let you salt yours how you like it."

"Thanks." The fact that Nikki's brief, light touch affected him so deeply meant he was in real trouble.

Moments later they were enjoying their snack in silence.

His throat tightened. "Your turn," he said gruffly.

"I'm surprised you're willing to answer questions."

He frowned. "What does that mean?"

"Fifteen years ago, it was like you disappeared off the face of the earth."

The tops of his ears got hot. "It wasn't that extreme," he said, feeling guilty all over again. "I sent the occasional text or email to my brothers. First question, please."

"I know you're good at playing the stock market. But day-trading isn't a full-time occupation, at least not in your situation. What else have you done for the past fifteen years? I wanted to write to you, but I never worked up the nerve to contact Joshua and ask for your addresses, snail mail or otherwise."

"Why would you have to 'work up the nerve'?"

She gnawed her bottom lip. "You blamed me for what happened. I thought Josh might, too. Believe me, I've wished a million times that I could turn back the clock and beg my father not to get involved with yours."

Jake's chest was tight. Mostly because he knew Nikki was right. Even as a twenty-two-year-old, Jake had known that his dad must have orchestrated whatever convoluted plan led to the painful implosion of Black Crescent. With Vernon Lowell missing and presumed dead, and Everett killed in a car chase, the details weren't all that important.

"I can't believe I'm saying this," he muttered, "but I'd rather talk about me than what happened fifteen years ago."

Nikki nodded. "Fair enough." She poked at the un-popped kernels at the bottom of her bowl. "You can hit the high spots. What does a twentysomething do when he sets out to seek his fortune?"

Jake leaned his chair back on two legs, completely willing to narrate a travelogue. That was a hell of a lot easier than dealing with messy emotions. "Everyone expected me to head to Europe, so I started out in Wyoming instead," he said simply. "Working for a mountain-climbing school. Teaching inexperienced tourists the basics, so they could climb Grand Teton. It was a dangerous job at times. And I pushed the edge more than I should have. I wasn't suicidal. But I didn't really care what happened to me at that point."

"How long were you there?"

"About eighteen months. One day I heard some guys whispering and snickering. They shut up when I walked by. I found out later that one of our climbing school pupils was from Jersey and recognized my face and my name from the news."

"That must have been awful."

"It was shocking. Humiliating. So I decided that North America was too close. I set out for Australia. I always wanted to travel more, so that's what I did. A couple of weeks here. A month there. Gradually, I worked my way around the globe."

"Sounds like fun."

"It was. Mostly. Still, there were days I was so homesick I could hardly stand it. It was as if I was living life in slow motion. But that slow pace was the only way I knew how to handle the upheaval. Every time I thought about flying back to New Jersey, I remembered there was nothing left to return to."

"How can you say that? Joshua and Oliver were here…and your mom."

"I sent Oliver a few texts over the years, but he never answered. I thought he was still angry with me for leaving, but now I know he was busy partying, doing drugs. And I couldn't face Joshua. I had run out on my twin… Left him to clean up my father's mess."

"My father's mess, too…"

"Yes."

"What about your mom?"

"She was in deep denial when I left. The few times I called home it was the same. 'Vernon will be back. This is just one of his stunts.' After six months, I still called her occasionally, but I quit talking about anything that happened at Black Crescent. I didn't mention my dad's name. It was too damn sad."

"I'm sorry, Jake."

"She and Oliver went to see him recently. Before I got back. Joshua couldn't get any details out of them."

"In a way, your mom was right. Vernon *did* come back. Don't you wonder what happened to the money?"

"Every damn day."

After a heartbeat of silence, Nikki smiled. "Still my turn," she said. "What about you, Jake? Did *you* ever get married?"

The question stopped him dead in his tracks. "No," he said bluntly.

"Any close calls?"

The expression on her face reflected mild curiosity, but he suspected she was hiding her true feelings. "None. I like my freedom too much."

Nikki surprised him when she reached across the table and squeezed his arm briefly. "We have to get past this and move on. We've both played the hands we were dealt. I don't hold any grudges, Jake. You are who you are. Maybe we could tell Emma the truth when she turns eighteen."

"And have her resent me for missing her childhood?"

"You can't have it both ways."

He had to get out of this house. His head threatened to explode with a million unanswered questions, and his libido wanted to get laid.

Not with just any woman. With Nikki. Nikki of the pale white skin and the fiery hair and the eyes that went moss green or forest green depending on her mood. She was a fascinating, desirable female.

Even though he had gone an entire decade without seeing her, he could have used the encounter in Atlantic City to build something new, something more than his vagabond existence offered him. But he hadn't had the guts to try again.

His own lazy, selfish choices had brought him to this point.

Jake had run away fifteen years ago. He had wanted to be left alone, and he had succeeded in his quest. As he wandered the globe, he'd kept his friendships and his sexual relationships on a shallow plane. Expedient. Disposable. Forgettable.

The one woman he had never been able to forget was Nikki Reardon.

Now it was too late.

He stood up abruptly, nearly tumbling the chair. "I need to go," he said. "I'll call you later."

Nikki stood, too, seeming hurt or relieved or maybe both. "Okay."

"Joshua is getting married soon. I'll need a plus-one."

She gave him a loaded look. "Is that an invitation?"

"You know it is," he said, feeling more irritated by the minute.

Nikki shook her head slowly. "Charming. You

sure know how to make a girl feel wanted. I'll think about it."

"What's to think about? Who else would I take?"

Nikki poked her finger in the center of his chest. "You need to learn some manners, Jake Lowell. I don't know what kind of women you've been hanging around with, but I'm not some floozy you can pick up and put down when the mood strikes you."

"Floozy?" He laughed out loud despite his uncertain temper. "This is the twenty-first century, Ms. Reardon. Women aren't judged for their romantic entanglements anymore. Haven't you heard?"

She poked him a second time, eyes flashing. "You know what I mean. You're the absolute definition of a man who keeps a woman in every port. Just because you and I share a history doesn't mean I'm going to let you push me around. Are we clear?"

They were toe-to-toe now. He could feel her breath on his skin, hear the uneven hitch in her angry words. "Poke me one more time, Nik. I dare you."

Her chest heaved as she sucked in a breath and exhaled. "I'm not scared of you." One feminine finger prodded his sternum.

"Well, you should be, you frustrating woman." He groaned the words and snatched her up in his arms, backing her into the refrigerator. "Because you make me insane."

Six

Nikki was a rule follower, a straight arrow.

Even as she recognized that Jake was neither of those things, she was drawn to him inescapably.

He hitched her legs around his waist and buried his face in the curve of her neck. "You smell good, Nik."

As he nibbled the sensitive skin below her ear, she shuddered. "You like the scent of tomato sauce?"

"On you I do." He caught her earlobe between his teeth. "Tell me to go home." He begged her with as much sincerity as she had ever heard from him.

She smoothed his hair. "You told me you don't have a home."

"You know what I mean."

He let her slide to her feet, but where their bodies were pressed together, she could feel the hard length of him. Her memories of Atlantic City undermined her good sense. "I've dreamed of you holding me like this, Jake."

"I did more than hold you five years ago," he said huskily.

She unbuttoned two buttons of his shirt and slipped her hand inside to test the warm contours of his chest. "Yes, you did. I was there, remember?"

Sexual tension pulsed between them.

Jake shifted his feet. "At the risk of jumping the gun, are there any condoms in this house?"

"What do *you* think?" She kissed his chin and tasted his lips, loving the way he shuddered at her touch. "Don't you have one or two?"

"Not on me."

His disgruntled response might have been funny if Nikki wasn't so wound up. Being a single mom for the past four years had been a monastic existence. Life was hard. Busy and good, but hard. Not much time for a woman to indulge her sexual needs. And now here was Jake—sexy, gorgeous, every inch the man of her dreams.

She wanted badly to undress him and explore his taut, hard body. But if she wasn't going to have sex with him, there were rules to follow. Fair play. Self-denial.

Though it took remarkable willpower on her part, she moved away. "Would you like some coffee?" she asked, trying to pretend as if everything was normal.

Her kitchen looked the same as always, despite Jake's presence. Pine cabinets. Faded Formica countertops. Beige walls. This little house was dated and homely, but the community was friendly, and crime was low. Nikki's neighbors were Black and white and Hispanic. Young and old.

The man with the laser gaze stared at her, his jaw rigid. "Coffee? That's your answer?"

"I don't want to fight with you, Jake."

"And you don't want to have sex with me."

She shook her head slowly. "Not like this." She dealt with the coffeepot and turned it on. When she faced him again, he was leaning in the doorway, arms crossed over his broad chest, a dark scowl doing nothing to diminish his sexual pull. "Have you bought a return airline ticket?" she asked. No point in pretending.

"I have an open-ended one. Because the judge has fast-tracked the trial, I want to catch the opening arguments. Apparently, my father is planning to make a statement. Given the nature of the case, the judge is also allowing wronged parties to face the man who stole from them. Perhaps even let them speak."

"Poor Vernon."

Jake raised an eyebrow. "You have more charity than I do. My father *deserves* public condemnation. In fact, that's the tip of the iceberg. He should be—"

Nikki held up her hand, halting the flow of angry words. "Stop." She poured a cup of coffee and handed it to him. "Bitterness will destroy you. Mom and I spent the first several years of our exile constantly in the midst of grief and emotional upheaval. It was only when we decided to forgive my father that we were finally able to move on."

"I've moved on," he said, his tone defensive.

"You moved *away*," Nikki said. "Ran away. By your own admission. It's not the same thing. I know you're in Falling Brook for a brief time, but why don't you use these weeks to find closure with your dad? Actually, closure with the whole dismal experience?"

He stared down at his coffee, his expression moody. "Can we take this outside? I need some air. It's not all that cold."

"Sure." She grabbed a coat and the baby monitor. Jake retrieved his jacket from the living room.

"A baby monitor?" he said. "Still?"

"It gives me peace of mind."

"I can understand that."

They settled on the porch, skipping the swing in favor of sitting on the top step. Nikki didn't bother with the light. Because the stoop was narrow, she and Jake were hip-to-hip. She wanted badly to lean her head on his shoulder and dream of a future that included everything she wanted.

But that was futile. She sipped her coffee in silence. They weren't the only people taking advantage of the unexpectedly mild evening. Older kids still played up and down the street.

Without warning, Jake put a hand on her knee, making her jump.

"Why don't you and Emma come to Switzerland with me when this is all over?" he said. "For a visit," he clarified, as if wanting to make sure she understood. "The mountains are magnificent, and I think Emma would like it."

"What's in Switzerland?" Nikki kept the question light and casual, though her guts were in a knot.

"I own a small house there. I have a great housekeeper who handles things when I travel."

When I travel. There it was. The truth of Jake Lowell.

Nikki clenched the handle of her cup. "I have a job," she said evenly. "And other responsibilities."

"Emma's not in regular school yet. Besides, with the money from Black Crescent, you could quit the diner, right? I'll cover all the Europe expenses."

She sucked in a breath. "Being poor is not as bad as you think it is, Jake. But even if I decide to take the money from Black Crescent, it's a long time until January. Besides, I think Emma is a little young for a trip like that. I appreciate the offer."

They were both being so damn polite. As if roiling currents of emotion and discord didn't threaten the foundation beneath their feet.

Jake stood abruptly and set his empty coffee cup on the porch railing. "When can I swing by tomorrow?"

Nikki stood, too. The night was cloudy. She couldn't read his expression. "Tomorrow is not good. I work a double shift. Maybe you could come to a movie with Emma and me late Friday afternoon."

"Joshua's bachelor party is Friday night."

"The wedding's so soon?" The prospect of seeing people from her old life sent anxiety coursing through her veins.

"The actual ceremony is a week from Saturday. You never answered me. Will you be my date?"

She saw a challenge in his eyes, a dare. She weighed the prospect of attending a romantic wedding with Jake against her very real concerns. "I will," she said. "But I'll be nervous about seeing Falling Brook folks."

"You didn't do anything wrong. We'll face them together."

"Okay." It might be the only carefree time she had with Jake. An evening that would have to sustain her for the long, lonely years to come. "Good night," she muttered. Jake was too tempting. Too everything.

He cupped her neck in his big, warm hands and pulled her head to his. "I'll dream about you, Nik."

This kiss was lazy and slow. As if he had all the time in the world.

She put her hands on his shoulders to steady herself when her knees went weak. He tasted like coffee and dreams. Her dreams. All the ones that shattered when Black Crescent imploded, and Jake left her.

For long seconds, she let herself kiss him back. It was exhilarating. Toe curling. She felt like a princess at the end of a fairy tale. A very hot, flustered, needy princess. Only this particular prince was never going to stick around for the happily-ever-after.

When she realized she was running her fingers through his hair, she made herself step back. Take a breath. Reach for reason. "I should go in," she said.

"I have a few mommy jobs to accomplish before I head to bed."

"I'll pay child support," he said gruffly. "Even if we decide not to tell her."

Nikki's temper flared, but she held her tongue. He was trying to do the right thing. "I don't need your money, Jake. Emma and I are fine. A child is a huge responsibility, but money is the least of it."

"You're saying you want emotional support?"

Is that what she was saying? She honestly didn't know. Having Jake around as a part-time dad would be awkward and painful. Maybe it *would* be better if he simply went away. She was convinced he still saw her as a version of her teenage self. He didn't understand or want to admit how much she had changed. "I only meant that it's eighteen years of hard work."

"Longer for some families whose kids never move out."

"I suppose so. Either way, I need you to know that you're off the hook. Your life doesn't accommodate fatherhood. Let's think about it. Maybe we can come up with a solution that suits us both."

"And Emma."

"Of course."

He moved toward the sidewalk. When a streetlight illuminated his features, she saw that Jake looked tired, sad. Maybe even uncertain. She had never seen him so vulnerable. Her heart squeezed. "You're good with her," Nikki said. "Truly, you are. She's lucky to have your brains and your fearlessness."

"You're wrong about one thing, Nik."

"Oh?"

He shoved his hands in his pockets and kicked at one of the small rocks Emma loved to collect. "I'm not fearless at all right now. Falling Brook. My father. My brothers. You. I feel like I'm stumbling around in a fog. I'm not even sure if I should have come back."

This time, her heart hurt when it pinched. "I'm glad you came, Jake. Really glad."

Jake always slept with the drapes open in a hotel room. In big cities, he liked seeing the array of colored lights on decked-out skyscrapers. Here in Falling Brook, the lights were fewer and less impressive, but they still lit the night with a comforting glow.

He was lying on his back with his hands behind his head. It was three in the morning. He'd barely slept. A few days ago, when he was flying across the ocean, he'd worried about reuniting with his twin. But the thing with Joshua had gone well.

The two brothers had fallen into their old relationship without drama.

Jake still had to face his mother and Oliver. Those reunions weren't something to dread, not really. The harder encounter had been finding out that he and Nikki had created a child, a daughter.

Suddenly, unable to be still a moment longer, he rolled out of bed, threw on some clothes and went down to the twenty-four-hour fitness center. On the treadmill, he set a punishing pace. If he ran hard enough and long enough, maybe he could outrun the demons at his heels.

At last, exhaustion claimed him. Back in his room, he showered and tumbled into bed, comatose almost instantly. When the alarm went off at eight, he opened his eyes and groaned. Insomnia had rarely been a problem in his adult life, except for the occasional bout of jet lag. Clearly, being back in Falling Brook was bad for his health.

He sat up on the side of the bed and reached for his phone. If peace and closure were his aims, he needed to work his list. Oliver was Jake's next priority. After thinking for a moment, he sent a text asking if his younger sibling could meet him at the Drayhill Quarry at ten thirty. It was a spot where the three Lowell brothers had often hiked and played around.

On one memorable hot summer day, they had even taken a dip despite the warning signs posted everywhere. Their mother had found out and grounded them for a month. After that, they still returned now and again to the abandoned quarry, but not to swim.

What appealed most was the isolation. At the quarry, they were free to be on their own. No parents breathing down their necks. No teachers demanding excellence.

But that was a long time ago.

Jake dragged his attention back to the present. While he was brushing his teeth, the text *ding* came through. Oliver would be there.

Jake was nervous. Once upon a time, the three brothers had been tight. But Jake had let his father's actions drive him away. He'd lost Nikki, his brothers, everything. Now a chance for reconciliation beckoned.

Jake knew he didn't deserve anyone's forgiveness—least of all, his baby brother's.

After a few sprinkles of rain overnight, the mild weather had continued today. A weak sun shone down, making the morning slightly more cheerful. The drive out to the quarry was familiar but different. The old rutted road was worse now. Jake's fancy rental car took a beating. He parked by the gated fence and waited.

Soon, Oliver showed up in a late-model sedan. When the other man climbed out, Jake felt a wave of emotion he rarely allowed himself to acknowledge. This was his sibling, the man who was part of him. His blood and kin.

The two men embraced without speaking. Jake's eyes were damp when he pulled back. "Good to see you, Ol."

Oliver's brilliant blue eyes twinkled with happiness. "Took you long enough to contact me. I started to think you hadn't really come home at all."

"Sorry about that. I had to deal with some urgent business first."

"Yeah. Joshua told me. You have a baby. Right?"

"Well, Emma is four. But yes."

"Must have been quite a shock." Oliver's eyes held empathy.

Again, Jake's throat was tight. "On a scale of one to ten, I'd say a fifty. I don't know what I'm going to do about it."

"Joshua told me Nikki Reardon is the mother?"

Jake nodded. "I assume you remember her?"

Oliver snorted. "Are you kidding me? Of course I remember Nikki. You panted after her for years. It was painfully obvious that you were a one-woman kind of guy."

"Well, I screwed that up, too. I abandoned her just like I abandoned my brothers. I'm sorry, Oliver. Sorry for what happened to you."

"I doubt you could have done anything. Josh tried to reach me. Mom did, too. But I was so damn angry. The anger ate me alive."

"Will you tell me what happened? If you want to," Jake said quickly. "I only had snippets from Josh."

"Sure," Oliver said. "But do you mind if we walk out to the falcon? I need to stretch my legs."

They climbed the fence and set off, striding along the makeshift trail that wound around the quarry. The underbrush was heavy. At times they had to scale fallen trees. After three quarters of a mile, they reached their destination. The falcon was an enormous boulder, shaped vaguely like Han Solo's famous spaceship. The broad, flat surface was perfect for hanging out, drinking beer or simply enjoying the summer sun.

Today, the November water below wasn't blue. It was murky and threatening. No temptation at all to chance a swim.

They sat down and got comfortable.

Oliver pitched a pebble into the quarry, his expression pensive. "I headed out for Harvard just a few weeks after you left. I was glad to leave Falling Brook, even though my tuition was only paid up for a year. I was furious with Dad. That anger moved with me, fueling the usual freshman-year screwing around. But I couldn't let it go, even though those feelings were poisoning me. Drugs and alcohol dulled the pain."

Jake's stomach twisted with guilt. He was silent for a moment. Stunned. "I'm sorry I wasn't there for you."

Oliver shrugged. "I needed to sort myself out. Things are good for me now, and I've been sober for years. I'm finally happy. But our father still has a lot to answer for."

"Josh said you went to visit him?"

"I did. He looked old, Jake. Old and pitiful. But when I saw him, all that anger came back, and it scared the hell out of me. He immediately criticized me for being a photographer. Same old crap. I asked about the stolen money. He said it was his. At that point, I knew he'd never change. I walked out. I won't let him destroy me a second time."

"I'm really proud of you, you know. You're very good at what you do. Our father is an asshole. Josh and I went, too," Jake said slowly, remembering and sorting through his own emotions. "Actually, we were summoned. But when we got there, the old man apparently changed his mind. Sent us away."

"What a bastard. But then again, perhaps you were lucky. Did you really want to talk to him?"

"Maybe. I don't know. I became a man without a country because of him. Falling Brook was unbearable. I went on my graduation trip and just never came back. Because of him, I've lived my life in slow motion. Slow to forgive, slow to process my feelings. Slow to mend the rift with you and Joshua."

"And Nikki?"

"Her most of all. I ran into her five years ago in Atlantic City. We had a…thing. But I let her slip through my fingers again. When Josh called and said Dad had been found, I took it as a sign that maybe it was time to deal with my own failures."

They sat there in silence. Although Jake couldn't speak for Oliver, he suspected the two of them were juggling the same mishmash of regrets.

Finally, Jake exhaled. "So, are there any women in *your* life?"

Oliver's broad grin caught Jake off guard. "As a matter of fact, there *is* a woman. Samantha. We just got engaged. And we're expecting a baby."

"Well, hell, man. You buried the lead. Congratulations." Jake envied the fact that his brother was clearly thrilled about fatherhood. Oliver wasn't conflicted, like Jake.

"Sammi is a firecracker. You'll love her. She's had a tough life, but she's one of the strongest women I know."

"How did you meet?"

Oliver ducked his head, his expression sheepish. "A one-night stand. But it turned into something more, really fast."

Jake winced inwardly. His one-night stand with Nikki was at the root of his troubles. Did he regret it? How could he? It was arguably the best night of his life. But he'd been terrified by what he felt for her after a decade of nothing. She had changed, grown up. Though he wouldn't have thought it possible, she'd been even more intensely appealing than the teenage girl he had known all those years ago.

The tsunami of feelings had swept him under, drowned him. And so he had run.

Was he any better equipped to deal with her now?

Since there were no clear answers to his current dilemma, he changed the subject. "I assume you're going to the bachelor party tomorrow night?" One of Joshua's friends had put together a fun evening in Atlantic City.

"I'll be there," Oliver said. "It's not every day a Lowell man gets married. How about you?"

"Yep. I'm coming. Have you bought him any kind of gift?"

"No. Damn. I'll get something tomorrow."

"Well, here's the thing. When I was in Paris earlier this fall, I stumbled on a small Matisse at auction. It's a window scene from Morocco. I immediately thought of Joshua. You know how much he always loved Matisse. Of course, I had no idea Josh was going to get married soon, but when he told me, I had my assistant package the painting and send it to me. I should have it at the hotel tomorrow morning. I'd like to put your name and mine on the gift. You know, to acknowledge the fact that Josh is starting a new career, a new life. We left him to clean up the mess fifteen years ago. I know he didn't have to do it, but he did. What do you think?"

The words had tumbled out in a rush.

Oliver nodded. "That's perfect."

"Good. I want this gift to come from both of us. Together. I want to mend fences. To heal our family. We used to be the three Lowell brothers, unbreakable, unshakable. I'm sorry for my part in breaking us up. This is a gesture. A peace offering. Are you in?"

"I'm in."

Oliver ran a hand through his hair, his profile stark as he stared out across the quarry. Jake felt the coals of guilt burn hotter. Oliver had been a teenager when Jake left. Jake had failed him. Had failed Joshua. And Nikki. And his mother.

Could he ever do penance for his neglect? Sometimes he thought he'd simply been too lazy to look for a reason to return home. The truth was…he'd been scared. Scared that the people he loved would judge him. Or turn their backs on him.

Now it seemed that both of his brothers were willing to forgive and forget. That realization filled him with quiet satisfaction.

But what about Nikki? He had wronged her, most of all.

Would the mother of his child be willing to accept his regrets and his determination to do better?

And, if she did, was Jake willing to deal with the consequences?

Seven

It had been a very long time since Nikki shopped the designers on Fifth Avenue or Madison Avenue. But some memories never faded.

If she was going to Joshua's wedding—as Jake's date—nothing in her closet was remotely suitable. She had a credit card for emergencies. This didn't qualify. But even if the promised payments from Black Crescent didn't come through, Nikki could pay off a purchase over the coming months.

She had trained herself, out of necessity, not to live on credit. Today, she was going to break her own rule. A woman deserved the occasional fantasy, and this was hers.

After working the very early morning shift at the diner and then spending time with her daughter,

Nikki changed clothes and said goodbye to her mom and Emma. Because the wedding was close, she decided to postpone the movie date with her daughter. Catching a train into the city at one o'clock didn't leave Nikki much time for shopping.

She dozed en route, exhausted. Yesterday's double shift, followed by a 4:00 a.m. alarm this morning, had drained her. Even so, adrenaline pumped in her veins when she arrived at Grand Central.

In better days, Roberta Reardon had employed a full-time chauffeur. Now, Nikki was happy to use the subway. It was cheap and easy and took her where she wanted to go.

The first two stores she tried were a bust. Her mother had shopped with her at both when Nikki was a teenage girl. But Nikki's tastes had changed.

She was getting discouraged when she spotted a small boutique wedged in between two well-known fashion houses that took up most of the block. The modest shop had a name on the glass door that Nikki didn't recognize. The items in the window told her to go in and take a look.

Inside, a pleasant saleswoman honored Nikki's intent to browse undisturbed. There were casual outfits aplenty. Deeper into the salon, Nikki found what she was looking for. Jake had told her the wedding would be in the early afternoon. Which meant tealength was perfectly appropriate. The dress she spotted was a beautiful shade of ivory. Strapless. With a ballerina skirt that frothed out in layers of soft tulle.

"I'd like to try this one," she said impulsively, although the price tag made her gulp.

"I'll put it in a changing room for you," the woman said. "And if you're interested, that small rack over there is marked down. Last year's items. You know the drill."

Nikki wondered if the clerk had scoped out her customer and noted the inexpensive jeans and generic top. It didn't matter. False pride was a commodity Nikki couldn't afford. Though she had planned only to flip through the discounted items, her hand landed on a scoop-neck red cashmere sweater that might or might not clash with her hair. The black wool pencil skirt was a no-brainer. It would go with everything.

In the curtained cubicle, she tried the sweater and skirt first. They fit perfectly. A small pulled thread on the sleeve of the sweater and a missing button on the skirt explained another reason the items were on sale. The small imperfections didn't daunt Nikki. She had learned to be handy with a needle. Jake wanted to see her again. If that involved a night out, this outfit would bolster her confidence.

Her choice for the wedding was even better. She smoothed her hands over the skirt and tugged at the bodice. The only thing holding her back was the color. Some people insisted that only a bride should wear white to a wedding.

The saleslady knocked on the door frame. "Any luck?"

Nikki held back the curtain. "I love this, but I don't

know if I can wear it to a wedding. You know, because of the color."

The woman tilted her head and studied Nikki. "It fits you like a dream. And I don't think most people care anymore. Besides, it's a deep, rich ivory, not white. What if you add a pop of color? Hold on."

When the woman returned moments later, Nikki nodded. "That might work." She took the proffered scarf and draped it around her shoulders. It was soft, watered silk in pale, pale pink. When Nikki looked in the mirror, she smiled. "Thank you. I'll take it."

As the clerk rang up the purchases, Nikki battled her conscience. Any extra money she made over and above her household expenses went to doing things with her daughter and her mother. Movies. Meals out. This self-indulgence was hard to justify.

The saleswoman excused herself for a moment to deal with a call on the store's landline. While Nikki waited perched on the edge of a chair, her cell phone dinged. Her heart gave a funny little jump. It was a text from Jake…

Dinner tomorrow night? Just us? Let me know…

There was no reason to get flustered. Jake wasn't making a romantic overture. He clearly wanted to speak with Nikki about the future and how he would be a part of Emma's life. Or how he might not. Nikki knew it was an important conversation. One she needed to have with Jake alone. She would have to act like a mature thirtysomething single mother and not the giddy cocktail waitress who had still adored Jake Lowell and let him coax her into bed.

Even more importantly, she absolutely *had* to decide what it was she wanted from him. She needed his body, his intense lovemaking. His rakish charm. But common sense said she couldn't sleep with him and still make smart decisions about Emma.

What happened if Nikki didn't make the right choice?

If she agreed to this dinner, she had little more than twenty-four hours to figure it out.

Other customers entered the store, and Nikki got up, rattled by the unexpected text. When the employee handed over two lilac-and-navy shopping bags, Nikki winced inwardly. On the other hand, a little part of her was already thinking about how perfect her new sweater and skirt would be for a night out with her daughter's father.

Elegant. Not too fussy. Nothing that would suggest Nikki misunderstood Jake's motives. But definitely flattering.

Outside, the wind had picked up, and the sky was gray. The pleasant temperatures were gone, replaced by a bone-chilling cold. Nikki leaned against the building only long enough to answer the text.

She dithered over what to say, even as her fingers began to freeze. Finally, she pecked out a response…

Dinner is fine. Can we do seven?

Her phone dinged again…

Works for me. I'll pick you up then.

She gnawed her lip. But decided to add one more note…

Have fun at Joshua's bachelor party!

After a long silence, all she got was the thumbs-up emoji. Jake could be busy. Or he wasn't interested in a long text exchange.

No need to feel rejected.

When she glanced at her watch, she saw that she had a little time to kill before she caught the train. Too bad the Rockefeller Center tree wasn't up yet. Maybe she could bring Emma in a few weeks. At four, her precocious daughter was more than old enough to enjoy the treat.

Since Nikki's shopping errand had been accomplished with time to spare, she decided to walk despite the gloomy weather. She could definitely use more exercise. Everywhere she looked, retail establishments were beginning to deck the halls for the holiday season.

Thanksgiving was the weekend after Joshua's wedding. Barely two weeks away. Nikki and Roberta never made a big deal about the holiday. Nikki often baked a pumpkin pie. And sometimes they cooked a small turkey breast. But the celebration was low-key.

When Nikki was in high school, she remembered huge Thanksgiving spreads, mostly put together by the Lowell cook and housekeeper. As a kid, Nikki had never really thought about the work it took to pull off something like that. Or the expense.

Vernon Lowell had loved hosting lavish celebrations and inviting fifteen or twenty of his friends and business associates. The enormous cherry dining-room table could seat two dozen. The chandelier was actual Venetian glass. The priceless Persian silk rug and the enormous sets of china, crystal and heavy silver had all been sold off after the patriarch's disappearance.

Nikki had nothing of that era to pass down to her own daughter.

It didn't matter, she told herself firmly. Emma knew she was loved, and that's what mattered.

Eventually, Nikki made her way back to Grand Central and caught the train home. This time she didn't sleep. She worried. Did she and Jake have anything in common anymore? Could she step back into his world even temporarily? Could she sleep with him and let it be no more than that? And what about the fact that he didn't understand how much she had changed?

She knew he wasn't staying. But she badly wanted him to acknowledge all the ways she had survived and thrived. Something deep inside her craved his approval and his love.

And if that wasn't the most dismal admission a woman had ever made, she didn't know what was.

Arriving on the doorstep of her familiar small house calmed some of Nikki's nerves. She and Emma had made it this far and had a good life. Whatever came next, they would handle.

When Nikki opened the front door, the aroma of homemade chicken-noodle soup wafted out. Though her mom and Emma had finished eating, the soup was still warming on the stove.

Nikki shrugged out of her coat and hung it up on a hook near the door. Her shopping bags went in a nearby closet. Then she hugged Emma and smiled at her mom. "Thanks for keeping her this afternoon." She tried never to take her mother's help for granted, even though Roberta enjoyed time with Emma.

Emma demanded to be picked up. Nikki nuzzled her daughter's hair. "You smell like dessert," she teased.

The routine of the next hour and a half was comfortable and familiar. At Nikki's request, Roberta stayed. When Nikki told her mother they needed *to talk*, Roberta raised an eyebrow, but nodded.

At last, Emma was asleep. The two women made their way to the tiny living room, turned on the gas logs and put up their feet.

Roberta sighed. "This is nice. Did you find a dress for the wedding?"

"I did," Nikki said. "I'll try it on for you sometime soon. Thanks again for keeping Emma. I tried to get back as quickly as I could."

Roberta cocked her head. "You said we needed to talk. Is this about Jake?"

"Not directly. He and I are having dinner tomorrow night to discuss Emma and the future."

"What's to talk about? He's her father."

"Jake being Emma's daddy isn't what I wanted to talk to you about, Mom."

"Oh?"

Carefully, and as calmly as possible, Nikki shared what Joshua had told her about his plan to compensate Roberta and Nikki for all they had lost. She went on to explain that all of the Black Crescent clients who lost money fifteen years ago had received payments at an agreed-upon rate. It had taken Joshua a very long time, but the ethical and legal obligations had been met.

Roberta listened in silence, though her eyes widened, and her cheeks flushed.

When Nikki finished, Roberta sat up on the edge of her seat, clearly agitated. "Vernon stole that money. Why should you and I get anything?"

"That's what I told Joshua, Mom. But he says Dad stole from us, too. Joshua wants to do this."

"Dear Lord." Roberta seemed dazed.

"The payments will begin January first. It's a lot of money. Not like what you had before, but plenty if we're careful. We'll need to invest some and save some. You don't want to get to the end of the ten years and find yourself right back where you are now."

Roberta nodded. "I didn't know a single thing about finances when I married your father. I've regretted that more than once since he left us."

"I'll help you. And I suspect Joshua will be willing to advise us."

"And Jake, too. If he's such a financial genius."

"Yes," Nikki said hesitantly. She'd told her mom how Jake had supported himself for years by day-trading. "Jake, too. Think about it, Mom. You can go back to your old friends. Pick up the good pieces of your old life."

Roberta's face hardened. "They turned their backs on me."

"No. To be fair, you and I disappeared. We didn't give anyone a chance to help us. We were embarrassed and too humiliated to show our faces. I'm sure there were a few of your friends who might have shunned you for what Daddy did, but I have to believe that at least some of them would be glad to reconnect. I think that's true even now. But we haven't wanted any contact. Maybe we were wrong, Mom."

"I suppose."

It was a lot to digest. Nikki was glad her mother didn't turn the tables and ask what Nikki wanted to do. Life was comfortable now. Hard and demanding, but comfortable in its predictability.

Did Nikki want to uproot all she had worked for and return to the town of her childhood? Emma could attend the same Falling Brook prep school where her mother got a good education. Nikki could be a stay-at-home mom for a few years. Volunteer at school. Pay attention to her physical and mental health. Not be so exhausted all the time.

Maybe see Jake when he came home to visit his mother and brothers.

Nikki yawned. "We've got a lot to think about. Thankfully, nothing has to be decided tonight."

The more important questions surrounded Jake. Despite the changes happening all around her, Nikki was most conflicted about Jake. Fascinating, sexy, unpredictable Jake Lowell. What would tomorrow night bring?

Jake sipped his scotch and loosened his tie. Joshua's bachelor party was proving to be a good distraction from thinking about Nikki. A friend of Joshua's had reserved a large room on the top floor of one of Atlantic City's glitziest casinos. Jake didn't know the man. It was someone Josh had become friends with after college— a relationship that began after Jake had left Falling Brook.

The dress code tonight was upscale, but Jake noticed that several guys had already shed their jackets. Enormous flat-screen TVs covered the walls, tuned to various sports channels. The open bar was stocked with top-shelf booze. Three beautiful pool tables were busy. Half a dozen female servers wandered among the partygoers handing out delicious hors d'oeuvres and smiles.

At the far end of the room, elegant tables were set for the steak dinner to come. Jake sat in a bubble of quiet at the moment, observing. He knew most of the men in the room, or he had at one time. Many of them had greeted him cordially tonight. They were understandably curious about Joshua's absent twin. When Jake left Falling Brook, he had cut all ties with surgical precision, preferring to look forward rather than dwell on the past.

That recollection brought him right back to Nikki. She, like Jake, had abdicated her place in Falling Brook society and had gone into hiding. Maybe that was a dramatic way of phrasing it, but the result was the same.

A waitress stopped at his elbow. "Would you like anything, sir?"

He looked up, noticing the woman's surgically enhanced breasts and the flirtatious look in her eyes. At one time, he wouldn't have thought twice about getting her number and hooking up after the party was over.

"Thanks, I'm good," he said, giving the woman his best noncommittal smile. Despite the fact that he was in the midst of a dry spell, sexually speaking, he wasn't interested. Nobody but Nikki pushed his buttons. Knowing that she was so close and yet so far away made him grumpy. Their brief text exchange had revved his motor to an embarrassing degree.

He found himself obsessing about tomorrow night's date. Clearly, he and Nikki had to come to a decision about Emma. Maybe Jake was a total jerk to think so, but dealing with his small daughter wasn't nearly as worrisome as understanding his feelings for Nikki.

Seeing her in Atlantic City five years ago had been both exhilarating and unsettling. He hadn't stuck around long enough to find out what was going on in her world. Despite the incredible sex, he'd been afraid to hear that she had a life that didn't include him, which was stupid, because of course she did.

His stomach tightened unpleasantly as he finally admitted the truth to himself. One reason he had stayed away from Falling Brook for so long—among many—was that he'd been afraid to come back and see that Nikki had moved on with another man.

And she had. By her own admission. She had married and divorced.

That was more of a relationship than Jake could claim. His hopscotching travels had, by design, left him little opportunity to get attached to any one place or person. He had anesthetized his pain over his father's betrayal with new experiences, fresh vistas.

For a very long time, he had been satisfied with the status quo. Or, at least, he had convinced himself he was. When Joshua's phone call came out of the blue saying that Vernon was alive, it had been an electric shock to the system.

The Jake who lived day by day and never worried about anything was suddenly jerked back into the truth that he was indeed tied to other people. Despite time and distance, he was still a son, a brother. And now, a father, too.

What he was to Nikki remained to be seen…

Oliver approached him and bumped his knee. "Play me some pool?"

Jake finished his drink and set it aside. "I'd be happy to kick your ass. Lead the way."

It wasn't as easy as he had imagined. Though Jake was a shark when it came to the pool table, his baby brother was a different kind of wizard. Jake lined up his shots with cool precision, sinking ball after ball.

Oliver, on the other hand, played wildly, taking dumb chances that paid off. After four games, they had each won twice. Both men had shed their sport coats and rolled up their shirtsleeves. Jake raised an eyebrow. "Best three out of five?"

"Nope."

"Nope?"

Oliver wiped his forehead with the back of his hand. "I learned in recovery to be satisfied with 'enough.' That who I am is sufficient. Now, when those competitive rushes try to drag me into deep water, I step away."

Jake frowned. "You know we weren't playing for money, right?"

"Doesn't matter. I still have that killer instinct. And it can get me in trouble. So I stop and take a breath and ask myself what's really important. You should try it, Jake. It's good for the soul."

Oliver excused himself, leaving Jake a lot unsettled and a little bit pissed. He was damn glad his sibling had beaten addiction, but Jake didn't have similar problems. He didn't drink to excess. He'd never done drugs. Why did Oliver's implication sound so judgmental?

Maybe Jake was making a big deal out of nothing. So Oliver didn't want to play the tiebreaker. So what?

Jake was leaning against the momentarily empty pool table, brooding and watching the nearest TV screen, when the man of the hour crossed the room in his direction. Joshua looked relaxed and happy. For a split second, Jake was jealous. Jealous that his twin had found love and challenges and purpose in his life.

The truth was, if anybody deserved that trifecta, it was Josh.

Jake grinned at him. "I still can't believe you're getting married. And leaving Black Crescent."

Joshua lifted an eyebrow. "The job is still yours if you want it."

The urge to say yes came out of nowhere. Jake quaked inside. Here was an opportunity to fit back into the fabric of Falling Brook, to grow close to his family again, to build a bond with his daughter. To make Nikki proud. The temptation dangled. But it would require stepping up to the plate. Changing. Growing.

His gut clenched. *Back away.*

"Lord, no," he said, managing a chuckle. "I'd be terrible at it. It's one thing to take risks with my own cash. I wouldn't want the responsibility of handling other people's money, but I don't mind helping you with the CEO search."

"Then what *do* you want to do, Jake?"

The serious question caught Jake off guard. He hadn't expected to be grilled in the middle of a party. "Same thing I always do, I guess. Be me."

Joshua's gaze showed concern. "We all have to move forward. Whether we want to or not. Don't let Dad control your life."

The expression in his twin's eyes baffled and bothered Jake as much as Oliver's pseudo lecture about being *enough*. "That's bullshit," Jake said angrily, keeping his voice low. "Dad doesn't control me. I haven't seen the man in fifteen years. Are you nuts?"

"He casts a long shadow. And now even more. He's going to spend the rest of his life in prison, by all accounts. It would be foolish of us to let him affect our choices. I'll admit that I'm being selfish. I lost you for a decade and a half. I don't want to lose you again."

Joshua bumped Jake's shoulder with an affectionate fist and walked off, leaving Jake with the strongest urge to run out the door and keep on running. That's what he did when things got tough. But this was his brother's bachelor party. His twin. His other half. He couldn't bail on Joshua. Not tonight. He'd done it too often already. He owed Josh.

He certainly didn't *deserve* Josh's goodwill and forgiveness. Jake had left his brother holding the proverbial bag. When Vernon disappeared, Joshua had dealt with the feds and the insurance companies and their mother and everything else in the midst of panic and grief and confusion.

What had Jake done to help? Nothing. Nothing at all... He had disappeared, severing the ties that might have sustained him in his grief. He might be slow, but he was finally beginning to understand how much he had lost.

Eight

The bachelor party was a huge success. Even the guys who imbibed heavily were classy enough not to get falling-down drunk. Or maybe Joshua picked his friends carefully. Maybe he surrounded himself with men of depth.

Whatever the reason, the evening was going well.

When it was time for dinner, the men moved as one to the tables, where shrimp cocktails and Caesar salads sat waiting. As everyone dug in, Jake noted that Joshua had perhaps intentionally *not* set up a head table. In most families, the groom-to-be might be flanked by his two brothers. But the Lowell relationships, though cordial, were strained by the events of the past.

Jake sat with Oliver to his right and a Black Crescent employee he had just met on his left. The meal was fabulous. And it must have cost a fortune. Again, Jake felt guilty. *He* should have been the one paying for this spread. He could certainly afford it. But, heck. He hadn't even known his brother was getting married.

Jake had kept himself out of the loop.

When the steaks and potatoes were only a memory, and there was a brief lull before dessert was served, Jake seized the moment to say a few words. He stood and cleared his throat. "As the twin brother of the groom, I believe it's my duty to make a toast."

Joshua grinned, his expression a mixture of surprise and pleasure. "By all means," he said. "But if you start telling childhood stories, I'll plead the Fifth."

Ignoring laughter and a few catcalls, Jake began his spiel. "Joshua…you were known as the good kid, and I was the bad apple. I guess some things never change."

A titter of laughter went around the room.

Jake continued. "For a decade and a half, you've managed to find the best in a really crappy situation. Now, although I've only met Sophie briefly, I can already tell that the two of you are a perfect match."

"Thanks," Joshua said, his posture slightly guarded as if he didn't know what was coming next.

Jake reached beneath the dinner table and picked up the small package that was loosely wrapped in brown butcher paper. "Oliver and I want to give you something to mark this occasion. It's not exactly a wedding gift. It's more of a thank-you for being a damn good human being, and our steady-as-a-rock brother. We love you, man."

Jake walked past several people and handed over the small package, then returned to his seat.

Joshua stood and carefully peeled back the paper. He examined the painting intently, his fingers clenched on the frame. His face went pale. He looked up, startled, staring at his two brothers. "My God. Is this really a…" He trailed off, his expression gobsmacked.

"It's a Matisse," Jake said quietly. Joshua's reaction made him damn glad he'd come up with this idea.

Oliver, shoulder-to-shoulder with Jake, spoke up. "We're pumped as hell that you're jump-starting your art career, and I hope you know we'll both be first in line to hang a few Josh Lowell masterpieces on our walls."

Jake lifted his glass of champagne. "To Josh. May your marriage be as long lasting as this old master."

"To Josh." The chorus rose around the tables.

Amid the laughter and applause, Joshua stood and hugged each of his brothers tightly, then pulled them both in for a triple embrace. "Thanks, guys. This means the world to me."

Oliver held up his hands. "We're heading for the mushy zone. Time for more red meat and male bonding." He returned to his seat with a chuckle.

Joshua kept his hand firm on Jake's shoulder. "I'm not letting you hold me at arm's length ever again. You got that?"

The words were low, only loud enough for Jake to hear. But they packed a punch. Jake nodded, his throat tight. "Understood."

The remainder of the evening passed in a haze for Jake. He was more of a watcher than an active participant. The men in this room admired Joshua. It was evident in the way they joked with him and laughed with him and thanked him for inviting them to be part of his bachelor celebration.

Oliver was equally popular and social, though he drank nothing stronger than sparkling water. Jake wondered how his brother felt being present at an event where the alcohol flowed freely, but Oliver never seemed tempted.

The room was booked until midnight. Gradually, the guests began making their goodbyes. Oliver had come with a trio of guys and was the designated driver. Eventually, quiet fell. Only Joshua and Jake remained.

Joshua yawned. "That was fun. But I sure as hell am glad the wedding is not tomorrow. I'm going to go home and crash hard."

"Sounds like a plan," Jake said. "You want me to drive you? I switched to coffee a couple of hours ago."

"Sure. I'd like that. My driver is waiting, but I'll send him on."

In the car, Jake adjusted the heat and made his way out of the crowded parking garage. "This may take a while," he said, grimacing at the line of cars.

Joshua took off his tie, reclined his seat a few inches and sighed deeply as he stretched out his legs.

"If you had told me six months ago that I'd be getting married soon, I'd have said you were crazy." He shook his head, but he seemed more smug than reflective.

Jake swiped his credit card and waited for the arm to raise. "What does it feel like?" he asked, easing out into the traffic. "Knowing that you've found someone for a life partner? Isn't it scary? What if you've made a mistake?"

"I know the statistics. But I also know Sophie. I didn't even realize I had been waiting for someone like her. She argues with me and pushes me and makes me a better person. Plus, she's hot as hell. Not that I'm bragging."

Jake horse laughed, wiping his eyes with one hand. "Of *course* you're bragging. That's what a groom is expected to do."

"And what about you and Nikki and Emma?"

Josh shrugged, keeping his eyes on the road. "Nikki and I are having dinner tomorrow night to talk about the situation."

"A date?"

"Not a date." The clarification was irritating, mostly because he had asked himself the same question a dozen times.

"What are you going to say? About the daddy thing, I mean."

Jake rotated his shoulders. He felt as tight as if he had been driving for hours. "I'm not sure. I don't think I can walk away from my own flesh and blood."

Several seconds passed. Long, suddenly awkward seconds.

Joshua ran a hand across the back of his neck. "Not to belabor the point, bro, but you did before. I can understand where Nikki is coming from. She wants to protect her daughter from getting hurt."

Suddenly, all the warm fuzzies Jake had been feeling as he reconnected with his twin evaporated. Was he always going to be the bad guy? Was there nothing he could do to make up for his fifteen-year hiatus? Nikki insisted she had changed, but did no one entertain the possibility that Jake might be changing, too?

He reached for the radio and tuned it to a station that played current music. It wasn't long before Joshua was snoring.

It was just as well. Jake knew where he stood now. He was always going to be on the outside looking in, wishing for something he couldn't even name...

Nikki worked the eight-to-four shift on Saturday, then rushed home to shower and change. Emma was pouty because her mom was leaving again, but it couldn't be helped. And, honestly, except for work, Nikki seldom left her daughter to go out. Mommies had needs, too.

She gave herself a mental slap. Tonight wasn't about a single mother's *needs*. She and Jake were getting together to discuss his role in Emma's life, her future.

The red sweater and black skirt, both newly mended, gave Nikki's confidence a boost. She paired the outfit with spiky black heels and silver snowflake earrings. Her black wool coat was at least seven years old, but it had classic lines. The forecast called for spitting snow, so she had no choice but to dress for the cold.

Roberta had been with Emma during the day, but Nella came over at five thirty to help with Emma's dinner and stay until Nikki returned.

"Enjoy yourself, Ms. Reardon," she said. "I brought stuff to do when Emma is in bed. If you're late, it won't matter. I'll doze on the sofa."

"Thanks," Nikki said, hoping her cheeks weren't as red as her sweater. "Text me if you need anything. And I'll check in with you a time or two." When the doorbell rang, Nikki kissed her daughter. "Be good, sweetheart. You and I will spend the day together tomorrow, I promise. Bye, Emma."

When she went through the house to the front door, she slipped her arms into her coat, then picked up her cell phone and purse. Jake wasn't coming in. Not with a babysitter who might or might not gossip.

As she pulled open the door, she smoothed a flyaway strand of hair. "Hi, there. I'm ready." Though she thought she was prepared, the sight of him made her weak. Those beautiful greenish-hazel eyes. The tousled hair. Broad shoulders. Flat belly. She felt the zing between them and forced herself not to react.

He blinked when he saw her, as if he, too, felt something. She saw the muscles in his throat work. "You look nice, Nik. I hope I didn't rush you too much."

"Not at all. Actually, I'm starving." They were back to being polite again. She hated it. At least when they fought, they were honest with each other. Now she felt the need to guard her words to preserve the peace.

Jake had suggested eating at the restaurant in his hotel. Nikki looked it up online while she was getting ready. It was one of the top-rated eateries in Falling Brook. Upscale. Jackets and ties required.

The fact that Jake had a king-size bed a few floors above was incidental.

"How was the bachelor party?" she asked when they were in the car.

Watching Jake's capable hands on the wheel made her tummy feel funny. *Sexual attraction. Animal attraction.* She recognized it for what it was, just like she had recognized it that night in Atlantic City. No point in denying the truth. But her physical response to Jake complicated the conversation about Emma.

When he helped her out of the car at the hotel, he put his hand under her arm momentarily. She came close to leaning into him the way she used to when they were together as teenagers, but she stopped herself.

He smelled warm and spicy and masculine. As they walked quickly toward the building, icy snow pellets dotted her coat. She turned up her collar and shivered. Neither of them was wearing gloves. When they entered the lobby and were enfolded in warm air, she inhaled the scents of fresh gardenias and furniture polish.

They bypassed the registration desk and walked down a long, carpeted hallway. The decor was understated and elegant, with no expense spared. It had been a very, very long time since Nikki had found herself in such sophisticated surroundings.

Their table was waiting for them. A single white orchid bloomed alongside a lit hurricane lamp. The restaurant was already swathed in holly and gold ribbons. The smells wafting from the kitchen promised culinary delights.

When Jake helped Nikki out of her coat, the warmth of his breath on the back of her neck made her shiver. He draped the coat over one of the extra seats and held her chair as she sat down. Then he took his place on the opposite side of the table and stared, his gaze hot and hungry.

"Don't," she said.

"Don't what?" His eyes danced, though he didn't smile.

"Don't look like you're going to gobble me up. It's disconcerting."

"I'd forgotten how beautiful you really are."

"I'm older and five pounds heavier, and I have stretch marks."

Now his beautiful lips curled upward in a sexy grin. He shrugged. "I know what I see, Nik."

"Can we eat right away?" she asked, unable to look straight at him. It was as dangerous as peering at the sun. Everything inside her heated and churned. "I don't want to be out too late." Was she reminding herself or him?

"Of course." Jake lifted a hand and summoned the

waiter. "My friend is famished. We'd like to order, please."

"Yes, sir. As you wish."

Nikki glanced blindly at the specials. "I'll have the prix fixe menu," she said. "Bruschetta. Shrimp bisque. The chicken piccata."

The dignified older man nodded. "And for dessert?"

"I'll decide later if that's okay."

The server turned to Jake. "And you, sir?"

"I'll order the other choices, so we can try them all. A house salad, the sweet-potato puree and the pork tenderloin."

Soon, Nikki and Jake were alone. Again. She worried her bottom lip with her teeth. "This feels awkward."

Jake nodded solemnly. "Very. Shall we discuss Emma now or later?"

"Let's get it over with." She clasped her hands on the table and took a deep breath. "Have you thought about who you want to be in her life?"

His response was instantaneous. "I'm her father," he said firmly. The possessive words sent a thrill through Nikki. They had made a baby together. "That's who I am and who I want to be," he said. "But I understand that I'm new to this game. I don't want to step on your toes or cause a problem for you."

Too late. Nikki kept her dark humor to herself. She cleared her throat, acknowledging the butterflies in her stomach. Though she spoke prosaically, she wanted to crawl across the table and drag his lips to hers. "I'm glad. A girl needs her father. How often do you think you might be available? I know you live a long way from here, and you have a busy travel schedule."

"It's the twenty-first century. We have jets and Wi-Fi conversations. I'll make time for Emma, I promise. I want to know her. I want to know her well."

Nikki found herself on the brink of tears. She realized in that moment that she hadn't known for sure Jake would claim his fatherhood. The fact that he had made her wildly emotional. "I'm so glad," she said, her throat tight. "I suppose we can work out the details later."

"I suppose we can." He reached across the table and took one of her hands, stroking his thumb across the back of it, giving her goose bumps. "Now that we've settled the big topic, let's talk about us."

"Us?" Her heart raced.

His tight smile held a hint of determination. "I ran away from you twice, Nikki. Once in Atlantic City, but even worse when you were almost eighteen."

They both winced. By the time Nikki's birthday rolled around that June, she had lost her innocence, but not because of Jake. Her world had been in ashes. Law-enforcement vehicles in her driveway. Uniformed men and women inside her house, boxing up her father's office. Opening the safe. Confiscating computers.

"I wish I could have spared you all the awfulness," he said, the words gruff and raw. "You were in so much pain. It broke my heart."

"You stayed for the funeral before you took off. I always appreciated that."

"It was a circus, as I recall. Paparazzi everywhere we turned. My mother and your mother weeping in a corner. I still get nauseous when I smell carnations."

"It was all a long time ago," she said softly. "We're different people now."

Suddenly, their food arrived, and the intimate conversation was shelved. Though Nikki was the furthest thing from calm, she ate, anyway. Soon, the flavors and textures of the various dishes coaxed her into enjoying the meal.

Beneath their conversation, a current of heated lust ran strong. She saw it in Jake's laser gaze, recognized it in her trembling body. They laughed and flirted and shared something rare and wonderful.

But Nikki knew in her heart it was temporary. Ephemeral.

Jake seemed relaxed, more relaxed than she had seen him since he had returned to Falling Brook. She asked the question she had been avoiding. "What did you do Thursday when I was working? I felt bad about turning you down."

"You have a job, Nik. I understand that. Oliver drove in from Manhattan, and we reconnected. Then we went to my mom's."

"How did that go?"

"Mom hugged me. Cried a little. I'm worried about her, Nik. A few years back, my father was declared legally dead. Mom took off her wedding ring. Thank

God she didn't date anyone seriously. It would have killed her, I think, to know she had committed adultery."

"Is she glad your father is alive?"

"I'm not sure. It's a devil of a mess. The hell of it is, there's not much my brothers and I can do for her."

"Except be there."

"I suppose."

"Sorry," Nikki said. "I didn't mean to ruin the mood."

Jake's face lightened. "Well, that's promising. I didn't even know we had a mood," he said, teasing. "Have I told you that your very lovely red sweater gives me all sorts of naughty ideas?"

"It's new," she admitted. "I bought it even though I shouldn't have, because I wanted to look good for you."

"Mission accomplished." The words were intense. Now he had both of her hands in his.

"Seeing you again after all this time has surprised me, Jake."

"How so?"

"You know the phrase *slow burn*?"

"Of course."

Her bottom lip trembled. "You severed our relationship. But the burn didn't end. I used to fantasize about you sometimes when I was having sex with my husband. How awful is that?"

He went pale. His pupils dilated. "Why are you telling me this? The truth, please."

She pulled her hands away and wrapped her arms

around her waist, trying not to fall apart. "I know there's nothing between us, Jake. You've been gone almost half my life. Fifteen years. We've lived apart. Separate. No connection at all except for that one insane night in Atlantic City five years ago. But that slow burn rekindled when I saw you again. And I have to know. Do you feel it, too?"

Now his face was grim, almost angry. "You know I do."

She swallowed hard, wondering if she was making a huge mistake, but feeling the urgency of the moment. "I'd like to sleep with you again. I'm living like a nun. I miss physical intimacy. I miss you."

The server brought dessert. For a moment, Nikki thought Jake might come unglued. The glare he gave the poor man sent him scuttling away.

"This looks good," Nikki said inanely.

Jake's jaw was hard as iron. "Please tell me you don't really expect me to eat anything right now."

"Shall I ask for to-go boxes?"

The sexual frustration and hunger rolled off him in waves. She had unleashed a sleeping dragon. A beautiful creature capable of creating great destruction.

He stared at her, his gaze hot. "Fine."

This time, Nikki was the one to summon the waiter. Soon, the check was taken care of, and Nikki had a paper bag in front of her. It was imprinted with the restaurant's name and held two clear plastic boxes, one with tiramisu, the other pecan pie.

She stood up on shaky legs. "Are we done?"

Jake stood, as well. His feral smile made the hair rise on the back of her neck. "We're *not* done, Nikki. Not even close."

Nine

Jake wondered if he was dreaming. He'd had a number of vivid dreams about Nikki Reardon over the years. With color and sound and all the visuals he could handle. But tonight was different. She stood at his elbow in the elevator, her gaze downcast, her fair skin tinted with a noticeable flush.

When the elevator stopped on his floor, they both got out, but still he didn't touch her. His hand shook as he tapped his key card on the electronic panel and waited for the tiny light to turn green.

Inside, he turned on lamps and kicked up the heat a couple of notches.

"This suite is amazing," Nikki said.

"I'm glad you like it."

Suddenly, he found himself looking at the room

through her eyes. He wasn't the neatest traveler. His laptop was plugged in on the desk by the window with papers scattered nearby. His suitcase was open on a luggage stand revealing his tumbled clothing.

For a man who traveled constantly, he'd never had any interest in being anal about organization. He was more likely to toss things in and hope for the best. His system hadn't failed him yet.

Now that he finally had Nikki within ten feet of his bed, his brain seized up and threatened to shut down. He was hard all over. And breathless. A thirty-seven-year-old man who could barely speak.

"Um," he said, as he undid his tie and tossed it aside with his jacket. "Would you like something to drink?"

Nikki set the desserts on a table and removed her coat. "I'd rather not. That's what got us into trouble in Atlantic City. If we're doing this, I want to be all in, not woozy."

"Fair enough." So much for smoothing anyone's nerves with alcohol. "There's an extra robe in the bathroom. If you'd like to get comfortable."

She kicked off her sexy high heels and padded across the room to where he stood. "I kind of thought you'd be the one getting me out of my clothes."

Holy hell. "Nikki…" He nearly swallowed his tongue when she placed her small hand, palm flat on his chest, right over his heart. Her fingers burned his skin through the expensive fabric of his dress shirt.

She went up on her tiptoes and kissed him. "I have

a babysitter on the clock. And I'm *interested*." She hesitated. "Have I shocked you?"

"Lord no." He lifted her off her feet and walked toward the bed, her legs dangling. When he set her down, the smile she gave him fried a few more synapses. "I didn't think this would happen tonight," he said. "Or ever. Forgive me if I'm off my game."

She ran her hands through his hair while he reached behind her to unbutton her skirt and lower the zipper. What he saw then paralyzed him even more. Nikki stepped out of the skirt casually, as if undressing for an audience was no big deal.

The lacy white garter belt, thong panties and silky stockings she wore were pure fantasy. He touched her warm thigh. "Damn, Nik. If I'd known you were hiding this, we'd have skipped dinner altogether."

Her small smile was smug. The little tease was enjoying his discomfiture. "I ordered all of it online after you left my house Wednesday. I'm glad you approve."

He removed her sweater next, lifting it over her head, trying not to mess up her hair. The bra he found matched the rest of her undies. Except that it had a panel of fine mesh on the top edge that revealed her raspberry nipples.

With his heart slugging in his chest, he scooped her up in his arms, folded back the covers one-handed and laid her gently on the bed. "Don't move," he croaked.

He began to strip with a marked lack of coordination, tossing pieces of clothing wildly until he was down to his black knit boxers.

Nikki no longer smiled. Her gaze fixed raptly on his erection, outlined in stretchy cloth. "You are a beautiful man, Jake Lowell," she said softly. "I thought I might have embroidered the memory of you naked, but it seems not."

He dispensed with his underwear and joined her on the bed.

When he touched her, he understood that time really could stand still. The room was hushed. Traffic noise from the street below barely penetrated his consciousness.

He ran his fingers through Nikki's golden-red tresses, spreading her hair on the pillows. She was a sensual woman. A siren. A goddess.

He refused to dwell on his grief for the years he had missed.

Timing. It all came down to timing.

"Jake?" She said his name softly, with concern. As if she could sense his turmoil. "Are you okay?"

He nodded slowly, running one hand from her shoulder to her belly to her silken-clad legs. "Oh, yeah," he said. "I'm good." He removed the panties but left everything else in place. When he played with her nipples through the bra, she moaned and arched off the bed. Her cheeks flushed. Her eyelids fluttered shut.

For one breathless moment, she was there in front of him. Ripe for the taking.

That one night in Atlantic City was a blur to him now. This felt like another first. A second chance.

Was karma offering him closure, or an opportunity for redemption?

Slow burn. Yes. That's what it was. The need to take her rose through him like a forceful, uncontrollable wave.

"Nikki…" He whispered her name, not even sure what he wanted to tell her. If he hadn't run away all those years ago, *this woman* might have been his.

Emotion burned his throat, scored him with pain, but not as much as the regret crushing his chest.

He wouldn't let the negative emotions ruin this. Not now. Not tonight.

Carefully, he touched her center and found her wet and slick with heat.

Belatedly, he remembered the condoms in his shaving kit. He rested his forehead on her belly, breathing hard, shaking like he had a fever. "I'll be right back."

When he returned seconds later, Nikki turned her head and smiled at him. The look in her eyes nearly brought him to his knees.

He joined her again, but when she tried to curl her fingers around his shaft, he grabbed her wrist and held her at bay. "Later," he said gruffly. "I don't think I can wait."

He took care of protection and moved over her, spreading her thighs and fitting the head of his sex at her entrance. They both gasped when he went deep. So much for wooing her with his technique.

Nothing about this was smooth or practiced. Just two people yearning, straining against each other. Her skin was soft and warm. When he lifted one stocking-clad ankle onto his shoulder, the sight of her shot another bolt of heat through his gut.

"I adore these stockings, Nikki. You look like a pinup girl from a wartime calendar."

Her smile was sleepy and happy. "Glad you approve." She raised her hips, urging him on.

Fear like he had never known intruded—a fear he didn't want to admit. This was a mistake. Like that night in Atlantic City, he was rocked with wild emotions. He didn't know how to control the feelings. This was more than sexual desperation. So much more…

What did it mean?

Now he and Nikki were forever connected because of Emma. He couldn't pretend he was a ship passing Nikki's in the night.

He had left her twice before.

In the midst of unprecedented passion, the knee-jerk instinct to run was strong. But even scarier was the yearning, the need to stay.

She cupped his face in her hands, testing the late-day stubble on his chin. Her eyes searched his. "It's okay, Jake. Don't worry about it. This is just you and me scratching an itch. No declarations. No promises. Give me what I want."

"Gladly." He closed his eyes and pumped his hips, breathing raggedly, blind with need and confusion. Nikki's body welcomed him, drew him in, squeezed him. If he had been the kind of man to believe in love, this might have changed him.

But he wasn't and he didn't, so he concentrated on taking Nikki with him to the top and then holding her as they tumbled over the edge.

When it was over, they were both breathing heavily, the sounds audible in the silent room. He felt dizzy and warm and limp with satisfaction.

As he rolled onto his back, Nikki curled her body into his, her head resting on his shoulder. "Wow. You're good at this."

"I'm glad you think so." He mumbled the words, his eyes closed. He was so tired suddenly that he teetered on the brink of unconsciousness.

After a few moments, Nikki stirred. "I have to go, Jake. It's a long way back. Please don't get up. You're in a warm bed. I'll grab a cab or a ride share."

He tried to process her words. And then it hit him. Nikki wasn't free to spend the night. He knew that, of course, but the knowledge had been pushed to the back of his brain. "I'll take you," he said.

"No, really." She climbed out of bed and scooped up her underwear and clothes, then went toward the bathroom, still wearing the garter belt and stockings. God help him. "Stay where you are," she said. "I'll text you when I get home."

He stumbled after her, pulling up short in the doorway to the small en suite. The long mirror over the sink reflected a woman who looked like a weary angel…if angels had red hair and white skin and a stubborn tilt to their chins.

"Don't be ridiculous," he said. "I'm getting dressed."

His clothing was scattered all over the floor and the furniture. He grabbed everything except his sport coat. When he was ready, he avoided looking at the bed. Would he be able to sleep there tonight?

Nikki wasn't like the other women he had bedded. She never had been.

What was he supposed to do with that knowledge?

They made their way down to the car in silence. The snow had picked up, but it wasn't sticking to the roads.

Nikki tried once again to convince him to let her leave without him. He shut her up by leaning her against the car and kissing her hard. Then he tucked her into the passenger seat and closed the door. Once the engine fired, he turned up the heat.

"You okay, Nik?"

She nodded. "I'm good."

When she reached out and put a hand on this thigh, he felt like he had won the lottery. "What's your schedule like this week?" he asked.

"On Wednesday, I only work half a day. I could fix dinner and you could have some time with Emma."

"Any chance I might spend the night?" His hands gripped the steering wheel.

The long silence made his stomach curl. He heard his passenger sigh. She sounded conflicted. "I'll have to think about it, Jake."

"Is there a downside?" He asked the question lightly, as if he was merely curious instead of stung by her palpable reluctance.

"I want you, but I don't want to get involved. My

life and yours are both complicated. You've left me twice now. And both times nearly killed me. So I like to think I'm smarter than I used to be."

"You don't think much of my character, do you?"

"It's not your character. It's *my* self-control."

The rest of the trip passed in silence. Jake chewed on her words, unable to put a positive spin on them. She cared about him, but she didn't want to get hurt when he inevitably left again.

She wasn't wrong. He wasn't cut out for Falling Brook. Hell, he wasn't cut out for anywhere permanent. That was why he wandered. But could he change? Did he want to?

"Will you still come to Joshua's wedding with me?" he asked.

"Of course. I said I would. Besides, it will be fun. Your brother is a super guy. I'm so glad he and Sophie found each other."

The snow was coming in heavier bands. Jake focused his attention on the road, glad of the excuse to drop the conversation. Talking about his brother's happy nuptials made his own life seem empty and meaningless.

When they finally pulled up in front of Nikki's modest house, she leaned over and kissed his cheek— a brief peck, nothing to get hot and bothered about.

"I enjoyed tonight, Jake. Thanks for dinner…and everything."

"I'll walk you to the door," he said.

"No. Keep the car warm. I'll talk to you soon."

And then she was gone, though her scent lingered.

Jake waited for the front door to open and close. Then he put the car in gear and headed back to Falling Brook. The long drive gave him plenty of time to think. Too much time. Why were people so complicated?

As soon as Josh's wedding was over, there would be no reason to stay. Except for the trial, of course. But even those legal proceedings didn't demand Jake's presence. He didn't care what happened to his father.

Not at all...

But he couldn't lie to himself. He was falling for Nikki all over again. Which scared the hell out of him...

Nikki spoke briefly with Nella, and then urged her to go home before the roads got any worse. She handed the girl an envelope with cash in it. "Thank you so much for staying late. I really appreciate it."

"No problem, Ms. Reardon. She was a lot of fun, and she went to sleep as soon as I put her to bed. Call me again anytime."

When the babysitter left, Nikki closed the front door and leaned her back against it. She had shed her coat when she walked in, but now her cashmere sweater and wool skirt felt too hot. Nella must have run up the thermostat.

It was fine, really. Emma sometimes tossed off her covers during the night. Nikki wanted her baby girl to be warm.

In the bathroom, she tried to avoid looking at herself in the mirror. She felt as if she was wearing a neon sign—*I had sex tonight...with Jake Lowell.*

Who really cared? If Nikki kept her head in the game and didn't lose sight of the fact that Jake would leave New Jersey sooner than later, she couldn't get hurt. Right?

After a long hot shower, she put on her oldest, comfiest pair of flannel pajamas and climbed into bed. When she closed her eyes, Jake was there in the bed with her. He had touched her hungrily but with such tender care. As if she was breakable.

She wasn't. Not anymore. Life had knocked her down more than once, but she had picked herself up and kept going.

Though it was late, and her daughter would be up early, Nikki couldn't sleep. She replayed the night with Jake over and over, stirring restlessly in her lonely bed.

No other guy she knew was as smart or as funny... or as dangerously masculine and attractive.

The sex tonight had been revelatory. Nikki responded to Jake like no other partner she had ever known. Not that there was even a handful to compare.

He drew something from her. Some deep expression of her femininity. With Jake, she felt sexual, sensual, elementally human in the best possible way.

For the first time, she let herself wonder if there was a way forward that included the two of them as a couple. They shared a child. It wasn't so far-fetched an idea. They certainly had sexual chemistry. And a deep history. Similar backgrounds. Shared values.

What if she allowed herself to open up to him? To drop her resentment and anger and disappointment? What if she took Jake into her bed and into her life with a blank slate? Was there any possibility she might really be able to love him again? Did there exist a part of her that never *stopped* loving him?

If she lowered her defenses and let her emotions run wild, would Jake be able to reciprocate? It was scary to think of saying "I love you" and then being rejected.

When he had suggested that she and Emma visit Switzerland, the invitation had been couched in very temporary terms. To say Jake was skittish about commitment was like saying a zebra had stripes.

Nikki wanted more from a man. She deserved more. A life partner. Someone who would encourage her to grow and flourish, and who would love and support her.

Being honest with herself about the current situation was getting harder and harder. She wanted to dream.

By the time Wednesday rolled around, she had second-guessed herself a million times. She picked up Emma after Mom's Day Out, stopped by the store and then rushed home to throw together a homemade lasagna. Soon, the kitchen was all warm and cozy and filled with the wonderful smells of tomato sauce and cheese and garlic.

Jake had sent a text, offering to pay for a babysitter so they could go out to dinner again, but Nikki had declined politely. Perhaps it was unfair, but she felt the need to test Jake's reactions in a boring family setting. He couldn't always splash his money around and expect to make problems go away.

Nikki liked being pampered as much as the next woman, but this relationship with Jake had three sides, not two. Tonight's focus would be Emma. After Emma went to bed, all bets were off. Nikki hadn't planned that far ahead. Some things were best left to chance.

Jake hadn't asked again about staying over, and she hadn't brought it up.

Unfortunately, the weather had taken a raw turn. The flurries they'd had for a few days were predicted to become accumulating snow sometime during the night. She wondered if Jake would cancel, and then felt sheepish when she realized how very much she dreaded that phone call.

She could tell herself all she wanted that she was keeping an emotional distance, but the truth was far different. Jake was deeply involved in her life already. She had allowed it, encouraged it and enjoyed it.

The real question was…did she want him to *stay* involved?

When the doorbell rang at five thirty on the dot, she dried her damp palms on her pants and took a deep breath. Emma was playing in her room, but she would soon be asking for dinner.

Nikki had decided to dress casually. Her stretchy black leggings and gold ballet flats were comfortable and cute. The off-the-shoulder sweater was turquoise. She looked like what she was—a middle-class suburban mom home for the evening.

The bell rang a second time. Evidently, she had dithered too long.

Scuttling through the house, she swept her fingers through her clean hair and checked her reflection in the hall mirror. Not bad. Her eyes were perhaps too bright, her smile too big. She inhaled sharply and let the air escape slowly. *Calm, Nikki. Calm.*

It took her two tries to grab the doorknob. At last, she flung open the door, letting in a rush of cold air and revealing the identity of her visitor, not that she'd had any doubt.

"Jake. Hi. Come on in."

In a quick glance, she saw everything about him. Leather jacket unzipped over a tailored blue cotton shirt. Jeans that were just the right amount of worn. Jeans that hugged his legs and man parts in a very distracting fashion. And my gosh, were those…?

She blurted it out. "Are you wearing *cowboy boots*? Mr. Sophisticated World Traveler, Jake Lowell?"

"Let me in, Nik. It's freezing."

"Sorry." She stepped back quickly.

He brushed past her, bringing in the scents of the outdoors. "These are for you."

The large bouquet of deep yellow roses definitely didn't come from a run-of-the-mill supermarket. The blossoms were huge and fragrant. She took them automatically. "You didn't have to bring me flowers."

He shot her a glance that included irritation and banked lust. "I know that. Put them in water, Nik."

He glanced down the hall. "I brought Emma something, too."

"Honestly, Jake. Gifts aren't necessary. She'd just a little kid."

Without warning, he kissed her, his lips lingering, pressing, summoning memories of the night in his hotel room. "She's more than just a little kid. She's my daughter."

Ten

Jake noted the stricken look on Nikki's face, but he couldn't quite pinpoint the cause. Was he being too abrupt about claiming his parental rights? Did his words sound like a threat? He hadn't meant them that way.

Giving Nikki a chance to regain her composure, he shrugged out of his jacket and rolled up his sleeves. The little house was cheery and warm. "Dinner smells amazing."

At last, Nikki's posture thawed. "I hope you like lasagna."

He followed her into the kitchen and watched as she rummaged under the sink for a vase. Her position gave him a tantalizing view of her perfect, heart-shaped ass.

Just as his libido began to carry him down a dangerous path, little Emma appeared in the doorway. "Is it time, Mommy? I'm hungry." She turned to Jake. "Hi! Are you eating with us?"

Jake nodded. "Sure am. And *I'm* hungry, too. Maybe we should get out of the way for a bit and let Mommy get everything on the table." He shot Nikki an inquiring look. "Unless you need help."

Her cheeks were pink. "I'm good. Give me five minutes."

In the living room, he handed Emma the gift that was wrapped in shiny red paper.

She cocked her head in a movement eerily reminiscent of her mother. "It's too early for Christmas."

"This isn't a Christmas present. It's just something your mom told me you liked." He had wrestled with his conscience and finally decided he wasn't above buying a child's affection if it landed him a few extra points in a sticky situation.

Emma's excited screech brought her mother running. Nikki stopped in the doorway, her expression frazzled. "What's wrong?"

Emma beamed and held up the toy, not realizing she had scared her mother. "Look what Mr. Man got me!"

Nikki mouthed at Jake, *Mr. Man?*

He shrugged. "I thought you told her to call me that."

"No."

Emma demanded her mother's attention. "Look, Mommy. It's the special one."

What Jake had procured at an appalling price was the princess from the latest animated movie. She was the deluxe edition with eyes that opened and closed and a fancy dress with two additional outfits. The doll had been advertised heavily on television and was out of stock in stores across the area despite the fact that Black Friday hadn't even happened yet.

Nikki squatted to give the princess her required admiration. "She's beautiful, Emma. Did you thank Mr. Jake?"

Without warning, Emma whirled and wrapped her arms around Jake's knees. "Thank you, thank you, thank you."

He touched her head, felt the long, soft golden hair. "You're very welcome." Emotions buzzed inside his chest. Alien emotions that weren't particularly welcome. He had decided he wanted to know his daughter. But that had been a cerebral decision. He hadn't anticipated actually *feeling* things.

Nikki rescued him. "Dinner's ready," she said calmly, rising to her feet. It almost seemed as if she could detect his internal agitation.

The meal could have been awkward. Emma's nonstop chatter made it less so. The roses were displayed in an inexpensive glass container. They matched the yellow stripe in Nikki's woven place mats.

Emma turned up her nose when her mom put a small serving of salad on her plate. It must have been a battle the two females had fought before, because the younger one sighed and gave in to the older.

The three of them ate in harmony, though Jake was

unable to keep from imagining Nikki naked and at his mercy. Such inappropriate mental pictures probably reflected poorly on his qualifications to be a dad, but he couldn't help it. Three entire days and most of a fourth had passed since he had seen his lover.

Though Jake had kept busy, the mental movie reel made him itchy and restless and disrupted his sleep. He'd brought an overnight case this trip and left it in the trunk of the car. He couldn't read Nikki on this particular subject, but he wanted to be prepared.

Emma liked her mother's lasagna and cleaned her plate.

Jake ate three helpings himself and groaned when he finally pushed back from the table. "I had no idea you could cook like that."

"Thank you." Nikki served her daughter a very small dollop of warm apple pie with ice cream.

When she offered some to Jake, he shook his head ruefully. "I overdid it with dinner. I'll have to wait for some of this to shake down."

"Of course."

Emma asked to be excused and was given permission. Just like that, the atmosphere in the kitchen went from homey to horny. At least on his part.

Nikki's face wasn't giving away anything.

Jake finished his glass of wine and poured himself another. "I'm glad she liked the doll."

Nikki stiffened visibly. "Presents aren't a substitute for quality time."

He stared at her. "I only found out I was a father

a short time ago. You could cut me some slack, Nik. Are you trying to pick a fight with me?"

All that wild red hair was caught back in a pony-tail at her nape, but it didn't take much effort to re-member it fanned out across his sheets.

Her jaw jutted. "I want to make Christmas special for her. You just undercut me."

He frowned. "Were you planning to give her that doll?"

"No. You know I can't afford it. But now, what-ever Santa brings will look paltry in comparison."

"I doubt she knows the word *paltry*, and you're her mom. She's going to love whatever you and the jolly old man put under the tree."

Nikki's ire deflated visibly. "Whatever." She chewed her lip. "You could make it up to me."

He grinned. "I like the sound of that."

"Get your mind out of the gutter, Lowell. I'm talk-ing about actual useful *work*."

He glanced around him at the dishes. "You want me to clean up the kitchen? Sure. I'd be happy to—"

"No. Not that. I need help with the Christmas tree."

"What Christmas tree?"

She looked at him and rolled her eyes. "The one in the closet. I like to put up the tree the day after Thanksgiving. But since I've asked off for the wed-ding this coming Saturday, the diner has me down to work Friday *and* Saturday of Thanksgiving week-end. With you here tonight, we could put up the tree together in no time, and Emma could hang a few or-naments before she goes to bed."

"If you want, I could buy you a tree, fully decorated, and have it delivered tomorrow." Which would free up time for the two grown-ups to fool around later.

Nikki touched his arm briefly, making his skin hum. "Trimming the tree is part of the magic of Christmas," she said. "I appreciate the thought, but I love decorating. It makes me feel good."

"I get it. But why artificial?"

"For one, Emma has allergies. Besides, a live tree can't go up this early. They dry out. Surely, you've done this before."

"As a kid," he said, feeling defensive and trying not to show it.

Nikki stared at him, her beautiful eyes wide. "Are you telling me you haven't put up a Christmas tree in fifteen years?"

"Why does that shock you, Nikki? I live alone. I'm always on the road. It's a lot of hassle for one person."

"But what about the holidays? What about Christmas Day? How did you celebrate?"

Her inquisition brought back memories that weren't always exactly pleasant. "Well, for starters, sometimes I'm in a country that doesn't observe the Christmas holiday."

"Okay. I get that. But other years?"

"Occasionally a friend will invite me over. Or if I'm traveling, I'll find a church and go to a service. It's not a bad thing to skip the commercialism and the sappy sentiment. I haven't missed much."

Her eyes darkened with some emotion he couldn't

name. "Oh, but you have, Jake. You just don't realize it."

"Where's this damn tree?" he growled. "Let's get it over with."

Nikki pointed him toward the closet, though she seemed troubled. Jake carried the long, rectangular box into the living room and opened it. Fortunately, the tree was one of those prelit deals. All he had to do was lock together the three sections and make sure the stand was attached tightly.

At Nikki's direction, he positioned it in front of the window. Though he wouldn't dare say so out loud, the poor fake evergreen was not the snappiest tree in the forest. Honestly, it looked a bit dilapidated. Even sad…

"I know it's not great," Nikki said, studying the tree with her nose wrinkled. "I got it on clearance the year I was pregnant with Emma. But the decorations cover up its imperfections. Emma," she called. "We're ready to put ornaments on the tree."

Emma came running, holding her doll from Jake. "Can I do the first one?"

"Sure, baby."

Jake had planned to sit back and watch while the womenfolk did their thing. He was sadly mistaken about his role. First Emma, and then Nikki, chided him.

Soon, he was selecting ornaments from a jumbled plastic container and placing them on the tree. When the ornament box was finally empty—hallelujah— the adults added shiny silver tinsel, starting at the top and winding it around the tree. Nikki got down on her stomach and spread out a red velvet tree skirt, twitching and pulling until it was straight enough to meet her exacting standards.

Jake would have offered to help, but he was afraid he would be tempted to do more than twitch if he was down on the floor with Nikki. She looked like a holiday treat in her fluffy turquoise sweater. It was the color of the Aegean Sea. Maybe he could convince her to take a trip with him to Greece. Sunshine. Warmth. Blue skies.

He cleared his throat and tried to think about icebergs and cold showers. "Are we done?" he asked.

Nikki stood, stretched her back and nodded. A piece of her hair had tangled with one of the lower branches. Jake smoothed the strand and rubbed his thumb over her cheek. "The tree looks great, Nik."

It was true. Somehow, the collage of ornaments had transformed a shabby artificial tree into something beautiful.

Emma stared at it, her doll in her arms. "Turn the lights off, Mommy."

In the dark, the tree was even better. Jake pressed a surreptitious kiss beneath Nikki's ear and nipped her earlobe with his teeth. "I keep picturing you naked," he confessed, his words too quiet for the child to hear. He slid a hand under the back of Nikki's sweater and caressed the length of her spine.

Nikki shivered, but didn't move away. Instead, she leaned into him, letting him support her weight. Her hair tickled his nose.

Finally, she turned in his loose embrace, touched his lips with her fingers and spoke as he had, in a low voice. "It's snowing really hard now. You shouldn't drive back to Falling Brook. Why don't you spend the night?"

A rush of heat settled in his groin. His mouth dried. "On the sofa?"

He saw the multicolored lights from the Christmas tree reflected in her laughing eyes. "In my bed."

"What about Emma?" His voice sounded funny, perhaps because he was struggling to breathe.

Nikki gave his chin a quick kiss, then eyed her daughter. "We'll set an alarm," she muttered. "You can move to the sofa at five. It will be fine."

Nikki bathed her daughter, washed her hair and dressed her in warm pajamas. The temperature was dropping and would soon leave a crust of ice on the new-fallen snow. As Nikki tucked Emma into bed, her daughter cuddled the new doll sleepily. "Why isn't Mr. Man reading me a story tonight?"

"It's late, baby. Decorating the tree took all our time."

Emma yawned and snuggled deeper in her covers. "I like the tree. It's bootiful."

Nikki grinned. "Yes, it is. But remember, it's still a long time until Christmas. We put up the tree a little early this year. You and I will enjoy it every day and every night, and I'll let you know when it's time to look for Santa."

"I can wait, Mommy. I'm good at waiting."

"Can I ask you a question, love?" She smoothed her daughter's still-damp hair. "Why do you call Jake 'Mr. Man'?"

Emma yawned again, her eyelids drooping. "He's a boy and we're girls. I like Mr. Man."

Nikki managed not to laugh. "Fair enough."

When she turned off the light and tiptoed out, she was pretty sure her daughter was already asleep. Nikki found Jake in the kitchen wiping the last of the countertops. The dishwasher was humming, and the kitchen was spotless.

"Jake," she said, feeling guilty. "You're our guest. I would have done all this."

His grin curled her toes. "First of all," he said, "I needed to earn my keep. And second of all…" He crossed the room and scooped her up on her toes for a fast, breath-stealing kiss. "I wanted you to be free for whatever comes next."

"And what would that be?"

"Lady's choice."

She nuzzled her cheek against his broad, hard chest, listening to the steady *ka-thump* of his heart. "What if we start by drinking cheap wine in the dark and enjoying the Christmas tree?"

"Cheap wine?"

"You tell me." She threw open the cabinet where she kept a single bottle of red and then opened the fridge and pulled out two bottles of chardonnay. "Your pick."

He winced. "I could have brought some."

"I suppose a man who visits fancy vineyards in France and Italy is above five-dollar vino?"

Jake's expression was droll. "If you paid five dollars for these, you were robbed."

His disgust made her giggle, though she was breathless with wanting him. "How about coffee? I have some beans in the freezer. And a grinder. Though it's probably dusty," she admitted.

He cupped her face in his big hands and kissed her eyelids one at a time, his expression searing and intense. "How about a glass of water, and then we go make out on your couch?"

"I'm fine without the water," she gasped. They were pressed together so closely she could feel the hard length of him against her abdomen. "And we *could* go straight to the bedroom."

Jake was suddenly the one with patience. "Tree first, woman. We worked hard on that masterpiece."

He took her by the hand and drew her down the hall to the living room. Nikki had opened the drapes before she put Emma to bed. Now, streetlights illuminated the heavily falling snow. The tree cast a warm glow over the room.

"You couldn't have driven home, anyway," Nikki muttered. "Look at it out there. Did you bring an overnight bag? You should grab your stuff from the car before it gets any worse."

Jake sat down and pulled her onto his lap. "You agreed to make out with me. Don't change the subject. And yes. I packed a few things. Just in case."

Nikki shivered. How many times over the years

had the two of them fooled around like this? When she was in high school and Jake was in college, she had lived for the weekends when he came home to Falling Brook. He'd told his mother he needed to wash clothes. He'd told Nikki he needed *her*.

Now, Jake's hands were everywhere…caressing, arousing. When he stroked the center seam of her leggings, the one that lined up with her aching sex, she arched into him and whimpered. "Yes, Jake. Yes."

They kissed ravenously, straining to get closer and closer still. His lips bruised hers. His hands tangled in her hair. "I want you, Nik. I haven't been able to think about anything else but making love to you since I brought you home Saturday night. Please tell me I'm not the only one with this obsession."

"You're not," she panted, her tongue soothing the small hickey she had left on his neck. "Where are the condoms? Don't say they're in the car."

He shoved her aside and jumped to his feet, reaching for his billfold. "Two," he croaked. "Right here."

"Good." She stood also, then stripped her sweater over her head. The house was warm, but her nipples furled tightly when Jake reached for her, his gaze hot.

"Let me help you with that bra," he said. Seconds later, the bra was in the air and Jake was sitting on the sofa again with her on his lap so he could play with her breasts. He plumped them between his hands and buried his face between them, inhaling her scent. "You still wear the same perfume," he said softly.

"Yes."

"I caught a whiff in a department store one time

and got a hard-on. I love the way it smells on your warm skin. I could eat you up, Nik." Then he caught one nipple between his teeth and tugged. That simple contact sparked fireworks all over her body.

When she cried out, he glanced up at her, his cheeks flushed. "Too much?"

She smoothed his hair with a shaky hand. "No, Jake. Never too much."

He rewarded that confession by giving the neglected nipple equal time. In moments, Nikki's knees were weak and the thrum of arousal low in her belly was impossible to ignore. "Take off my pants," she begged, standing up clumsily.

The stretchy fabric cooperated easily when Jake slid his hands inside and dragged her pants down her legs. He took her ballet flats, too, leaving her in nothing but a pair of lacy black undies.

"God, you're beautiful," he breathed, his expression reverent.

"You have too many clothes on."

She started unbuttoning his shirt, but his patience ran out. "I'll do it."

Suddenly, she realized the drapes were still open. "Oh, my gosh." The living room was dark, but still. Scuttling backward into the shadows, she hissed at Jake. "My bedroom. Now."

They tiptoed down the hallway, past Emma's closed door, and made it unscathed into the master bedroom. *Master* was a misnomer. The bedroom was scarcely larger than Emma's, but it did have a bathroom, so the lady of the house didn't have to use the one in the hall.

Jake exhaled. "Does this door lock?"

The room was dark. "Yes. Hang on." She found the bedside table and turned on the lamp. When she saw Jake's face, her heart stopped. He looked like a pirate intent on capturing a prize.

Rapidly, he removed the rest of his clothes. He made her feel young again, and reckless.

She turned back the quilt and the sheet and climbed onto the bed.

Jake joined her quickly. "This feels good," he said as they rolled together, their limbs tangling.

"The mattress isn't great," she mumbled, wrapping her hand around the most interesting part of him.

He shuddered. "I don't give a damn about the mattress. I'd take you outside in the snow if that was the only way to have you. You excite me, Nik. I guess that's obvious. I'd like to see you sunbathing nude on a private terrace in Greece. Just the two of us. Drinking ouzo and eating cheese. How does that sound?"

Since he was touching every erogenous zone on her body and a few that were surprisingly mundane most of the time, she was in a cooperative mood. "Sounds wonderful. Would you buy me a gold anklet and let me ride a donkey down to the sea?"

He choked out a laugh. "I'd buy you a whole damn town. And every man who walked by our dinner table at night would see you in candlelight and be jealous that they weren't me." He moved away long enough to don protection, then came back to her.

Reclining on his hip, he entered her with two fingers, feeling the slick warmth of her body. Gently, he stroked the spot that centered her pleasure. "I want to take you hard and fast, but I also want it slow and easy."

Nikki skated her palm over his sculpted, warm shoulder, loving the feel of him, the intimacy. "Why choose?" she asked quietly. "We can have it all."

He rose over her and thrust hard, making both of them gasp. She wrapped her legs around his waist. The movement forced him deeper. He thrust again, and she climaxed, the world going hazy as she concentrated on wringing every bit of pleasure from her release. It had come too fast. She wanted more. But already Jake was finding his own nirvana, taking her body and making it his own.

At last, breathing hard, he rolled away, linking her hand with his. "That was amazing, Nik." The words were slurred. His breathing deepened as he fell asleep.

She reached for the lamp and turned it off. Then with one hand, she set an alarm on her phone. In the dark, tears stung her eyes. Christmas was the season of miracles, but something told her Jake Lowell wouldn't stick around long enough for Santa to show up.

Nikki squeezed his hand, holding on as if she could keep him forever. "I love you, Jake," she whispered.

Eleven

When Jake opened his eyes, he was disoriented by the dark. This wasn't his hotel room. And then he was fully awake.

Shifting carefully to the side of the bed, he stood and stumbled to the bathroom. When he returned, his eyes had adjusted fractionally to the black of night. Nikki must have installed room-darkening shades on her windows.

A glance at his watch told him it was only two. In the silence, he could hear the almost imperceptible sound of Nikki's breathing. He climbed back under the covers and turned into her warmth. The curves and valleys of her body had him hard again.

But he was cold inside, and there was a block of ice where his heart should have been. Nikki had thought he was asleep when she said those four incredible words. *I love you, Jake.*

Had she really meant it? How could she? After everything that had happened...

As he tried to steady his panicked breathing, a memory popped into his head. He'd been twelve, maybe thirteen, camping with a friend and his family at Yellowstone. A park ranger gave a talk about the west's low humidity and had warned that if the remnants of a campfire were not separated and scattered well enough, an ember, a slow burn, might remain for hours, days. And then spring back to life when the wind conditions were right.

Now here Jake was. Did he still love Nikki? Or did he even care enough to try? And with a kid in the mix, what was the fallout if he wanted to be the man Nikki deserved, but failed?

His erection mocked his indecision. *Take her*, the devil on his shoulder urged. *Protect her*, said his better self.

In the end, he knew the answer. Moving her gently in the bed, he shook her awake. "I need you, Nik. Again? Please?"

She nodded sleepily, murmuring her pleasure when he kissed her long and deep, teased her lips, thrust his tongue inside to stroke her tongue. The fire burned hot again.

Reaching for the nightstand on his side of the bed, he found the remaining condom and managed to rip it open. When he was ready, he faced her on his side.

Carefully, he lifted her leg over his hip, pulled her close and joined their bodies.

It was perhaps the most intimate thing they had done. Their breath mingled. They met as equals. Neither in charge. Both of them taking pleasure and giving it in return.

Nikki curled her arm around his neck and kissed him. "I'm glad you stayed tonight," she whispered.

Her kiss took him higher. He felt invincible. "Me, too, Nik," he groaned. Fire swept down his spine, flashed in his pelvis. His fingers dug into the soft curve of her ass. He wanted to say something, to tell her how he felt, but the storm swept him under. He came so hard he might have lost his wits for a moment.

He rolled to his back at the end. Her cheek was smashed against his chest. Stroking her glorious hair, he tried to steady his breathing. His brain spun out of control, and he tasted fear. How could he hurt the woman who had been his whole world?

"Jake?" she said, petting his chest like he was a big jungle cat.

"Hmm?"

"I'm wide-awake now. Tell me about the wedding. I know you said it's at two o'clock, but is it going to be a huge affair? Where are they getting married?"

He tried to focus. "You remember the Bismarck Hotel downtown?"

"Yes."

"They've remodeled the top floor into a large entertainment space. Josh and Sophie had the choice of including only family and close friends or planning for a crowd of a thousand or more. You know how it is in Falling Brook. Once you start inviting people, it's hard to draw the line. Plus, with all the Black Crescent mess in the news again this year, my brother and his fiancée thought it would be in poor taste to spread a bunch of money around. Last I heard, the guest list hits around fifty. Small and intimate."

"What about a rehearsal dinner?"

"Nope. Not even that."

"Good for them."

The conversation was a pleasant diversion, but Jake had arrived at the moment of truth. Things were getting far too cozy. He released her and scooted up against the headboard, forcing himself not to touch her.

Nikki reached for the lamp and flipped the switch. He hated that. He didn't want her to see what was coming.

If he had any guts at all, he wouldn't let her have hope. He raked his hand through his hair, feeling the cold sweat on his forehead. "I don't think I'm going to stay for my father's trial, Nikki."

She sat up, too, pulling the sheet to her chest, covering her breasts. Her hair was a tumbled, fiery cloud around her face. Her eyes were huge. "I don't understand. Why not? You need closure, Jake. If you don't face Vernon, you'll never get over what he did. He'll always be the bogeyman."

Perhaps there was truth in what she said, but he didn't want to hear it. He didn't want to admit it. "He's nothing to me. I don't care what happens to him. He destroyed us, Nikki. I can't forgive him for that."

Every bit of color leached from her face. He thought for a moment she might be sick. "That's not true," she said. The words were sharp.

He stared at her. "Of course it is."

The heartbreak dawning in her eyes was familiar. He'd seen it fifteen years ago. He might have seen it five years ago in Atlantic City if he'd left when she was awake. She lifted her chin, visibly angry. "*You* destroyed us, Jake. Not your dad. He disappeared, but you could have come back anytime, and you didn't."

The attack came out of nowhere.

He gaped at her. Nikki was always on his side. Always. "I *had* to leave. He'd made my life impossible. Everywhere I went, reporters followed me. One of them shimmied up a ladder and tried to climb into my bedroom. It was hell, Nikki. And all of it, his fault."

"I know it was hell. I was there, remember?"

"Well, at least your dad died. He paid for his sins. You didn't have people thinking that you and your mother were hiding a fortune somewhere."

"That's a terrible thing to say." Her pallor increased. "I loved my dad, even though I hated what he did. I also hate how your dad and mine tore lives and families apart. But time moved on, Jake. I'm not stuck in the past. I've had to build a new life from the ground up. I have a child who loves me and a mother who depends on me for emotional support. I'm not that frightened high-school girl anymore."

"The implication being that I'm a coward?" His temper simmered.

She hesitated. "Not a coward. No. Not that. But you're emotionally stunted. You've had every resource in the world at your fingertips, and yet you couldn't bring yourself to grow up and come back and do your part. We all needed you, Jake. Oliver. Your mother. Joshua. Me."

Her words chipped away at him, exposing his weaknesses. It wasn't that he'd been too lazy or immature to share the burden—he'd been afraid. Afraid that he would come home and make things worse. "I offered Josh my help more than once. But he assumed I was a screwup, so he wasn't interested."

"That was in the past. My God, Jake. He offered you the helm of the company recently. How much more does he have to do to prove he believes in you?"

"I've lived on the road too long to change my ways. People aren't always who you want them to be, Nikki. You expect too much."

Her eyes were wet. Her jaw wobbled. "Do I? Maybe so." One tear broke loose and ran down her cheek. "I think you should go sleep on the sofa now."

There it was. The death blow.

He had brought it on himself. Provoked this confrontation. The ice in his chest melted, leaving a gaping hole. It hurt. Dear God, it hurt. But he didn't know how to fix it.

Nikki stared at him, anguish on her face. "What about Emma?"

"I'll still see Emma. She has nothing to do with my father."

Now Nikki's smile was bitter. "I think you're wrong, Jake. How you relate to your daughter has everything to do with this chip on your shoulder. You've carried it far too long. It's crippled you."

He took the hit stoically, but he fought back, lashing out. "What did you say your college degree was in? Surely, not psychology." He heard the sarcasm and condescension in his words, but he couldn't seem to stop this train wreck of a conversation. "I'm a grown-ass man, Nikki. I think I can handle my own life."

She huddled against the headboard, her knuckles white where she gripped the sheet. "Maybe you can. But I have to ask, what about the wedding? I don't want to be rude to Joshua and Sophie."

"You'll come to the wedding with me. My family is expecting it. I've told them about Emma, so they'll want to see you."

"Won't that be fun," she said bitterly. "I'll find my own way there, Jake. I wouldn't want to inconvenience you."

"Don't be absurd. I'll pick you up at noon."

"And what happens to you and me after the wedding?"

He saw it then. Despite everything he had said and done, in Nikki's despairing gaze he saw one last remnant of hope amid her pain. "I don't think there is a 'you and me,'" he said, the words brusque and flat. "Lots of people share custody of children. I know who I am. And who I'm not." He slid out of bed and found his knit boxers. Grabbing up his shirt and pants, he started getting dressed.

Nikki wrapped the sheet around her body, toga-style, and went to her closet. "I'll get you some sheets for the sofa," she said.

Suddenly, he couldn't stand to be near her for another second. It was tearing him apart. "No," he said curtly. "I'm leaving."

She whirled around, frowning. "Don't be stupid, Jake. The snow is deep. And it's still coming down. You'll wreck your car."

He shrugged, staring at the woman who had shown him a glimpse of what his life *could* be like. "Don't worry, Nik. I always land on my feet."

As he grabbed his cowboy boots and the rest of his things and walked to the living room, he waited for her to follow him. Instead, the house was still and quiet. It would be a few more hours until dawn arrived. No need to worry about Emma getting the wrong idea. By the time she woke up, Jake would be back in Falling Brook at his impersonal hotel.

The Christmas tree mocked him with a cheerful glow. It was still lit, because Jake and Nikki had been too desperate for each other to pay attention. When he was completely dressed, he listened one more time to see if Nikki was going to waylay him. To lecture him about road safety. To tell him what a stubborn, closed-off bastard he was.

But nothing happened.

The front door had one of those twist locks that didn't require a key to be secured from the inside.

When he was bundled up, he opened the door, stepped out into the hushed silence and waded through the snow.

He was alone in a deserted landscape.

Nikki cried for an hour, cried until her nose was stuffed up and her chest hurt. For long minutes, she had expected a knock on the front door. She had strained to hear it. Because it would be Jake admitting that the weather was too bad to leave.

Apparently, risking life and limb was preferable to staying with her.

How could he make love to her so beautifully and feel nothing?

If Jake had shown any glimmer of interest in a permanent relationship, Nikki would have fought for their future. She would have traveled anywhere with him. Emma hadn't started school yet. And Roberta might soon be going back to the friends she had known for decades.

But Jake had run from Nikki yet again, because of shadows from his past. She was long beyond what had happened fifteen years ago. She wasn't reliving old hurts, not anymore. She deserved a man who would love her, body and soul. Maybe he was out there somewhere.

In the meantime, she had to let Jake go. The hurt was like severing a limb, but it would only hurt worse if she refused to face the truth. Jake Lowell didn't love her. He couldn't. He was too empty inside.

The trouble with heartbreak and emotional meltdowns was that the world kept on turning. Emma bounced into Nikki's bedroom at seven, her impish personality bolstered by a good night's sleep.

Nikki managed not to groan. "Hi, baby."

"Where's Mr. Man?"

"Why would you ask that, hon?"

"It was snowing last night. You told me we couldn't drive in snow. Remember?"

"Ah. Well, that was us. Mr. Jake is a very good driver. So he went home after you were in bed."

"When is he coming back?"

"I don't know." Nikki, in desperation, changed the subject. "Let's get you some breakfast, so you'll be ready to play when Grandma gets here."

In typical Jersey fashion, the weather pattern had shifted again. It was too early in the season for sustained cold temps. The snow was already melting, and the sun was out. The streets were a slushy mess. But not particularly dangerous.

Nikki's shift at the diner started at ten today. Though she was glad it wasn't any earlier, she still didn't know how she was going to make it through eight hours of on-your-feet work. Lots of caffeine maybe. And a stone-cold commitment not to think about stupid, emotionally stunted rich men.

Roberta Reardon didn't spare Nikki's feelings when she arrived. "You look terrible. Are you getting the flu?"

"No, Mom. I'm fine. I just didn't sleep well."

"I see you have your tree up. How did you manage that since I last saw you?"

Emma answered, innocently. "Mr. Man helped."

Roberta's eyebrows went up. "Mr. Man?"

"Jake. He had dinner with us." Nikki glanced at her daughter. "Go take off your pajamas and get dressed, please."

When Emma headed for her bedroom, Roberta pressed for more. "And?"

"And nothing. He's getting to know Emma. He wants to be part of her life."

Her mother's smile was gentle. "You don't seem happy about that."

"It will be difficult," Nikki admitted, her throat tight.

"Because you're in love with him?"

"Mom!" Aghast, Nikki turned to look down the hall, making sure Emma hadn't picked up on the adult conversation. "She'll hear you."

"So it's true?"

"No, Mother," Nikki lied. "Jake and I are friends who share a child. That's all we'll ever be, and I'm okay with that."

She waited for the lightning to strike or for a huge sinkhole to open up and swallow her for telling such a whopper.

Roberta seemed disappointed. "Okay then. I believe you."

"I have to finish getting ready."

Nikki fled the room, telling herself she absolutely would *not* break down and cry. She was a grown woman. Not some fragile schoolgirl fixated on romantic fantasies that had no base in reality.

She made it to work with ten minutes to spare, so she grabbed a cup of coffee and took it to the store-room. This place, this small restaurant, had become a familiar home. She liked her coworkers, and she liked her customers. The days had a comfortable routine.

Everybody needed to eat. And, surprisingly, a lot of people needed someone to talk to when their lives were empty. Nikki could do worse than stay here at the cozy retro diner indefinitely.

But the truth was, the salary for assistant manager wasn't all that great. When Emma was older and her needs were more expensive, Nikki would need a different job. Perhaps one that made use of her degree in communications.

She had thought about working for an ad agency. Maybe doing PR for a local business. She was a decent writer, and she didn't mind speaking in public.

Her moment of quiet time ended abruptly when one of the line cooks swung open the door and grabbed a can of baked beans. He glanced at the clock with a grin. "You hiding out in here, Nikki? Rough morning?"

Her face must have looked worse than she thought. She managed a smile. "Not enough sleep. You know. Kids…"

"Don't I ever."

The door closed, and she took a deep breath. Nothing had to be decided today. She would stay the course until after Christmas. January was a good month for resolutions and starting over. Maybe Falling Brook was the answer. Maybe Joshua really would offer Nikki and her mother a lifeline. Who knew what the future held?

The only certainty was that *Nikki's* future didn't include Jake Lowell.

Twelve

After Jake left Nikki's house in the predawn hours, he made a concerted effort to spend time with his family. If he was leaving after the wedding, he needed to fulfill his responsibilities as a son and a brother.

Oddly, the movie with Oliver, the rushed lunch with Joshua at Black Crescent and the afternoon tea at his mother's Friday afternoon were cathartic. He'd had in mind offering his support to *them*, but he ended up being the one who felt comforted.

His mother, especially, surprised him. They bypassed the pleasantries quickly and waded into deep water. "How are you doing, Mom? Really, I mean. I know you went to see Dad."

Eve Lowell looked much as she always had. Younger than her years. Dignified. Stylish. She was older now, of course. But she still had the posture of a beauty queen.

She wrinkled her nose at his question. "It was all small talk. But enough to show me that it's time to move on. I'm not the same person I was. It took me a long time to find my strength, but I did. I still have my rough days, but I'm in a good place now, just like Oliver. When Oliver told me about his visit and how he came to the same conclusions, I was glad he went. It was healthy and positive for both of us."

"Do you still love Dad?" Jake hadn't known he was going to ask that question. When his mother was silent, he wished he hadn't. Finally, she shook her head slowly. "It depends on what you mean by love. Your father was declared legally dead. I'm no longer bound to him by law. But I said vows a million years ago. Vows I meant at the time. I certainly didn't know my husband was going to become a felon."

"So, is that a yes or a no?"

She looked at him wistfully. "We can't always choose whom we love, and we can't always stop loving them simply because they don't deserve our love. I know your father sent you away, Jake."

"He didn't send me away." Anger snapped in each word. "He left. He left you. He left me. He left all of us. And I couldn't handle the gutter press. They hounded our family and made us miserable. Because of *him*." Jake shook with sudden fury—fury he hadn't realized he'd pushed down, and had pushed down forever, it seemed.

"My poor boy. He left you homeless, didn't he?"

Jake felt raw suddenly. And he hated that vulnerability. "I owe you an apology, Mother," he said formally. "I never should have left you to face everything on your own. I'm sorry I didn't stay. I'm sorry I didn't come back."

"I had Joshua," she said, waving a hand. "We got by."

Though her words weren't meant to wound, Jake felt them cut deep. He loved his brother dearly, but always being cast as the screwup was not a role Jake relished.

"Is there anything you need?" he asked. "I've done well financially."

"Jake, dear boy." She patted his hand. "Over the years you've sent me jewelry and artwork for my birthdays and Christmas. I never felt forgotten. I knew why you couldn't come home. But I hoped that one day the hurt would fade." She paused, her expression turning crafty, mischievous even. "Now tell me about Nikki and this baby of yours. Joshua has filled me in on the basics."

Jake hunched his shoulders. "Emma is four. She's mine. I'm making arrangements with Nikki, so I can fly in for the occasional visit. And, of course, we can video chat."

His mother's face fell. "I don't get to see my granddaughter?"

"I suppose that's up to you and Nikki."

"It strikes me that I haven't heard you talk about Nikki and *you*."

"There's nothing there, Mom."

"You made a baby together."

"That was five years ago. We bumped into each other one evening in Atlantic City and…well, you know."

Eve's smile was sweet. "I may be getting older, son, but I do understand sexual chemistry."

"We've been apart fifteen years. Whatever we had is gone."

"I find that hard to believe."

"Why?" He frowned at her.

"Because you've never found another woman to settle down with and make a home. That strikes me as odd. You have a huge heart, Jake. A generous spirit. And though you'd chew glass before you'd admit it, you're a sensitive and loving and wonderful man."

"I thought you were disappointed in me," he said gruffly, caught off guard by her praise. "I failed you."

"Nonsense," she said stoutly. "You followed your own path. Don't hide in the shadows forever, dear boy. You may not get too many chances for happiness. Seize this one before it's too late."

In that moment, he knew he was tired of running, tired of being so slow to change and grow. Despite all evidence to the contrary, he felt a fillip of hope that something new might be close at hand. He was ready to reach for happiness. But he still wasn't sure he could handle it or how to get there.

Maybe it was too late…

Though Jake appreciated his mother's support, his intentions were all over the map. Maybe Falling

Brook wasn't as bad as he remembered. After all, the town had been nothing more than an excuse, a convenient bogeyman.

He'd had no contact at all with Nikki. He couldn't bring himself to text her. What would he say? Her words still rang in his ears. *You destroyed us, Jake. Not your dad.*

Apparently, Nikki Reardon was not as forgiving as Eve Lowell. Mothers always made excuses for their misbehaving sons. Lovers simply walked away.

Though, in all fairness, Jake had been the one to leave. He'd given up the wild, glorious uncertainty of Nikki's bed for the cold comfort of his iron-clad, selfish rules.

Never stop moving. Never put down roots. Never look back.

On the morning of the wedding, he ran out of options. He sent a brief text: I'm picking you up at noon.

It took ten minutes for Nikki's reply: I'll be ready.

He sighed. Thanksgiving was five days away. Maybe he should get out of New Jersey. The sooner, the better. Nothing was the way he thought it would be. Too many messy emotions. Too many people. Too many regrets.

He pulled up in front of Nikki's now-familiar house at twelve sharp. Before he could exit the car, she started down the walk, her long legs shown to advantage in silver heels. He met her halfway. "Hello."

She eyed him coolly. "Hello."

Though she carried a winter coat over her arm, the

silvery-pink scarf around her shoulders protected her from the light breeze.

She looked stunning. Her golden-red hair was caught up on top of her head in a fancy knot of loose curls. The lustrous strand of pearls around her neck complemented the fabric of her dress. He wondered if Roberta had managed to hang on to one piece of valuable jewelry for her daughter, or if the pearls were costume.

The dress's strapless bodice and fitted waist fluffed out in what Emma would probably call a princess skirt. It ended midcalf. Jake opened the passenger door for Nikki and helped her in, carefully tucking in her skirt so the door wouldn't catch it.

When he ran around and slid behind the wheel, Nikki's familiar scent enveloped him. Her perfume wasn't heavy. Perhaps she had barely spritzed her throat. But he was intensely aware of it. And of her.

He started the engine. "You look beautiful, Nik. That dress was made for you."

She stared out the windshield. "Thank you."

"Are we going to act normal today?"

"I don't know. You tell me."

"C'mon, Nikki. Can't we call a truce?"

Now her head snapped around in his direction. Her eyes shot fire. He'd always thought that was just an expression, but Nikki nailed it. "You mean a truce during the wedding or until you leave town?" she asked.

He counted to ten. "For my brother's wedding. It's an important day."

"I know what weddings are, Jake. I had one, re-member?"

The reminder hit him hard. He'd tried to forget that. "I know," he said, reeling from the pain of imag-ining it. Suddenly, he wanted details. "Was it a big wedding?"

"Mom and I were broke. Timothy and I went to the courthouse."

"I'm sorry it didn't work out." He said the words quietly, but he meant them. "You deserve to be happy."

"Thank you." She crossed her arms. The curves of her breasts peeked over the silky fabric that cov-ered her chest. She looked lush, untouched, intensely feminine.

She belonged to him. The certainty came out of nowhere. Implacable. Undeniable. What was he going to do about it?

They arrived in Falling Brook and parked in a ga-rage near the hotel. The half-a-block walk wasn't bad. Nikki put on her coat. Jake helped. The bare nape of her neck gave him ideas, but he reined in his im-pulses. It would be hours until he could get her alone.

Weddings happened every day, all the time. Half of them ended. He hoped his brother and Sophie would not be one of the failures, but who knew? Jake wasn't a sentimental man, or at least he hadn't been. But today, the woman beside him and his brother's big day were making Jake *feel* things.

At the Bismarck, they left Nikki's outerwear at the coat check in the main lobby. In the elevator, riding up to the twentieth floor, he studied her. She wasn't looking at him, so it was easy to sneak a peek.

She was so beautiful, it made his chest hurt. As a seventeen-year-old teenager, she had been cute and pretty and full of life. Now, she carried the maturity of a woman—a woman who had faced many of life's challenges and persevered.

Her magnolia skin, so often associated with redheads, was still the same. Soft, unblemished. Begging to be touched. Lust stirred uneasily in his gut. Today was about his brother, his twin. But despite the occasion, or perhaps because of it, Jake was drawn to his wedding date, his Nikki. He had missed her fiercely the last two days. The strength of that feeling convinced him he needed to move forward carefully.

He cleared his throat, feeling claustrophobic in the small space. "Joshua and Sophie asked their guests, in lieu of gifts, to make a donation to Haley Shaw's charity. I wrote a check. But I also sent Sophie a large potted orchid this morning from you and me with best wishes for a wonderful wedding day."

Nikki's head came up, and she actually smiled. "That was a lovely gesture. Thanks for including me."

The elevator dinged, and they exited. The entire top floor of the Bismarck had been completely transformed. Plate-glass windows in every direction showcased the view. One section of the giant room was set up with rows of white chairs and a center aisle marked with a satin runner. At the front, seasonal live flowers covered a trellised arch. Along the center aisle, candles burned inside crystal globes atop brass stands.

"This is beautiful," Nikki said, scanning the room with interest.

"C'mon. Let's get a seat." The front row on the right-hand side was reserved for Jake's mother, for Oliver and his fiancée, Samantha, and for Jake and Nikki. Jake watched as Nikki greeted each member of his family. Then they sat down.

Eve shot her son a knowing glance, but he ignored it.

The area set aside for the ceremony filled up quickly. The guest list might have ended up closer to sixty than fifty, but the crowd was still small enough to be described as intimate. A buzz filled the space as anticipation mounted.

Suddenly, Jake needed air. He had been blind for far too long. He was beginning to know what he wanted, but he had to make plans. Now he was trapped by the time. Three minutes before the hour.

From a side alcove, Joshua appeared, beaming. The minister accompanied him. The two men took their positions. A stringed quartet had been playing for the last twenty minutes. Now they paused and began the first notes of "Pachelbel's Canon."

Nikki touched his forearm. He jumped at the unexpected contact. His skin felt too tight for his body, and his chest was constricted.

She looked at him with concern. "Are you okay?" she whispered.

Nikki knew without any doubt that Jake was definitely *not* okay. He ignored her question. They stood

with the other guests as the bride began to walk down
the modest aisle. The expression on Sophie's face
when she looked at Josh made Nikki's eyes damp
with emotion.

Weddings always got to her, but this one more than
most. Joshua had borne the weight of his father's sins
and had worked for years to restore the community's
trust in Black Crescent. He deserved to be the man
of the hour.

His bride was stunning in an off-the-shoulder
white satin gown with dozens of cloth-covered buttons down the back. Her hair was twined with tiny
white flowers. She had opted for no veil.

Sophie and Joshua held hands and faced the minister. Their voices as they spoke their vows were clear
and strong. They had chosen a traditional wedding
liturgy with phrases like "love, honor and cherish"
and "'til death do us part."

At last, the minister placed his palm over the couple's hands for a blessing. Then he said words that
rang out over the small assembly: "I now pronounce
you husband and wife. You may kiss the bride."

Everyone cheered and clapped. Josh bent Sophie
over his arm and kissed her enthusiastically, not
seeming to mind that they had an audience.

Nikki, without thinking, twined her fingers with
Jake's, fighting a flood of feelings that threatened to
overwhelm her. When he shot her a surprised sideways glance, she realized what she had done and
dropped his hand immediately. But it was too late.

She had inadvertently let him know how much she cared about him. Her face heated with humiliation.

The bride and groom exited. Everyone stood up and moved toward the reception area, talking and laughing.

Nikki spoke in Jake's direction without actually looking him in the eye. "Excuse me," she said stiffly. "I'd like to speak to Haley Shaw." She fled, managing not to run.

Fortunately, Haley was nearby. She had been sitting with Chase Hargrove. But Chase had moved away to chat with someone else.

"Hi, Haley," Nikki said. "You look beautiful."

Haley beamed. "Thanks. So do you."

"I didn't get a chance to say everything I wanted to the day I showed up at Black Crescent to talk to your boss."

Haley seemed surprised. "Oh?"

"I never thanked you for all those years you've stood by Black Crescent. Your loyalty to Vernon and my dad. And the way you stayed to help Joshua after everything fell apart."

Haley grimaced. "Well, I felt guilty, to be honest."

Nikki gaped at her. "Why?"

"Because I saw both of them that morning—Vernon and your dad. And I knew something was going down. But I never said anything to anybody. And then it was too late."

"Oh, gosh no, Haley. What could you have done? None of us had a clue what they were planning."

"Maybe. But you should know—I stayed with

Black Crescent because I loved working there, and Joshua is a great boss."

Nikki shook her head slowly. "Life is strange. I've felt guilty all these years, too. I was still living at home back then. I overheard pieces of several odd phone calls. Conversations that made me uncomfortable. But I never said anything, either. I blamed myself afterward. Jake blamed me, too."

"Well, he must have gotten over it. The way he looks at you gives me the shivers. The man is in love with you in a bad way."

"Oh, no," Nikki said quickly. "You're mistaken. We're old friends, that's all. He asked me to be his plus-one because he's been gone forever and doesn't really know any women in Falling Brook."

Haley wrinkled her nose, unconvinced. "I think you're kidding yourself. Chase and I had our ups and downs and misunderstandings before we got engaged. Relationships are difficult. We had to learn to trust each other."

"I didn't know you were engaged."

Haley held out her hand, showing off her ring. "Yep. No wedding date yet. I'm waiting to see if Josh is going to be able to find a new CEO before making plans."

"I thought he had been interviewing candidates."

"He has. For months. But it has to be the right fit. Look at the Lowell men over there. It's probably what they're talking about right now."

The groom had separated from his bride for the moment. Sophie was surrounded by a crowd of family and friends. Joshua stood in a tight circle with Oliver and Jake. The three men were gorgeous. With both twins in dress clothes, Jake looked far more like his identical brother than usual.

"You're probably right," Nikki said. "I think I'll go get some food. I skimped on lunch. And I see that your handsome fiancé is headed this way."

Joshua, Jake and Oliver were deep in conversation when Nikki slipped past them. She picked up enough words here and there to know Haley was right. They were talking about the CEO search. Maybe the Lowells should sell Black Crescent. She wondered if any of the three had floated that idea.

Feeling somewhat out of place, Nikki picked up a plate and began filling it with appetizers. The cake would be cut later. She found a corner and sipped her champagne. The day, unlike the expensive alcohol, had gone flat. She shouldn't have come. Things with Jake were rocky at best.

She was looking down at her glass when a deep voice startled her. "There you are."

"Jake," she said.

"So you do remember my name. That's a start."

His attempt at humor failed.

"Don't feel like you have to entertain me," she said. "I know you have lots of catching up to do with old friends." Even after fifteen years, she and Jake knew many of the guests personally.

"How about a dance?" he said, taking her empty plate and glass and setting them on a nearby tray.

"I don't think so."

"We agreed to a truce, remember?"

His gentle smile and half-hearted grin made her stomach curl with anxiety and heartbreak. "Sure."

He tucked her tiny beaded clutch in his jacket pocket, then took her by the hand and led her out onto the dance floor. Other couples had the same idea. Jake put an arm around her waist and pulled her close. The string quartet had yielded to a bluesy band that began playing romantic standards.

When the musicians launched into "I Only Have Eyes for You," Nikki stumbled and gasped. "I don't want to dance," she said, trying to pull away.

Jake held her tightly, looking almost as miserable as she felt. "Dance, Nik. For old times' sake."

He might as well have stabbed her through the heart. She wanted to run away. This was agonizing. She loved him, but he didn't feel the same.

No matter the pain, she wouldn't cause a scene at Josh and Sophie's wedding.

She kept her gaze focused on the third button of Jake's pristine white dress shirt, trying not to cry. His body was big and hard and warm, and he smelled amazing. His hand clasping hers was strong and tanned. He had mentioned Greece. Probably because he had a favorite villa there that he rented whenever the mood took him.

What kind of women did Jake *entertain* when he went to the Mediterranean? The odd thing was that Nikki didn't really care about all those faceless females. She loved him as he was—imperfect, fierce, generous, sweet with Emma…and the perfect lover in Nikki's bed.

Once, he had been her whole world. Having him back in Jersey now, even fleetingly, had shown her why her marriage hadn't worked out. It had also underlined the truth that some feelings never die. She loved Jake Lowell, and she probably always would.

The dance finally ended. Jake and Nikki stood at the edge of the floor, not speaking, and watched as the bride and groom enjoyed their first dance. After that, the tempo picked up. Alcohol flowed freely, and the crowd became more raucous.

"I have to go to the restroom," Nikki said. She pulled her clutch from Jake's pocket and slipped away before he could say anything. In the ladies' lounge she found a seat and repaired her lipstick. One glance in the mirror told her she was hiding her feelings fairly well. Only her eyes gave her away. She pinched her cheeks and put a wet paper towel on the back of her neck.

She wanted badly to go home. But it was a very long way. If she hired a car, it would cost a fortune.

When she returned to the reception, Jake was nowhere in sight. Some kind of buzz circled the room. Clumps of guests stood here and there, looking either startled or worried or both.

Nikki found Haley, who looked shell-shocked. "What happened?" Nikki asked. "I can't find Jake. What's going on?"

Haley lowered her voice. "Somebody just brought word that Vernon has escaped from custody."

"Oh, no. Poor Joshua. Poor Sophie. What a dreadful thing to happen today of all days."

Suddenly, Joshua strode across the room in their direction. His face was stormy. When he stood right in front of the two women, he sighed. "Jake is gone, Nikki."

She gaped at him. "What do you mean *gone*? I don't understand."

"He and Oliver left to go find our dad."

Nikki shook her head slowly. "No. That doesn't even make sense."

Josh rubbed his forehead and pinched the bridge of his nose. "I know that. Neither of them was particularly rational when we got the news."

"Vernon could be anywhere," Haley said.

Nikki felt sick. "I'm so sorry, Josh. Is Sophie upset?"

At last, he smiled. "My new bride is a saint. We're going to contact the travel agency and delay our honeymoon for a few days. Once again, Vernon has screwed me over. I don't know how this keeps happening."

Nikki touched his arm. "Is there anything I can do?"

"Maybe keep my twin from losing his mind."

She winced. "I don't have any control over your brother. Sorry. He told me he was leaving Falling Brook as soon as the wedding was over. He was pretty insistent about it. I tried to talk to him, but we had a big fight."

Haley frowned. "But you came to the wedding together."

"We had a temporary truce," Nikki said. "I guess it's over."

Joshua glanced over his shoulder, clearly looking for his bride. "I've got to get back to the lovely Mrs. Lowell. Jake sent you a text, Nikki. Check your phone. I'll see you ladies later. God help us if they don't find Vernon. I don't know if this town can handle that kind of news."

Thirteen

Nikki kicked off her high heels and stared at the message on her phone for the hundredth time:

I called a limo to take you back to your place. The driver will be in the lobby to greet you at five. Sorry I had to leave...

She didn't know whether to laugh or cry. Here she was, sitting in a fancy, over-the-top hired car heading home from the ball without the handsome prince. It was a miracle her dress hadn't turned into rags and the car into a pumpkin. In the whole history of bad wedding dates, today had to rank right up there in the top five.

This was the end. Jake was who he was. She was

never going to change him. Perhaps she should be glad Jake even remembered he *had* a date. *Damn* Vernon Lowell to hell and back. How could he do this to his sons, his ex-wife, the citizens of Falling Brook? Nikki's heart ached for the man she loved. But at the same time, she was angry and hurt. How could Jake treat her this way? Whatever she thought she had with him was over.

In fifteen years, Jake hadn't managed to deal with his father's betrayal. This stunt would rip open the wound for sure. She wanted to talk to Jake, but she was afraid that if she called, he wouldn't answer. And that would hurt even more.

It was better not to know. It was better to call time of death on this relationship.

She huddled into her coat and listened to her stomach growl. The original plan with Jake had been to go out to dinner after the wedding. As it was, Nikki was destined to eat peanut butter and jelly with Emma.

Finally, the ride ended.

Roberta lifted an eyebrow when her daughter walked into the house. "Was that a *limo*, Nicole Marie Reardon?"

"Yes, Mom." Nikki squatted and hugged her daughter. "Hi, baby. I missed you. But I brought you some bubbles from the wedding reception. And some M&M's." The candy was imprinted with the bride's name and the groom's. Yellow for Sophie. Navy for Josh.

"How was it?" Roberta asked.

"The ceremony was lovely," Nikki said.

"I hear the reception took an exciting turn."

Nikki shot her mom a startled glance. "You know?"

Roberta nodded. "It's all over the internet."

"Oh, lordy. Did you find out any details?"

"No. The story I read said they think he must have paid off one of the guards. The feds are investigating."

"Great. Just great."

"How did Jake react?"

"Not well, Mom. He and Oliver went haring off to try to find Vernon."

"Oh. I'm sorry."

"Yeah, me, too. That was the final straw for me. I can't wait forever for Jake to get his life together. I can handle the future on my own. I don't need a man who spooks like a skittish horse. I wanted him to share my world, but that's not going to happen."

Emma looked up, clearly not interested in the conversation. "I'm hungry. Can we eat now? And is Mr. Man coming over?"

Sunday evening, Nikki sat on the end of her bed and checked her texts…again. Nothing but yawning silence from Jake. Why was she surprised? Though she had hoped against hope that he might lean on her in the midst of his crisis, Jake was on his own…again.

If they'd had any chance at being a couple, it was gone. His silence said louder than words that he didn't need her.

It hurt, far worse than she could have imagined.

In the hours since law-enforcement officials had apprehended Vernon at the Canadian border—

midday today—the judge had issued a statement. On Tuesday morning at 10:00 a.m., anyone who had been wronged by Vernon Lowell and his partner, Nikki's father, would be given the opportunity to address the defendant directly. To state their grievances. To bear witness to the misery and pain Vernon and Everett had caused.

The only caveat was that in order for anyone to speak, he or she must first notify the judge via email and receive a confirmation.

Nikki was torn. She called her mother and posed the question. Roberta refused flat out. "I have no interest in going," she said firmly. "Anyone in that room will probably still assume I knew what my husband was doing. They'll hate me for what happened. My being there will solve nothing."

"Are you sure, Mom? Don't you even want to ask Vernon the questions you can't ask Dad? Aren't you curious?"

There was a brief silence, and then Nikki heard her mother sigh. "I can't change the past, Nikki. Go if you want to. I know you're worried about Jake."

"I'm not positive he'll be there. He was pretty insistent about leaving right after the wedding."

"Things have changed in the last two days. It's hard for me to believe he would simply walk away. I'll keep Emma. If it will make you feel better, go. Go see Vernon. Go speak to him. Ask what you want to ask."

"Maybe I will."

"When you sign up with the judge, you can always drop out if you change your mind."

"True."

"Do you *want* to speak to Vernon?"

"Maybe. Mostly, I just want to be in the room and see what happens."

"Then do it. There's not a downside. Judges are leaning more and more toward giving victims the right to face their abusers. Vernon hurt a lot of people and abused their trust. That pain runs deep. You've seen it in dear Jake. Go, Nikki. Be there to support the Lowell boys if nothing else. It will make you feel better, and maybe you'll get a few of the answers you've wanted for fifteen years."

Nikki slipped into the courtroom at twenty minutes before the hour. It had taken longer than she anticipated to get through security. The chamber was crowded, but she found a seat in the back corner. Many of the faces she recognized. Some she didn't.

The Lowell men were sitting in the front row with their mother, Eve. Sophie was there, too. And Samantha. Just looking at the back of Jake's head made Nikki tense and weepy. What was he thinking? How was he holding up?

The bailiff instructed everyone to stand. The judge entered. Then came Vernon Lowell in handcuffs, his gaze downcast. He was wearing a standard-issue orange jumpsuit. His scruffy beard and longish hair were a mix of gray and white. With his stooped shoulders and weary air, it was almost impossible to reconcile this version of the man with his past self.

At one time, Vernon had been one of the richest

men in the tristate area. The boutique hedge fund he created from scratch had been wildly successful. It was rumored years ago that there was a waiting list of would-be clients hoping for a chance to "get in."

Nikki didn't know if that was true or not, but it made sense. The very elite reputation of Black Crescent had made it all the more attractive to the high-profile citizens of Falling Brook. Those lucky enough to have their millions in Vernon's care had seen those millions multiply.

But then everything went south. The fiscal dreams rotted on the vine.

Vernon and Everett absconded with money that wasn't theirs.

The judge banged a gavel and made opening remarks, explaining why he had allowed this somewhat unprecedented hearing. Still, Vernon stared at the floor.

Nikki's stomach tightened as the first name on the list was read aloud. The judge instructed Vernon to lift his head and face his accusers. Nikki wondered if there was any particular order. The first person to stand and walk toward the front of the room was Zane Patterson. There was a small podium for the Falling Brook visitors. Zane's words were calm but held an underlying bitterness as he laid out for Vernon a litany of what had happened when the Pattersons lost everything.

Each person on the judge's list was allotted ten minutes. Some took the entire time. Some ended abruptly. Though the wounds were fifteen years old, the stories sounded fresh. Raw.

It was painful to hear. Jessie Acosta was on the list. Like Zane, her father had been a client of Black Crescent.

Nikki was shocked when Chase Hargrove stood. As far as she knew, his family hadn't entrusted their money to Black Crescent. But, apparently, Vernon had involved Chase's father with some scheme that ended with Chase's dad going to prison for fraud.

One after another, the people spoke. Many of them had been in their teens and twenties when the tragedy happened. Their lives had been shaped, broken, damaged by Vernon's actions.

Nikki held her breath, feeling waves of guilt for something that hadn't been her fault at all. But her father had been deeply involved.

Evidently, the judge was saving Vernon's immediate family for last.

Suddenly, the name read aloud was *Nicole Reardon.* She flinched. Why had she signed up? Why hadn't she had them strike her name when she first arrived?

"Ms. Reardon?" The judge repeated her name.

Nikki stood slowly, her heart thumping wildly in her chest. Dozens of people stared at her. Not Jake. He still faced straight ahead. Nikki swallowed, her mouth dry. "You can skip me, sir."

The judge frowned. "This is your moment, Ms. Reardon. I assume it's been a long fifteen years. I'm giving you a chance to speak your piece."

There was no backing out now. Nikki walked on shaky legs to the front of the courtroom. Not once did she cast her gaze sideways to see Jake. She stood at the podium and faced Vernon.

Until this very instant, she hadn't known what she was going to say to him. But the words came tumbling out as if she had rehearsed them for five thousand empty days. Not a single other person had asked Vernon a question. They had vented, accused, mourned. Now it was Nikki's turn.

"Mr. Lowell…" She paused, feeling overwhelmed. Hopefully, she wasn't going to keel over. "Mr. Lowell. You and my father were best friends, colleagues, business partners. Clearly, you both were involved with the destruction of Black Crescent. But tell me this. You got away scot-free. My father crashed his car fleeing the police. Why wasn't he with you?"

For a moment, emotion broke the stoic expression on Vernon's face.

The judge addressed him. "Please answer Ms. Reardon's question. She deserves to know the truth."

When Vernon spoke, his voice was almost defiant. "Everett wanted to say goodbye to you and your mother. I told him he was a fool. Partway back to the house, the chase started. He had to turn around. He never made it."

"Oh. Thank you." Why was she thanking Vernon Lowell? How stupid. She turned to go back to her seat. As she moved, Jake looked at her across the small distance that separated them. He didn't smile. He was visibly ashen.

Nikki kept on walking, comforted in the smallest possible way that her father had wanted to say goodbye.

Next up was Eve Lowell, Vernon's wife. When the judge read her name, she shook her head. Like Nikki, she must have changed her mind. The judge didn't press her. He went on. *Oliver Lowell.*

Oliver stood and shrugged. "I learned in recovery not to blame other people for my addiction," he said. "You're a wretched bastard of a father, and I'll spend the rest of my life trying not to be like you. End of story."

Joshua Lowell. Joshua went to the podium and spoke quietly about his regrets. Mostly, he mentioned his mother and his two brothers. He sat down.

Then came the name Nikki had dreaded hearing. *Jacob Lowell.* Surely, Jake was the last one. It was almost noon.

Jake walked to the podium, his shoulders stiff, his eyes blazing with strong emotion. When he reached the designated spot, he stood there for a moment. The courtroom was completely silent. Hushed. Waiting.

Outside, the noise of New York City was audible, but muted by the thick walls and closed windows.

Even Vernon seemed affected by the somber atmosphere.

Jake shoved his hands in his pockets as if he didn't know what to do with them. "I'm not going to address you as *Father* or *Dad*," he said. "You gave up that right long ago. But I will say that I have hated you for far too long. I've let your shadow hang over my life, blighting it. Constraining it. I told myself I traveled the world because I loved the freedom and the adventure. The truth is that I've been afraid to come home. What you did nearly destroyed me. Not because I was destitute or on the run from the law. But because you convinced me that my DNA carried some sort of poison. If you could do what you did, maybe I was doomed to be as black-hearted a person as you."

Jake paused, maybe to catch his breath, and then continued. "I'm not a perfect human being. I have my faults, plenty of them. But from this day forward, I will no longer let your treachery determine the course of my life. I don't hate you. I don't love you. You are nothing to me at all..."

The gathered crowd exhaled almost in unison as Jake returned to his seat.

Moments later, the judge tapped the piece of paper in front of him, shook his head slowly and gave the bailiff a nod.

"All rise," the uniformed officer instructed the gathering.

Another set of officers stepped forward, helped Vernon to his feet and led him away.

When the judge and the prisoner were out of sight, the bailiff said, "You're dismissed."

Nikki was sitting in the back corner. No one needed to climb over her. She wasn't in anyone's way. She remained as the room emptied. At last, Oliver and Samantha walked out. Then Joshua and Sophie and Eve.

Jake never stood up. She watched from the back

corner of the room as he leaned forward, elbows on his knees, and stared at the ground. His posture suggested that he was unapproachable.

Suddenly, Nikki couldn't bear the thought that he might speak to her or think she had been waiting for him.

She jumped to her feet and slid around the back of the last bench, escaping into the crowded hallway. When she saw the nearest stairwell, she made a beeline for it, not willing to wait for an elevator.

Six flights of steps. The courtroom had been higher up in the building than she had realized. At last, she popped out onto the street. The crisp, cool air felt good on her hot cheeks. She felt weird. Sad. Depleted. It had been an emotional morning.

But maybe there was closure now. Maybe everyone could move on.

She set off down the street, feeling tiny icy pellets of snow land on her face. Nothing that would amount to much. At least the weather felt Christmassy. Every shop she passed was fully decorated. Though Thanksgiving was still two days away, hardly anyone waited for that marker to get ready for the December season.

Behind her, someone called her name. "Nikki. Nikki. Stop. Wait up."

When she turned, she saw that it was Jake. She shivered, a combination of the cold and the way she always reacted in his presence. He'd had plenty of opportunity to speak to her in the courthouse. Why had he followed her now?

She stepped into the sheltered doorway of a large

building and waited. This was not a confrontation she relished. Prior to this morning, the last she had seen of Jake was when she went to the ladies' room at the wedding reception three days ago.

He caught up to her, panting. "Where's your car?" His hair was tousled, and his cheeks were ruddy with the cold. He looked like a male model in a winter catalog. Sophisticated. Gorgeous. Out of reach.

"In the garage on the next block."

"We'll take mine," he said, sounding as arrogant as a man who thought he had all the answers. "I'll get one of Joshua's guys to drive yours home."

"No, thank you," she said politely.

She left the alcove and continued her journey.

Jake took her arm. "Don't be ridiculous, Nik. We need to talk. We'll ride together. My car is more comfortable."

Anger swept over her, dissolving any squeamishness she had felt at facing him. "Don't you *dare* call me ridiculous," she said curtly, conscious of the many passersby. "I'm not the one who took a woman to his brother's wedding and then slipped out like a thief in the night."

His jaw tightened. "Maybe a poor choice of words."

"Sorry," she muttered.

"You knew where I was."

"I knew that you and Oliver lost your minds. You hadn't seen your father in fifteen years, and yet somehow you thought the two of you could track down Vernon better than the FBI? Sorry, Jake. That doesn't cut it."

"I made a mistake," he said. "I was running on shock and adrenaline."

"The mistake was mine," Nikki replied, her throat clogged with tears.

"Let me explain," he said urgently.

Nikki refused to be a pushover. "I know you're Emma's father. I won't play the villain. But when you decide on a visitation schedule that fits your life, I'll make plans for you to spend time with her in the company of either my mother or yours. I don't want to see you again."

His face was frozen in tight planes. His eyes burned. "Give me a chance, Nik. I have things I need to say."

She shored up her resistance. "I'm cold, and I'm hungry. Goodbye, Jake." She started walking again, blind to her surroundings. All she could think about was getting away. It hurt too much to be with him.

He followed her, took her arm in a gentle hold and spun her around, his eyes filled with anguish. "Don't go." He kissed her then, a kiss that held more desperation than passion. At first, his lips were cold against hers, but then the slow burn kindled again, and they were clinging to each other like survivors of a shipwreck.

In a way, the comparison was apt. Fifteen years ago, their love had crashed on the rocks of tragedy, and they had been one step from drowning ever since.

Jake's kiss was achingly sweet one second and roughly possessive the next. Nikki went on her tiptoes, striving to get closer. She was courting more heartbreak. She knew that. But how could she be strong when everything inside her was melting with yearning for him?

At last, he stepped back, but he kept her hands in his. "One hour," he said hoarsely. "That's all I'm asking. One hour."

"And you'll feed me?"

Not even a glimmer of humor lightened his face. "Yes."

They ended up at the same scruffy neighborhood grill where the two of them and Joshua had eaten after their abortive attempt to visit Vernon in jail. Jake asked for a booth in the back. As they took off their heavy coats, he tried to sit with Nikki like last time, but she waved him to the other side of the table. She needed a buffer zone.

Jake didn't ask her opinion about the meal. He motioned for a waitress. When the woman arrived, he ordered two burgers, medium, with no onions and extra pickles, plus a couple of Cokes. How many times as teenagers had they ordered that exact meal and then laughed that they were so perfectly matched?

While they waited for the food, awkwardness loomed between them, filling the space, making conversation almost impossible. Finally, Nikki broke the silence. "Have you learned anything at all about the stolen money?"

Jake scowled at his drink, poking his straw through it. "Mom spoke briefly to the lawyer this morning. According to him, Vernon claims there never was a theft. He told counsel that he and Everett were *hood-*

winked by an unscrupulous deal. They saw a chance to quadruple Black Crescent's coffers and took it. But the investment went belly up, and they were too ashamed to admit the truth, so they fled."

"Do you believe that?"

"I don't know. Maybe. I've read reports from the officers who apprehended my father. He wasn't living in luxury."

"I suppose that makes more sense than the two men suddenly deciding to embark on a life of crime. Doesn't that make you feel better?"

"No. Because they should have stayed and faced the music."

The server arrived with the burgers. Nikki dug into hers, ravenous despite the circumstances. Some women didn't eat when they were stressed. Nikki wasn't one of those. She had gained twenty pounds after her father's death and Jake's departure. Gradually, she had come out of her funk and started taking care of herself again, but it had been a struggle.

She and Jake barely spoke while they ate. The waitress brought drink refills and the check. Eventually, plates were clean, and the awkward silence returned.

Nikki looked at her watch. "It's been an hour," she said bluntly. "I have to go."

Jake frowned. "We haven't even talked."

She glanced around at the bustling eatery. "This place isn't exactly private, and it's too cold outside for a long walk. Let's call it quits, Jake. Please. You. Me. It's a no-go. There's nothing left." Her chest ached.

He was everything she wanted, but there might as well have been an ocean between them. Soon, there would be…when Jake returned to Europe.

The line of his jaw was grim. He flagged down their server one last time. Jake handed the woman the check and three one-hundred-dollar bills. "We'd like to keep the table for a bit. No interruptions, please."

The woman stared, dazed, at the cash in her hand. "You mean no change?"

"No change. No drink refills. No nothing. Is that okay with you?"

She nodded vigorously, wonder dawning in her eyes. "Yes, sir. Cone of silence. I've got it." Tentatively, she touched the sleeve of his jacket. "Thank you, mister. This will make Christmas pretty special at my house."

When the woman disappeared, Jake shrugged out of his suit jacket and rolled up his sleeves. It was warm in the small restaurant. They were tucked in a far back corner. No one had any reason to pass by their table. Because the lunch rush had now waned, the booth next to them was empty.

The situation wasn't ideal, but under the circumstances, it would have to do. Nikki fanned herself with a napkin, wishing she had chosen something other than wool when she got dressed that morning. She had worn the red sweater and black skirt again with more sensible shoes.

Jake must have read her unease. "I could grab us a hotel room for an hour. If privacy would make you more comfortable."

She gaped at him. "You'd spend two hundred and fifty dollars for one hour in a hotel?"

He shrugged. "More like five hundred probably. It's the holidays. But, yes. If you were there, I would."

Nikki knew what would happen if she found herself in a hotel room with Jake. The chemistry she had tried so hard to deny would spark and flame. That fantasy wasn't conducive to holding her ground. "No hotel," she whispered. "Just say what you want to say."

Jake stared at her. His eyes were more gold than green at the moment, and his gaze was hot and beautiful and determined. "I'm in love with you, Nikki."

Fourteen

Jake saw his companion flinch and knew he had his work cut out for him. Nikki's body language was guarded in the extreme. Her chin was up, and her eyes were dark with anxiety. He saw her throat work.

"No, you're not," she said quietly. "You've been under a tremendous amount of pressure, and you're trying to make a grand gesture. It's not necessary to placate me in order to see your daughter."

His temper flared. "That's not a very complimentary assessment of my character. I know my past behavior hasn't been exemplary, Nik, but I've changed. Or I'm trying to," he added, in the spirit of honesty. "I love you."

Tears spilled from her beautiful Irish-hued eyes, rolling down her cheeks unchecked. She swiped at the dampness with the back of her hand and reached for her purse and coat. "I can't do this."

"Don't leave me, Nik," he begged, his heart like shards of glass in his chest. "Don't be afraid of this, of us. We lost it all once before, but our time has come. You have to believe me. Things are different now."

She didn't slide out of the booth, but she was close to bolting.

"What makes you think so, Jake? I don't see it."

He swallowed hard. "I spoke to Josh this morning. Before we went to court. I told him I had changed my mind about Black Crescent. That I was prepared to take over as CEO." Even now, his stomach churned about his decision, but he wouldn't let Nikki misinterpret his nerves. "Josh was thrilled and supportive," he said.

Nikki seemed less so. She gnawed her bottom lip. Her restless fingers shredded a paper napkin. "You'll be bored with it in a month. And you'll disappear again."

It was his turn to flinch. "Wow," he said, stunned at how much she could hurt him. "You're not making this easy."

Now she was angry. "There's *nothing* easy about us, Jake."

"I heard you say 'I love you,'" he muttered. "That night I made love to you at your house. You thought I was asleep."

She closed her eyes and shook her head slowly. When she looked at him again, he finally saw how much his abandonment had cost her. "It was the sex talking."

"Don't be flip. Not now. I heard you say it, and I was too chickenshit scared to say it back. But I'm saying it now. *I love you*. I'm not leaving. I'm not running away. If it takes me ten months or ten years to convince you, I'll do it. I. Love. You."

"Stop," she begged, her gaze agonized.

He clenched his hand on the table as he resisted the urge to pound something. "When we ran into each other in Atlantic City five years ago, it was like being struck by lightning. You were everything I had left behind, everything I had lost. That night we spent together was incredible. But you weren't a teenager anymore. You'd lived your life far more bravely than I had. I was knocked on my ass and swamped with so many feelings I couldn't handle it. I'm sorry I left you, Nikki. I've regretted it every day since."

Nikki put her face in her hands, her shoulders bowed. He couldn't tell for sure, but he thought she was crying again. When she finally looked up at him, her mascara was smudged, and her eyes were still wet. "How can I believe you, Jake? I want to, but I'm afraid. Afraid you'll smash my heart again. I don't know how many more times it can recover."

Slowly, he reached for his wallet. "Maybe this will convince you," he said quietly. He opened the leather billfold and extracted a piece of paper that was ragged at the creases. It was yellow stationery with a row of pink daisies at the top. He handed it to Nikki. "Do you remember?"

She stared at the note, her eyes wide. Though the letter was upside down from Jake's perspective, he didn't need to read it. He had memorized the contents years ago. Nikki had slipped the plea to him at her father's funeral.

In the days before smartphones and texting, she had written, "Take me with you to Europe..."

Her hands shook as she traced the girlish handwriting with a fingertip. "I can't believe you kept this."

He sat back and sighed. "I tried to throw it away a hundred times. The guilt crushed me when I looked at it. Over and over."

"You shouldn't have felt guilty. It was outrageous of me to ask."

"Was it, Nikki?" He cocked his head and soaked in her grace and her courage, painfully aware of how his life might have turned out differently. "I kept this, too." He handed her a graduation picture, wallet-size. It was Nikki, smiling at the camera, her hair vibrant, her eyes filled with joy.

"Oh, Jake." She teared up again.

He inhaled sharply and dropped the last of his protective cloak of secrets. "I love you, Nikki Reardon. I suspected it in Atlantic City. I think I knew it deep down the moment I came back to Falling Brook and saw you face-to-face. And heard I had a daughter. But I couldn't accept the truth."

"But you—"

He waved a hand, cutting her off. "I'm not finished. I've loved you in one way or another my whole life, Nik. Everywhere I traveled, I wanted to share new adventures with you. Sunsets and storms. People and places. You were always in the back of my mind, those big emerald eyes telling me how much you cared. I was wrong, Nicole Marie Reardon. I was a coward. I let inertia keep me on a path that led nowhere." He reached across the table, across the miles and years of loneliness. "I love you. I adore you, in fact. I want to spend the rest of my life with you and Emma."

And finally, at long last, the sun came out.

She smiled at him through her tears. Her fingers gripped his. "Yes," she said, the word barely audible. "I love you, too, Jake. So much it hurts."

They sat there for seconds. Minutes. Their gazes locked. Their hearts healing.

Finally, Nikki glanced around the restaurant, seeming dazed, noting the people going about their business. She took a sip of her watered-down drink. "If you're still serious about that hotel thing, I'll take you up on it."

And just like that, his body went hard all over. Except for his heart. That organ was embarrassingly soft and filled with love for this incredible woman.

"Let's go," he said gruffly.

Outside the restaurant, he hailed a cab, not wanting to waste the time it would take to retrieve his car. Pulling Nikki against him in the back seat, he trembled when she laid her head on his shoulder.

He directed the driver to one of the city's premier luxury hotels.

Nikki balked briefly when she saw the iconic fa-
cade. "We don't have any luggage," she whispered.

"They won't bat an eye."

It was true. The front desk ran Jake's credit card
and confirmed his request for a suite. The man
handed over two keys.

Jake dragged Nikki with him to the small gift
shop. Her face turned bright red while he bought
protection.

Then they were on the elevator, streaking toward
the top floor. When they were in the room, Nikki
exclaimed over the view of Central Park. The light
snow had dusted the tops of the trees.

Jake took her hand and went down on one knee.
"Nikki, will you marry me? We'll shop for a ring together."

She tugged on his arm. "Yes, yes, yes," she cried.
Her eyes glowed with happiness.

He stood and scooped her up. "Is it too soon to
try out the bed?"

"Honestly," she said, with a mischievous grin, "I
thought you were moving kind of slow for a well-
traveled bachelor bad boy."

He carried her into the bedroom. Though the ache
in his body urged him to do everything in hyper
speed, Jake knew this occasion was too important to
rush. He set Nikki on her feet and started undressing
her, pausing to caress her smooth skin, soft curves,
lush hills and valleys.

Her body was a wonder to him. Feminine. Unbe-
lievably arousing.

While Nikki settled herself in the sumptuous covers, he stripped in record time and joined her. "I'm sorry," he groaned, burying his head between her breasts, feeling the ragged thump of her heart. "I'm sorry we've wasted so much time."

She stroked his hair, shivering when he tasted her nipples. "We've learned a lot, Jake. We've grown up. We've faced battles and won. Life won't ever tear us apart again, because we won't allow it. Make love to me, my dearest heart. Now. Like it's our first time. Like we have forever ahead of us."

"We do, Nikki. We do." He gave her his pledge and entered her slowly, stunned by the pleasure as her body welcomed his. The fit was snug, the stimulation almost unbearable. She deserved romance, but the lust he had bottled up for days and hours roared to life.

They moved together wildly, straining for dominance. It was heat and blessing, madness and perfect bliss. He took them to the peak and then slowed, tormenting them both. Trying to make it last.

Nikki arched and cried out beneath him, her fingernails scoring his shoulders. "Don't stop," she begged. "Don't stop."

He was beyond reason then, blinded by the need to find release, wrapped in the realization that their love had risen from the ashes against all odds.

The end was hot and hard and fast, draining, as close to perfection as mere mortals could get.

He held her after that, his breathing rough and jerky. Though it had been far too long since he had done so, he thanked the deity for not giving up on him.

Nikki's body was a warm, sweet gift in his embrace. "You're everything to me, Nik," he muttered hoarsely. "Now and always. I love you."

She smiled softly and reached for his hand, curling her fingers with his. "Emma and I will go wherever you go, Jake. You don't have to run Black Crescent if you don't want to…"

Shaking his head slowly, he exhaled. "I'm back where I belong. Here with you. And with my family and Falling Brook. I'm not leaving again."

A tiny hesitation betrayed her last reservation. "You're sure?"

He nuzzled her hair, letting sleep take him. "You can count on it, my love. You can count on it…"

* * * * *

*If you loved Dynasties: Seven Sins, then don't miss
the next Dynasties series from Harlequin Desire
and Joanne Rock—Dynasties: Mesa Falls!*

The Rebel
The Rival
Rule Breaker
Heartbreaker

All available now!

And...

The Rancher
The Heir

Available January and February 2021!

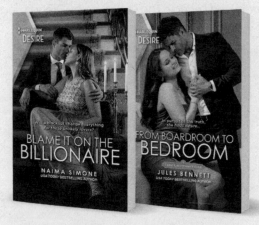

#2773 THE WIFE HE NEEDS

Westmoreland Legacy: The Outlaws • by Brenda Jackson
Looking to settle down, Alaskan CEO Garth Outlaw thinks he wants
a convenient bride. What he doesn't know is that his pilot,
Regan Fairchild, wants *him*. Now, with two accidental weeks together in
paradise, will the wife he needs be closer than he realized?

#2774 TEMPTED BY THE BOSS

Texas Cattleman's Club: Rags to Riches • by Jules Bennett
The only way to get Kelly Prentiss's irresistible workaholic boss
Luke Holloway to relax is to trick him—into taking a vacation with her!
The island heat ignites a passion they can't ignore, but will it be back to
business once their getaway ends?

#2775 OFF LIMITS ATTRACTION

The Heirs of Hansol • by Jayci Lee
Ambitious Colin Song wants his revenge—by working with producer
Jihae Park. But remaining enemies is a losing battle with their sizzling
chemistry! Yet how can they have a picture-perfect ending when
everyone's secret motives come to light?

#2776 HOT HOLIDAY FLING

by Joss Wood
Burned before, the only thing businessman Hunt Sheridan wants is
a no-strings affair with career-focused Adie Ashby-Tate. When he
suggests a Christmas fling, it's an offer she can't refuse. But will their hot
holiday fantasy turn into a gift neither was expecting?

#2777 SEDUCING THE LOST HEIR

Clashing Birthrights • by Yvonne Lindsay
When identical twin Logan Harper learns he was stolen at birth, he vows
to claim the life he was denied. Until he's mistakenly seduced by
Honor Gould, *his twin's fiancée*! Their connection is undeniable, but
they're determined not to make the same mistake twice...

#2778 TAKING ON THE BILLIONAIRE

Redhawk Reunion • by Robin Covington
Tess Lynch once helped billionaire Adam Redhawk find his Cherokee
family. Now he needs her again—to find who's sabotaging his company.
But she has a secret agenda that doesn't stop sparks from flying. Will
the woman he can't resist be his downfall?

"May I go on record to make something clear, Regan?" Garth
asked, kicking off his shoes.

She swallowed. He was standing, all six feet and three inches
of him, at the foot of the bed, staring at her with the same intensity
that she felt. She wasn't sure what he had to say, but she definitely
wanted to hear it.

"Yes," she said in an almost whisper.

"You don't need me to make you feel sexy, desired and wanted.
You are those things already. What I intend to do is to make you feel
needed," he said, stepping away from the bed to pull his T-shirt over
his head and toss it on a nearby chair. "If you only knew the depth
of my need for you."

She wondered if being needed also meant she was indispensable,
essential, vital, crucial…all those things she wanted to become to
him.

"Now I have you just where I want you, Regan. In my bed."

And whether he knew it or not, she had him just where she
wanted him, too. Standing in front of her and stripping, for starters.
As she watched, his hands went to the front of his jeans.

"And I have you doing what I've always fantasized about, Garth.
Taking your clothes off in front of me so I can see you naked."

She could tell from the look on his face that her words surprised
him. "You used to fantasize about me?"

"All the time. You always looked sexy in your business suits, but my imagination gets a little more risqué than that."

He shook his head. "I never knew."

"What? That I wanted you as much as you wanted me? I told you that in the kitchen earlier."

"I assumed that desire began since you've been here with me."

Boy, was he wrong. "No, it goes back further than that."

It was important that he knew everything. Not only that the desire was mutual but also that it hadn't just begun. If he understood that then it would be easier for her to build the kind of relationship they needed, regardless of whether he thought they needed it or not.

"I never knew," he said, looking a little confused. "You never said anything."

"I wasn't supposed to. You are my boss and I am a professional."

He nodded because she knew he couldn't refute that. "How long have you felt that way?"

There was no way she would tell him that she'd had a crush on him since she was sixteen, or that he was the reason she had returned to Fairbanks after her first year in college. She had heard he was back home from the military with a broken heart, and she'd been determined to fix it. Things didn't work out quite that way. He was deep in mourning for the woman he'd lost and had built a solid wall around himself, one that even his family hadn't been able to penetrate for a long while.

"The length of time doesn't matter, Garth. All you need to know is that the desire between us is mutual. Now, are you going to finish undressing or what?"

Don't miss what happens next in...
The Wife He Needs
by Brenda Jackson, the first book in her
Westmoreland Legacy: The Outlaws series!

Available November 2020 wherever
Harlequin Desire books and ebooks are sold.

Harlequin.com

Get 4 FREE REWARDS!

We'll send you 2 FREE Books <u>plus</u> 2 FREE Mystery Gifts.

Harlequin Desire® books transport you to the world of the American elite with juicy plot twists, delicious sensuality and intriguing scandal.

FREE Value Over $20

**IF YOU ENJOYED THIS BOOK
WE THINK YOU WILL ALSO LOVE**

⊕ HARLEQUIN

PRESENTS

Escape to exotic locations where passion knows no bounds.

Welcome to the glamorous lives of royals and billionaires,
where passion knows no bounds. Be swept into a world
of luxury, wealth and exotic locations.

8 NEW BOOKS AVAILABLE EVERY MONTH!

HPXSERIES2020

Love Harlequin romance?

DISCOVER.

Be the first to find out about promotions, news and exclusive content!

 Facebook.com/HarlequinBooks

Twitter.com/HarlequinBooks

Instagram.com/HarlequinBooks

Pinterest.com/HarlequinBooks

ReaderService.com

EXPLORE.

Sign up for the Harlequin e-newsletter and download a free book from any series at **TryHarlequin.com**

CONNECT.

Join our Harlequin community to share your thoughts and connect with other romance readers!
Facebook.com/groups/HarlequinConnection

HSOCIAL2020

BOOKS BY JUDE DEVERAUX

Jude Deveraux

The Blessing

POCKET BOOKS

New York   London   Toronto   Sydney

For information regarding special discounts for bulk purchases, please contact Simon & Schuster Special Sales at 1-800-456-6798 or business@simonandschuster.com

This book is a work of fiction. Names, characters, places and incidents are products of the author's imagination or are used fictitiously. Any resemblance to actual events or locales or persons, living or dead, is entirely coincidental.

Originally published in hardcover in 1998 by Pocket Books

 A Pocket Star Book published by
POCKET BOOKS, a division of Simon & Schuster Inc.
1230 Avenue of the Americas, New York, NY 10020

ISBN -13: 978-0-671-89109-1
ISBN -10:   0-671-89109-X

First Pocket Books paperback printing June 1999

20 19 18 17 16 15 14 13

Cover illustration by Lisa Litwack
Cover photos: woman and child © Ariel Skelley/The Stock Market; porch © Owen Franken/Stock Boston/PNI

Printed in the U.S.A.

CHAPTER ONE

"I OUGHT TO KILL YOU, YOU KNOW THAT? JUST OUT-right murder you," Jason Wilding said, looking at his brother from under straight black eyebrows that were topped with a lion's mane of steel gray hair.

"What else is new?" David asked, smiling at his older brother, giving that smile of such great charm that people trusted him with their lives. David Wilding, or Dr. David as he was known to the people of Abernathy, Kentucky, picked up his glass of beer and drank deeply, while Jason sipped at his single malt whiskey.

"So what do you want?" Jason asked, arching one brow. It was a look that had made many a businessman's knees quake.

"Now what makes you think I want anything?"

"Years of experience. The rest of this one-horse town may think you're ready for sainthood, but I know you. You're up to something and you want something from me."

"Maybe I just wanted to visit with my illustrious older brother and the only way I could get you to come home for Christmas is to tell you that Dad was about to die."

"Cheap trick," Jason said with tight lips. He began to look in his suit pocket for a cigarette, then remembered that he gave them up over two years ago. But there was something about being in a bar in the town where he grew up that brought out the good ol' boy in him.

"It was the only thing I could think of," David said in defense of what he had done. He'd cabled his rich, overworked brother in New York that their father had suffered a heart attack and probably had only days to live. Within hours Jason's private jet had landed in an airfield fifty miles from Abernathy, and an hour later Jason was standing in their living room. When Jason had seen his father drinking beer and playing poker with his buddies, for a few minutes, David had feared for his life. But, as he well knew, Jason's bark was worse than his bite.

"I'm not staying," Jason said, "so you can get that idea out of your head."

"And why not?" David asked, trying to sound

innocent. It had always been a family joke that David could get away with anything while Jason got blamed for everything. It was their looks. David had blond hair and blue eyes and a pink-and-white complexion. Even at thirty-seven he looked like an angel. And when he had on his doctor's coat, a stethoscope about his neck, every person who saw him breathed a sigh of relief, for any man who looked as divine as he did had to be able to save lives.

On the other hand, Jason was as dark as David was fair, and as his father had often said to him, "Even if you didn't do anything, you look like you did," for Jason was born with a scowl.

"Let me guess," David said, "you're booked for four weeks in Tahiti and you'll be bedding three women at once."

Jason just took a sip of his whiskey and looked at his brother archly.

"No, no, don't tell me," David said. "I really can guess this one. Maybe it's Paris and you're having an affair with a runway model. One of those tall, cool creatures with plastic breasts."

Jason looked at his watch. "I have to go, Leon is waiting."

David knew that Leon was his brother's private pilot and, in cases like this trip, he doubled as his chauffeur. David also knew that Jason's staff served as his family, since he never bothered returning home and he'd always been much too busy to create a family of his own.

Jason gave his brother a look, then finished his whiskey and rose. "Look, you know how much I'd love to stay here and listen to you make fun of me, but I have—"

"Let *me* say it," David said heavily. "You have *work* to do."

"Right, I do, and I would imagine that just because it's Christmas people don't stop getting sick, even in charming little Abernathy."

"No, and they don't stop needing help, even in Abernathy."

At that Jason sat back down. David asked for help only if he really needed it. "What is it? Cash?" Jason said. "Whatever you need, if I have it it's yours."

"I only wish that were true," David said, looking down at his beer.

Jason signaled the waiter to bring another single malt, and David looked up at him in speculation. Jason wasn't much of a drinker. He said it dulled his brain and he needed his wits about him if he was going to work. And, of course, work was Jason's be-all, end-all of life.

"I'm in love," David said softly; then when his brother was silent, he looked up and saw one of Jason's rare smiles.

"And what else?" Jason asked. "She from the

wrong side of the tracks? Are the biddies of this town up in arms because their precious Dr. David is no longer available?"

"I wish you didn't hate this town so much. It's a great place, really."

"If you like small-minded bigots," Jason said cheerfully.

"Look, what happened to Mother— No, I'm not going to get into that. I like this town and I plan to stay here."

"With your new ladylove. So what's the problem with this girl that you think you need me? What do I know about being in love?"

"You know about dating. I see your name in all the society columns."

"Mmmm. I need to network at those charity functions . . . and it helps to have a woman on my arm," Jason said without much feeling.

"It's nice that the women you escort happen to be some of the most beautiful women in the world."

"And the most avaricious," Jason said, this time with feeling. "Do you have any idea how much jet fuel costs? If you did, you'd get on with whatever has happened to make you lie and connive your way into getting me here."

"I figure one trip costs less than an EKG machine."

Jason didn't miss the hint. "You got it, so stop

begging and get on with it. Who are you in love with and what's the problem? You want me to pay for the wedding?"

"Believe it or not," David said angrily, "some people on this earth want something from you other than that money that seems to be your life."

Immediately, Jason backed down. "I apologize for the insinuation. Just tell me about this woman and how in the world I can be of help to you."

David took a deep breath. "She's a widow. She's . . ." He looked up at his brother. "She's Billy Thompkins's widow."

At that Jason gave a low whistle.

"She's not like that. I know Billy had problems, but—"

"Yeah, the three *d*'s: drugs, drink, and driving."

"You didn't know him in his last years. He settled down at the end. He went away on some job across the river, and he came back two years later with Amy, and she was four months pregnant. He seemed to have turned over a new leaf. He even bought the old Salma place."

Jason raised an eyebrow. "Is that heap still standing?"

"Barely. Anyway, he bought it with his mother's help. She co-signed the mortgage."

"But then who in Abernathy would lend Billy money?"

"Exactly. But it didn't matter, because he died

four months later. Plowed into a tree doing about eighty."

"Drunk?"

"Yeah, drunk, and his wife was left alone except for Mildred. You remember her? Billy's mother?"

"I always liked her," Jason said. "She deserved better than Billy."

"Well, she got it in Amy. She's the sweetest person you ever met."

"So what's your problem? I can't imagine that Mildred is standing in your way. Don't tell me Dad—"

"He loves Amy almost as much as I do," David said, looking down into his beer, which was already half empty.

"If you don't get on with it, I'm leaving," Jason threatened.

"It's her son. I told you that Amy was pregnant when she came back with Billy. Well, it was a boy."

"You deliver it?" Jason asked, one eyebrow arched.

"No, and don't start that again. It's different when you're a woman's doctor."

"Mmmmm. What about her son? Is he like his father?"

"Billy had a sense of humor. This kid is . . . You'd have to meet him to see what I mean. He's ruthless. Utterly without conscience. He is the most manipulative, conniving little monster I have ever met. Jealous doesn't begin to describe him. He completely controls Amy."

"And she has no idea what the kid's doing, right?" Jason said, his lips tight. He had been in David's position. Years before, he'd met a woman to whom he was more than just physically attracted. After one date he had begun to think that maybe there could be something between them. But then he'd met the woman's thirteen-year-old son. The kid was a criminal-in-the-making. He used to rifle through Jason's coat pockets and steal whatever he could find. Once he took Jason's car keys, which forced him to leave without his Jaguar that night. A week later the car was found at the bottom of the East River. Of course the kid's mother didn't believe that her son could do anything like that, so they had broken up. The last Jason had heard, the kid was now working on Wall Street and was a multimillionaire.

"You've had some experience in this area?" David asked.

"Some. You can't get any time with her unless the kid gives permission, right? And the mother dotes on him." There was bitterness in his voice.

"Like you've never seen in your life. She never goes anywhere without him. I've tried to persuade her to let me hire a baby-sitter, but she's too proud to accept my help, so the kid goes with us or we don't go. And it's impossible to stay at her house."

David leaned halfway across the table. "The kid doesn't sleep. I mean it. Never. He's either a freak or a spawn of the devil. And of course Amy gives him one hundred percent of her attention all the time he's awake."

"Drop her," Jason said. "Trust me on this. Get away from her fast. If you did win her, you'd have to live with that kid. You'll wake up one morning with a cobra in your bed."

"He'd have to fight Max for space."

"The kid is still sleeping with his mother?" Jason said in disgust.

"When he wants to."

"Run."

"It's easy for you to say. You've never been in love. Look, I think I could handle the kid if I could just win over his mother. But the truth is, I have no time alone with her." At that, David looked up at Jason in a way he'd seen a thousand times before.

"Oh, no, you don't. You're not getting me into this. I have engagements."

"No, you don't. How many times have I heard you complain because your employees want to take time off at Christmas? So this year you can stay here and help me out and give that secretary of yours some time off. How is that gorgeous creature, by the way?"

"Fine," Jason said tightly. "So what is it you

want? You want me to kidnap the kid? Or maybe we should be done with it and have him murdered."

"The kid needs a father," David said, his mouth in a grimace.

"You do have it bad, don't you?"

"Real bad. I've never felt this way about a woman, and I have competition. Every man in town is after her."

"What's that, a whopping ten men or so? Or did old man Johnson die?"

"Ian Newsome is after her."

"Oh?" Jason said, giving his brother a one-sided grin. "Is that the boy who was the captain of the football team and the swimming team and also single-handedly won the state debating championships? The boy the girls used to throw themselves at? Didn't he marry Angela, the captain of the cheerleader squad, the one with more hair than brains?"

"Divorced. And he's back in town and he took over the Cadillac dealership."

"Must be making a lot of money there," Jason said sarcastically. There wasn't much call for Cadillacs in Abernathy.

"As a sideline, he sells Mercedes to the Arabs."

"Ahhhh," Jason said. "You do have problems."

"All I need is some time alone with Amy. If I could get her alone, I know I could—"

"Make her love you? That's not the way it works."

"Okay," David said, "but at least I'd like to get a chance."

"All Newsome has to do is send her over a red Mercedes convertible and she's his. Maybe you could give her free—"

"She's not like that!" David almost shouted; then when half the people in the bar looked at him, he lowered his voice. "I wish you'd stop joking. I'm not sure I want to live without her," David said softly.

For a moment Jason studied the top of his brother's head. David didn't ask for help often, and he *never* asked for help for himself. He had put himself through med school, refusing his brother's offer of a free education. "I won't appreciate it if it's handed to me on a platter," David had said. So now Jason was sure that David was still up to his neck in debt for that education, but he still wouldn't accept financial help.

But now David was asking his brother for something personal, something that didn't involve Jason's copious wealth. It had been a long, long time since anyone had asked Jason for anything that didn't have to do with money.

"I'll do what I can," Jason said softly.

David's head came up. "You mean it? No, no, what am I saying? You won't do what I have in mind."

Jason was by nature cautious, so now he said, "What exactly did you *have* in mind?"

"To live with her."

"What!?" Jason sputtered, again causing the patrons to look their way. He leaned toward his brother. "You want me to *live* with your girlfriend?"

"She's not my girlfriend. At least not yet, anyway. But I have to get someone in that house who can keep that kid away from her. And she has to trust him or she won't allow him to baby-sit."

"And then there's Newsome you have to deal with."

"Yeah, and all the other men who are after her."

"All right. I'll call Parker and she can—"

"No! It has to be you! Not your secretary. Not your chef or your pilot or your cleaning lady. You." When Jason looked at his brother in consternation at his vehemence, David calmed. "This kid needs a man's touch. You're good with brats. Look what you did with me."

Jason couldn't help being flattered, and it was true that he had been as much a father to his much younger sibling as he had been a brother. Their mother was gone and their father worked sixty hours a week, so they just had each other.

"Please," David said.

"All right," Jason answered reluctantly. In New York he was known to never give in on any deal, but then only David had the power to persuade him.

And, besides, there was part of Jason that wanted to replay one of the few battles in his life that he'd lost. A spoiled monster of a kid had kept him away from one of the few women Jason had ever thought he could love, and in the many years since then, he'd regretted not staying and fighting for her. Just last year he'd seen the woman again. She was happily married to a man Jason was doing business with and she looked great. They had a big house on Long Island, and they'd even had a couple of kids of their own. Now, at forty-five years old, Jason wondered what his life would have been like if he'd stayed and fought for the woman, if he hadn't let a thirteen-year-old con artist beat him.

"I'll do it," he said quietly. "I'll stay and see that the kid is occupied while you go out with your Amy."

"It won't be easy."

"I guess you think the rest of my life *is* easy."

"You haven't met this kid, and you haven't seen how attached Amy is to him."

"Don't worry about a thing. I can handle anything you throw at me. I'll take care of the brat for one week, and if you don't win this woman in that time, then you don't deserve her."

Instead of gushing with gratitude, as Jason thought he would, David looked down at his beer again.

"Now what is it?" Jason snapped. "A week isn't

enough time?" His mind was racing. How many Little League games could a man attend without going insane? Thank God for cell phones so he could work while sitting on the bleachers. And if he got into a jam, he could always call Parker. She was capable of handling anything at any time, any-where.

"I want your sacred promise."

At that, Jason's face grew red. "Do you think I go back on my word?"

"You'll turn the job over to someone else."

"Like hell I will!" Jason sputtered, but had to look down so his brother couldn't see his eyes. If the men he dealt with in New York knew him as well as his brother did, he'd never close a deal. "*I'll* take care of the kid for one week," he said more calmly. "I'll do all the things that kids like. I'll even give him the keys to my car."

"You flew; you don't have a car, remember?"

"Then I'll buy a car and give him the damn thing, all right?" David was making him feel decid-edly incompetent. "Look, let's get this show on the road. The sooner I get this done with, the sooner I can get out of here. When do I meet this paragon of loveliness?"

"Sacred promise," David said, his eyes serious but his voice sounding as if he were once again four years old and demanding that his big brother promise that he wouldn't leave him.

Jason gave a great sigh. "Sacred promise," he murmured, then couldn't help looking around to see if anyone in the bar had heard him. In a mere thirty minutes he had gone from being a business tycoon to a dirty-faced little boy declaring blood oaths. "Did I ever tell you that I hate Christmas?"

"How can you hate something that you have never participated in?" David asked with a cocky grin. "Come on, let's go. Maybe we'll be lucky and the kid will be asleep."

"Might I point out to you that it is two o'clock in the morning? I don't think your little angel will appreciate our dropping in."

"Tell you what, we'll go by her house and if all the lights are out, we'll go past. But if the lights are on, then we'll know she's up and we'll stop in for a visit. Agreed?"

Jason nodded as he drained the last of his whiskey, but he didn't like what he was thinking. What kind of woman would marry a man like Billy Thompkins? And what kind of woman stayed up all night? A fellow drunk seemed to be the only answer.

As they left the bar and headed toward the sedan where Jason's driver waited, Jason began to make up his own mind about this woman who had enticed his brother into wanting to marry her. The facts against her were accumulating fast: a drunken husband, an incorrigible child, a nocturnal lifestyle.

Inside the car, Jason looked across at his younger brother and vowed to protect him from this hussy, and as they rode toward the outskirts of town, he began to form a picture of her. He could see her bleached hair, a cigarette hanging out of her mouth. Was she older than David? He was so young, so innocent. He'd rarely left Abernathy in his life and knew nothing of the world. It would be easy for some sharp-witted huckster to take advantage of him.

Turning, he looked at his brother solemnly. "Sacred promise," he said softly, and David grinned at him. Jason turned away. For all that his brother was often a pain in the neck, he had the power to make Jason feel as if he was worth what his accountant said he was.

CHAPTER TWO

THE OLD SALMA PLACE WAS WORSE THAN HE REMEM-
bered it. It couldn't have had a coat of paint in at
least fifteen years, and the porch was falling down
on one side. And from what he could see by the
moonlight, he didn't think the roof was going to
keep anyone dry.

"See, I told you," David said eagerly, seemingly
oblivious to the house's decrepitude. "The lights
are all on. That kid never sleeps; he keeps his
mother up all night."

Jason glanced at his brother and thought that the
sooner he got him away from this harpy, the better.

"Come on," David said, already out of the car
and halfway up the broken sidewalk that led to a
fence that had half collapsed. "Are you afraid of
this? If you are—"

"If I am, you'll double dare me, right?" Jason said, one eyebrow raised.

David grinned, his teeth white in the moon-light; then he half ran up the porch steps toward the front door. "Don't step on that, it— Oh, sorry, did you hurt yourself? The house needs some work."

Rubbing his head where a board from the porch had smacked him, Jason gave a grimace to his brother. "Yeah, like Frankenstein needed some fine tuning."

But David didn't seem to hear his brother as he eagerly rapped on the door, and within seconds it was opened by a young woman. . . . And Jason's mouth fell open in disbelief, for this woman was not what he had been expecting.

Amy was not a Siren luring men to her; she wasn't going to inspire sonnets written to her beauty. Nor was she going to have to worry about men falling at her feet in lust. She had long dark hair, which looked to be in need of a washing, pulled back at the nape of her neck. She wore no makeup, and her pale ivory skin had a few off-white-ish spots on her chin. Her dark eyes were huge, seeming to almost swallow her oval face; they certainly overshadowed her tiny mouth. As for her body, she was short and fragile-looking, and from the way her bones protruded from her clothes, she needed a good meal. The only thing of substance about her were her breasts, which were huge—and were marked by two large wet circles.

"Damnation!" she said as she looked down at herself; then she scurried back into the house. "Come in, David, make yourself at home. Max is—thank you God—asleep for the moment. I'd give you some gin, but I don't have any, so you might as well help yourself to the fifty-year-old brandy, which I don't have any of either."

"Thanks," David said brightly. "In that case I think I'll have champagne."

"Pour me a bucket full of it too," came the answer from a darkened doorway.

David looked at Jason as though to say, Isn't she the wittiest person you ever met?

But Jason was looking around the room. It had been a long time since he'd left what David referred to as his "house in the clouds." "You live so much in private jets and private hotels and private what-evers that you've forgotten what the rest of the world is like," he'd said too often. So now, Jason looked about the room in distaste. Shabby was the word that came first to his mind. Everything looked as though it had come from the Goodwill: nothing matched, nothing suited anything else. There was an ugly old couch upholstered in worn brown fabric, a hideous old chair covered in what looked to be a print of sunflowers and banana leaves. The coffee table was one of those huge, cast-off wooden spools that someone had painted a strange shade of fuchsia.

The nicest thing Jason could think about it was that it looked like a place where Billy Thompkins would live.

David punched his brother in the ribs and nodded toward the doorway. "Stop sneering," he said under his breath; then both men looked up as Amy reentered the room.

She emerged from the bedroom wearing a dry, wrinkled shirt, and most of the spots on her chin were gone. When she saw Jason glance at her, she gave another swipe, removed the remaining spots, then gave a half smile and said, "Baby rice. If he got as much in him as I get on me, he'd be one fat little hog."

"This is my cousin Jason," David was saying. "You know, the one I was telling you about. He'd be really grateful if you'd let him stay with you until his heart mends."

This statement so stunned Jason that all he could do was stare at his brother.

"Yes, of course. I understand," Amy said. "Do come in and sit down." She looked at Jason. "I'm sorry Max isn't awake right now, but you'll get to see him in about three hours. I can assure you of that," she said, laughing.

Jason was beginning to smell a rat. And the rat was his little brother. The brother he had helped raise. The brother he had always loved and cherished. The one he would have died for. *That* brother seemed to have done a real number on him.

Long ago Jason had figured out that if he kept his mouth shut long enough, he'd learn everything he needed to know. Many times his silence had achieved what words could not, so now he sat and listened.

"Can I offer you some tea?" Amy asked. "If I can't afford champagne, I can afford tea. I have chamomile and raspberry leaf. No, that one's good for milk, and I doubt if either of you need that," she said, smiling at Jason as though he knew everything that was going on.

And Jason was indeed beginning to understand. Now he noticed a few things about the room that he had overlooked before. On the floor was a stuffed tiger. No, it was Tigger from *Winnie-the-Pooh,* and there was a cloth book against the edge of the sunflower chair.

"How old is your son?" Jason asked, his jaw rigid.

"Twenty-six weeks today," Amy said proudly. "Six months."

Jason turned blazing eyes on his brother. "May I see you outside?" He looked at Amy. "You must excuse us."

When David made no move to get off the old brown sofa, Jason dug his hands into his brother's shoulders and pulled him upward. One advantage Jason had was that wherever he went he made sure there was a gym available so he could keep in shape. David thought that standing on his feet fourteen hours a day was enough exercise, so now Jason had the advantage and he nearly lifted his softer brother into a standing position.

"We'll only be a minute," David said, smiling at Amy as Jason half dragged him from the house.

Once they were outside, Jason glared at his brother, his voice calm—and deadly. "What are you playing at? And don't you dare lie to me."

"I couldn't tell you or you would have run back to your damned jet. But actually I didn't really lie to you. I just omitted some details. And haven't you always said that no man should assume anything?"

"Don't turn this back on me. I was talking about *strangers*. I didn't think my own brother would— Oh, the hell with it. You go in there and tell that poor young woman that a mistake was made, and—"

"You're going back on a sacred oath. I knew you would."

For a moment Jason closed his eyes in an attempt to regain strength. "We are no longer in elementary school. We are adults and—"

"Right," David said coldly, then turned toward the car that waited at the curb.

Oh, Lord, Jason thought. His brother could carry a grudge into eternity. In one step he caught David's arm and halted him. "You must see that I can't follow up on my promise. I could look after a half-grown boy, but this is . . . David, this is a *baby*. It wears *diapers.*"

"And you're too good to change them, is that it? Of course, the great and rich"—he sneered the word—"Jason Wilding is too good to change a kid's diapers. Do you have any idea how many times I have emptied bedpans? Inserted catheters? That I have—"

"All right, you win. You're St. David and I am the devil incarnate. Whatever, I can't do this."

"I knew you'd go back on your word," David muttered, then turned toward the car again.

Jason sent up a little prayer asking for strength, then grabbed David's arm again. "What is it you've told her?" he asked while envisioning his secretary flying to Abernathy and taking over the kid. No, the *baby.*

David's eyes brightened. "I told her you were my cousin and you were recovering from a broken love affair and it was the first Christmas you'd had without your lover, so you were very lonely. And that your new apartment was being repainted, so you had nowhere to stay for a week. I also said you loved babies and she'd be doing you a favor to let you stay with her for a week and take care of Max while she job hunts during the day." David took a breath.

It wasn't as bad as Jason had at first thought when he'd heard that "broken heart" remark.

David could see his brother relenting. "All I want is a little time with her," he said. "I'm mad about her. You can see that she's wonderful. She's funny and brave and—"

"And has a heart of gold, I know," Jason said tiredly as he walked toward the car. Leon was already out and had the back door open. "Call Parker and tell her to get here fast," he ordered. It felt good to give an order. David made him feel as though he were back in nursery school.

Jason turned back to his brother. "If I do this for you, you are never to ask anything from me ever again. You understand? This is the all-time, ultimate favor."

"Scouts' honor," David said, raising two fingers and looking so happy that Jason almost forgave him. But at least the good news was that now that David had lied to him, he felt free to do a little underhanded business of his own. He most definitely would get his competent secretary to bail him out of this.

David could see by his brother's face that Jason was going to do it. "You'll not regret this. I promise you."

"I already do," Jason muttered as he followed

David back into the house. And once they were inside, it took David all of about four minutes before he excused himself, saying he had to get up early; then he left the two of them alone.

And it was then that Jason felt especially awkward. "I . . . ah . . ." he began, not knowing what to say to the young woman who stood there staring at him as though she expected him to say something. What did she want from him? A résumé maybe? Such a document might list several Fortune 500 companies he owned, but it wouldn't say anything about his ability—or in this case his inability—to change diapers.

When Jason said nothing, the woman gave him a bit of a smile, then said, "I would imagine that you're tired. The spare bedroom is in there. I'm sorry, but there's only a narrow bed. I've never had a guest before."

Jason tried to give her a smile in return. It wasn't her fault if his brother was in love with her, but, truthfully, Jason couldn't see what there was to love about the woman. Personally, he liked his women to be clean and polished, the kind of women who spent their days in a salon having every hair and pore tended to.

"Where are your bags?"

"Bags?" he asked, not knowing what she meant. "Oh, yeah. Luggage. I left it at . . . at David's house. I'll get it in the morning."

She was looking at him very hard. "I thought—" She looked away, not finishing her sentence. "The bedroom's through there, and there's a little bathroom. It's not much but—" She broke off as though she weren't going to allow herself to apologize for the inadequacy of the room.

"Good night, Mr. Wilding," she said, then turned on her heel and went through another doorway.

Jason wasn't used to people dismissing him. In fact, he was more used to people fawning over him, as they usually wanted something from him. "Right," he muttered. "Good night." Then he turned and went into the room she'd indicated. It was, if possible, worse than the rest of the house. The bed stood in the middle of the room, with a clean, frayed old red-and-white quilt spread over it. The only other furniture in the room was an overturned cardboard box with a lamp on it that looked as though Edison might have used it. There was a tiny curtainless window and two doors, one that looked as if it might lead to a closet and the other the bathroom. Inside that room was all blazing white tile, half of it cracked.

Ten minutes later, Jason had stripped to his underwear and was huddled under the quilt. Tomorrow he'd send his secretary to buy him an electric blanket.

It couldn't have been more than an hour later

that he was awakened by a sound. It was a scraping noise followed by something that sounded like paper being crumpled. He'd always been a light sleeper, but years of jet travel had made things worse; he was now nearly an insomniac. Quietly, barefoot, he padded into the living room. There was enough moonlight that he could see the shadow outlines of the furniture and keep from bashing into it. For a moment he stood still listening. The sound was coming from the woman's room.

Hesitating, he stood outside the open doorway. Maybe she was doing something in private, but as his eyes adjusted he could see her in bed, see that she was asleep. Feeling like a Peeping Tom, he turned away to go back to his own bed, but then the sound came again. Peering into the darkness, he saw what looked to be a cage in the corner, but as he blinked, he saw it was an old-fashioned wooden playpen and sitting up in it was what appeared to be a baby bear.

Jason blinked, shook his head, then looked again as the bear cub turned its head and grinned up at him. He could distinctly see two teeth gleaming in the pale silvery light.

Without thinking what he was doing, Jason tiptoed into the room and reached down to the kid. He fully expected the child to let out a howl, but he didn't. However, the baby did grab Jason's face and pinch in a way that made Jason's eyes water with pain.

After removing the little hand from his face, Jason carried the child back into his own room and put him down onto the narrow bed, pulled the quilt about him, then said sternly, "Now go to sleep." The baby blinked up at him a couple of times, then squirmed around so he was lying crosswise on the bed, and promptly went to sleep.

"Not bad," Jason said in admiration of his own accomplishment. Not bad at all. Maybe David had been right when he said that his older brother had a way with children. Too bad Jason hadn't used his firmest tone with that horrid boy so many years ago. Maybe . . .

He trailed off as he realized that he now had no place to sleep. Even if he turned the kid around, the bed was too narrow for the both of them as the child was as fat as a Christmas turkey. No wonder his first impression of him was that he was a bear cub.

So now what? Jason thought, looking at his watch. It was four A.M. and New York wasn't open, so he couldn't do any business. Ah, he thought, New York might be closed, but London was open.

After putting his wool suit on to protect him from the cold, he retrieved his portable phone from his coat pocket and went to the window, where the signal would be better, and dialed. Five minutes later he was being hooked up to a conference call with the heads of a major company that Jason had recently bought. In the background he could hear sounds of an office Christmas party, and he could tell that the managers were annoyed to be missing the fun, but it didn't matter to Jason. Business was business, and the sooner they realized that the better.

CHAPTER THREE

I DON'T LIKE HIM, AMY THOUGHT AS SHE LAY IN BED. For some odd reason, Max was still asleep; she could see the great lump that was him in the old playpen that had once been Billy's.

"I don't like him, I don't like him, I don't like him," she said aloud, then glanced anxiously toward the playpen, but Max didn't move. She'd have to wake him in a minute or two or she was going to explode from milk, but it was nice to have these few minutes just to think.

When David had proposed that she allow his gay cousin to live with her for a week, Amy had readily said no. "What will I feed him?" she'd asked. "I can barely afford to feed Max and me."

"He, uh, he . . . He loves to cook. And, well,

I'm sure he'd love to have someone to cook for. He'll buy everything you'll need," David had said in such a way that Amy didn't believe him. "No, really, he will. Look, Amy, I know this is an imposition, but Jason and his boyfriend just broke up, and my cousin has nowhere to go. You'd be doing me a real favor. I'd let him stay with us, but you know how my dad is about gays."

Actually, Amy had met Bertram Wilding only once and she had no idea how he felt about anything except chili dogs (he loved them) and football (loved that too). "Isn't there someone else? You know everyone in town," she had wailed. David had been so good to her; he hadn't charged her a penny for either of Max's ear infections or the immunizations, and he'd sent over his nurse to help out when Amy was sick with the flu those three days. It wasn't easy being a single mother on a severe budget, but with David's help she'd been able to survive. So she owed him.

"You have a spare bedroom and you need him. You don't have anything against gays, do you?" he asked, implying that he may have misjudged her.

"Of course not. It's just a matter of space and, well, money. I can't afford to feed him much less pay him for baby-sitting services and—"

"You just leave that to me," David said. "In fact, leave everything to me. Jason will help you do everything, and he'll make your life much easier. Trust me."

So she had trusted him, just as everyone else in this town trusted him, and what did she get? A six-foot-tall sneering man who made her want to run and hide, that's what. Last night, or actually, this morning at the two o'clock feeding, she had had to bite her tongue to keep from making a snide remark as she watched him look about the house, his upper lip curled in distaste. He was wearing a suit that looked as though it cost more than her house had and she could feel his contempt. Right then she wanted to tell David to take him away, that she wouldn't let him near her son.

But then she remembered all that David had told her about this poor man and his broken heart. But to Amy the man didn't look depressed as much as he looked angry: angry at the world, maybe even angry at her in particular. When he'd demanded that David go outside with him, Amy had almost bolted the door against the two of them, then gone back to her warm bed.

But she hadn't, and now she was going to have to spend a whole week with the jerk, she thought. One whole week of her life being sneered at. One week—

She didn't think anymore because through the

thin wall came the heavy thud of something falling, and it was followed by Max's scream of terror. Amy was out of the bed instantly and into her boarder's room before he could pick up the child.

"Get away," Amy said, pushing at his hands, as she snatched up her baby and cuddled him to her. "Hush, sweetheart," she said, holding him tightly, her heart pounding. He had fallen off the bed. Had he hit his head? Was he all right? Concussion? Brain damage? Her hands ran over him, searching for lumps, for blood, for anything wrong.

"I think he's just scared," Jason said. "He fell on the pillow, and besides, he has enough clothes on that you could drop him off a building and he wouldn't be hurt." At that he gave Amy what she imagined he thought was a smile.

Amy glared at him. Max had stopped crying and was now bending at the waist as he moved his head downward, letting her know that he wanted to nurse.

"Get out," she said to Jason. "I don't want you here."

The man looked at her as though he didn't understand English.

"Get out, I said. You're fired."

She was having trouble holding on to Max as he jackknifed downward. "Take your . . . your telephone and leave." It was easy to see that he had been standing by the window talking on the thing while he'd left a baby alone on a narrow bed. She wasn't about to leave Max in the care of someone so careless.

"I've never been fired from a job before," Jason said, his eyes wide.

"There is always a first time for everything." When Jason didn't move, she tightened her lips. "I don't have a car, so if you want transportation, call David. I'll get his number."

"I know his number," Jason said quietly, still standing there looking at her.

"Then use it!" she said as she turned away, her arms around Max's squirming body. She stalked into the living room, put Max down on the two pillows on the couch, her hand behind his head, then angrily unfastened her nightgown to reveal her breast. Max made fast work of latching on, then he lay there looking up at his mother intently, obviously aware that something was going on.

"Look, I— Oh, excuse me," Jason said as he turned his back to her, and Amy could feel his embarrassment at seeing her breast-feeding. Pulling a baby blanket off the back of the couch, she covered herself and most of the baby.

"I'd like a second chance," Jason said, his back still to her. "I was in the . . ." He nearly choked on the word. "I was in the wrong to leave the baby alone on the bed. But I, uh, I meant well. I heard him, so I took him out of his pen. I just wanted to give you a couple more hours' sleep, that's all."

As far as Amy could tell, every word out of the man's mouth was a struggle. You'd think he'd never apologized before in his life. No, actually, hearing the wrench in his voice, you'd think he'd never done anything wrong in his life before.

"You're asking me to take a second chance with my child's life?" she asked calmly, still looking at the back of him.

Slowly, he turned around, saw that she was covered, then sat down in the sunflower chair. "I am not usually so . . . so lacking in vigilance. Usually I watch over several matters at one time and keep them all going at once. Usually I can handle anything that's thrown my way. In fact, I pride myself on being able to handle anything."

"You don't have to lie to me; David told me everything." When she said that the man's face turned an odd shade of lavender, and she renewed her vow to get rid of him. I don't like him, she repeated to herself.

"And what did Dr. David tell you?" the man said softly.

There was something about him that was a bit intimidating. She owed David a lot, but she wasn't going to repay anyone at the expense of her child.

"He told me that you're gay and you're recovering from a broken heart and—"

"He told you that I'm gay?" Jason said quietly.

"Yes, I know it's a secret and that you don't want people to know about you, but he had to tell me. You don't think I'd let a heterosexual man stay here with me, do you?" She squinted her eyes at him. "Or do you? Is that what kind of woman you think I am?" When he didn't reply right away, she said, "I think you'd better leave."

Jason didn't so much as move a muscle, but sat there staring at her as though he were pondering some great problem. She remembered that David had told her that his cousin had nowhere to stay, nowhere to spend Christmas. "Look, I'm sorry that this hasn't worked out. You're not an unattractive man. I'm sure you'll find . . ."

"Another lover?" he asked, eyebrows raised. "Now I must ask what kind of man you think *I* am."

At that Amy blushed and looked down at Max, who was still nursing, his eyes wide open and seeming to listen to every word that was being spoken. "I apologize," she said. "I didn't mean any slur on any group of people. Forgive me."

"Only if you forgive me."

"No," she answered. "I don't think that this arrangement will work. I don't—" Breaking off, she looked down at Max again. He was no longer sucking, but he wasn't about to let go of her. As she well knew, he thought she was one big pacifier.

"You don't trust me? You don't want to forgive me? You don't what?"

"Like you," she blurted. "I'm sorry, but you wanted to know." Sticking her finger in the side of Max's mouth, she broke his powerful suction and removed him from her breast, covering herself, all in one practiced motion. She put him on her shoulder, but he soon twisted about to see who else was in the room.

"And why don't you like me?"

At that moment she decided that her debt to David had been paid. "You have done nothing but sneer since you got here," she blurted. "Maybe we can't all afford to wear hand-tailored suits and gold watches, but we do the best we can. I think that somewhere along the way you lost your memory of what it's like to be . . . be part of the masses. When David begged me to take you in, I got the idea we could help each other, but I can see that you think you're above Billy Thompkins's widow." She said the last with a rigid jaw. She hadn't been in Abernathy for a week before she learned what people thought of Billy.

"I see," Jason said, still not moving from where he was, and he looked as though he had no intention of leaving either the chair or the house. "And what would I have to do to prove myself to you?

How can I prove that I am trustworthy and can do this job?"

"I haven't a clue," she said, wrestling with Max as all twenty-two pounds of him fought to stand on her lap, but his balance wasn't good, so he wobbled about like a very strong piece of wet spaghetti.

Suddenly, Jason leaned across the room and took the baby from her, and Max let out a squeal of delight.

"Traitor," Amy said under her breath as she watched Jason hold Max aloft, then lower him and rub his whiskery face against Max's neck. Max grabbed Jason's cheeks with his hands, and Amy well knew how he could hurt; twice Max had drawn blood with those little love holds of his.

After several minutes of tossing Max about, Jason sat the baby down on his lap, and when Max started to squirm, Jason said, "Be still," and Max obeyed. Sitting there on Jason's lap, looking utterly content, Max smiled up at his mother.

Amy hated being a single mother, hated that Max didn't have a daddy. It wasn't what she had planned. For all that Billy had lots of faults, he was a sweet man, and he would have made a good father. But fate had decreed differently, and—

"What do you want?" Amy said tiredly when she realized he was staring at her.

"A second chance. Let me ask you, Mrs.

Thompkins, has he ever fallen when you have been watching him?"

Blushing, Amy turned away. She didn't know how, but Max had fallen off the bed once and off the kitchen countertop once. The second time he'd been strapped to a thick plastic booster seat and he'd landed on his back, still strapped in, looking like a turtle in his shell. "There have been a couple of incidents."

"I see. Well, this morning was my first and only 'incident.' I can assure you of that. I thought he was asleep, and since he took up all the room in the bed, I couldn't go back to sleep, so I made a few calls. It was wrong of me to assume anything, but I wasn't negligent by intent. What else did David tell you about me?"

"That you were homeless for the moment and that you came home to mend your broken heart," she said. Max, the traitor, was sitting calmly on Jason's lap, playing with his big fingers, looking for all the world as though he'd found his throne.

"Have you noticed that your son seems to like me?"

"My son eats paper. What does he know?"

For the first time the man actually smiled, just a hint of a smile, but it was there. It was a bit like seeing the figures on Mount Rushmore smile. Would his face crack?

"May I be honest with you?" he asked, leaning

toward her. "I don't know diddly-squat about taking care of a baby. I've never changed a diaper in my life. But I'm willing to learn, and I do need a place to stay. Also, I think I'd like to change your opinion of me. I can be quite likable when I make an effort."

"Does this mean you can't cook either?"

"David told you I could?"

She nodded, thinking that she should demand that he leave this minute, but Max did seem to like him. Now her son was beginning to twist around and, easily, Jason held him in Max's favorite standing position. The books said that babies didn't start standing until about six months, but Max had been standing on her lap and trying to pull her arms from their sockets since he was five and a half weeks old. Maybe if Jason did watch after Max she could take a shower. A real shower. One of those where she could shampoo her hair twice, then put on conditioner and leave it. Oh, heavens! maybe she could shave her legs! And afterward maybe she could rub moisturizer into her dry skin. Making milk seemed to remove every bit of moisture from her body, and her skin felt like sandpaper.

Maybe she would fire him later. After she'd had a bath. After all, he couldn't be too bad if Dr. David had recommended him so highly. "Would you mind if I took a bath?"

"Does that mean I get my second chance?"

"Maybe," she said, but she smiled a bit. "You wouldn't let anything happen to my baby, would you?"

"I'll guard him with my life."

Amy started to say something else, but instead she scurried off to the bathroom, and an instant later the hot water was running.

CHAPTER FOUR

"DEAD," JASON SAID INTO THE PHONE, MAX SLUNG over his arm like a sack of potatoes. "Little brother, you are dead."

"Look, Jase, I have about twenty patients waiting to see me, so what exactly is going to cause my death this time?"

"Gay. You told her I was gay. She thinks I've just broken up with my *boyfriend*."

"I couldn't very well tell her the truth, could I?" David said, defending himself. "If I'd told her my rich and powerful brother who owns half of New York City had agreed to help me woo her, I don't think she would have agreed."

"Well, she didn't agree," Jason snapped. "She fired me."

At that David took a deep breath. "Fired you?"

"Yeah, but I talked her out of it."

David paused, then began to laugh. "I see. She gave you a way out of all this, but you were too proud to take it, so you used your powers of persuasion to keep your job. Now you don't know what to do with the job, right? Tell me, what did you say to persuade her?"

"The kid likes me."

"What? I can't hear you. We're giving flu shots today, and there's a lot of screaming. Senior citizens' day. It almost sounded like you said that Max likes you."

"He does. The kid likes me."

"Why would that horrible child like *you?*" David half shouted into the phone. "He doesn't like anyone. Has he bitten you yet? Don't tell me he lets you hold him? He only lets Amy hold him."

"I have him right now," Jason said smugly. "And you know what, Davy? I think your Amy likes me too." At that, he hung up the phone. Let his devious little brother contemplate *that* one.

Once the phone was down, Jason looked at the bundle hanging over his arm. "Is it my imagination or do you stink to high heaven?" Max twisted around and gave Jason a toothy grin, showing two teeth in his bottom jaw. Suddenly the thought of breast-feeding an infant with teeth went through his mind, and Jason shuddered. "Brave lady is your mother. Now, hang on, and she'll be out of the shower in a minute or two."

But Amy wasn't out of the shower in a minute. Or five. Or ten. And Max began to squirm. Jason put him down on the floor, but the baby lifted his legs high in the air and began to whimper, all the while looking up at Jason with big eyes.

"I am going to kill my brother," Jason muttered in what was becoming a chant; then he began to look for changing facilities. Not that he'd know how to use them, but he had seen movies and had occasionally watched TV. Wasn't there supposed to be a tall cabinet that you put the baby on and it had shelves full of diapers and whatever else was needed? On the other hand, maybe if he thought about all this long enough, Amy would get out of the shower.

But still the shower ran, and the baby was looking up at Jason mournfully. Didn't babies cry at the drop of a hat? he thought. But this little guy was a trouper and even a bucketload wasn't making him howl. "Okay, kid, I'll do my best."

Looking about, he saw a pile of plastic-coated diapers under a table, so he figured it was now or never.

CHAPTER FIVE

AFTER WHAT HAD TO BE THE WORLD'S LONGEST shower, Amy slipped into an old bathrobe that had raspberry stains on it and began to towel dry her hair as she went in search of her son. She was sure she would win the title of World's Worst Mother for leaving her son in the hands of someone she had tried to fire, but maybe Max was a better judge of people than she was, for, inexplicably, Max certainly did like this man. And considering that Max didn't like any men and only a few women, Amy was indeed intrigued.

The sight that greeted her had to be seen to be believed. Jason, wearing what had to be a hand-made shirt and very formal wool trousers, had Max stretched out on the kitchen countertop and was trying his best to change his diaper. And all the while he was fiddling with the thing, Max was staring at him in intense concentration, not wriggling as he did when Amy changed him.

Putting her hand up to stifle a giggle, Amy watched until she was in danger of being discovered; then she silently ran back into the bedroom to take her time dressing.

After a luxurious thirty minutes of putting on her clothes, combing her wet hair, and even applying a little eye makeup, she went into the living room, where Jason sat on the couch, looking half asleep, while Max played quietly on the floor. Max wasn't yelling for breakfast, wasn't demanding attention. Instead, he looked like an ad for Perfect Baby.

Maybe she wouldn't fire Jason after all.

"Hungry?" she asked, startling him. "I don't have much, but you're welcome to it. I haven't been to the grocery store in a few days. It's difficult since I have no car. My mother-in-law usually takes me on Fridays, but last Friday she was busy, so . . ." She trailed off, since she knew she was talking too much.

"I'm sure that anything you have will be fine with me," he said, making her feel silly.

"Cheerios it is then," she said as she picked up Max, took him to the kitchen, then strapped him into his plastic booster seat, which she placed in the middle of the little kitchen table. She did the best she could to make the table pretty, but it wasn't easy, not with a red, blue, and yellow baby chair in the middle and Max's feet kicking at everything she set out.

"It's ready," she called, and he sauntered into the kitchen, all six feet of him. He's gay, she reminded herself. Gay. Like Rock Hudson was, remember?

As she prepared Max's warm porridge and mashed banana, she did her best to keep quiet. It was tempting to chatter away, as she was hungry for the sound of an adult voice, even if it was her own.

"David said you were looking for a job," the man said. "What are you trained for?"

"Nothing," she said cheerfully. "I have no talents, no ambition, no training. If Billy hadn't shown me what's what, I wouldn't have figured out how to get pregnant." Again she saw that tiny bit of a smile, and it made her continue. Billy always said that what he liked best about her was her ability to make him laugh.

"You think I'm kidding," she said as she held the cup of porridge up to Max's mouth. He was much too impatient to give her time to spoon-feed him, so he usually ended up drinking his morning meal. Of course a third of it dribbled down his chin and onto his clothes, but he got most of it inside him.

"Really, I'm no good at anything. I can't type, can't take shorthand. I have no idea how to even turn on a computer. I tried to be a waitress, but I got the orders so muddled I was fired after one week. I tried to sell real estate, but I told the clients that the houses weren't worth the asking price, so I was asked to leave. I worked in a department store, but the perfume caused me to break out in a rash, and I told the customers where to buy the same clothes cheaper, and the shoes, well, the shoes were the worst."

"What happened in the shoe department?" he asked as he ate a second bowl of cereal.

"I spent my whole salary on the things. That was the only job I ever quit. It cost me more than I made."

This time he nearly gave a real smile. "But Billy took you away from all of that," he said, his eyes twinkling.

Amy's face lost its happy look, and she turned away to grab a cloth to wipe the porridge from Max's face.

"Did I say something?"

"I know what everyone thinks of Billy, but he was good to me and I loved him. How could I not? He gave me Max." At that she gave an adoring look to her messy son, and in response he squealed and kicked so hard that he nearly knocked over the booster seat.

Jason stuck out a hand and steadied the thing. Frowning, he said, "Isn't he supposed to be in a high chair? Something with legs on the floor?"

"Yes!" Amy snapped. "He's supposed to be in a high chair, and he's supposed to sleep in a bed with sides that lower, and he's supposed to have a changing table and all the latest clothes. But as you know, Billy had priorities for his money and . . . and . . . Oh, damnation!" she said as she turned away to hide her sniffling.

"I always liked Billy," Jason said slowly. "He was the life of every party. And he made everyone around him happy."

Amy turned around, her eyes bright with tears. "Yes, he did, didn't he? I led a pretty sheltered childhood, and I didn't know that the cause of Billy's forgetfulness and his—" Abruptly, she halted. "Listen to me. My mother-in-law says that I'm so lonely that I'd ask the devil to dinner." Again she stopped. "I'm not complaining, mind you; Max is all I want in life; it's just that—"

"Sometimes you want an adult to talk to," he said softly, watching her.

"You're a good listener, Mr. Wilding. Is that a characteristic of being gay?"

For a second he blinked at her. "Not that I know of. So, tell me, if you need to get a job to support yourself and you have no skills, what are you going to do? How are you going to support yourself and your son?"

Amy sat down at the table. "I haven't a clue. You have any suggestions?"

"Go back to school."

"And who takes care of Max all day? How do I pay someone to take care of him? Besides, I'm much too thick to go to school."

Again he smiled. "Somehow I doubt that. Can't your mother-in-law take care of him?"

"She has a bridge club, swimming club, at least three gossip clubs, and it takes time to keep that hair of hers." At that, Amy made motions of a bouffant hairdo.

"Yes, I do seem to remember that Mildred had a real fetish about her hair."

"Religious wars have been fought with less fervor. But, anyway, you're right, and I have to get a job. I was going for an interview this afternoon."

"Doing what?" he asked, and the intensity of his eyes made her look down at the banana she was mashing with a fork.

"Cleaning houses. Now, don't look at me like that. It's good, honorable work."

"But does it pay enough for you to hire someone to look after the baby?"

"I'm not sure. I'm not very good with numbers, and I—"

"I am very good with numbers," he said seriously. "I want to see everything. I want your check-book, your receipts, your list of expenses, what-ever. I need to see your income and your outgoing money. Give it all to me and I'll sort it out."

"I'm not sure I should do that," she said slowly. "Those things are private."

"You want to call David and ask him about me? I think he'll tell you to show me any papers you have."

For a moment she studied him. It had been so long since she'd been around an adult, and it seemed like years since she'd been around a man. Billy never cared about finances. If there was money, he spent it; if not, he found a way to per-suade someone to lend it to him. "There isn't much," she said slowly. "I have a checkbook, but I don't write many checks, and . . ."

"Just let me see what you have. You take care of Max, and I'll deal with the numbers."

"Do you always order people around?" she asked softly. "Do you always walk into a person's life and take it over as if they had no sense and you knew how to do everything in the world?"

He looked startled. "I guess I do. I hadn't thought about it before."

"I bet you don't have too many friends."

Again he looked startled, and for a moment he studied her as though he'd never seen her before. "Are you always so personal with people?"

"Oh, yes. It saves time in the long run. It's better to get to know people as they really are than it is to believe something that isn't true."

He lifted one thick black eyebrow. "And I guess you knew all about Billy Thompkins before you married him."

"You can laugh at me all you want, and believe me or not, but, yes, I did know. When I first met him I didn't know about the drugs and the alcohol, but I knew that he needed me. I was like water to a thirsty man, and he made me feel . . . Well, he made me feel important. Does that make sense?"

"In a way it does. Now, where are your financial records?"

It was Amy's turn to be startled at the abrupt way Jason dismissed her. What is he hiding? she wondered. Whatever secrets he had, he didn't want anyone to know what they were.

After she gave Jason her box of receipts and her old checkbooks, she spent an hour cleaning the kitchen and pulling Max out of one thing after another. If there was a sharp edge, Max was determined to smash part of his body against it.

"Could you come in here?" Jason said from the doorway, making Amy feel like a child being called into the principal's office. In the living room, he motioned for her to sit down on the couch, Max squirming on her lap.

"Frankly, Mrs. Thompkins, I find your financial situation appalling. You have an income well below the national poverty level, and as far as I can tell you have no way to replenish your resources. I have decided to make you a, shall we say, permanent loan so you can raise this child and you can—"

"A what?"

"A permanent loan. By that I mean you'll never have to pay it back. We will start with, say, ten thousand dollars, and—"

He broke off as Amy got up, walked to the front door, opened it, and said, "Good bye, Mr. Wilding."

Jason just stood there gaping at her. He wasn't used to people turning down money from him. In fact, he received a hundred letters a day from people begging him to give them money.

"I don't want your charity," Amy said, her lips tight.

"But David gives you money; you told me he did."

"He has given my son free medical treatment, yes; but in return, I have scrubbed his house, his office, and the inside of his car. I don't take charity, not from anyone."

For a moment Jason looked bewildered, as though her words were something he'd never heard before. "I apologize," he said slowly. "I thought—"

"You thought that if I was poor, then of course I

was looking for a handout. I know I live in a house that needs work." She ignored the expression on his face saying that that was an understatement. "But wherever I live and how I live is none of your concern. I truly believe that God will provide what we need."

For a moment Jason just stood there blinking at her. "Mrs. Thompkins, don't you know that nowadays people believe that you should *take* all that you can get and the rest of the world be damned?"

"And what kind of mother would I be if I taught values like that to my son?"

At that Jason stepped forward and took Max from Amy as the baby was trying his best to pull her arms from her shoulders. As before, the baby went to Jason easily and quickly settled against his chest.

"I do apologize, and you have to forgive me for not realizing that you are unique in all the world."

Amy smiled. "I hardly think so. Maybe you've just met very few people. Now, if you really want to help, you can take care of Max this afternoon while I go for the job interview."

"To clean houses," he said with a grimace.

"You find something else I'm qualified for and I'll do it."

"No," he said slowly, still looking at her as though she came from another planet. "I don't know what jobs are available in Abernathy."

"Not many, I can assure you. Now, I need to tell you all about Max, then I have to get ready to go."

"I thought you said the interview was this afternoon. You have hours yet."

"I don't have transportation, so I have to walk, and it's five miles. No! Don't look at me like that. You have 'I'll pay for a taxi' written all over your face. I want to make a good impression at this interview because they've said I can take Max with me if I leave him in a playpen. If I get this job, all our problems will be solved."

He didn't return her smile. "Who would you be working for?"

"Bob Farley. Do you know him?"

"I've met him," Jason said, lying. He knew Bob Farley very well, and he knew that Amy would be hired because she was young and pretty and because Farley was the biggest lecher in three counties. "I'll take care of the baby," Jason said softly. "You get dressed."

"All right, but let me tell you about his food." She then launched into a long monologue about what Max would and would not eat, and how he was to have no salt or sugar. Everything was to be steamed, not baked, and certainly not fried. Also, there was half a chicken in the refrigerator and some salad greens that could be Jason's lunch.

She went on to tell him that Max didn't really

like solid food, that he would much rather nurse, so, "Don't be upset if he doesn't eat much."

Jason only vaguely listened, just enough to reassure her that everything would be fine. Thirty minutes later she was out the door and he was on the phone to his brother.

"I don't care how many patients you have waiting," Jason said to his brother. "I want to know what's going on."

"Amy's great, isn't she?"

"She is . . . different. Wait a minute." He'd put Max on the floor, and the baby had half crawled, half dragged himself to the nearest wall socket and was now pulling on the cord to a lamp. After Jason had moved the baby away from the dangerous socket and put him in the middle of the floor, he went back to the phone.

"This woman," Jason began, "lives on a tiny life insurance policy left by that husband of hers, and she has no way to make a living. Do you know where she's going for a job interview today? Bob Farley."

"Ahhhhh," David said.

"Call that old lecher and tell him that if he hires her, you'll inject him with anthrax," Jason ordered.

"I can't very well do that. Hippocratic oath and all that. If I didn't know you better, I'd say you sound a little like a jealous husband. Jason? Are you there?"

"Sorry. Max was caught under the coffee table. Wait! Now he's eating paper. Hold on a minute."

When Jason got back, David spoke in frustration. "Look, big brother, I didn't mean for you to get involved with her, just take care of the kid so I could have time with Amy. That's all you're to do. Once I convince Amy we're made for each other, I'll support her and she won't have to work. Why don't you tell her wonderful things about me?"

"If she thinks you're going to take care of her for the rest of her life, she might not marry you. She has more pride than anything else. And can you tell me why a baby can't have salt or sugar or any form of seasoning on his food?"

"The theory is that he'll grow up to crave sweets if he has them as a baby, so if you eliminate those things, he'll be healthier as an adult."

"No wonder the kid only wants to nurse and won't eat much solid food," Jason muttered, then dropped the phone to move Max away from the door, where he was swinging it and trying to hit himself in the face.

When he returned, Jason said, "Do you think she'd allow me to give her a Christmas gift?"

"What did you have in mind? Buy a business and give it to her to run?"

Since this is exactly what Jason had in mind, he didn't answer. Besides, Max was now chewing on Jason's shoe, so Jason picked the baby up and held him, and Max grabbed Jason's bottom lip, nearly pulling the skin off.

"Look, Jason, I have to go," David said. "Why don't you use your brain instead of your money and figure out another solution to this problem? Amy's not going to take your charity, no matter how you disguise it."

"I wouldn't be too sure of that," Jason said as he looked across the room to a potted plant set on a folded newspaper. "You call Farley. I'd do it, but I don't want him to know I'm here, and you say whatever you have to, but he's not to hire her. Got it?"

"Sure. How's the monster?"

Wincing, Jason removed the baby's fingers from his mouth. "Fine."

"Fine? The kid is a brat. What's that sound?"

Max had grabbed both of Jason's cheeks painfully and pulled him closer as he planted a very wet raspberry on Jason's cheek. "I'm not sure, but I think the kid just kissed me," Jason said to his brother, then hung up before David could reply.

For a moment, Jason sat down on the couch, while Max stood on his lap. Strong kid, he thought, and not bad looking. Too bad he was wearing what looked to be hand-me-downs from someone's hand-me-downs. He could believe that every kid in Abernathy had worn these overalls and faded shirt. Shouldn't a smart little fellow like

Max have something better than this? So how could he arrange it?

At that moment, the newspaper caught his eye, and in the next moment he was fighting Max's hands to be able to dial his cell phone.

"Parker," he said when his secretary answered the phone. There was no greeting. She had been his private secretary-assistant for twelve years, so he didn't need to identify himself.

Within a few minutes he had told her his idea. She didn't make any complaint that it was Christmastime and he was telling her that she had to leave her home and family—if she had one, for Jason had no idea what her personal life was like— she just said, "Is there a printer's in Abernathy?"

"No. I wouldn't want the work done here anyway. Do it in Louisville."

"Any color preference?"

Jason looked down at Max, who was chewing on a wooden block that had probably been his father's. "Blue. For a manly little boy. None of those pink-and-white bunny rabbits. And add all the bells and whistles."

"I see. The whole lot."

"Everything. Also, buy me a car, something ordinary like a . . ."

"Toyota?" Parker asked.

"No, American." For all he knew Amy was against foreign cars. "A Jeep. And I want the car to be very dirty so I'll need to hire someone to clean it. And buy me some clothes."

Since all Jason's clothes were made for him, it wasn't unusual that Parker should ask if he wanted something sent.

"No. I want normal clothes. Denim. Blue jeans."

"With or without fringe?"

For a moment Jason stared at the phone. In twelve years he had never heard Parker make a joke. Was this the first one? On the other hand, did she even have a sense of humor? "No fringe. Just normal. Country clothes but not too expensive. No Holland and Holland; no Savile Row."

"I see," was Parker's toneless reply. If she had any curiosity about any of this, she didn't say so.

"Now call Charles and tell him to get down here and make this kid something good to eat."

There was a pause on the phone, which was unusual for Parker, as she usually agreed to anything he said instantly. "I was wondering where Charles would be staying, because he'll want proper equipment." Considering that Jason's private chef was a snob as well as a genius, this was an understatement.

Max was trying to pull himself to a standing position by dragging on the faded cloth on an old end table. If he pulled it off, three flower pots were going to crash onto his head. "Just do it!" Jason snapped into the phone, then shut it off and went to retrieve Max. Was this the fifth or sixth time the baby had tried to kill himself in the space of an hour?

"Okay, kid," Jason said as he untangled little hands from the cloth and picked the baby up. "Let's go see what we can do about lunch. A lunch with no sugar, no salt, no butter, no flavor at all."

At that Max again planted another wet raspberry against Jason's whiskery cheek, and Jason found the feeling not unpleasant.

CHAPTER SIX

"GET THE JOB?" JASON ASKED AS SOON AS AMY entered the house.

"No," she said despondently, then reached eagerly for Max. "And I'm bursting with milk."

To Jason's embarrassment, she plopped down wearily on the worn-out old sofa, unfastened her dress, unsnapped her bra, and proceeded to feed Max, who eagerly began sucking.

"How about dinner out tonight?" he asked. "My treat."

"Ow!" Amy said, then stuck her finger in Max's mouth and made him release her breast for a moment before he latched on again. "Teeth," she said. "You know, before he was born, I was in love with the whole romance of breast-feeding. I thought it would be something sweet and lovely, and it is, but it's also . . ."

"Painful?" he asked; then when she smiled in reply, he smiled back.

"I think I would have known that you were gay even if David hadn't told me. You're very perceptive, and for all that you look hard and unfeeling, you're really a bit of a softie, aren't you?"

"I've never been called that before," Jason said as he glanced at a faded and cracked mirror hanging to his right. Did he actually look hard and unfeeling?

"So what did Max get up to while I was gone?"

At that Jason smiled and soon found himself expending a great deal of energy into making a funny story of his afternoon with Max. "I think for Christmas I'll give him a set of knives, something he can easily hurt himself with. As it is now he has to work so hard to hit himself in the face and to try to crack his skull. I think I'll make life easier for him."

Amy laughed and said, "Knives with strings attached. Don't forget the strings, because how else can he choke?"

"Ah, yes. The strings. And I think I'll take him to visit a paper factory. I'll set him down in the middle of the place and let him eat his way out."

Amy switched Max to the other breast, and when she did so, Jason motioned for her to lift her arm so he could slide a pillow under it so she wasn't supporting the weight of Max's head. "And don't forget drawers that he can roll out then close on his fingers."

They were really laughing now, and Jason suddenly realized that for the first time in years a woman was genuinely laughing at his jokes.

"How about a pizza?" Jason said abruptly. "A huge one with everything on it. And giant Cokes and garlic bread?"

"I'm not sure I should because of my milk," Amy said hesitantly. "I'm not sure babies should have garlic-flavored milk."

"Doesn't seem to bother the Italians," Jason answered.

"That's true," Amy said, then smiled at him. "Pizza it is. But only if I can pay for my share."

Before he thought, Jason said, "You're too poor to pay for anything," then was shocked at what he'd said.

"Too true," Amy said good-naturedly. "Maybe over dinner we can figure out what to do with my future. Do you have any ideas?"

"None whatever," he said, smiling. "You could always marry some nice young doctor and never work again."

"Doctor? Oh, you mean David. He's not interested in me."

"He's mad about you," Jason answered.

"You are funny. David is in love with all the women in this town; that's why he's so popular.

Besides, I'm not a gold digger and I don't want to live off any man. I want to do something, but I'm not sure what I can do. If only I had a talent, like singing or playing the piano."

"It looks to me like you have a talent for being a mother."

Amy cocked her head to one side. "You're very sweet, you know that? Can you dial for pizzas on that phone of yours?"

"Sure," he said, smiling.

Later, as Max slept on the sofa, they lit candles and talked. He asked her about her life with Billy, and after an initial protest, she started talking, and he soon realized that she was hungry to talk.

And as she talked, he began to see the town drunk in a different light. Billy Thompkins had been a joke to the people of Abernathy since he was fourteen years old and began to drink. He wrecked cars as fast as he could get into them. His parents mortgaged their house to pay Billy's bail to get him out of jail time after time. But Amy saw something inside the man that no one else had.

Jason had ordered a giant pizza, and while Amy talked, she didn't notice that she ate three quarters of the thing. Long ago Jason had forgotten what it was like to be in a position that a pizza was a rare treat.

As soon as the last bit of cheese was gone, Amy gave a great yawn, and even though it was only nine P.M., Jason told her to go to bed. Standing, she bent to pick up Max, but Jason brushed her hands away, then scooped the baby up without waking him.

"You're a natural daddy," Amy said sleepily as she led the way into her bedroom.

Smiling at Amy's assessment, Jason put Max into the beat-up old playpen that was his bed, then quietly left the room. Oddly enough, he too felt sleepy. Usually he didn't go to bed until one or two in the morning, but something about pulling a baby away from one danger after another had exhausted him.

He went to his bedroom, pulled off his trousers, and fell into bed in his shirt and underwear and was aware of nothing until he heard a high-pitched scream from Max. Leaping out of bed, he ran into the kitchen, where he saw Max in his booster seat and Amy feeding him. They were both fully dressed yet it was still dark outside.

"What time is it?" Jason asked, rubbing his eyes.

"About six-thirty. Max slept late this morning."

"What was that scream?"

"Practice, I guess. He likes to scream. Shouldn't you get some clothes on?"

Jason glanced down at his bare legs. "Yeah, sure." Then he looked up at Amy's red face. She bared her breasts before him yet was embarrassed by his wearing more than he'd wear if he went swimming? With a smile at her turned head, he felt a little rush of pleasure that she was attracted to him.

David, he thought. David. David is in love with Amy.

"This was stuck in the front door this morning, and there's a car outside," she said, nodding toward a rolled-up newspaper on the kitchen table.

Ignoring her plea for him to get dressed, he rolled the rubber band off the newspaper and took out a note wrapped around the keys inside. It was a typed message saying that his clothes were in the back of the car and that the other matters had been taken care of. He would be contacted. "Sounds like a spy message," Jason said under his breath, then looked up to see if Amy had heard him.

But she hadn't heard anything, for her face was so full of excitement that at first he thought something was wrong with Max. But the baby was happily smearing oatmeal in his ear, so Jason looked back at Amy.

Looking like a mime, she was pointing speechlessly at the newspaper he had left spread on the table. There was a double-page ad about a huge sale in a baby store in a town about ten miles from Abernathy. The owner had put together entire nurseries, with furniture and bedding, and was selling the lot for two hundred and fifty dollars each. Amy was pointing at a photo of a bed, a rocking chair, a changing table, and a mobile that looked as though it had cowboys and horses on it. She was making a strangling sound that was a sort of, "Uh, uh, uh."

Maybe a devil got into him, but he couldn't help teasing her. "Is there any cereal in the house or has Max eaten everything?" He picked up the paper and opened it. "Looks like gold prices are down. Maybe I should buy some." He was holding the paper so the huge ad was right in front of Amy's face.

Amy finally recovered her voice. Ignoring him, she said, "Can I afford it? Can I? What do you think? Maybe I should call David and borrow the money from him. Oh, no, we have to be there when the store opens at nine. How can I get there? Maybe David—"

At that Jason put down the paper and held the car keys in front of her nose, jingling them.

"We'll go see David," she said hurriedly. "I'll pay you back for the gas later. Look here at the bottom. I wonder if clothes are included in the outfit? 'Everything for the baby.' Oh, heavens, but Max has never had any clothes that haven't been worn by someone else. May I borrow your phone to call David?"

"I'll lend you the money," he said, wishing he'd included clothes in his orders to his secretary.

"No. I can pay David back in work, but you don't need anything."

Jason frowned at that, and he wasn't sure why. Wouldn't it be better if she did borrow from David? After all the whole idea was to get David and Amy together. And when it came to that, why hadn't David come over to visit last night?

"Go look at my car," Jason said. "Then come back in here and tell me how much you'll charge to clean it."

With a "Watch Max" tossed over her shoulder, she scurried out the front door. Ten minutes later she returned. "One hundred dollars," she said grimly. "How can you be such a pig?"

All Jason could do was give her a crooked grin. Had Parker overdone it on the car?

"And another hundred and fifty to do something with those clothes in the back. Really, Mr. Wilding, I had no idea you were such a slob."

"I, uh," he began, feeling like a little boy being bawled out by his mother.

"Now go put some clothes on, then come and eat your breakfast. I mean to be at that store when the doors open. He says he has only eight sets to give away. You know, I bet this has to do with a divorce. That's why he'd give this furniture away rather than let his wife have the money. Some people have no conscience. I wonder if there are children involved. Why are you standing there looking at me? Go and get dressed. Time is wasting."

Blinking in disbelief at the astonishing story Amy had just concocted, Jason went to his bedroom to shower and put back on his dirty, wrinkled clothes. How had Parker known to fill the car with dirty clothes that needed Amy's attention?

When he went into the kitchen to get his measly bowl of cereal, Amy was looking like the cat that stole the cream. She was up to something, but he had no idea what.

"I borrowed your phone," she said sweetly. "I hope that was all right."

"Sure," he said, then looked down at his bowl. "Couldn't wait to call David?" The words were out of his mouth before he caught them.

"Oh, no. Just a few girlfriends. But I'm afraid a couple of the calls were long distance. I'll pay you back . . . somehow."

"I have an apartment," he said, and they both laughed when Amy groaned at the thought of cleaning the place.

Amy made them leave the house at seven-thirty, and when Jason opened the car door, he was appalled. What in the world had been done to the vehicle? The inside was plastered in mud, which had seeped down into every crevice. He doubted if the windows would work because of the mud that had oozed down between the glass and the door. In order to clean the car, the door would have to be taken apart. In the back was a pile of clothes that had been given the same mud bath.

Having seen the car already, Amy was prepared and she spread an old quilt over the passenger seat, then climbed in, Max on her lap. "You don't have to tell me," she said softly, once the door was closed, "but your lover retaliated by driving your car and your clothes into a lake, didn't he?"

"Something like that," Jason muttered, thinking he was going to have a word with his secretary. When he'd said dirty, he meant, maybe, soda cans and potato chip bags.

"It's odd that the engine isn't clogged with mud, though," she said as the car started easily. "Oh, no!"

As Jason swung the car into the street, he looked at her in question.

"He filled the car full of mud, didn't he?"

"Could we not talk about my personal life?" Jason snapped. He was sick of this talk of his male lover.

For a moment Amy didn't say anything, and he regretted his outburst. "I hope they have a car seat," he said as he glanced over at her, and she smiled back.

"Do you have any cash? I don't—"

"Lots," he replied, glad the moment's discomfort was gone. "So what other jobs have you tried to get besides cleaning?" Jason asked as Amy held Max firmly on her lap. If they were spotted by the police, they'd be arrested because Max was unrestrained. And Jason refused to think what would happen to Max if they had a wreck. On impulse he reached out and gave Max's little hand a squeeze and was rewarded with a toothy grin.

Amy didn't seem to notice, as she was telling Jason about all the jobs she had applied for and even been hired to do, yet had lost for one reason or another. "Twice I've had to quit because the boss . . . Well . . ."

"Chased you around the desk?"

"Exactly. And it's just so difficult to find a job around here. I've thought I might be a good aromatherapist. What do you think?"

Jason was saved from answering that question by the sight of the store just ahead. But he was shocked at what he saw. Under the sign, Baby Heaven, there were about fifteen women with baby carriages waiting for the store to open.

"Oh, dear," Amy said. "I only called seven friends. They must have called their friends, and, oh, no, there are more cars arriving and they have to be for Baby Heaven because the other stores don't open until ten."

"You called all these people?" Jason asked.

"I was afraid they wouldn't see the ad and afraid they might miss the sale. You know, it's odd that there aren't more people here than there are. What about the other people who saw the morning paper? Maybe they know that this is just a sales gimmick and it isn't real. Maybe the owner has done this before and there isn't any merchandise. Maybe—"

Before she could launch into one of her fanciful stories, Jason got out and opened the car door for her. "Come on, let's go around the back and see if we can get in a few minutes early."

"Do you think that's fair?"

With his back to Amy, Jason rolled his eyes. "Probably not, but then this is for Max, isn't it?" he said as he took the baby from her. "Besides, it's too cold to wait out here and the store doesn't open for thirty minutes yet."

Amy gave him a dazzling smile. "You do know how to fix things, don't you?"

As Jason turned away, Max snuggled comfortably in his arms, he couldn't help smiling, for Amy had a way of making him feel at least ten feet tall. When he pounded on the back door and it opened, he was startled to see one of his top executives from his New York office standing there wearing a gray coverall, a broom in his hand.

"You wanta see the stuff early?" the man asked, sounding as though he was not a graduate of Harvard Business School.

Annoyed, Jason could only nod. He didn't like it

when his employees did things he hadn't first sanctioned. Even when Amy briefly took his arm and squeezed it, Jason was still not appeased.

Once they left the back storage area and walked into the store, Jason was even less pleased, for there were two of his vice presidents, both men wearing coveralls, both moving baby furniture around.

"You are our first customer so you can have the pick of the lot," came a feminine voice and they turned to see a striking woman standing behind them. She was, of course, Jason's secretary, only she wasn't dressed in her usual Chanel suit but in something he was sure she had bought at Kmart, and her long red hair was pulled into a bun on top of her head. And there were three yellow pencils stuck into the lump of hair. Even so, she couldn't hide the fact that she was five feet ten inches tall and as stunning as any runway model.

Parker didn't blink at Jason's or Amy's speechlessness. "What would you like?" she asked. "Blue? Pink? Green? Yellow? Or would you like to see our one and only designer set?"

"Oooohhhh." Amy emitted a sound that came straight from her heart and out her lips, then started following Parker as though she were in a trance.

Parker kept up a running stream of chatter as she walked. "It's all closeout goods. Nothing is used, but it's all discontinued merchandise. I hope you don't mind that these are really last year's goods."

"No," Amy said in a voice unnaturally high pitched. "No, we don't mind. Do we, Mr. Wilding?"

She didn't wait for Jason's answer because before her was a sample room and even Jason had to admit that his secretary had outdone herself. He could smell wallpaper paste, so she must have worked through the night to get this done, and he must say that they'd created a fabulous room. And with his eye for merchandise, he knew that what he was seeing was the top of the top line. Parker must have bought everything in New York and brought it to Abernathy in his jet.

It was a room for a little boy, with blue-and-white striped wallpaper with a border of boats sailing a rough sea. The bed looked like a new version of a sleigh bed, but with safety bars and sides that lowered; a whole set of *Winnie-the-Pooh* characters were tucked into a corner. The linens of the bed were hand embroidered with tiny animals and plants, something that Jason knew Max would love to look at. To test his theory, he put Max in the bed, where he immediately pulled himself up, then began to grab at the mobile until he got a horse's head in his mouth.

The rest of the room was filled with furniture of equal quality. There was a rocking chair, a changing table, a car seat, a high chair, a toy box that had to have been decorated by Native Americans, and in the corner was a stack of white boxes.

"More linens and a few necessities," Parker said as she followed Jason's eyes. "There are a few pieces of clothing, but I wasn't sure of the size . . ." She trailed off.

"This costs more than I have," Amy said, and there were tears in her voice.

"Two hundred and fifty dollars for the lot," Parker said quickly.

Amy squinted her eyes at the woman. "Are these things stolen? Is this an outlet for stolen goods?"

"I would imagine that in a way, yes, they are stolen," Jason said quickly. "If these things are still in the possession of the store owner come tax time, he'll have to pay taxes on what they're worth. But if he sells them at a loss, he can write off the loss and be taxed on the amount he has received, which is a pittance. Am I right?" he asked Parker.

"Perfectly," she said, then turned back to Amy. "Perhaps you don't like this room. We have others."

"No, it's perfect," Amy said, then before she could say another word, Jason spoke up.

"We'll take it. Have it delivered today." As he said this, he glanced at his two executives leaning on brooms and watching the scene with smug little smiles. By tomorrow everyone in all his offices would know about this. "And I think you should throw in someone to hang the wallpaper."

At that Amy gave a little whimper that said she was sure Jason was going to make the woman retract the deal.

"Certainly, sir," Parker said without a hint of a smile, then turned to Max in the bed. Now he was on his back and trying to kick the sides off, the sound reverberating through the store. "What a beautiful child," she said, then held out her arms as though she meant to pick Max up.

The baby let out a howl that shook the bed. Immediately, Amy was there, her arms out to Max. "Sorry," she muttered. "He doesn't take to strangers very well." And at that Max made a leap into Jason's arms.

Jason wasn't going to look at his two vice presidents because he knew that they would assume that Max was his. How else to explain that Jason wasn't a "stranger" to the child?

"I'll pay while you look around," Jason said as he followed Parker to a nearby counter. "The pencils are overkill," he snapped as soon as they were out of earshot of Amy.

"Yes sir," she said as she removed them from her hair.

"And what are those two doing here?"

"You had to buy the store in order to pull this off. I didn't feel that I had the authority to negotiate with that much money."

"How much could a tiny shop like this cost?"

"The man said to tell you that his name is Harry Greene and that you'd understand."

Jason's eyes rolled upward for a moment. In high school he had stolen Harry's girlfriend the day before the prom. "Did you manage to buy it for under seven figures?"

"Just barely. Sir, what do we do about the people waiting outside? The newspaper ad appeared in only your paper, but somehow . . ."

"They're friends of Amy's." For a moment he looked around Max, who was trying to grab the telephone off the desk, to see Amy running her hand lovingly over the baby furniture. "Give them the same deal. Give everything away at a loss. Make sure everything is given away for what they can afford. Split the rooms up so every woman out there gets something she needs."

When he looked back, Parker was staring at him with her mouth open. "And get those two back to New York right after they hang the wallpaper."

"Yes, sir," Parker answered softly, looking at him as though she'd never seen him before.

Jason removed Max's hands from around a curtain hanging from the top of a cradle. "And, Parker, add some toys to that lot when you deliver it. No," he contradicted himself. "Don't add anything. I'll buy the toys myself."

"Yes, sir," Parker said quietly.

"Did Charles get here?"

"He came with me. He's at your father's house, as all of us are." By her expression she looked to be on the verge of shock.

"Now close your mouth and go open the door to the other customers," he said as he peeled Max's hands off the curtain again and went back to Amy.

CHAPTER SEVEN

JASON WAS EXPERIENCING AN EMOTION HE HADN'T felt in a long time: jealousy.

"Isn't it wonderful?" Amy was saying in a breathless way he hadn't heard from a female since he'd left high school. "Isn't it the most beautiful room you ever saw? I never thought I could love the IRS, but since it was the cause of Max getting all these beautiful things, I could grow to love them. Don't you think so, Mr. Wilding? Don't you think the room is beautiful?"

"Yes," Jason said grumpily, while telling himself that it was better to give anonymously than to flaunt your gift. At least that's what he'd heard. But he rather wished Amy would look at him with her eyes sparkling like that.

He took a deep breath. "It is nice. The room looks great. Do you think the clothes will fit?"

"If they don't now, they will next week," she said, laughing. "See, I told you that God would provide."

Before Jason could give a cynical reply as he thought about how much these few pieces of furniture had actually cost him, since he'd had to buy the store, there was a loud, insistent knock on the door.

Instantly, Amy's face went white. "They made a mistake and they want everything back."

Jason's bad mood left him and he couldn't help putting a reassuring arm around Amy's thin shoulders. "I can assure you that everything here is yours. Maybe it's Santa Claus come early."

When she still hesitated, Jason picked up Max from the crib, where he was trying to eat the legs off a stuffed frog, then led the way to the front door, where he was greeted by the sight of a huge evergreen tree.

"Ho ho ho," came David's voice as he shoved his way inside the house. "Merry Christmas. Jase, ol' boy, you want to bring in the boxes from outside?"

"David!" came Amy's squeal of delight. "You shouldn't have."

Outside in the cold, Max sitting on his arm, Jason muttered, "Oh, David, you shouldn't have," in a falsetto voice. "I paid heaven only knows how much for a bunch of furniture and she thanks the

IRS no less. But David shows up with a twenty-dollar tree and it's, 'Oh, David.' Women!"

Max laughed, raked his nails across Jason's cheek in an attempt to pat him, then bit his other cheek in a kiss. "Why don't you do that to the divine Dr. David?" Jason said, smiling at the boy as he hoisted a big red cardboard box under his arm and took it into the house.

"You can't do this," Amy was still saying but looking at David adoringly.

"Dad and I don't want a tree. We're just a couple of old bachelors and we don't need the needles everywhere, so when a patient gave me this tree, I thought about the attic full of ornaments and thought Max would love the lights. Don't you think he will?"

"Oh, yes, I'm sure he will, but I'm not sure—"

David cut her off by going toward Jason and holding out his arms to Max. "Come here, Max, and give me a hug."

To Jason's great satisfaction, Max let out a howl that made the tree drop quite a few needles. "Doesn't seem to like you, does he?" Jason said smugly. "Come on, boy, let's go try on some of your new clothes."

"New clothes?" David asked, frowning. "What's this about?"

"Oh, David, you can't believe what has happened. This morning we went to a store where the man was selling everything cheaply so he wouldn't have to pay taxes on it and Mr. Wilding made them come and hang the wallpaper and arrange the furniture and . . . and . . . Oh, you'll just have to see it to believe it."

With a look at Jason, David followed Amy through the old house with its peeling paint and water-stained wallpaper, to have her open a door to a dazzling nursery. It didn't take much of an eye to see the quality of everything inside. The linens, the furniture, the pretty little prints on the wall, the painted wardrobe that held a few pieces of fabulous baby clothes, were all the finest that could be bought.

"I see," David said. "And how much did you have to pay for all this?"

"Two hundred and fifty dollars, sales tax included," Amy said proudly.

David lifted a hand-embroidered sheet from the side of the crib. If he wasn't mistaken, he'd seen these in a catalog for about three hundred dollars each. "Great," David said. "By contrast my tree and old ornaments look like nothing."

"How silly," Amy said as she took his arm. "Your gift is from your heart, while this is merely from the IRS."

At that, David shot a triumphant smile at his older brother as he led Amy back into the living room.

"And I brought dinner," David said happily. "A grateful patient of mine gave me a free dinner for two at a restaurant in Carlton, but I persuaded the chef to make it a carryout for three. I hope it's still hot," he said as he looked up at his brother. "The food boxes are on the front seat of my car. Oh! and I hope you don't mind, but I signed you and Max up as guinea pigs to try a new baby food." At that he began to unload his pockets of baby food jars with hand-lettered labels, and Jason recognized his secretary's neat script.

"Rack of lamb with dried cherry and green peppercorn sauce," Amy read. "And salmon cakes with cilantro sauce. They sound a bit high fashion for a baby, and I'm not sure he should have peppercorns."

"I think the company is trying to reach the top-end market. It's just in the planning stages now, so if you'd rather not be one of their test babies, I could get Martha Jenkins to try them."

"No," Amy said, taking the jars David held out to her. "I'm sure Max will like them." Her tone said she wasn't sure at all. "Who is the manufacturer?"

"Charles and Company," David said as he winked at Jason, still standing by the door, still holding Max, still scowling. "Come on, old man, don't just stand there; let's get everything inside so we can eat, then decorate the tree."

Jason handed the baby to Amy, then followed his brother outside.

"What in the world is wrong with you?" David snapped as soon as they were away from the door.

"Nothing is wrong with me," Jason snapped back.

"You hate it here, don't you? You hate the noise and the falling-down old house, and Amy is boring compared to the women you're used to. Didn't you date some woman with a Ph.D. in anthropology? Didn't she save tigers or something?"

"It was fish. She saved whales, and she smelled like seaweed. There is nothing wrong with me. So Charles made the dinners and the baby food?"

"Is that what's bothering you? That I took credit for what you'd paid for? Look, if you want, we can tell her the truth right now. We can tell her you're a multimillionaire, or is it a billionaire by now, and that you can afford rooms full of baby furniture from what you carry in your pocket. Is that what you want to do?"

"No," Jason said slowly as David loaded his arms with boxes of Christmas ornaments. They were boxes he'd seen all through his childhood, and he knew everything that was inside them.

Suddenly David stopped and stared at his brother. "You're not falling for her are you? I mean, you and I aren't going to have to compete for a woman, are we?"

"Don't be ridiculous. Amy isn't my type at all. And she has no concept of the future. I don't know how she means to support that child on the small amount of cash she has coming in. She has no work or prospect of work. She can't do anything at all except clean things. But in spite of her situation, she has more pride than anyone I've ever met. If you told her who I was, she'd kick me out, and no doubt throw all the furniture into the street after me. She spent this afternoon scrubbing that car Parker gave me so she could pay me back the two fifty. If you knew . . ."

They were walking toward the house, and Jason was still talking.

"Knew what?" David asked softly.

"The women I date ask for five hundred just to tip the maid in the toilet. That fish woman. She was dating me only so I'd make a donation to her whales."

"So what's your problem then?" David asked. "Why are you so surly?"

"Because my little brother duped me into spending time in this one-horse town and going to baby stores and carrying old Christmas ornaments. Get the door, will you? No, the other way. You have to pull inward, then turn the knob. Is that your phone ringing or mine?"

"Mine," David said as soon as they were in the house. "Yeah," he said into the receiver. "Yes, yes,

that's good. I'll be there as soon as I can get there."
As he turned the phone off, he looked up at Amy, Jason, and the baby with regret. "I can't stay. Emergency."

"I'm so sorry," Amy said. "After you did all this work and now you can't stay."

"Yeah, it's a shame," Jason said as he held open the door for his younger brother. "But when work calls, you have to go."

Frowning, David made his way to the door. "Maybe we can put up the tree tomorrow. I'd really like to see the baby's expression when he first sees the lights."

"We'll make a video," Jason said quickly. "Now, I think you'd better go before somebody dies."

"Yeah, right," David said after one last look of regret tossed to Amy. "I'll see you—" He didn't finish his sentence because Jason shut the door in his face.

"You weren't very nice to him," Amy said, doing her best to frown at Jason, but he could see a hint of a smile about her lips.

"Horrible," Jason said agreeably. "But now there's more food for the two of us. And, besides, I'm much better at tree decorating than he is."

"Is that so? You have to go some to beat me. Why I've decorated trees that have made Santa weep."

"I decorated a tree so beautiful that Santa wouldn't leave my house and I had to push him out into the snow, and when he still wouldn't leave, I had to drive his sleigh and deliver all his gifts."

Amy laughed. "You win. Let's see what's in these boxes."

"Nope. We eat first. I want to try this new baby food on Max and see what he thinks. Does this fireplace work?"

"Better than the furnace," Amy replied.

"I repeat, Does this fireplace work?"

Amy giggled. "If you open the damper very wide and build the fire way back against the wall, it's okay. Otherwise it smokes a lot."

"Had experience with it, have you?"

"Let's just say that I had some pork chops in the freezer and after the first time I tried to make a fire in there, they were smoke-cured hams."

It was Jason's turn to laugh, and when he did, Max started to laugh too, banging his hands on his legs and nearly knocking his mother down.

"You think that's funny, do you?" Jason said, still laughing as he took the boy and tossed him into the air. Max was so delighted at this that he squealed until he got the hiccups, then Jason tickled him and he squealed some more.

When Jason stopped, hugging the sweaty baby close to him, Amy was looking at him in a way no woman had ever looked at him before.

"You're a nice man, Mr. Wilding. A very nice man."

"Want to call me Jason?" he asked.

"No," she said as she turned away. "I'll heat dinner while you light the smoker."

For some reason her refusal to call him by his first name pleased him. He set Max on the floor, then started building the fire. It took a while because every three minutes he had to pull Max away from a life-threatening situation. But at last he had the fire going without too much smoke, he had Max interested in his Breitling watch (it would never be the same again), and Amy entered the room with an enormous tray full of food. There was also a bottle of wine and two glasses.

Jason held up one of the glasses, watching the colors in the lead crystal. Waterford. "David does know how to live, doesn't he?"

"I feel guilty eating this without him," Amy said. "After all, it was his skill as a doctor that earned the meal."

"We could always wrap it up, put it in the refrigerator, and he can have it tomorrow."

Amy looked down at the beautiful meal on the tray. There was a salad of baby lettuces and vegetables, roast lamb, potatoes . . .

She looked back up at Jason. "I don't have any plastic wrap."

"That settles it then. We'll just have to eat it ourselves."

"I guess so," Amy said seriously; then they laughed and dug in.

Max sat on Jason's lap, a huge bib around his neck, and ate everything that was offered to him. Whatever Amy had thought about his not liking solid food was disproved by the way he downed a whole jar of lamb with peppercorns; then he started in on Jason's mashed potatoes with garlic.

"But I thought babies liked bland food," Amy said in amazement.

"No one likes bland food," Jason said under his breath.

Thirty minutes later Amy had nursed Max until he fell asleep, an angelic smile on his face. "Do you think it's the food or the new room that's made him look like that?" Amy asked as she looked adoringly down at her son in his new crib.

"I think he's happy because he has a mother who loves him so much," Jason said, then smiled when Amy blushed.

"Mr. Wilding, if I didn't know better, I'd think you were flirting with me."

"I guess stranger things have happened," he said; then when she looked confused, he said, "Come on, woman, there's a tree to decorate."

In all his life, Jason knew that he'd never had as much fun decorating a Christmas tree as he had with this one. As children he and David had complained every minute they had to spend on the task. Without a woman in the home, there was no smell of cookies baking, no music playing, just their dad, who was his usual grumpy self. He put up a tree or his sister would hound him all the rest of the year, saying that she should raise the boys, not her lazy brother.

Now, as Jason strung lights that Amy had untangled, he found himself telling her about his childhood. He didn't bother explaining why he had lived with David when he was supposedly only a cousin, and she didn't ask. In return Amy told him about her childhood. She had been an only child of a single mother and when she'd asked who her father was, her mother told her it was none of her business.

Both of their stories were rather sad, and definitely lonely, but when they told them to each other, they made jokes, and Amy started a contest to see who had the grumpiest parent. Amy's mother was a fanatically clean woman and hated Christmas because of the mess. Jason's father just hated having his routine disrupted.

They began fantasizing about what a marriage between the two of them would be like, what with Jason's father playing poker and flipping cigar ash all over the room and Amy's mother with a vacuum cleaner permanently attached to her right arm.

They went on to speculate what kind of children

these two would produce and decided that they themselves were actually perfect examples of what would happen if their two parents mated. Jason was so serious his face nearly cracked when he laughed, and Amy lived in a house that would make her mother's heart stop beating.

"It's beautiful," Amy said at last, standing back to look at the half-finished tree.

"I wish I had a camera with me," Jason said. "That tree deserves to be immortalized."

"I don't have a camera, but I can—" She broke off and grinned at him. "You finish with the tinsel while I make a surprise. No, don't turn around, look that way."

He heard her scurry off into the bedroom, then return and sit down in the ugly old sunflower chair. He was dying to see what she was doing, but he didn't look. Not until he'd strung the last of the tinsel did she tell him he could turn around.

When he turned he could see that she was holding out a piece of printer paper and there was a pencil and a book on her lap. He took the paper and looked at it. It was a delightful sketch of him struggling with the wires of a dozen strings of lights, the tree just behind him. The picture was whimsical, funny, and at the same time poignant, making him look as though he was putting a lot of love into the project.

Jason sat down on the sofa, the sketch in his hand. "But this is good."

Amy laughed. "You sound surprised."

"I am. I thought you said you had no talents." He was very serious.

"Not any marketable talents. No one wants to hire someone to draw funny pictures."

Jason didn't respond to her remark. "If you have more of these, get them and bring them to me."

"Yes, sir!" Amy said, standing and saluting him. She tried to sound lighthearted, but she rushed to obey his command, and in seconds, she handed him a fat, worn, brown envelope tied with a drawstring.

Jason was very aware that Amy was holding her breath while he looked at the drawings, and he didn't need to ask if she had shown them to anyone else, for he knew she hadn't. For all that she put on a brave act, life with a drunk like Billy Thompkins had to have been difficult.

"They're good," he said as he lifted the papers one by one. The drawings were mostly of Max, from birth to the present, and they were quite clever, showing all the things a baby could get into. There was one of Max with wonder on his face as he looked up at a balloon, his hands reaching for it eagerly.

"I like them," he said as he carefully put them back into the envelope. The businessman inside him wanted to talk to her about publication and royalties, but he reined himself in. Right now he thought that all he should do was give her praise.

"I like them very much and I thank you for showing them to me."

Amy gave him a smile that threatened to break her face in half. "You're the only one who's ever seen them. Except my mother and she told me to quit wasting my time."

"And what did she want you to do?"

"Become a lawyer."

At first Jason thought she was joking, but then he saw her eyes twinkling. "I can see you defending a criminal. 'Please, Your Honor, he promises that he won't do it again. He gives his word, hope to die. He'll never murder more than the twenty-two little old ladies that he has already. Pleeeeaaaaasssse.' "

It was such a good imitation of Amy's tone of voice that she picked up a pillow and tossed it at him, watching him do an elaborate duck as though he might get hurt by the flying object. "You are a horrible person," she said, laughing. "I would have made an excellent lawyer. I'm quite intelligent, you know."

"Yes, very, but you do tend to love the under-dog."

"If I didn't, *you* wouldn't have had any place to spend Christmas," she shot back.

"That's true," he said, grinning. "And I thank you for it." As Jason said this, he looked down into her eyes and realized he wanted to kiss her. Like he wanted to continue living, he wanted to kiss her.

"I think I better go to bed," she said softly as she got up and went toward her bedroom. "Max is an early riser and there's a lot to do tomorrow." She was halfway into the room when she turned back to him. "I didn't mean to sound as though I was doing you a favor by allowing you to stay here. The truth is, you've made this Christmas wonderful for Max and me. Both of us enjoy your company very much."

All Jason could do was nod in thanks. He couldn't remember anyone ever telling him that he was enjoyed just for his company. "Good night," he said, then sat for a long time before the dying fire, thinking about where he was and what he was doing.

CHAPTER EIGHT

A SMELL WOKE JASON. IT WAS A SMELL THAT HE knew but couldn't exactly place. It was from a time long past and only vaguely remembered. Following his nose, he got out of bed, pulled on his wrinkled suit pants, and went toward the light. He found Amy in the kitchen, Max in his high chair, his face and hands covered with food, and wet clothes were everywhere. Shirts, pants, underwear, hung from the light fixture, the door jambs, the crack in the plaster over the stove. And in the middle of it all Amy stood over an ironing board using an iron that should have been in a museum.

"What time is it?" Jason asked sleepily.

"About five, I think," Amy answered. "Why?"

"How long have you been up?"

She turned the shirt she was ironing so the wrinkled sleeve was exposed. "Most of the night. Little rascal, he does love to mix up his days and nights."

Yawning, rubbing his eyes, Jason sat down at the table beside Max's high chair and handed him a dried peach. Wordlessly, he motioned to the wet clothes hanging around the room. It had been a long time since Jason was a child and his father had spread their wet clothes about to dry, but it was a smell one never forgot. "What happened to the dryer?"

"It broke about a year ago and I haven't had the money to get it fixed. But the washer works great."

Standing, Jason put his hands in the small of his back, stretched, then walked behind Amy and unplugged the iron.

"I have to finish this. It needs to be—"

"Go to bed," Jason said quietly. "No, not a word of protest. Go to bed. Sleep."

"But Max . . . And the clothes, and . . ."

"Go," Jason ordered in a quiet voice, and for a moment he thought Amy was going to cry in gratitude. With a smile, he nodded toward the bedroom, and gratefully, she went into the room and shut the door.

"Now, old man," Jason said, "let's see if we remember how this is done." At that, Jason plugged the iron back in and picked it up.

At eight A.M., Jason's cell phone rang and he put it on his shoulder as he finished ironing a shirt.

"Did I wake you?" David asked his older brother.

"Of course," Jason said. "You know how lazy I am. No! Max, leave that alone! What do you want, little brother?"

"I want time alone with Amy. Remember? That's what this is all about. I want to take her out tonight and tomorrow. I even got tickets to the Bellringers' Ball."

Jason well knew that the Bellringers' Ball was the only social function worth attending in the entire western half of Kentucky—and it was nearly impossible to get tickets. "So who did you have to kill to get the tickets?"

"I didn't kill; I saved. I saved the life of the chairman of the committee to something or other. Anyway, he got me the tickets. Christmas Eve. I'm going to pop the question. Jason? Jason? Are you there?"

"Sorry," Jason said once he came back to the phone. "Max was pulling on a lamp cord and about to bite into it. What was it you were saying?"

"I said that tomorrow I'm going to ask Amy to marry me. Jason? Are you there? What's Max doing now?"

"He's not doing anything," Jason snapped. "He's a great kid and he doesn't do anything bad."

There was a pause from David. "I didn't mean

to insinuate that he was doing something 'bad.' It's just that children Max's age do tend to get into things. It is a normal and natural process of growing up, and they will—"

"You don't need to take on that doctor tone with me," Jason grumbled.

"Boy! Are you in a bad mood this morning. Where's Amy anyway?"

"Not that it's any of your business, but she's in bed asleep and I'm taking care of Max. And doing the ironing," he added, knowing that David would nearly faint at that information.

"You're doing what?"

"The ironing. Parker dumped mud on the clothes she sent me, so Amy washed them, and now I'm ironing them. You see anything wrong with that?"

"Nothing," David said softly. "I had no idea you knew how to iron, that's all."

"So who do you think ironed your clothes when you were a kid?" Jason snapped. "Dad? Ha. He had to earn the money to buy the food, so I had to . . . never mind. What was it you wanted to tell me? Wait, I have to get Max."

"Jason, dear brother," David said minutes later, "I think I'd better talk to Amy in person. I want her to go out with me tonight and tomorrow night, and I think I should ask her myself."

"She's busy."

"Is something going on that I should know about?" David asked. "You and Amy aren't . . ."

"No, we aren't!" Jason said quickly. "The last thing I need in my life is a daffy, head-in-the-clouds female like her. The man who takes her on will have his hands full taking care of her. It's a wonder she can tie her shoes. She can't even feed herself, much less a child, and—"

"Okay, okay, I get the picture. So, what do you think?"

"Think about what?"

David gave a great sigh. "Do you think it would be all right if I took Amy out tonight and tomorrow? Can you keep the kid?"

"I can keep Max forever," Jason said with some anger. "Sure, you can take Amy out. I'm sure she'd love to go."

"I think I should ask her myself."

"I'm not going to wake her up just to talk on the phone. What time should she be ready tonight?"

"Seven."

"All right. Now give me Parker."

"She's, ah, she's not up."

Jason was so shocked at this that he left the iron on the back of a shirt until it began to scorch. "Damnation!" he said, lifting the iron. "Wake her," Jason ordered, then was surprised to have his secretary get on the line almost instantly.

After a moment to recover from his shock, Jason

told Parker to get two more tickets to the Bell-ringers' Ball.

"You do know that that is next to impossible," she said, and again Jason paused in shock. What in the world was wrong with his secretary? The impossible never daunted her.

"Get them," he said, annoyed. In fact, what was wrong with his whole world? First, two of his executives get themselves involved in his private affairs without his permission, and now Parker was telling him that something he wanted was going to be difficult. If he'd wanted someone who couldn't do the impossible, he wouldn't be paying her the outrageous salary he did.

"I'll need my tux from my apartment in New York," he went on to say, "and Amy will need something appropriate to wear to the ball. What's that shop on Fifth?"

"Dior," came Parker's instant reply.

"Right. Dior."

"And who shall I get for your escort?" she asked.

"My— Oh, right, my date," he said, and realized that he hadn't given that a moment's thought. But then he wasn't giving any of it a thought or he'd be wondering why he was going to the ball when he was supposed to stay home with the baby. And if both he and Amy left, who would take care of Max?

"I believe there are any number of women who would be available at a moment's notice to go with you," Parker was saying in that efficient, no-nonsense way of hers.

For a moment Jason paused to think over the many available women he knew. And when he thought of them, he knew how nasty all of them would be to Amy—and how nosy. "Get yourself a dress, Parker. You'll go with me as my date."

It was her turn to be shocked, and it almost made Jason smile to hear the hesitation in her voice. "Yes, sir," she said at last.

"Oh, and get hair and makeup people over here for Amy. Think up some story so she doesn't know it's a gift from me."

"Yes, sir," Parker said softly. "Anything else?"

Jason looked down at Max happily chewing the tail of a yellow duck pull toy. From the look of the thing, his father had probably chewed on it thirty years ago, and Jason wondered if the paint was lead-free. "Everything all right there at my father's?"

"I beg your pardon?" Parker asked.

"I asked if you and Charles are comfortable at my father's house."

"Oh, yes," she said hesitantly. "I'm sorry, sir, you don't usually ask personal questions, but, yes, we are doing well. Now."

"What do you mean? Now?"

"Charles had to make a few adjustments, but he's all right now. He should be at your house soon. And your father reminds you that you and Mrs. Thompkins and the baby are to come here for Christmas dinner. Would three P.M. be all right with you?"

Jason ignored most of what she said and got to the point. "What kind of adjustments?"

"The kitchen needed . . . augmentation."

"Parker!" he warned.

"Charles tore out the back side of your father's house and added what is actually a kitchen for a small restaurant. He had to pay the men triple time to work twenty-four hours a day to get the room done quickly. Then he bought enough equipment to furnish the room, and, well, your father is having rather lavish dinner parties each night and—"

"I don't want to hear any more. We'll be there at three on Christmas Day and don't forget the clothes."

"Certainly not, sir," Parker said as he hung up.

Ten minutes later Amy wandered into the kitchen, looking like the most grateful woman on earth—until she saw that the ironing had been done. "How will I repay you for the furniture now?" she wailed as she sat down on a rickety kitchen chair. Max was happily sitting in his new high chair, his face smeared with half a dozen various colored substances.

"I promise to get everything dirty today so you'll have more to do tomorrow," Jason said, smiling, obviously unworried about how he was to be repaid. "Now, would you mind watching Max while I take a shower? I've been in this shirt for days and I'd like to get out of it."

"Yes, of course," she murmured as she picked Max up. As soon as he'd seen his mother, he'd started to whine and wanted out of the chair.

For a moment Jason paused in the doorway. Nothing bad could happen in the next fifteen minutes, could it? he asked himself, then gave one last look at Amy and the baby and left the room.

CHAPTER NINE

"MR. WILDING," AMY SAID ENTHUSIASTICALLY THE moment he stepped back into the kitchen thirty minutes later. "Come and meet Charles."

As soon as Jason saw his randy little chef, he knew that he was in trouble. Charles was about five feet four, handsome as any movie star, and utterly devastating to women. He flirted outrageously, and Jason was sure that more than one of his dinner guests had succumbed to the man. But Jason never asked; he figured it was better not to know the details of his chef's private life. As it was, the man traveled wherever Jason went and prepared the most delicious meals imaginable. In return for the food, Jason overlooked certain personal foibles.

But now, seeing Charles sitting by Amy, her

hand in his, he wanted to tell his chef to get out and never return.

"This is the man responsible for the wonderful food Max loves so much. It seems that David told a bit of a fib. It isn't really a company trying to open a line of baby food, but Charles is trying to go into business. And he lives right here in Abernathy. Isn't that amazing?"

"Yes, truly," Jason said as he took an electrical cord out of Max's mouth.

"And I've been encouraging him to open his own business. Don't you think he should?"

Charles looked up at his employer with sparkling eyes, obviously enjoying the whole masquerade.

"I hear he has a kitchen that can handle a catering company," Jason said as he glared at his chef. Only someone of Charles's caliber could get away with what the man did.

"Oh, yes," Charles said in that tone he used with women. In his kitchen he used a whole other tone, one of command that brooked no disobedience, but now he practically purred to Amy. "I have the most divine kitchen. Copper pots from France, a cook stove as big as my first apartment. You must come and see it."

"I'd love to," Amy said eagerly. "Maybe you'd give me a few cooking lessons."

"I will give you anything you want," Charles

said seductively as he raised her hand to kiss the palm.

But at the exact moment that Charles's lips were to touch Amy's flesh, Jason accidentally knocked over Max's high chair and the clatter made her jump away. Max was frightened by the noise, so he started to scream, and Amy grabbed him from the floor.

After a moment she had him settled, and she turned back to Jason. "So, what do you think about Charles's opening his own business? I told him you'd have good advice."

When Jason just stood there in silence, she looked nervously at Charles. "Yes, well, I think it's a good idea. Max has eaten more of your food in the last day than he has in his whole little life. If you want to do more testing, I can get some other women you can supply baby food to and they'll be your guinea pigs. And we'll all write letters of recommendation for you."

For a moment Jason smirked at this idea. Charles and baby food! The idea was laughable. Charles was such a snob that he complained about what people *wore* when they ate his food. "That woman crumbled crackers in my soup," he once said, then refused to ever again cook for her, saying that she wasn't worth his time. And later Jason found out he was right: the woman was a gold digger of extraordinary greed.

But now Jason could see that Charles was thinking about Amy's idea of going into business. Which would mean that he'd *lose* his chef!

"You don't know how difficult it is cooking for a baby," Amy was saying. "If you cook a butternut squash, you have enough for a dozen meals and who wants to eat butternut squash for a solid week?"

"I see. It is a problem. I had never tasted baby food from jars until this week. Awful, dreadful stuff. No wonder American children hate proper food and prefer living on hamburgers and hot dogs."

"Exactly. So that's why—"

She broke off because Jason suddenly stepped between them. "I think we need to get ready to go now, so you'd better leave," he said to Charles.

"But we were just getting started. I'd like to hear more about this baby food idea. Maybe I could—"

"Maybe you couldn't," Jason said as he pulled the chair back so Charles could stand. So help him, if he lost his chef to this whole fiasco of David's, he was going to—

"For you, my beautiful lady," Charles was saying, "I will deliver free dinners every night for the next two weeks. And perhaps lunch too."

"Oh, really, I haven't done anything," Amy said, but she was blushing prettily as Charles once again reached for her hand to kiss.

But Jason stepped between them and in the next moment Charles was out the door. "I could have stayed in the most expensive hotel in the world for less than what this trip is costing me," Jason muttered as he leaned against the door.

"You were awfully rude to him," Amy said, frowning. "Why?"

When Jason could think of nothing to explain his actions, he picked up Max and started toward the living room. "I think we should go shopping today," he threw over his shoulder. "Unless you have all your Christmas shopping done already."

"Oh, no, I haven't. I, uh, yes, I'll get ready in a moment," she said, then disappeared into her bedroom.

"Lesson number one, ol' man," Jason said as he lifted Max high over his head, "if you want to distract a woman, mention shopping. The worst you'll have to do is spend the day in a mall, but it's better than answering questions you don't want to answer."

CHAPTER TEN

"WAS CHARLES YOUR LOVER?" AMY ASKED AS SOON as they were in Jason's car. The vehicle was much cleaner now that she'd spent hours cleaning it, but the interior, including the upholstery, had been ruined.

"My what?" Jason asked as he swung the car into the street.

"Why do you always say that when I ask about your personal life? You can see all about my life, but I know nothing about you. What was Charles to you? You obviously know him well."

"Not as well as you think," Jason said, looking in the rearview mirror at Max as he chewed on his fingers and stared out the window. "Where did you get that coat Max is wearing?"

"Mildred," Amy said quickly, giving her mother-in-law's name. "What about Charles?

Would you rather that I didn't take food from him?"

"Charles is a brilliant chef, so of course you should take his food. Can Max choke on that?"

Instantly, Amy turned around in her seat, entangling herself in the seat belt, only to see that Max wasn't chewing on anything. "I guess that means you don't want to talk about that side of your life," she said heavily as she turned back around.

Jason didn't answer but kept his eyes on the road—and his mind imagining ways to murder his little brother.

"Have you ever thought of going to a therapist?" Amy asked softly. "Being gay is nothing to be ashamed of, you know."

"Where do you think we should park?" Jason asked as he pulled into the lot of the mall. Since it was a mere two days before Christmas, there were few places. "Looks like we're going to have to hike," Jason said cheerfully, as he found a place that looked to be half a mile from the stores.

Amy was sitting still, not moving an inch, and when Jason opened the back door behind her to get Max, she still sat where she was.

"You going with us?" Jason asked, somehow pleased by her disgust with his refusal to talk about his personal life.

"Yeah, sure," she said as she climbed out of the

car, then stood back as Jason unfastened Max from the car seat and inserted him into the new stroller.

"Maybe I can change," Jason said when Max was strapped into the stroller. "Maybe I can find the right girl and she could change me." With that, he started pushing Max toward the stores.

"Right," Amy said as she hurried after them. "And tomorrow I'm going to go the other way."

"Could be," Jason said. "I guess stranger things have happened. Now, where do we begin?"

"I have no idea," Amy said, looking at the huge crowds moving from one store to another, their arms straining under the weight of the bags they carried. "Shopping isn't something I do a lot of." She was feeling as though he'd snubbed her, and she hated the way he laughed at her every time she asked him a personal question.

"I think Max needs a new coat, so where's the best shop?"

"I really have no idea," she said aloofly, turning away from him to look at the crowds. When he didn't speak, she turned back and he was looking at her with an expression of, *I don't believe a word you're saying*.

"There's a BabyGap—"

"Where would you *like* to buy Max's clothes? Money no object."

For a moment Amy hesitated; then she gave a sigh and pointed. "Down that aisle, take a left at the second intersection, four stores down on the right. But it's no use going there. The clothes cost much too much."

"Would you let me worry about the money?" he said.

For a moment she squinted at him. "Is this the way you ordered your lover around? Is this why he kicked you out?"

"My last lover threatened to commit suicide if I left, so do you want to lead or follow?"

"Why?"

"Because I don't think we can travel through these crowds side by side," he answered. He was having to speak almost into her ear to be heard over the noise.

"No, I meant why did he threaten to commit suicide?"

"Couldn't bear the thought of living without me," Jason answered, then thought, *and my money*. "Could we continue this later? Max is going to be hungry soon, you'll be dripping milk, and I'd like to watch a football game this afternoon."

With another sigh, Amy gave up, then turned and started making her way toward the baby store.

Jason watched her moving ahead of him and Max, and he felt better than he had in weeks, maybe in years. He wasn't sure what was making him feel so good, but something was.

It took them several minutes to make their way through the crowds to the little store at one end of an aisle off the main artery of the mall, and as soon as Jason saw the place, he admitted that Amy had taste. If she was going to fantasize about what to buy her son, then she was going to start at the top.

The walls were full of double rows of the most beautiful clothes, for boys on one side, girls on the other. Each set was a whole outfit, with shirt, trousers, hat, shoes, and jacket to match. By the time Jason made his way into the store, Amy was already looking up at the expensive little sets with stars in her eyes. As Jason entered, he saw her put out her hand to touch a little blue jacket, but she withdrew it as though she couldn't allow herself such a pleasure.

"So what do you like?" Jason asked, maneuvering Max between the stands of clothing.

"All of it," Amy said quickly. "So now that we've seen it, let's go."

Jason ignored her. "I like this one," he said, holding up a yellow-and-black set that had a matching raincoat. Little yellow boots had eyes on them, and he knew Max would like trying to get the eyes in his mouth. "What's his size?"

"Nine to twelve months," Amy said quickly. "We have to go—"

"What is it?" Jason asked, for Amy's face seemed to drain of color.

"Out. Now," she gasped, then tried to hide behind him.

Jason found he rather liked her hands on his waist and the way she hid behind him, but when he looked up, he saw nothing but another woman with a baby about Max's age entering the store.

"It's Julie Wilson," Amy hissed up at him. "Her husband owns the John Deere store and has horses."

Jason didn't see what this information had to do with anything in the known world.

"We went to prenatal classes together," Amy said; then she tightened her grip on his waist and started to pull Jason out of the store, using his big body to hide her from view of the woman.

"Aren't you forgetting something?" Jason whispered down to her, then nodded toward Max, who had managed to pull eight boxes of shoes off a shelf and was now busily eating the ties off two mismatched shoes.

"Heaven help me, I have failed motherhood," Amy gasped; then, crouching low, she made her way back to her son.

"Hello, Mrs. Wilson," the shop clerk was saying in a fawning way. "I have your order in the back. If you'll just come this way, we'll see if it fits little Abigail."

Jason recognized that tone of voice, since he'd heard it many times. It said that the clerk knew the woman and knew that she could afford anything in the shop. The snobby little clerk had not so much as asked Jason and Amy if they needed help when they entered, so he suspected that Amy was known to the girl. Abernathy was a tiny place, and even though this mall was a few miles out of the town, Jason guessed that it was known that Amy couldn't afford the clothes in this shop, therefore she was ignored.

"Let's go!" Amy said as soon as the woman had disappeared into the back.

"I have no intention of leaving," Jason said, and there was anger in his voice.

"You don't understand," Amy said, nearly in tears. "Julie married the richest boy in town, while I married—"

"The most likable boy in school," Jason said quickly, and instantly there were tears of gratitude in her eyes.

"Did she marry Tommy Wilson?"

"Yes. I told you, his father—"

"When we get home, I'm going to tell you all about Tommy Wilson and his father; then you won't be hiding from any woman who had the misfortune to marry either one of them. Now, help me here," Jason said as he began pulling one outfit after another off the shelves and slinging them over his arm.

"What in the world are you doing?" Amy gasped. "You can't—"

"I can buy everything now and return them later, right?"

"I guess so," Amy said, hesitantly; then as she began to think about what he was saying, she picked up a little outfit with a blue teddy bear on the front of it. "I just love this one."

"Think quantity and forget about choosing."

Amy giggled, then got into the mood of pulling clothes off the racks and plonking them down onto the sales counter. There were yellow overalls with a red giraffe embroidered on the bib, a red shirt, a red-and-yellow jacket, with the most adorable red-and-yellow sandals to match. For once in her life, Amy didn't look at a price tag as she tossed things onto the counter.

When the clerk returned, Julie Wilson behind her, she stopped so suddenly that the baby carriage hit her in the heels. "Sir!" she said sternly, then opened her mouth to let Jason know that she didn't appreciate the mess they had made. But Jason held up a platinum American Express card, and the woman's frown turned into a smile.

"Did you see her face?" Amy was saying as she licked her ice cream cone. She and Jason were sitting on a bench by the fountain in the mall, Max in his carriage between them. All around them were bags and bags of clothes for Max.

"Of course, I'll have to hear the lecture from

that snippy little salesgirl when I take all of it back, but it was worth it to see Julie's face. And you were marvelous." Amy was swinging her legs back and forth like a child, licking the ice cream before it melted and smiling as she watched Jason sharing his cone with Max.

"Was she really awful to you in class?"

"Worse than you can imagine," Amy said cheerfully. "She couldn't wait to tell me every rotten thing Billy had done at school. Not that she was there, but her husband was. Heavens, that must mean he's as old as you are."

At that Jason raised an eyebrow at her. "I hardly think I'm at death's door yet," he said archly.

"Got ya," Amy said, laughing. "Oh, but you were wonderful. But you shouldn't have told her that you and I were an item. You don't remember what Abernathy is like. Within two hours everyone in town will think I'm living with some great virile hunk of a man and they won't have any idea of the truth."

"And what is the truth?"

"That you've been having an affair with Charles, of course."

"I did not say—"

"And you didn't deny it, either. Hey! What are you doing?"

"I'm putting a new shirt on Max, that's what. I'm sick of this worn-out thing."

"But we have to take them back, and—" She broke off to stare at him. "You have no intention of taking these clothes back, do you?"

"None whatever."

"I wish I could understand you. Why *did* you agree to stay with Max and me in my leaky old house?"

"To give David a chance with you," Jason said simply.

"I didn't think you'd tell me the truth. Come on, Max, let's go see what the bottom half of you has done." She took the handles of the carriage and wheeled Max toward the women's restroom.

When he was alone, Jason looked around the mall. Two weeks ago he would never have believed that he would be spending his Christmas holidays like this. Usually he celebrated Christmas at some extravagantly expensive resort, and his customary gift to the woman he was with was a pair of diamond earrings. Her gift to him was something in bed. Maybe he was getting old, but sometimes he wished the women would shell out for a tie or a pair of socks.

"You are getting old, Wilding," he muttered, then got up to give his place on the bench to a woman who looked about ready to deliver twins. He picked up the bags, then walked a few stores down as he waited for Amy, and he saw in a window the perfect dress for her to wear on her date with David tonight. It was a lavender short-sleeve sweater with a matching cardigan, and a pleated skirt of dark purple with tiny tulips on it.

Jason didn't hesitate in entering the store, and immediately three attractive saleswomen ran to help him. He told them he had about five minutes, and he wanted the outfit in the window with hose, shoes, and jewelry to go with it.

The tallest of the women, a striking redhead, didn't bat an eyelash. "Underwear?"

Jason nodded curtly. "She's about that woman's size," he said, glancing at a shopper. Minutes later he'd signed the charge slip and the clothes were in the bag.

"Big one," Amy said as soon as she saw Jason, referring to Max. "Sorry we took so long. What did you buy now?"

Jason grinned at her. "I bought you something to wear tonight."

"You— Oh, I see. Gay men are good at that, aren't they? I mean, you like to choose women's clothes, don't you?"

Jason bent over her until his nose was almost touching hers. "Do you know the words 'thank you'? Or is my wanting to hear them more evidence of my sexual orientation?"

"Sorry," Amy murmured. "It's just that I—" She broke off, her eyes wide as she stared at something behind Jason. The next minute, she pushed him aside, stretched out her arms, and squealed, "Sally!" and a short, very attractive young woman came running toward Amy.

Jason stood to one side as he watched the two women hug each other and talk over the top of one another, their words tumbling out in a cascade.

"How long—"

"When did you—"

"Why didn't you—"

"This is Max," Amy said at last, then stepped back to show her friend her son.

But the woman only glanced at the baby in the carriage, for her attention was on the gorgeous man who had his long-fingered hand on the back of the stroller. "Who is this?" she breathed, and Jason was quite pleased to be seen as a handsome man. Amy sure didn't seem to notice!

Jason couldn't help himself, but he picked up the woman's hand and kissed the back of it, then looked at her with what he'd been told were very seductive eyes. Since the woman looked as though she were going to melt and run down into her shoes, he felt good.

"This is Mr. Wilding and he's gay," Amy said in a cold voice.

"But I'm thinking of changing," Jason practically purred.

"You can practice on me," the woman said, and looked at Jason with hot eyes.

"Is Max all right?" Amy said sharply. "Mr. Wilding is Max's nanny. Gay men are good at that sort of thing, you know."

"I've been thinking of having a baby," Sally said, never taking her eyes off Jason, "and I think I'm going to need a nanny."

"How about a maternity nurse as well?" Jason said in a low voice.

"Honey, I need a *donor.*"

"Sally, could you disentwine yourself from my nanny so we could go get something to drink? You can manage Max by yourself for a while, can't you?" she asked Jason, her lips a tight line as she glared up at him.

"I might be able to handle him," Jason said, his eyes still on Sally, as though she were the woman of his dreams. "You two go on. Max and I will take these packages to the car, then I have some, ah, personal shopping to do." He made the last sound as though he meant to buy something sexy and silky.

Before her friend could reply, Amy firmly took Sally's arm and led her to a nearby fake English pub and sat down heavily in the nearest empty booth.

"I want to know everything there is to know about him," Sally said eagerly.

"So what brings you to Abernathy over Christmas and why didn't you tell me you were going to be here?"

"I'm in a mall, not in Abernathy, and I'm here because I live six miles away," Sally said slowly. "You want to tell me what's going on? Are you having an affair with him? Or do you just look at him like he's a work of art?"

"Do you have to come on to every man you meet?" Amy snapped as she grabbed a menu and looked at it. "Are you hungry?" When Sally didn't answer, she looked up.

"Out with it," Sally said. "I want to know everything."

"I've already told you everything. He's gay; he has no interest in me as a female, and we talk like two old hens. That's the end of it."

"I want details," Sally said as she ordered two cups of coffee from the waitress.

"No, give me a large orange juice. Milk production, you know."

Sally gave a slight shudder. "No, I don't know and don't want to know. Now, get on with it. Are you *sure* that hunk is gay?"

It didn't take Amy but a moment to get over her unusual reticence with her friend, and she was quite annoyed with herself for feeling what could almost be described as jealousy at Sally's reaction to "her" Mr. Wilding. And his to her, she thought with a grimace.

"I think his ex-lover came to the house this morning," she said, then described Jason's encounter with Charles. "There was lots of eye rolling while Charles was kissing my hand. There was definitely something going on between them. And the day before, Mr. Wilding kept glaring at two men at Baby Heaven. He paid no attention to the saleswoman, who was a knockout, but gave a hundred percent of his interest to the two men."

"Okay, so where did you find him?"

"He found me. I just opened the door and there he was. David brought him over and gave him to me."

"You mean like an early Christmas present?"

"Sort of, but don't get any ideas. He really is gay."

"He doesn't seem gay."

"And what stereotype do you have in mind for a person to appear gay?" Amy asked defensively.

"Hey! Don't jump down my throat. I was just asking, that's all. Gay or not, he's divine, and I want to know all there is to know about him."

"I don't know much, really. David insisted that his cousin needed a place to stay and to recover from a broken heart, so I let him stay."

"He could mend his broken heart in my bed any day he wanted to."

"You've been reading too many romantic novels. There is nothing between us, and there never will be. I told you: he's gay. Besides, he's very elegant, isn't he? When I first saw him, he had on a suit that probably cost more than my house."

"Amy, this cup of coffee is worth more than that rat trap of a house of yours. If you set it on fire, the fire would put itself out out of pity."

"It's not that bad."

"It's worse. Tell me more about him."

"He's odd, really. He doesn't say much, but he . . ." She looked up at her friend. "He brings me luck. Isn't that an odd thing to think about someone? But it's true; he brings luck to Max and me. Since he arrived, some lovely things have happened."

"Such as his going on one knee and telling you he can't live without you, and—"

"Stop daydreaming. First of all, Max adores him."

"Hmm . . . What else?"

"I don't know how to explain him. The truth is that I don't think I understand him myself. It's as though he's a . . ." Her head came up. "He's a bit of a turtle really. Or maybe an armadillo. He has a hard outer covering, but I think that inside he's really quite soft. I don't think he realizes it, but he adores Max just as much as my son adores him."

For a long moment, Sally leaned back in the booth and stared at her friend. "Are you in love with him?"

"Don't be ridiculous. He's a nice man and we

have fun together, but he really is effeminate. He likes to shop and cook and do all the things that men don't."

"You mean, all the things that Billy didn't like, don't you? Look, Amy, I know you were the only girl in school who graduated a virgin, and I know you were saving yourself for your husband. I also know that you gave yourself to a drunken dope addict. Don't give me that look. I know Billy had his good points, but I'm a realist. You've been to bed with one man, lived with one man, and all you know is the kind of man who doesn't know how to open a refrigerator. There are other kinds of men, you know."

"Why are you always trying to make a romance out of everything? I didn't guess that the man is gay; I was told so. By David."

"Dr. David? Now, there's a hunk. You know, your Mr. Wilding reminds me of him."

"They're cousins."

"Ah, I see. So what happens next? Do you keep living with this gorgeous hunk who you can't have or do you have to return him after Christmas?"

"I have no idea."

At that Sally laughed. "Amy, you haven't changed. Only you would be living with a man and have no idea why he's there or how long he means to stay."

Amy didn't answer that, but looked down at her empty glass.

"Okay, I'll lay off. What about the other men in your life? What happened to that beautiful used car salesman?"

"Oh. Ian. He *owns* the Cadillac dealership. He's very rich, I suppose." Amy gave a sigh.

"I can see how you'd consider him tedious. Poor guy is only handsome and rich, so of what interest could he possibly be to you?"

"He's of more interest to himself than to anyone else. He seemed to think he was doing me a great favor by showing up every night. He kept calling me 'Billy Thompkins's Widow' as though he were saying that I was an untouchable."

"Welcome to small-town life. Why don't you get out of here and go somewhere where no one has ever heard of Billy and his problems?"

But before Amy could reply, Sally looked as though someone had stuck a pin in her. "What time is it?"

Amy looked around to find a clock but didn't see one.

"I have to go," Sally said urgently as she gathered her things and started sliding out of the booth; then she saw Amy's face. "Don't tell me you don't know?"

When Amy shook her head, Sally gave a grimace. "Didn't you see the signs? They're all over the mall.

You know Candlelight Gowns? That shop in Carlton that's about to go out of business?"

"Out of my league," Amy said, finishing her orange juice and sliding out to stand by Sally. "I could never afford to even window shop there."

"Nobody could afford that place. I don't know how they expected to sell those ritzy dresses in eastern Kentucky, but they did. Anyway, everyone knew they were about to go under, but it seems that some mysterious buyer from New York, no less, has bought the place and to launch the new shop, they're giving away a Dior dress."

When Amy said nothing, just kept walking beside her friend, Sally said, "Hello! Dior. Doesn't that *do* anything to you?"

"No, I'm more into Pampers and Huggies. Why would anyone want a Dior dress?"

"You poor baby," Sally said. "You know, I have a theory that having a baby takes away about fifty points on a woman's IQ. I think she gets them back when the kid goes off to school, but until then she's an idiot."

Amy laughed. "You just think it's true, but I *know* it is. So what do you want with a Dior dress?"

At that, Sally rolled her eyes to let Amy know that she was hopeless. "Come on, the drawing's about to begin, and you have to enter the contest."

"Me?"

"Yes, and if you win, you have to give me the dress."

"All right," Amy said, "that's a deal."

But first Amy had to find Jason and Max, and an hour later, the three of them were standing in front of the fountain in the center of the mall and waiting for the drawing to be held. And when they drew Amy's name, somehow, she wasn't surprised. In the last few days it was as though nothing but good luck came her way.

"Sally is going to be so happy," Amy said as the crowd turned around to look to see if the winner was in the audience.

"Why?" Jason asked, smiling down at her, Max in his arms.

"Because I promised her that if I won, I'd give her the dress."

Jason grabbed her arm as she turned away. "You did what?"

"I have no need for a dress like that. Where would I wear it?"

"Oh. I forgot to tell you. David got tickets to the Bellringers' Ball for tomorrow and he wants you to go with him."

For a moment Amy just blinked at him, as though she didn't understand what he was saying. Then she grinned and said, "I hope Sally doesn't mind having a dress that's been worn once," and the next moment she went up to the podium to accept her prize. She wasn't surprised when she found out that the dress was in her size and that the prize included a free hair and makeup makeover by Mr. Alexander from New York on the night of her choice. When she told them she wanted it tomorrow night, she wasn't shocked to hear that Mr. Alexander was going to be in the Kentucky area tomorrow.

When she said all this to Jason, he said, "That's because Mr. Alexander is probably Joe from the local beauty shop. He went to New York once, so he now bills himself as being from there."

"Still . . ." Amy said, "a great many odd things have happened to me since . . ." She looked up at him.

"Since David started courting you?"

"David? Courting me? Are you out of your mind?"

"I think you're missing something if you can't see what everyone else can. Dr. David is in love with you and wants—"

"Oh, you are ridiculous. Look, it's nearly time for lunch and I have to feed Max, so we better go home."

Jason didn't answer her, but put his hand on the small of her back and half pushed her into a very nice Italian restaurant. They were first served bread with a dish of oil from a bottle filled with garlic cloves. The oil was much too spicy for either of the adults, but Max sucked the oil off three pieces of bread.

After lunch they went to three toy stores, and amid Amy's protests that grew weaker by the minute, Jason bought Max sackfuls of toys. In the car on the way home, she wailed, "How am I going to repay you? You *must* return all those clothes and you have to take back those toys. There is nothing you own that's dirty enough for me to make the kind of money that I'd need to repay—"

"David's going to pick you up in an hour, so you'd better hustle to get ready."

"Hustle?" Amy asked, sounding as though she'd never heard the word before.

"Mmmm," was all Jason said as he swung the car into the driveway. "You have to nurse Max before you go or you'll be in pain all night, and—"

"Would you mind!" she said, annoyed. "I think I know my own milking needs better than you do."

She had meant to put him in his place, but instead, she'd made herself sound like a cow. When he didn't say anything, she looked at him sideways and said, "Maybe I should apply for a job at the local dairy," and they both burst into laughter.

But as she got out of the car, she said, "I can't go. I have nothing decent to wear out with a doctor," and Jason thrust a heavy dark green bag into her hands. Amy opened it only enough to see that something gorgeous was inside. "How did you know that I love lavender?" she asked softly.

"Intuition. Now go and feed Max and get out of here."

"Mr. Wilding, you are my fairy godmother," she said, smiling up at him; then she put her hand over her mouth at the use of the word *fairy*. "Oh, I didn't mean . . ."

"Go!" he ordered. "Now."

Grabbing Max from him, she ran into the house, and all three of them were smiling.

CHAPTER ELEVEN

As soon as Amy left with David, Jason picked up his telephone and called his father's house. When his father answered, he was startled at the noise in the background. "What's going on?" Jason half shouted into the phone.

"If it isn't my newly turned gay son," Bertram Wilding said. "So how's the gay scene?"

Jason looked toward heaven and again vowed to kill his brother. "Could you cut the jokes, Dad, and put my secretary on the line?"

"Cherry?"

"What? I can't hear you. No, I don't want a cherry pie; I want Parker."

"Cherry Parker, old man."

"Ah. Right. I knew that." And he did, he told himself. Vaguely, he remembered thinking that

Cherry was an odd name for an icy woman like Parker. "Would you put her on?"

"Sure thing. I think she's in the kitchen with Charlie."

At that, he put the phone down, and Jason could hear his steps on the wooden floor. "Cherry?" Jason whispered. "Charlie?"

"Yes, sir," Parker said when she picked up the phone, and for the life of him, Jason couldn't imagine a more inappropriate name for her than "Cherry." "What can I do you for?" When Jason was silent, she said, "Sorry. I've spent too much time in Kentucky."

"Yes, well," Jason murmured, not knowing what to say in reply. "I need you to do something for me."

"I assumed as much. I didn't think it was a social call."

For a moment Jason held the phone away from his face and looked at it. When this was over and he got back to New York, he was going to pummel his staff back into shape.

"I'm going to dictate a list of toys that I want you to buy; then I want you to wrap them up in white tissue paper and tie them with red or green ribbon. You are to put labels on the gifts saying they're from Santa Claus. Got that?"

"Rather easily," Parker said.

Again, Jason grimaced. His secretary was really

being too insolent. "And I want you to deliver them into the house on Christmas Eve. Put them under the tree."

"I see. And how do I get into the house?"

"I'll leave a key under the back doormat."

"Ah, the pleasures and safety of small-town life. How I miss it."

"Parker, when I want your personal comments, I'll ask for them."

"Yes, sir," she said, but she didn't sound contrite in the least. "Is there anything else?"

For a moment Jason felt a bit guilty for his outburst. It was just that too many things in his orderly world were coming apart. "Do you have your dress for tomorrow night?" he asked in an attempt to be less dictatorial.

"You bought me an Oscar de la Renta, quite expensive."

"Good," he said; then, not knowing what else to say, and hearing laughter in the background, he hung up without a farewell.

In the next moment, he made another call and issued an invitation.

"Well, well, well," Mildred Thompkins said when Jason opened the door, Max on his arm. "So you're the angel Amy keeps going on and on about. Don't just stand there; let me in; it's cold out here."

"You're not going to tell her, are you?" Jason asked, sounding like a little boy begging her not to tell his mother.

"Tell Amy that her gay guardian angel is really one of the richest men in the world?"

"Not quite. And, before you ask, I'm *not* a billionaire."

"Come here, darlin'," she said to her grandson, and the baby went to her. "So you want to tell me what's going on here? Why are you masquerading as some gay man when I happen to know that you pursued every female in Abernathy all during high school, and how many homes do you have around the world?"

"I can see you haven't changed," Jason said, smiling and looking with fascination at the lacquered mass of hair on Mildred's head. The strands wove in and out in an intricate pattern that wouldn't have moved in a hurricane. "Still nosy as ever."

"I'm interested in Amy," Mildred said simply. "I want what's best for her."

"Since Billy isn't here to give it to her?" Jason asked.

"That was a low blow and you know it. My son may have had his faults, but he did one good thing in his life: he married Amy and produced this child." She gave Max a hug and a kiss, pulled his hands away from her glasses, then said, "No, that's not true. He did another good thing. On the night he died Billy was drunk, very very drunk, and he was driving about sixty on the twisty old River Road. But he was sober enough—and kind enough—that he turned his car into a tree rather than hit a busload of kids coming back from a ball game."

"I always liked Billy," Jason said softly.

"I know you did, and you were always good to him. And that's why I came by to see how you and Amy were getting along. Amy is the best. She sees the good in people. Don't get me wrong. She's not one of these idiots who thinks that everyone who doesn't have a tail and horns is a good person. It's just that Amy can see good in a person when others can't. And her belief in them makes them try harder. Maybe if Billy hadn't died, she'd have made something good out of him. But then . . . Oh, well, it's better not to speak ill of the dead. Billy left behind a beautiful wife and Max."

Her head came up. "So now, you want to tell me what's going on and why you're living with my daughter-in-law in this falling-down old heap?"

Jason ignored her question. "You want to baby-sit tomorrow? I have to go somewhere."

She narrowed her eyes at him. "You know, a lot of odd things have been happening lately, like someone buying Baby Heaven and Candlelight Gowns and—"

"What? Someone bought a dress shop?"

"Yeah. That shop in Carlton that put on the drawing today for that Dior gown. Now, we may be pretty country in Kentucky, but we do know that a place like Candlelight Gowns doesn't carry a one-off Dior gown. Do you know what that dress cost?"

"I imagine I'll be told," Jason said heavily. "Tell me, did you hear the name of the buyer for this dress shop?"

Mildred smiled at him as she shook a rattle for Max. "Only that he was from New York. Did you know that the owner of the shop was an old football rival of yours? I seem to remember one game where you were to pass him the ball, but you didn't. Instead, you ran with it, and made the touchdown that won the game. What was that boy's name?"

"Lester Higgins," Jason said heavily.

"That's it. He married a girl whose father owned that shop, and Lester tried for years to make a go of it but couldn't." She was watching Jason's face and her smile was broadening. "So now maybe he finally found someone to take that shop off his hands. Someone who can afford it."

"Don't look at me. I used to be rich, but then I came to visit Abernathy and my resources have plummeted."

"Can't make a profit on a dress shop in Kentucky

even when you give away twenty-thousand-dollar gowns as a sales gimmick?"

Suddenly, Jason grinned at her. "You are still the nosiest gossip in four counties. You want to baby-sit tomorrow?"

"So you can go to the Bellringers' Ball? I hear that that jet of yours is paying so much to Jessie Green to use his landing strip that he's thinking of retiring."

Jason groaned. "All right, you win. You get your gossip, but I get someone to take care of Max tomorrow. Deal?"

"Sure. You call and order pizza while I get the bottle of bourbon from the car. It's no use looking to see if Amy has any in the house. She'd probably be afraid that Max would drink it."

"You haven't changed, Mildred. Not one bit."

"Neither have you," she said, smiling. "And you were always my favorite."

"Along with all the other boys in town," he said, smiling as he picked up the phone.

"And you should see him play with Max!" Amy was saying. "He'll spend twenty minutes encouraging Max to crawl; he has endless patience. And everything good seems to happen when he's around. I win things, find great bargains, and did I tell you that he does the ironing and lets me sleep?"

"Twice," David said, looking down at his salad.

"Oh, sorry. It's just that I've never lived with anyone so unselfish. Not that I'm really living with him, but, you know . . ." She trailed off, moved her fork around in her lettuce, and wondered what Mr. Wilding and Max were having for dinner.

"Amy, would you rather go home?" David asked, leaning across the table to her.

"No, of course not. I'm having a wonderful time. It's great to get out of the house."

"You certainly look nice. That color suits you."

"Mr. Wilding bought this for me," she said before she thought. "All right, that's it. I promise not to mention his name again. Tell me, did you save any lives today?"

"Half a dozen at least. Would you like to go dancing after this?"

"Can't," she said, stuffing her mouth full, trying to make up for lost time, since David was nearly finished and she had been talking too much to eat. "Milk," she muttered.

"What did you say?"

Amy took a drink of her lemonade. "Milk. I have to feed Max. I told him that I should work in a dairy, since I can't get a job anywhere else."

"You told Max that?"

"No, uh, I told . . ."

"Jason. I see." For a moment David was silent; then he looked up at Amy. "Did he tell you about the ball tomorrow night?"

"Yes, but not until after I'd won a dress by Dior."

"You won a dress? And by Dior, no less. You have to tell me about this."

Amy couldn't help herself as she rattled off about the whole day, starting with Jason's ironing, then seeing Julie Wilson in the mall and how Jason bought Max all those clothes. "Of course he has to take them back," she said, her mouth full of steak, "and he will, but he hasn't done it yet. We just have to talk about it."

"What about the dress?"

"Oh, yes, the dress." Amy told him what Sally had said about the store in Carlton going out of business, then having been bought by a new owner, so they were giving away a dress. "And I won it. And a makeover, so tomorrow I should look presentable."

"You always look presentable," David said, but Amy didn't seem to notice the compliment.

"In my case I'm glad the dress is strapless, as it makes for easy access." She had meant that as a joke, but when she looked up at David's intense stare, she turned red. "Sorry. I'm forgetting where I am. I make breast-feeding jokes all the time and I shouldn't. They're tasteless." Heaven help her, but she couldn't stop herself. "Well, maybe not tasteless to Max. Especially after I eat something hot and spicy." She gave David a weak smile. "Sorry."

"Do you and Jason share jokes?" David asked softly.

"Yes. He's a good audience, and he laughs at my jokes no matter how tasteless they are."

"But not to Jason."

"I beg your pardon."

"You just said that your jokes weren't tasteless to Max, and I said they weren't tasteless to Jason either."

Amy looked at him blankly, still not understanding. "Yes, of course. This is good; what is it?"

"Beef."

"Ah, yes. Did I tell you about Charles?"

"This is another man?"

"No, silly, he's the one who makes the baby food you gave me. He's a beautiful man, and you should have told me the truth."

"Yes, I should have. Why don't you tell me the truth?"

"You'd be bored."

"No, honest," he said. "I'm beginning to find this whole story fascinating. I'm meeting new people I've never met before. There's the very funny and unselfish Jason. And there's Max the Huggable. And now there's Charles the Beautiful. Who else is in your life?"

Amy jammed a piece of meat the size of a golf ball in her mouth, then made motions that she couldn't talk until she'd chewed it.

"Amy!" came a masculine voice from beside them. "Don't you look divine? Are we still on for New Year's Eve?"

Amy waved her hands and pointed toward her full mouth as she looked up at Ian Newsome.

"I think Amy is going to be busy on New Year's Eve," David said firmly, glaring up at the man.

"Is that so? Did you get my Christmas gift, Amy?" Ian asked, smiling down at her.

Amy, still chewing, shook her head no.

"Oh? Then I'll have to bring it over myself on Christmas morning. Or maybe I should say that I'll *drive* it over." He turned to David. "How's that little clinic of yours doin', Doc? Still beggin' people to donate to it? And are you still livin' in that tiny house over on River Road?" Before David could reply, he turned back to Amy, winked, waved, and was gone.

"I really hate that bastard, don't you?"

Amy found that she hadn't yet finished chewing the huge piece of steak.

"You want some dessert?"

"Milk," Amy mumbled. "Max."

"Yeah, sure," David said, then signaled for the waitress to bring the check. "Might as well leave. What a night!"

Amy wouldn't allow David to walk her to the front door. She felt guilty that she didn't, since, after all, he had paid for such a nice dinner for her and he was taking her to the ball tomorrow, but still, she just wanted to be inside. "I'm home," she called out softly, and when there was no answer, she had a moment of panic. Had Mr. Wilding gone? Had he taken Max?

But in the next second Jason appeared, Max in his arms, tears on the baby's face. "Gimme, gimme," Amy said, stretching out her arms. "I'm bursting." In seconds, she was on the couch and Max was happily sucking.

"Have a good time?" Jason asked, standing over her.

"Oh, sure. Great. Is there any of that casserole left from lunch?"

"I think so," he said, smiling down at her pleading look for a moment; then he went into the kitchen and filled a plate full of cold salad and cold meat. "You need one of those quick ovens," he said as he handed her the plate.

Amy took the plate with one hand, but she had no lap to set it on. While looking about, Jason took the plate from her, cut off a bite, and fed it to her on a fork. "A microwave," she said when her mouth was empty. "But Charles's food is good cold or hot. Did you have dinner?"

"Yes, and I thought you did too, so why are you hungry?" He fed her a piece of potato in a dill sauce.

"You know," she said, waving her hand; then she turned sharply. "What's that?"

"The coffee table," he said, scooping up cold beef cooked with red wine. "Or it's supposed to be, I guess. Maybe we could find a furniture store that's going out of business." He was referring to the big electrical spool that she had in the middle of the room.

"No, *that*," Amy said, mouth still full.

"The glass? It's a glass. Haven't you seen one before?"

She ignored his attempt at humor. "What is on the glass?"

Jason turned, stared at the single glass sitting on the table; then, with his back to Amy, he smiled. He was sober when he looked back at her. "Lipstick," he said. "Red lipstick."

"It's not mine." She was looking at him as hard as she could as he put more food into her mouth.

"Don't look at me. It's not mine either."

"I know that all gays aren't cross-dressers," she said. "So whose lipstick is that?"

"Ahhhhh."

"Jason!"

"What happened to 'Mr. Wilding'?"

As she switched Max to the other side, she still glared at him. "Did you have a guest?"

"I did, actually. Nice of you to ask."

"I don't think you should have," she said tightly. "You never know what a person has in mind when a baby is involved. I am very concerned about Max's safety."

"Me too, but then this was a woman I've known for a while." He fed her the last bite on the plate.

"I think you should have asked my permission

before you invited a woman into this house. Into my house, that is."

"I'll do that next time. You want something to drink? I have some beer. Max would probably like it."

"So who was she?"

"Who was she who?"

"The woman who left red lipstick on that glass, that's who."

"Just a friend. What about a Coke? Or a Seven-Up?"

Amy glared at him. "You're not answering me."

"And you're not answering me. What do you want to drink?"

"Nothing," she said, inexplicably feeling very angry. Max had fallen asleep before he'd finished nursing, and she knew she should wake him, but she didn't have the heart to do it. Instead, she just wanted to go to bed. What business was it of hers if he had visitors, male or female? "I'm very tired," she said, picking up Max and turning toward her bedroom. "I'll see you in the morning."

"Good night," he said cheerfully, then went to his own bedroom.

Hours later Jason awoke to the sound of glass breaking and immediately swung his long legs off the bed. He had fallen asleep in his clothes, the light still on as he went over a market report for a company he was trying to buy.

In the kitchen he found Amy, a broken glass on the floor, and she was trying to pick up the pieces with her bare hands while walking about in her bare feet.

"Get back from that," he said, annoyed. "You're going to cut yourself." When she looked up at him with pain-filled eyes, he knew that something was wrong. Striding across the glass in his bedroom slippers, he swept Amy into his arms and carried her to a chair by the kitchen table. "Now, tell me what's wrong."

"Just a headache. It's nothing," she managed to whisper, but even that slight sound made a look of pain cross her face, and she shifted uncomfortably on the seat.

"Nothing?" he said. "How about if I drive you to the emergency room of the hospital and let a doctor have a look at you?"

"I have some pills," she said, then gestured vaguely toward her bedroom. "They're in—"

She broke off because Jason had left the room, but in seconds he was back with his cell phone to his ear. "I don't care what time it is or whether you ever get any sleep," he said into the receiver. "I'm not a doctor, but I can see when someone is in serious pain. What do I do with her?"

"Right," Jason said into the phone. "And how long has she had these? Uh huh. Uh huh. I see. I'll call you if I need you again."

Jason put down the phone and looked at Amy. "David said hot compresses and massage. And he's given you pills that you were to take at the first sign of pain. Why didn't you take them?"

"I was busy," she said, looking up at him with mournful eyes. "I'm sorry to keep you up, but my head hurts so much."

Jason went to the sink, turned on the tap, let it run to get hot, then soaked a tea towel in the hot water. "Here, now," he said, handing it to her. "Wrap this around your forehead and tell me where the pills are."

But when Amy started to speak, she had to close her eyes against the pain, so Jason bent, swept her into his arms and carried her into the bedroom. In her bathroom medicine cabinet he found a bottle of pills that were labeled "For migraine," so he brought two of them and a glass of water to Amy.

He meant to leave her then, but she was curled into a ball and he knew that tension and lack of sleep had as much to do with the headache as anything else. David said on the phone that new mothers often got headaches and what they needed more than pills was TLC.

When Jason sat down on the bed beside Amy, she started to protest, but he didn't listen to her. Instead, he leaned back against the headboard and pulled her up so she was leaning against his chest. The washcloth had grown cold, and her hair around her forehead was damp, either from the compress or from sweat, he didn't know which.

Gently, he put his long, strong fingers to the back of her neck and began to massage. At the first groan from Amy, that was all the encouragement he needed. Slowly, he stroked her neck and up to her head, and as the minutes ticked by, he could feel her neck and head relaxing. "Trust me," he said when she didn't want to seem to relax completely.

But his deep strokes made her forget any awkwardness of their being in bed together, and seemed to make her forget everything else in the world. His hands moved down her back, running along her spine, then outward over her ribs, then back up her arms. There was a lot of tension in her upper arms, and he managed to release it.

After about thirty minutes she was limp in his arms, fully supported by him, as trusting of him as Max was.

In another ten minutes Jason realized that she was asleep, so he gently put her down on the pillow and eased his long legs from under her body. When he was standing by the bed, he pulled the cover over her; then, on impulse, he kissed her cheek and tucked her in as though she were three years old.

Smiling, he turned away to leave the room.

"Thank you," he heard Amy whisper as he started back to his own bedroom, and Jason smiled in answer.

CHAPTER TWELVE

WHEN JASON FIRST HEARD THE SOUNDS IN THE KITCHEN and knew they weren't the sounds of Amy and Max, he frowned. Already it had become part of his life to hear Max's high-pitched squeal and Amy's laughter at the morning antics of her son. But then, on second thought, maybe it was just Amy in the kitchen.

With a wicked grin on his face, he got out of bed wearing only the bottom of his pajamas and sauntered into the kitchen. Then, to his pure disgust, he found it was Charles in there, puttering around with the knobs on the stove.

"Expecting someone else?" he asked, one eyebrow raised as he looked Jason up and down, noting his bare chest.

Jason returned to his bedroom to pull on jeans and a shirt before he spoke to his chef. "What are you doing here at this hour?" Jason growled as he sat down at the table and ran his hand over his unshaven face. "And how did you get in here?"

"I'm trying to work this powerless range, and you told Cherry that there was a key under the mat, remember? And, besides, it's after nine in the morning. And what were you doing last night to make you sleep so late?" Charles asked with a lascivious little smirk.

"I remember telling Parker where the key was, not you," Jason said pointedly, ignoring Charles's insinuations.

Charles was unperturbed. "She's not really your type, is she?"

"Parker?" Jason asked, his voice filled with horror.

"No, her." Charles nodded toward Amy's bedroom door.

"You could be fired, you know," Jason said, glaring at the little man.

Silently, Charles turned to a porcelain bowl on the counter behind him, lifted the lid and held it under Jason's nose. It was crepes with hot strawberry sauce, Jason's favorite.

In reply, Jason just grunted and looked toward the overhead cabinet that held the dishes. Within seconds he was eating double forkfuls. How was Charles able to always find the best produce no matter where he was? Jason was willing to bet that these lusciously ripe strawberries didn't come from the local supermarket. On the other hand, based on what the last few days had cost him, he thought it best not to ask where the strawberries had come from.

"I really am thinking of starting a baby food business," Charles said seriously. "Maybe you can advise me in what I should do to get started in my own business."

It was on the tip of Jason's tongue to tell him to forget it, because to help Charles meant that he'd lose him as his personal chef. Instead, Jason acted as though his mouth were too full to talk. Some part of his conscience said, "Coward!" but the strawberry crepes won over his higher moral values.

"Of course I guess everything depends on Max," Charles was saying. "Do all babies have such educated palates?"

Here Jason was on safe ground. "Max is unique in all the world, one of a kind. Speaking of which . . ." He trailed off as he listened silently for a moment, then rose and went to Amy's bedroom door, opened it, and tiptoed inside. Minutes later he came out with a sleepy-looking Max and a clean diaper.

"I didn't hear anything," Charles said. "You must have great ears."

"When you get to be a—" Jason didn't say

"father," as he meant to, but stopped himself. "Get to be a man of experience," he finished, "you learn to listen for things."

But Charles wasn't listening to a word his employer said, because his wide-eyed interest was on the fact that Jason had thrown a dish towel down on the kitchen table and was changing the baby as though he'd done it all his life. All Charles could think was that this was a man who had everything done for him. His clothes were chosen and purchased for him by his valet, his car was driven for him, meals cooked for him, and anything that was left over, his secretary did for him.

Charles recovered himself enough to smile at the baby. "And how do you like strawberries, young gentleman?" Max's reply was a toothy grin, but Charles's reward was when Max grabbed the crepes with both hands and sucked and chewed until there was nothing but sauce on his hands. And on his arms, face, hair, and even up his nose.

"How utterly gratifying," Charles said, standing back and watching Jason clean Max with a warm cloth. "He is without prejudice. Without preconceived ideas. His culinary gusto is the purest form of praise."

"Or criticism," Jason said, annoyed that Charles was still hinting that he wanted to start his own business.

"Afraid of losing me?" Charles asked, one eyebrow arched, knowing exactly what was in his employer's mind.

Jason was saved from answering by a pounding on the front door. As he went to open it, Max draped over his arm, Amy came out of the bedroom, a ratty old robe over her nightgown and blinking sleepily. "What's going on?" she asked.

When Jason opened the door, he was shoved aside by a thin blond man who was followed by two other thin young men and one woman who were carrying huge boxes, plastic cloths slung over their arms. All four of them wore nothing but black, lots of black, layers of it. And all of them had hair bleached to an unnatural white blondness that stuck out at all angles from their heads.

"*You* must be the one," the first man, who was carrying nothing, said as he pointed at Amy. He had three gold earrings in his left ear and a heavy gold bracelet on the wrist he was extending. "Oh, dearie, I can see why I was told to come early. That *must* be your natural color of hair. What was God thinking when He did that to you? And, dear, where did you get that robe? Is it kitsch or have you had it since the Nixon administration? All right, boys, you can see what we have to do. Set up here and there, and over there."

He turned, looked Jason up and down, and said, "And who are you, darling?"

"No one," Jason said emphatically, then tossed a look at Amy. "Max and I are going *out.*"

Amy gave him a look that begged him to take her with him, but Jason had no pity. Heartlessly, he grabbed jackets for him and Max, then was out the front door before it closed. When he'd told Parker to have someone do a makeover, he'd meant maybe hair rollers for half an hour and a little eye shadow. Amy possessed natural beauty; she didn't need the help of an army of beauticians to prepare for a party.

For all that Jason pretended to leave the house because of the arrival of the makeover people, the truth was that he was glad to have Max to himself for a while. It was amazing how important the adoration of a child could make you feel, he thought. And it was even more amazing the lengths that a person would go to to entertain a child.

Jason knew that he had a whole morning before Max would have to nurse again, so he had the baby to himself for hours. The carriage was in the back of the car, so he drove to the tiny downtown of Abernathy and parked. Since Max was still in his pajamas, the first thing he had to do was buy him something to wear.

"Haven't I seen you somewhere before?" the man who owned the Abernathy Emporium said, squinting at Jason. Since the man had served Jason, David, and their father hundreds of times while the boys were growing up, he should remember him.

"Mmmmm," was all Jason said as he put the baby overalls and T-shirt down on the counter along with a snowsuit for a two-year-old. It would be too big for Max now, but it was the best-looking one they had, and Max did have his pride.

"I'm sure I know you," the man was saying. "I never forget a face. Did you come with them city people this mornin' to do up Amy's face?"

"I need diapers for a twenty-pound kid," Jason said, starting to take out his credit card, then paying instead with cash. He didn't want the man to read his name on the card. Maybe it hadn't been such a good idea to come to Abernathy; he should have gone to the mall.

"It'll come to me," the man said. "I know it will."

Jason didn't say anything, but put his hand through the handles of the plastic bags, then wheeled Max out of the store. That was a close one, he thought as he pushed Max back toward the car. But the encounter had taken him back in time to when he lived in Abernathy, and now he could see the place with the eyes of an adult, an adult who had traveled all over the world.

The town was dying, he thought, looking at peeling paint and faded signs. The little grocery store where his father had shopped twice a week and where Jason had stolen candy once had a broken pane of glass in front. He had stolen only once in his life. His father had found out and had taken

Jason back to the store. Attempting to teach Jason not to steal again, his father had arranged for him to sweep the store's wooden floors and wait on customers for two weeks.

It was during those two weeks that Jason got his first taste of business and had loved it. He found that the more enthusiastic he was, the more he believed in a product, the more he could sell. At the end of the two weeks both he and the store owner regretted having to part company.

The Abernathy dime store windows looked as though they hadn't been washed in years. The Laundromat was disgusting.

Dying, he thought. The malls and the larger cities had killed poor little Abernathy.

By the time Jason reached his car, he was feeling quite bad about the place, as he did have a few good memories there, in spite of what he told David. Thinking of whom, he wondered why his brother would want to go through med school, then move back to this funeral-waiting-to-happen of a town.

Jason got into the car, turned on the ignition, waited awhile until the car was warm, then got into the back with Max and proceeded to dress him in his new clothes. "Well, *you* won't have to live here," he said to Max, then halted for a moment as he thought about what he was saying.

There would be David to consider, of course, but

Jason figured he could talk his brother 'round. David couldn't possibly love Amy more than he, Jason, did. And no man on earth loved Max more than he did. So of course they'd spend their lives together.

"Want to go live with me in New York?" Jason asked the silent baby as he chewed on the laces of his new shoes. "I'll buy you a big house out in the country, and you can have your own pony. Would you like that?"

Jason finished dressing the baby, put him in his car seat, then headed for the clean, homogenized mall. Since it was Christmas Eve, there were few shoppers, so he and Max could stroll at their leisure and look in all the windows. But Jason saw nothing as he thought about what he wanted to do.

It wasn't difficult to see what the last few days had meant to him. Max and Amy were now as much a part of his life as breathing, and he wanted them with him always. He'd buy a huge country house within commuting distance from New York and Amy and Max could live there. Amy would never have to worry about cooking or cleaning again, as Jason would make sure that they were taken care of.

And they would be there when he got home, just waiting for him. And their presence would make life easier, he thought. He'd return from long, hard days at the office and there would be Amy with oatmeal on her chin and Max in her arms.

On impulse, he stopped in an art store and bought Amy a huge box of art supplies: watercolors, chalk, pencils, and six dozen sketchbooks of the finest quality paper they had.

"Either somebody likes to draw or you're tryin' to get a girl into bed with you," the clerk, who looked to be all of seventeen, said as he rang up the sale.

"Just give me the slip to sign," Jason snapped.

"Aren't you in the Christmas spirit?" the young man said, undaunted by Jason's scowl.

After he left the art store, he passed a jewelry store, and as though a hand pulled him inside, he entered. "Do you have engagement rings?" he asked, then was horrified to hear his voice crack. He cleared his throat. "I mean—"

"That's all right," the man said, smiling. "It happens all the time. Now, if you'll just step over here."

Jason glanced down at the tray of diamond solitaires in front of him with contempt, then back up at the man. "You have a vault in this store?"

"Oh, I see, you're interested in our security system," the man said nervously, and from the way his hand was hidden under the counter, he looked as though he were about to push a button and summon the police.

"I want to see some of the rings you have in the vault."

"I see."

Jason could tell that the stupid little man didn't see at all. "I want to buy something much nicer than any of these. I want to buy something expensive. Understand?"

It took the man a moment to stop blinking, but when he did, he grinned in a way that Jason found quite annoying, but the next moment he scurried into the back, and twenty minutes later Jason left the store with a tiny box in his trouser pocket.

Jason took Max back home at noon to allow him to nurse. Neither male recognized Amy at first, as her head was covered with pieces of aluminum foil. Max looked as though he were about to cry as he always did with strangers, but Amy's arms felt familiar, so he settled down.

"How adorable," one of the thin young men said with sarcasm, his lip curled in distaste as Amy nursed Max, every inch of her flesh hidden from view.

"Don't hit him, Mr. Wilding," Amy said without looking up.

At that, the young man looked at Jason with such interest that he went into the kitchen, but Charles was still there, and now he was cooking lunch for the whole lot of them. Finally, Jason went into his room and called Parker.

As was becoming a habit with her, she took a long time to get to the phone. He told her he wanted her to call a realtor in the surrounding areas around New York and fax him details of estates for sale. "Something suitable for a baby," he said. "And, Parker, I hope I don't have to tell you to mention this to no one, especially my little brother."

"No, you don't have to tell me that," she said, and Jason wasn't sure, but he thought he heard anger in her voice. And, oddly, she hung up before he did.

Jason took Max out to lunch. They shared a huge steak, butternut squash, and tiny green beans with almonds—and Jason had them grind the almonds so he could share them with Max. When that wasn't enough, they had crème brûlée, with burnt sugar on top and raspberries on the bottom.

After the meal, Max slept in his stroller while Jason bought more gifts for everyone. He bought things for David, for his father, for Amy (a new bathrobe and four cotton nightgowns that buttoned from neck to hem), and, on impulse, something for Parker. He got her a pen-and-pencil set. When he saw a cookware store, he bought Charles something the clerk assured him was unique: tiny ice cream molds in the shape of various fruits. For Max he bought a set of hand puppets and a bubble gun that ran on batteries and produced huge, glorious soap bubbles.

Feeling quite proud of himself, Jason headed home with a car full of gaudily wrapped packages.

When he entered the house, a tired, fussy Max in his arms, Amy stood there in all her glory, the product of many hours of work—and Jason didn't like what he saw. She looked beautiful in the long ivory column of satin that was the dress. It was rather plain, strapless, tight about Amy's prodigious bosom, then opening to a pleat in front and flowing to the floor.

She was gorgeous, true, but she looked too much like all the women he had dated for so many years. This was a woman who didn't need any man; she could have them all if she wanted them. And she was a woman who knew she was beautiful. She had to know it if she looked like that.

Looking at Jason's face, Amy laughed. "You don't like it, do you?"

"Sure. It's fine. You're a knockout," he said without expression.

"Meow," said one of the thin men. "Jealous, are we?"

Jason gave the man a quelling look, but the thin hairdresser just turned away, laughing.

"It doesn't matter," Amy said, but her voice said that it did matter and that she was hurt by Jason's lack of enthusiasm. "David's the one who counts, since I'm going with him."

"Ooooh, the kitten has claws," the thin man said.

"Lance!" snapped the head hairdresser. "Shut up. Let the lovebirds alone."

At that Amy laughed, but Jason put Max on the floor, then went to plop down heavily on the old sofa in the living room. Everyone else was in the kitchen, either eating or cleaning up and putting supplies away. Amy followed her son and Jason into the living room.

"Why don't you like it?" she asked, standing before him.

Jason had a newspaper in front of his face and didn't put it down. "I don't know where you got that idea. I told you that you look great. What else do you want?"

"For you to look at me and say that. Why are you angry with me?" There were almost tears in her voice.

Jason put the newspaper down (it was three weeks old anyway) and looked up at her. "You look great, really, you do. It's just that I think you look better the way you are naturally." He thought that would appease her, but it didn't, and he watched her frown, then turn away to look at Max as he sat on the floor chewing on a small cardboard box.

"He'll bite off a piece and choke on it," Amy said, letting Jason know that he wasn't being a very good nanny. Lifting her heavy satin skirt, she strode out of the room, leaving Jason to wonder what he had done wrong.

"Women," Jason said to Max, who looked up and gave him a grin that showed all four of his teeth.

Thirty minutes later David arrived with a flat velvet box, a dozen white roses, and Jason's limo. "I knew what the dress looked like," David was saying, "but then everyone everywhere knew what the dress looked like, and, well, Dad and I thought pearls might look nice with it. They aren't real, but they look good."

With that, he opened the box and revealed a six-strand choker with a clasp of carved jade surrounded by diamonds. And Jason knew very well that the pearls and the diamonds were quite real. And, he had no doubt what David had paid for them.

"I've never seen anything so beautiful," Amy gasped.

"They're nothing compared to you," David answered, and Jason had to repress a groan.

But maybe he didn't do well at repressing it, because Amy said, "Don't mind him. He's been like that since he got back. I think he believes I should wear a straw hat and calico."

"It's his image of Abernathy," David answered, speaking about Jason as though he weren't standing there and glaring at the two of them.

"And we should be attending a hayride, not a ball," Amy said, laughing.

David held out his arm as though they were

square-dancing and Amy took it. "Now claim your partner and do the Strutter's Walk," he said, sounding like a square dance caller.

"Yee haw!" Amy kicked the back of her skirt out of the way as she followed David around the room.

"All right, that's enough," Jason said, grimacing at the two of them. "You've had your fun, now get out of here."

"We should go, David," Amy said. "I'll probably fall asleep by nine o'clock."

"Not while *I'm* with you, you won't," David said mischievously as he leered down the front of her gown.

"The only thing you're going to get there is dinner."

"I'm a hungry man," David answered, making Amy giggle.

"I think that 'man' is the key word here," Jason said ominously. "You need to remember that Amy is a mother and that she needs—"

"You are not my father," Amy snapped, "and I don't need to be told—"

"I'm ready, how about you?" David said loudly. "And the limo is waiting. Shall we go?"

Once they were in the car and Amy was staring out the window, David said, "What was that all about?"

"What was what about?"

David gave her a look that told her she knew exactly what he was talking about.

"I don't know. Mr. Wilding and I have gotten along beautifully, but ever since the hairdressers arrived this morning, he's been insufferable. He stomped around like a bear and made the whole staff, who were so nice to me, run and hide in the kitchen. Charles says the most devastating things about him, and—"

"Like what? What does Charles say?"

"That Mr. Wilding once walked past a cow and immediately turned it into frozen steaks. But he also says that Mr. Wilding can boil a kettle of water by looking at it. And, oh, other things. I don't understand why Mr. Wilding's been so nice these last days, but today he's so awful. If the people who came today are gay, shouldn't Mr. Wilding be nice to them since he's gay too?"

"It doesn't always work that way," David said, but he could hardly speak because of the effort it took not to laugh. "Ah, what else did Charles have to say?"

Amy looked at David, blinking for a moment. "Oh, you mean, like that Mr. Wilding doesn't sweat, doesn't excrete anything, if you know what I mean." She turned away for a moment to hide her red face. "That Charles really does have a wicked tongue."

David was about to burst with laughter. "And

what about women? Surely Charles must have said something about Jason's women."

"You mean his men, don't you?"

"Yeah, sure. Whatever. What did Charles say?"

"Marble goddesses. Charles said that if a woman, ah, burped around him, Mr. Wilding would die of apoplexy. But, David, that's not true. Last night Mr. Wilding helped me get rid of a migraine. He stayed with me for a very long time, rubbing my temples until I fell asleep."

"He did what? I think you should tell me everything."

When Amy finished, David was looking at her in astonishment. "I've never heard of Jason doing anything like that. He's . . ."

"He's a very unusual man, is what he is," Amy said, "and I can't figure him out at all. I just trust Max's judgment and Max adores him. And I think Mr. Wilding adores Max too."

CHAPTER THIRTEEN

"YOU REALLY ARE THE MOST WICKED MAN," AMY said, laughing. They were in Jason's damaged car, driving back to the old, drafty place they called home. "I can't believe you managed to get a date *and* tickets to an event like that on such short notice. And *what* a date! Although I can't say that she seemed to like you very much."

"Parker? I mean Miss Parker? She likes me fine. And I got a date because I'm a damned good-looking guy, in case you haven't noticed."

"Mmm. Well, you're passable, when you aren't scowling, that is. So tell me *everything*."

"My hair is natural, my teeth are all mine—"

"No, idiot," she said, laughing more. "Tell me about Miss Parker. Whatever did you say to make her laugh like that?"

"Laugh? I don't remember her laughing," Jason said seriously.

"She is a bit solemn, isn't she? But you danced with her and she laughed. I heard her. I *saw* her and it was a real belly laugh."

He gave a one-sided grin. "Jealous, are you?"

"So help me, if you don't tell me, I'll . . ."

"You'll what?"

"Tell Charles to stop sending food over and I'll cook for you."

"You are a cruel woman. Okay, I'll tell you, but all I did was ask her if she was one of those women who falls in love with her boss." When Amy looked at him in puzzlement, he continued. "You know how some women pine away for their handsome, rich, powerful boss, so they never marry, never have a family of their own?"

"I've seen that in movies but never in real life," Amy said. "But I don't understand. Who is the owner of Baby Heaven?"

"Some guy I know."

"Ahhh, I see."

"See what?"

"That you're not going to tell me. Is her boss gorgeous?"

"Makes that Gibson guy look like a troll."

"Somehow, I doubt that. But, anyway, Miss Parker found the idea of being in love with her boss hilarious?"

Jason frowned. "Actually, she did."

"So why does that bother you?"

"Who said it bothers me?"

Amy threw up her hands in helplessness. "I can't imagine why I thought it bothered you. But then maybe it was just because when she laughed and walked off the dance floor, you stood there for a full two minutes glaring at her back. I was afraid her hair was going to catch on fire."

"And well it should!" Jason snapped. "Her boss has been good to her, paid her well for years."

"Oh."

"What is that supposed to mean?"

"Nothing. Just that money is no substitute for personal feeling."

"Maybe he didn't want personal feeling; maybe he just wanted a competent assistant!"

"What are you getting so angry about? How long did she work for him?"

"Several years. And what do you mean, 'did' work for him? She still does as far as I know."

"Well, it won't be for long."

"And what does that mean?" he asked as he swung into the driveway and parked beside Mildred's Oldsmobile. He knew he was being irrational and short-tempered, but he couldn't help it. The evening hadn't gone as he'd hoped. Now that the ball was over, he didn't know what he'd been hoping for, but maybe he'd wanted, even expected,

Amy to . . . What? he asked himself. Declare undying love for him?

Over the course of the evening he'd tried to keep his attention on Parker, and the others at the party, but he'd only had eyes for Amy. But she had seemed oblivious. But David had noticed.

"What were you and David arguing about?" Amy asked as he helped her out of the car, taking care that her satin dress didn't touch the gravel of the drive. She'd looked divine tonight. Pearls and white satin suited her. He gave a little smile at her back as he thought of the engagement ring burning a hole in his pocket. Maybe tonight he'd give it to her.

Inside the house, Mildred was holding a fretful Max, and when the baby saw Amy, he leaped into her arms, and for a while the two of them held on to each other as though they'd been separated for years.

"So how did it go?" Mildred whispered as she and Jason stood by the front door.

"All right," Jason answered. "Nothing special." He wasn't going to tell the town gossip anything.

"If nothing unusual happened, how come *you're* bringing Amy home when she left with your brother?"

"Sssh," Jason warned. "Amy thinks David and I are cousins."

Mildred turned her head sideways to look up at him. The weight of her hair moved to one side, and for a moment Jason thought she must have astonishingly strong neck muscles to hold something like that up.

"Have you thought about what Amy's going to say when she's told that you've played her for a fool?"

"It's not quite like that," Jason said stiffly.

"Oh? You don't think buying a baby store, then telling her all that furniture cost two hundred and fifty dollars isn't assuming she's an idiot?"

"She believed it, and that's all that counts."

Amy had taken Max into his bedroom, so he and Mildred were alone in the room. "Look, I'm planning to tell her tomorrow."

Mildred gave a low whistle. "Merry Christmas, Amy."

"Don't you think you should go home?"

"I think *you* should go home," Mildred retorted. "I think Amy should be given a fair chance at a man and not be involved in this sick game you and David are playing."

"Sick?" he asked, one eyebrow raised. "Isn't that a bit strong?"

"So, Jason, how are the men in your life?"

At that, he opened the front door. "Thanks for taking care of Max."

Mildred gave such a great sigh that Jason almost thought he saw the curtains by the door move, but the older woman's hair stayed perfectly in place. "Don't say I didn't warn you."

"I consider myself warned." The second he closed the door, Amy stuck her head around the bedroom door.

"Clear?" she whispered.

"Yes," Jason answered, grinning. "You can come out now."

She was wearing her old bathrobe, and Jason thought of the new one wrapped and placed under the tree. "How's Max?"

"Asleep and snoring. He was exhausted, poor baby."

"I know how he feels," Jason said.

"Oh," Amy said flatly. "You want to go to bed?"

He couldn't help teasing her as he yawned. "Yeah. I'm bushed." He pulled the tie to his tux open and gave a greater yawn.

"Me too," she said, but she didn't sound tired.

"On the other hand," Jason said slowly, "we could build a fire—if we can get the damper open—make some popcorn and you can tell me what you enjoyed most about the evening."

"You fire. Me pop," she said before she hurried off to the kitchen.

In record time a blazing—if smoky—fire was going and Amy and Jason were in front of it, a huge tub of buttered popcorn and glasses of ice water between them.

"So what were you and David fighting about?" Amy asked.

Jason groaned. "Not that again. What did you think of that blonde's dress?"

"I think she'll be a good mother."

Jason looked at her in consternation.

"With a set like that she'll be able to produce a *lot* of milk," Amy said, deadpan, making Jason smile.

"All plastic."

"And how would you know?" she asked.

"I danced with her, remember?"

Laughing, Amy said, "So what made David leave early so that you ended up taking me home? And don't you *dare* tell me it was an emergency at the hospital."

"Difference of opinion," Jason said tightly.

For a moment Amy stared at the fire. "All night, I felt as though all of you knew something that I didn't," she said quietly.

"It's Christmas and we all have secrets."

"Right. Stupid little Amy can't be told."

"What are you talking about?"

"Oh, nothing. What were you and my mother-in-law whispering about?"

"Are you going paranoid on me?" Jason asked, trying to distract her. "Did you have a good time?"

"Yes," she said hesitantly.

"But?" he asked as he ate a mouthful of popcorn.

"Something was missing tonight."

"And what could have been missing? You were the most beautiful woman there."

"You're sweet. No, it was something else. It was . . . Well, for one thing, there was the woman in the restroom."

"What woman? She say something catty to you?"

"No, actually, she talked about you."

Jason took a while before speaking. "Does she know me?"

"Would it be a crime if she did?"

"Depends on what she knows. What did she say?"

"That you'd break my heart."

"Ah," Jason said flatly. When he said no more, Amy looked at him in the firelight.

"Do you often break women's hearts?" she added softly.

"Every day of the week. Twice on Sunday."

Amy didn't laugh. "What's going on?"

"What do you mean, 'what's going on'?"

Suddenly, Amy put her face in her hands and began to cry. "Stop it! Just stop it! I *know* something is going on, but no one will let me in on the joke. Sometimes I think *I* am the joke."

"The woman in the restroom upset you, didn't she?"

At that, Amy got off the floor and started toward the bedroom. "I'm going to bed," she said, and her voice was without emotion.

Jason caught her before she reached the door, his hand closing about her arm. "Why are you angry with me?"

"Because you're part of it. Tonight . . . Oh, you'd never understand."

"Try me."

"It was all so beautiful. I know it's a cliché, but I felt like Cinderella. Poor little Amy Thompkins with her leaky house at a real live ball. Everyone looked so beautiful. And the jewels! If they'd lit one candle in the middle of the room, the sparkle of the diamonds would have illuminated the whole place. It was all like a dream, a fantasy."

Gently, Jason led her back to the living room to sit on the sofa. "But what was wrong?"

"I felt a sense of . . ." Looking up at him, there were tears in her eyes. "I felt a sense of doom. That's it. I feel that something awful is about to happen and I have no way to stop it. Everything has been so wonderful lately and my mother warned me to be suspicious of good things. She said we were put on this earth to suffer and if something good happened, it was the work of the devil."

"That isn't always right," Jason said softly, then he lifted her hand and kissed her fingers one by one.

"What are you doing?" she asked suspiciously.

"Making love to you."

Angrily, she jerked her hands from his and tried to get up, but he blocked her way.

"Would you mind?!" she said, her voice full of steel.

"Yes, actually I do mind." Again he lifted her hand and began to kiss the back of it.

"I changed Max's dirty diaper with that hand and didn't wash," she said to the top of his head.

"You know how much I love the kid," he said, but didn't stop kissing. In spite of herself, Amy smiled; then she put both hands on his shoulders and pushed. When he was upright she glared into his eyes. "You're gay, remember?"

"Actually, I'm not. David lied." Jason went back to kissing her hand; Amy pushed him away, and her expression said it all.

"All right," he said, leaning back against the old sofa. "David wanted me to stay with you and baby-sit Max so he could take you out. He's in love with you."

When Amy said nothing, he turned to look at her. She had the oddest expression on her face. "Go on," she said.

"David didn't want any hanky-panky between us, so he told you I was gay."

"I see. Is that it?"

"More or less," he answered, then bent down to get his glass of ice water and drank deeply.

"So you two have been fighting over me?" she asked softly.

Jason swallowed. "Well, actually . . . Well, yes, we have. I was just supposed to keep Ian Newsome away, but I . . ."

"You what?"

"I fell in love with you and Max," he said, but he stared at the fire, not at her. He'd never before told a woman he loved her. He had a feeling that most of the women he'd known in New York would have responded by getting a calculator and figuring their cut of his wealth. When Amy said nothing, he turned to look at her. Her oval face was pale and she was staring straight ahead.

"What else have you lied to me about?" she asked softly.

"Nothing of any consequence," he said quickly, his breath held. If she said she loved him now, when she had no idea of his wealth, he'd know forever after that she loved him for himself. Suddenly he knew his whole life could change in this moment and if he'd ever tried to sell anything, he'd better sell himself now.

"I love you, Amy. I love you and Max, and I want you to marry me. That's what David's so angry about. He wanted you for himself, so he conned me into staying with you, but Max . . . Max was a blessing from the beginning. He liked me, and you know how I adore him, and I want—"

"Oh, shut up and kiss me," Amy said, and when Jason turned and saw that one side of her mouth was turned up into a smile, he felt as though he'd been freed from slavery.

Quickly, he swooped Amy into his arms and carried her into her bedroom. He didn't need to be told that she'd want to be where she could hear her son. Our son, Jason thought. His wife; his son; his family.

"I love you, Amy," he said as he nuzzled her ear. "I love the way you make me feel. I love how you need me."

There was something about what he was saying that bothered Amy, but she couldn't pinpoint what it was, for at the moment she couldn't think much of anything. He was kissing her neck, sliding the gown from her shoulders.

It had been so very, very long since she'd been touched by a man. And she'd die before she said anything to further sully her late husband's memory, but, at the end, Billy was drunk most nights. But Jason was sober and clean and, oh, so beautiful. His long-fingered hands were moving over her body in a way she'd only dreamed of. Inch by inch he removed her robe, then her old gown, kissing as he removed her clothes. His warm hands ran up the sides of her breasts. How long it had been since her breasts had been anything but utilitarian!

"That's nice," she said, closing her eyes, letting sensation overtake her. His hands moved between her thighs, kissing and caressing.

"I like this," she said dreamily. "Does it have a name?"

"Foreplay," he said, smiling into her eyes. "Like it?"

"Oh, yes. May I have some more please?"

"I'll give you all I have," he said as he kissed her breasts.

When he entered her, Amy gasped, because, for the first time ever, she was ready for lovemaking.

"Oh, my goodness but that is nice," she said, and the way she said it made Jason laugh as he rolled onto his back and pulled her on top of him.

"Now *you* do the work."

Obviously this was a novel experience to Amy, and Jason was pleased by her expression. "A virgin mother," he murmured, his hands on her hips, guiding her.

"Don't ever stop," Amy murmured as her hips moved up and down. When she exploded against him, she collapsed, limp and sated.

"Yes," was all she could say, and feeling as secure as Max must feel in her arms, she snuggled onto his chest and let him hold her. Jason pulled the sheet over both of them, and they fell asleep in each other's arms.

A loud thud awoke Amy, and she sat bolt upright, immediately afraid that Max had fallen, but when she checked on him she saw that her son was fast asleep in his new crib. His knees were tucked up under him, his well-padded rear end stuck into the air, his head was turned toward her, drool running down the side of his mouth.

Walking into the nursery, she went to her baby, gently blotted his mouth, tucked the quilt about him, then returned to her room to fetch her nightgown. It was flung over the end of the bed, and she was careful not to wake Jason as she put it on. But she needn't have worried, for both her men were in what she called "coma sleep"—you could perform major surgery and they'd not know it.

Smiling, Amy bent and kissed Jason's forehead, then put on her old robe and went into the living room. For a moment she was disoriented, as the Christmas lights were on and the pile of gifts was as tall as the sofa.

"Santa Claus," she read as she looked at tag after tag on the white packages.

"David," she whispered, then felt a bit guilty at the way she'd treated him at the ball. She went into the kitchen to fix herself a cup of tea. She was wide awake, and now, in the middle of the night, when Max was asleep, was the only time she had to think. As the water boiled and she got out a cup and a tea bag, she thought about the ball. She was sure that every other woman in the world would have loved the ball, but Amy had been bored by it. Sure, it was lovely and everyone had looked splendid, but all she'd wanted to do was go home to

Jason and Max. There she was wearing a Dior gown and pearls—fake but who could tell?—and all she really wanted was to be home in her old bathrobe with her son and her gay boarder.

Everyone at the ball knew everyone else, and of course everyone knew Dr. David, so Amy had had time to sit alone at a table with a nonalcoholic drink and think—and remember. In all her life she didn't think she'd had a happier, more secure feeling than she'd had in the last few days. Every minute had been an adventure. Since David had entered her house with his gorgeous gay cousin, Amy's life had been turned upside down. Mr. Wilding—or Jason, as she called him to herself—seemed to have a magic wand he could wave to fix anything. It wouldn't surprise her to wake up one morning and find that the roof over the dining room had been repaired.

And, now, tonight, she thought with a sigh. Tonight he'd said he loved her, told her he wasn't gay, said . . . Oh, she couldn't remember all she'd heard or felt tonight. All she knew was that this ball had changed her life.

When the kettle boiled, she poured hot water over the tea bag, liberally added milk, then went into the living room to sit and look at the Christmas tree. Now she could smile when she remembered how she'd felt tonight when she'd looked up to see Jason walk in with that gorgeous redhead on his arm. At that moment if someone had handed Amy a shotgun, she could have blown a hole through Miss Cherry Parker's tiny never-had-a-baby waistline. Better yet, Amy thought, she'd have liked to fire a cannon and hit both of them.

When Jason and that woman sat down at the table with Amy and David, she wasn't in the least surprised. What had surprised Amy was the instant animosity that came from mild-mannered David. Immediately, the two men had said things to each other under their breath, things Amy couldn't hear.

Taking a deep breath, Amy had leaned toward the tall, divinely beautiful Miss Parker and said, "What will happen to Baby Heaven now?"

The woman was closer to Jason, so maybe she could hear what the two men were saying. And maybe the fact that she could hear and Amy couldn't was why Amy decided to engage her in conversation.

"Baby Heaven?" the woman said, reluctantly pulling away from where Jason and David were engaged in furious conversation.

"Where you work," Amy said loudly. "That *is* where I saw you, isn't it?"

"Oh, yes, of course."

The two men stopped arguing for a moment, and Miss Parker turned to Amy. "What was it you asked me?"

Amy cleared her throat. "What will happen to

Baby Heaven now that all the merchandise is sold? Will you have a job?"

"Oh, yes." The woman kept looking at the two men to see if they were going to start arguing again.

"So you *will* have a job," Amy said loudly, demanding the woman take her attention away from the men.

"Job? Oh, yes. The owner has many businesses. Baby Heaven is just one of them." She looked back at the men, who'd started again.

"I see," Amy said even louder. "Where will you work? Abernathy or somewhere else?"

"New York," the woman said over her shoulder, her eyes and ears on the men.

"Ah, so you're slumming. I thought so. You have the look of a big city about you. Ever seen a tractor, Miss Parker?"

The woman turned and gave her full attention to Amy. "Mrs. Thompkins, I grew up on a farm in Iowa. I was driving a harvester at twelve years old because I was nearly six feet tall even then and I could reach the pedals. By the time I was sixteen I was cooking daily for twenty-three ravenous farmhands. So tell me, Mrs. Thompkins, how many calves have *you* delivered?"

Amy gave the woman a weak smile and excused herself to go to the restroom. So much for her attempt at being catty. "Better stick to what I do best," she said to herself, then wished with all her might that she knew what that was.

It was in the restroom that she had the strangest encounter. A woman with long dark hair, expertly pulled back into a chignon, wearing a slinky red satin dress, was putting on lipstick to match her dress. When she saw Amy, she nearly jumped, and for a moment Amy thought she was supposed to know the woman. It's the dress, she told herself. Not too many Diors in Kentucky, but when Amy left the stall, the woman was still there and she made no pretense that she was doing anything except waiting for Amy. And, for some reason, Amy wanted to bolt. She had her hand on the door before the woman spoke.

"So, you're with Jason Wilding."

Amy took a breath and straightened her spine before turning back to the woman. "Not really. I'm with Dr. David, his cousin. Miss Parker is with Jason." And Amy had no doubt that Miss Parker could handle anything this woman was about to dish out.

"Oh? That's not what I saw and heard," the woman said. "From what I could hear David and Jason were fighting over *you.*"

"What did they say?" Amy said before she thought to control her tongue.

"Are both those men in love with you?" the woman asked as she looked Amy up and down.

At that Amy relaxed, smiled, and decided to wash her hands. "Oh, yes," she said. "They want to fight a duel over me. Pistols at dawn. Or maybe they'll use swords."

The woman turned back to the mirror. "More like scalpels and cell phones."

Amy laughed and decided the woman wasn't predatory, as she'd first thought. "How about fax machines versus color copiers?"

"Or your Internet dialer against mine," the woman said, smiling at Amy in the mirror; then she paused for a moment. "That's some dress you're wearing. Buy it around here?"

"Hardly. I won it in a contest. It's a Dior from a shop in New York."

"Ah, I see. A contest."

Again Amy wanted to leave, but somehow, she couldn't. "Do you know Mr. Wilding?" she asked tentatively.

"Dr. David?"

Amy had a feeling the woman was teasing her. "Jason."

"Ah, *that* Mr. Wilding. I've met him. How do you know him?"

"He's living with me," Amy said brightly, then smiled smugly at the woman's look of shock. But she soon recovered.

"Living with him? Not married to him?"

Amy laughed. "You don't know him very well,

do you?" She'd love to tell the woman Jason was gay, but, on the other hand, let her think Amy had reeled in a hunk like Jason. The woman didn't answer Amy's question.

"I think I should ask how well *you* know him. And what's he doing at a dud of a thing like this?"

That snobby question made Amy's lips tighten. "Jason Wilding is here because he *likes* it here, because this state makes him happy."

At that, the woman put away her lipstick and looked at Amy in amusement. "I don't know what's going on, but a man like Jason Wilding doesn't attend some cheap affair in Nowhere, Kentucky, because it makes him *happy*. Jason Wilding only does things because they earn him more money. He's the only man on this planet who actually does have a heart of gold."

"I don't know what you're talking about," Amy said, confused. "Jason, Mr. Wilding, is staying with us, my son and me, that is, because he has nowhere else to stay and no one to spend Christmas with."

At that the woman laughed. "My sister used to be just where you are now. She too felt sorry for Jason Wilding and she took him in, and he repaid her by— Oh. I can see you're not going to believe anything I say, so maybe I'll just send you something."

"No, thank you," Amy said as she put her nose in the air. But the woman wasn't listening as she withdrew a tiny cell phone from her evening bag and began to dial.

Amy didn't wait to hear half of the conversation but rushed back to the table with the intention of telling either Jason or David about the woman, but when she got there, the table was empty.

"What did I expect?" she said aloud. "That they'd all be worried about why I'd taken so long?"

"*I* was worried and I don't even know you," said a handsome man standing about six inches away from her. "What a beautiful . . . necklace," he said, but he wasn't looking at Amy's pearl necklace; he was looking down her cleavage. "Are they real?"

"As real as mother's milk," she said, smiling up at him, and he laughed.

"Would you like to dance? Or would your escort die from the absence of your company?"

"Yes, her escort would die," came Jason's voice over the top of her head, and to Amy's delight she looked from one handsome, scowling face to another.

"On the count of three, draw your cell phones and *dial!*" she said.

The man looked at her in puzzlement, but Jason clamped down on her upper arm and pulled her to the dance floor.

"Where in the world were you? Is Max all right?"

"Shouldn't I ask you that, since I left him with you?"

"Mildred has him," Jason said tightly. "Who was that man and what was he saying to you?"

"That I have a nice set of pearls," she said, glancing down at her cleavage.

"Have you been drinking?"

"No, I've had two encounters with female piranhas though, so maybe I should have a drink. But then, I survived both attacks and I still have my skin."

"Amy . . ." Jason said in a warning voice. "What is going on?"

"Other than the fact that my date seems to have dumped me? And my gay nanny has turned my child over to someone else so he can attend a ball with a woman so gorgeous she puts tulips to shame? And a woman in the restroom—"

"Tulips? Why tulips?"

"I like them," Amy said, sighing. Why couldn't he stay to the point? "Why are you here?"

"Just looking out for things." He was holding her in his arms, and she had to admit that it felt wonderful.

"How did you get tickets to this event?" she murmured as her head touched his shoulder and stayed there.

"Long story," he murmured back, his cheek against the top of her head, but he didn't elaborate.

After that they danced together to one old song after another. No rock and roll that would separate partners was played at the Bellringers' Ball. When they at last returned to the table, they found a note from David saying he'd taken Miss Parker home and would Jason please escort Amy? It was a tense note and Amy felt guilty at ignoring her date, but then Jason's big hand closed around hers and he said, "Let's go home, shall we?" and the way he said "home" almost made Amy cry.

So now she was sitting on the sofa, staring at the Christmas tree lights, and wondering whether it was Jason or David who'd played Santa and put all the white wrapped gifts under the tree.

It was cool in the room, so she snuggled her feet under her, her hands wrapped around the still-warm mug. Her tenant wasn't gay, and they'd made love, and this morning was her son's first Christmas. Standing, she took a deep breath, stretched, and thought she might just go back to bed and wake Jason up and . . . Well . . .

Smiling, she started back to the bedroom, but paused because she saw a fat brown envelope on the floor by the front door. The heavy oak door had an old-fashioned brass mail slot in it, and someone had pushed the thick envelope halfway through it. Must be the thump I heard, Amy thought, then wondered who would drop a package through a door slot at two o'clock in the morning on Christmas Day.

Idly, she picked up the envelope, yawned, started to put it on the table with the broken leg that stood by the door, but curiosity got the better of her. "Probably just a particularly aggressive advertiser," she murmured as she opened the top of the envelope.

When she first pulled the papers from the envelope, she didn't know what she was seeing. They seemed to be photocopies of newspaper articles. "Entrepreneur Closes New Deal," "Wilding Buys Everything!" were some of the headlines.

"Wilding?" she said aloud, then thought of David. But what had David done to engender articles written about him? Had he saved so very many lives? By the fourth page she'd flipped, the name "Jason" began to jump out at her.

Taking the package to the kitchen, she put the kettle back on to make herself another cup of tea to sip while she read. But the kettle boiled dry, and Amy turned off the stove while she continued reading.

It was four A.M. when she finished, and she wasn't surprised when she looked up to see Jason standing in the doorway wearing only the trousers to his tux.

"Come back to bed," he said seductively, but Amy didn't move. "What's wrong?" he asked, but he didn't seem too concerned.

"You're very rich, aren't you?" she asked softly.

Jason had been heading toward the teakettle, but he paused to look at the articles spread out on the table. They were all faxes, so someone had called and had this information faxed to Abernathy.

"Yes," he said as he picked up the kettle, then filled it and put it back on the stove. When he turned back to Amy, she was wearing an expression he'd never seen before.

"Look Amy, about last night—"

She interrupted him. "Last night wasn't important. Sex isn't important, but the lies that led up to the sex are *very* important."

"I never meant to lie," he said softly. "It started out quite innocent but . . ."

"Go on," she said. "I'd like to hear this. I was told you were gay and that turned out to be a lie, but I forgave that. Of course, I admit that it was in my own selfish interests to forgive that. I was also told that you desperately needed a home over Christmas, and that seems to have been a lie too. According to what I've just read, that last one was a very *big* lie. And you certainly do date some smashing-looking women."

"Amy—" He reached out to touch her, but she lifted her palms to let him know he was to stay away.

Jason turned off the kettle, then sat down across from her. "Okay, so I lied. But when I told you I loved you, that wasn't a lie." He took a deep breath.

"Now I guess I'm to fall into your arms and we live happily ever after."

"That would be the ending I have in mind," he said with a one-sided smile.

Amy, however, didn't smile. "Who is Miss Parker?"

"My secretary."

"Oh, I see. And I guess she arranged the two-hundred-and-fifty-dollar nursery set."

"Yes," Jason said, his eyes burning into her.

But Amy kept looking at the articles. "And the contest for the dress? Was it arranged by her for you?"

"Yes."

"My, my, but you've been busy. Santa Claus should work as hard as you."

"Look, Amy, it started as something I was doing to help my brother, and—"

Her head came up. "Brother? David? Ah, yes, of course. How stupid of me. Did you two have a couple of great laughs at the impoverished widow and her half-orphaned child?"

"No. Amy, believe me, it hasn't been like that. I think you should listen to my explanation."

She leaned back in the chair, her arms folded across her chest. "Okay, so tell me."

Jason had earned a lot of money in his life because

he just didn't care about the outcome of the deal. If he won, good; if he lost, that was okay too. It was the game that he enjoyed. But now he very much cared about the outcome of this "meeting."

"My brother, David, believed he was in love with you. I say believed because last night I set him straight on that one. Anyway, he said Max was such a tyrant that—"

"Max? A tyrant?"

"Well, I mean, I didn't know how old Max was until after I accepted David's bet so—"

"Bet? You made a *wager* over me?" Her voice was rising. "You mean like a man betting the plantation on the turn of a card?"

"No, not at all," he said, but his eyes didn't meet hers. "Please, Amy, let me explain."

She waved her hand then leaned back against the chair.

"David wanted me to be Max's nanny, so to speak, so he could have some time alone with you. He bet me that I couldn't handle the job. That's all it was. And he told you I was gay so you'd let me stay here. It was that simple."

"I see. And where does the nursery furniture and the dress come into this farce?"

"You needed the things, so I, uh, I arranged for them. . . ." He trailed off at the look in her eyes.

"I see," she said again, but her facial muscles were rigid and her eyes cold.

"No, Amy, I don't think you do see. I have fallen in love with you."

"Sure you have. It says in here that you give quite a bit to charity. How gratifying it must have been to make a donation directly to the poor."

"That isn't the way it was. Well, maybe it was that way in the beginning, but it changed. I've come to love both you and Max."

"And what do you plan to do with us now?"

Jason looked bewildered. "I want to marry you."

"Of course. What was I thinking? You didn't by any chance buy me a great big diamond ring, did you?"

Based on her tone of voice, Jason started to lie but decided against it. "Yes," he said simply. "A huge diamond."

"That makes sense. That fits. I guess you've planned our futures too, haven't you?"

Jason didn't answer, just looked at her across a table covered with reprints of everything that had ever been published about him. His mind was racing as he tried to figure out who had sent these to her, but he had a suspicion. At the ball he'd seen the sister of a woman he used to date. After going out for a few weeks they had parted ways amicably. Then she had approached him several months later and wanted to begin things again. When he'd turned her down, as gently as he could, she'd flown into a rage and sworn she'd get even with him. So now, Jason wondered if the sister he'd seen last night across the room, her eyes staring at him coldly, had had these pages faxed here and had made sure Amy received them.

When Jason didn't reply to Amy's question, she continued. "Let me guess. You plan to buy Max and me a huge house within commuting distance of New York City and you plan to visit us on weekends. Maybe you'd helicopter in, right? And you'd open accounts for us everywhere so I could buy Dior any time I wanted. And Max could have all the finest toys and clothes. Nothing but the best for *your* family, right?"

For the life of him Jason could see nothing wrong with the picture she was painting.

Slowly Amy began to smile. "Sounds good to me," she said at last. "How about some tea to celebrate?"

"Yes. Please. I'd like that."

Slowly, Amy got up from the table, with her back to him, filled the kettle, and opened a few tins as she looked for the tea bags.

But Jason was so relieved he didn't pay any attention to what she was doing. "How about a summer home in Vermont?" he was saying. "We'll get some place with stone walls and acres of . . . of fruit trees."

"Sounds great," Amy said, her voice flat. But she

knew he wasn't listening to her. He was in his own little daydream of a happy, idyllic life in which he had a loving wife and child to come home to. Whenever he could find the time, that is.

"Here you are," she said, smiling.

Jason tried to take her hand and kiss it, but she pulled away to sit down at the opposite side of the table.

"Did you see the movie *Pretty Woman*?"

"Can't say as I did." He was smiling at her sweetly.

"It's about a businessman, a billionaire, who falls in love with a prostitute."

"Amy, if you're implying that I think of you as a—"

"No, let me finish. The movie was a great success, and everyone I know loved it, but—"

"You didn't."

"No, I did, but I was worried about what happened later. What would happen five years down the road when they had an argument and he threw it in her face that she'd turned a trick or two? And what about his education versus hers? His money against her lack of it?"

"Go on," Jason said cautiously. "What's your point?"

"Drink your tea before it gets cold. You and I are like the couple in that movie. You've done everything, proven everything to yourself."

"I hardly think—"

"No, it's true. You have."

"Amy, you're a lovely woman, and—"

"And women don't need to prove anything, is that right?"

"I didn't mean that."

"Look," she said, leaning toward him. "If I left here with you, you'd swallow me up like the Richard Gere character would have swallowed the young woman played by Julia Roberts."

"What?" Jason asked, rubbing his hand over his eyes. Now that the crisis had passed, he found that he was quite sleepy. Why did women always want to discuss things in the middle of the night? "Could we talk about this in the morning?"

Amy didn't seem to hear him. "Why do you think I've refused to take charity?" she asked. "Everyone knows me as the drunk's widow, but I needed to prove that I was worth more than that. I don't want Max known as the drunk's kid." She leaned toward him. "And I most certainly don't want him known as the billionaire's kid."

"I'm not a billionaire." Jason could barely keep his eyes open. The clock over the stove said five A.M. "Amy, sweetheart," he said. "Let's discuss this in the morning." Rising, he took her hand and led her back to the bedroom, where he removed her robe then held the covers back from the bed. When she was under the covers, he slipped in beside her and snuggled her in his arms. "Tomorrow we'll go over all of this, I promise. I'll explain everything, and we can talk about all the movies you want. But right now I—" He broke off to give a jaw cracking yawn. "Now I . . . love you . . ." He was asleep.

Beside him, Amy took a deep breath. "I love you too," she whispered. "At least I think I do, but right now I have an obligation that is more important than my love for a man. I'm Max's mother, and I have to think of him first before my own needs."

But there was no reply from Jason.

When Amy saw that he was asleep, she angrily threw back the covers and stood, glaring down at him. "It takes more than a private helicopter to be a father," she said quietly, then turned on her heel and went to the hall closet, where she pulled out an old duffel bag; then, without realizing what she was doing, she began to throw clothes into it. "To be a father, Jason Wilding, you need to be a teacher as well as a money provider," she said under her breath. "And what would *you* teach him? To *buy* whatever he wants? To lie his way into a woman's heart? Would you teach him that he can do any devious, underhanded, sly thing he wants to a woman, then all he has to do is say 'I love you,' and those three words erase all the lies?" She leaned very close to his sleeping face. "Jason Wilding, I don't *like* you. I don't like the way you use your money to trick people, to connive behind their backs. You have treated me, Max, and, actually, this whole town with contempt."

The only reply she received was that he rolled to his other side and kept on sleeping.

Drawing back, she looked down at him, and suddenly, she was calm and she knew what she had to do. "Max and I aren't for sale. Unless the currency used is good deeds," she said as she almost smiled. "I'm going to leave now, but please don't look for me, because even if you find me, you still won't be able to buy me."

With that she turned away and went into her son's room.

CHAPTER FOURTEEN

ONE YEAR LATER

"MR. EVANS TO SEE YOU, SIR," MRS. HUCKNALL SAID to Jason's back.

Jason didn't bother to turn around, but gave a nod as he continued staring out the floor-to-ceiling windows. Manhattan lay thirty stories below, the people and cars looking like toys. He didn't know why he still bothered hiring the private detectives. Twelve months ago his whole life revolved around the reports of the first one he'd hired. The reports were called in daily, and Jason took the calls wherever he was. But when the detective could find no trace of Mrs. Amy Thompkins and her baby son, Jason had fired the man and hired someone else.

In the last year he'd hired and fired more detectives than he could count. He'd tried everyone from sleazy guys whose ads promised to catch any cheating husband to men retired from Scotland Yard. But no one could find the single woman and her little boy.

"You have nothing to go on," he'd been told again and again—and it was true. First of all, there were no photos of Amy past the age of twelve. Mildred, her mother-in-law, had taken pictures of her grandson, but Amy wasn't in them. The people in Amy's hometown said that the house Amy had grown up in burned down the week after Amy's mother's death, so maybe all the pictures of her had been destroyed then. Maddeningly, Amy seemed to have been absent every time photos were taken for the high school yearbook.

The detectives said that all she had to do was go to some two-bit lawyer in some one-horse town and change her name. The lawyer would run the announcement in some local rag sheet and, "Not even God would read it," one detective said. And with a new name, Amy could be anywhere. America was full of single women with kids and no fathers.

One by one, Jason fired each man; the truth was too painful to hear. So now he'd spent a whole year paying people to look for one woman and one child and they'd come up with nothing.

Jason heard the current detective enter the room, but he didn't bother to turn around. It wasn't until the man cleared his throat that Jason whirled about. "What are *you* doing here?" he snapped, for David stood there.

"Wait!" David said as Jason was about to press the button that called his secretary into the office. "Please, five minutes; that's all I ask."

Jason moved his finger off the buzzer, but by his stance, he wasn't softening. "Five minutes, no more. Say it, then get out."

Instead of opening his mouth to speak, David thrust his hands in his trouser pockets and walked about the room. "I always hate your offices," he said conversationally. "They're always so cold, all that glass and these pictures! Who chooses them for you?" When he looked back at his brother, Jason was scowling.

"Four minutes," Jason said.

"Want to see pictures of my wedding?"

Jason didn't answer, just glared at his brother. A year before on that horrible morning when Jason woke up to find Amy and Max gone, he and David had had a fight in which they'd nearly killed each other. David blamed Jason for everything, saying he drove Amy and Max out into the snow, with no means of support, no friends or family, no help of any kind.

And Jason blamed his brother for having started it all in the first place. But in spite of the argument, Jason had a search party looking for Amy within an hour of waking up. But by then the trail was already cold. A woman traveling alone with a baby was too common a sight and an unremarkable one; no one had noticed either of them.

It was after the disappearance that the real rift between the brothers came, because Parker took David's side. Jason's loyal secretary, a woman who had been Jason's right arm for years, was suddenly his enemy. For the first time since he'd known her, she'd stood against her employer and told him what she thought of him.

"No wonder she left you," Parker had said, quietly at first, but her voice came from deep within her and carried more volume than the loudest siren. "You have no heart, Jason Wilding. You look at people as goods to be bought and sold. You think that because you pay me a high salary, you can treat me as though I'm not human. You thought because you bought Amy's baby a roomful of furniture that she would fall down at your feet in everlasting gratitude. But the only thing men like you foster is greed. You made me want more and more money from you until I was beginning to despise myself.

"But I need my self-respect back, so I'm leaving your employment."

Nothing in the world could have stunned Jason more than Parker's defection. When he turned away, he expected never to hear from her again, but that was far from what actually happened, for three months later he received an invitation to the wedding of Dr. David Wilding and Miss Cherry Parker.

To Jason, still trying his best to find Amy and Max, the marriage seemed the ultimate betrayal. Now, he could hardly bear the sight of his brother. If David hadn't called him and made up that lie that their father was dying . . . If David hadn't thought he was in love with a widow with a baby . . . If Jason hadn't fallen for David's hard-luck story . . .

"What do you want?" Jason demanded, glaring at his brother.

"Family, that's all. Getting married, settling down, changes a man. I want you to come to Christmas dinner. Cherry's a fine cook."

"She has a nice kitchen to do it in," Jason said, remembering the bill he'd received for the addition of a fabulous kitchen to his father's house. And that was another thing: his chef had left him to try to start his own business in gourmet baby food. Jason had tried to be pleased when he heard that Charles wasn't doing very well, but instead he felt bad for his former cook. Charles's cocky arrogance didn't go over too well with bankers, and he'd had no luck in finding the funds to back his business.

"Is that still bothering you?" David snapped. "Damnation, but I'll pay you back for the bloody kitchen. I don't know how, but I'll do it."

Suddenly, David sat down on a chair across from Jason, who was standing rigid behind his desk. "What do you want from all of us? What do you want from *life?* Do you think that if you find Amy, she's going to come back to you and live inside your golden cage? She didn't want to be a prisoner, no matter how beautiful the surroundings. Can't you understand that? Can't you forgive her? Forgive *me?*"

Jason didn't move, but stood still as he stared at his brother. How could he explain that for a few short days he had been happy? Plain, old-fashioned *happy.* During his time with Amy and Max, it had given him pleasure to buy things for other people, to do things, to listen, to laugh. Amy had a way about her—

He had to cut himself off from thinking about her or he'd go crazy. There wasn't a day that went by that he didn't think about how old Max was now. He was walking by now, maybe even talking.

Or maybe he wasn't. For all he knew, Amy and Max were dead. There were some awful people out there in the world and—

"I can see that you won't give up," David said as he stood. "But then, that's what makes you strong. And makes you weak. Look, it's Christmas Eve and I need to fly home. I want you to come with me, and—"

"I have plans," Jason said, glaring at his brother.

Tonight his apartment would be full of people, for tonight was the anniversary of the last time he'd seen Amy and Max. Tonight he was going to drink champagne until he was drunk, and tomorrow he was not going to wake up alone.

"All right, I tried," David said as he started for the door. "If you need us you know where we are." He started to say more, but at the stony look on his brother's face, he shrugged, then walked to the door. But he paused with his hand on the knob. "I know you're still grieving for Amy and Max, but there are other people in this world. There are even other children." When Jason made no reply, David sighed and left the office.

Jason buzzed his secretary. "Call Harry Winston's and have them send me a selection of engagement rings."

"Engagement?" Mrs. Hucknall said.

"Yes!" he snapped, then punched the button to cut her off.

CHAPTER FIFTEEN

"OH, JASON, DARLING," DAWNE PURRED AS SHE rubbed her perfectly toned body against his. "The party is perfect." Somehow, she made the word sound like "Purrrrrfect." "I have never seen so many famous people in one room before."

Jason sat on the chair in silence as he sipped what had to be his fifth glass of champagne and looked at all the people. They were indeed famous and rich, he thought, as well as beautiful. The women had that glossy sheen that came from many hours spent in beauty salons the world over. Their skin and hair glowed with health and cosmetics that cost more than the resources of several small countries combined.

"What's wrong with you?" Dawne asked, a slight frown marring her perfect forehead, although Jason knew that it hadn't been perfect when she was born. It had been "lifted," as most of her had been lifted and augmented. She looked about twenty-seven, but Jason chuckled as he realized that it wouldn't surprise him to find out that Dawne was seventy-five years old.

"Why are you looking at me like that?" she asked. She was perched on the arm of his chair, her long, lean, well-muscled thigh within reaching distance.

"I was wondering how old you are."

Dawne almost choked on her drink, and he could see spots of anger growing on her perfectly made-up cheeks. "You're in a mood tonight, aren't you?" she said, her lips tight. "Why don't you get up and talk to your guests?"

Suddenly her face brightened, as though she wouldn't allow herself to get angry with him. "I know what would cheer you up. How about if I give you your Christmas gift now?"

"I have enough ties," he said.

"No, silly, it's not a tie; it's . . ." Leaning over so her breasts were against his shoulder, she whispered her plans for seduction.

Drawing back, Jason gave her a small smile. "Don't you think I should stay out here with my guests?"

At that, he could see a look of hurt in her eyes. She got up and walked away, leaving him alone.

When she was gone, Jason didn't know whether to be glad or to feel even more alone than he usually did. Damn his brother, he thought yet again. He'd been doing fine until David showed up with his talk of marriage and a family. That visit, combined with its being Christmas Eve and the anniversary of Amy's disappearance, was about to unhinge him.

Jason had anticipated that tonight would be difficult, so he'd hired a well-known interior designer to put on a party in his apartment that would take his mind off his troubles. And Jason had to admit that the designer had done a bang-up job, as the party was exquisite. The decorations were magnificent, with crystals sparkling in candlelight in the designer's theme of silver and white.

The food was wonderful, each mouthful a delight. Or at least that's what Jason had been told; personally, he hadn't touched anything but the champagne.

So if everything in his life was wonderful, why was he so miserable? Sure he'd lost a woman he thought he loved, but didn't other people break up every day? And did they go into a decline that a year later still haunted them?

Jason knew that if he had any sense, he'd do what he had been advised by everyone from the detectives to his own brother and forget about finding one woman and a little boy. As one of the detectives had said, "If I had your money, I wouldn't be worried about any woman; I'd buy myself all of them." Jason had fired the man on the spot and had tried to clear the words from his head.

But now, looking at the glittering people in the glittering apartment, he remembered them. "Buy myself all of them," the man had said. And wasn't that what Amy had said, more or less? That Jason was trying to *buy* himself a family?

He signaled the waiter to refill his glass, then kept on staring at his guests. In the last year Jason had done everything he could to forget that last night with Amy. Twelve whole months of refusing to think about it, to remember it. Twelve long months of hanging on to his anger. If she'd just listened to him . . . If she had thought about his side of things . . . If she'd just been willing to wait until the morning to talk . . .

Jason drained the glass, then held it up for another refill. But tonight, in spite of the fact that he was in very different surroundings and the giant tree in the corner bore no resemblance to the one he and Amy had decorated, it was as though he were back with her.

Images came before him until he could hardly see the roomful of people. He remembered Amy laughing, Amy teasing, Amy's excitement at being able to buy her child some furniture.

The waiter started to fill Jason's glass again, but he waved him away; then Jason put his hand over his eyes for a moment. For the first time since Amy left he thought, Why didn't I listen?

His head came up, and he looked about him.

No one was looking at him. No, they were all too busy looking at each other and enjoying Jason's food and drink to give a thought to their host, who was quietly sitting in a corner and going mad.

I am going mad, he thought. For one whole year he hadn't had a moment's peace. He'd tried to carry on a life, but he hadn't been able to. He'd dated women, beautiful women, and today he'd even thought that he'd ask this latest one, Dawne, to marry him. Maybe marriage was what he needed to make him forget. Maybe if he had a child of his own . . . .

Breaking off, his breath caught in his throat. What was it David had said? There are "other children." In Jason's mind there was only one child: Max.

But he'd lost that child because he had—

Again Jason rubbed his hand over his eyes. Maybe it was all the alcohol he'd consumed; maybe it was the anniversary, but tonight he couldn't work up his usual anger at himself, at David, at the town of Abernathy, at his father, at anyone.

"She left because of me," Jason said to himself.

"Jase, come and join us," said a man to his right.

Jason recognized him as the CEO of one of the largest corporations in the world. He'd come to the party because he was afraid he was about to be fired, so he was trying to get a job with Jason. In truth, every person in the room was there because he wanted something from Jason.

Shaking his head, Jason turned away from the man. Amy left because Jason had wanted to put her in a house and leave her there. He'd wanted to take away her freedom, her free will, all while causing himself no inconvenience whatever.

It was a hard truth to look at, Jason thought, very, very hard. And if he'd succeeded in persuading Amy to marry him, where would he be tonight?

He'd be here, he thought, just as he was right now, because he would have continued to think that CEOs were important people.

And where would Amy be? he wondered, and he knew the answer. He would have bullied her into attending also. He would have told her that, as his wife, she had an obligation to attend his business parties and help him earn money.

Money, he thought as he looked about at the people in the room. The sparkle of the jewelry on them was enough to blind a person. "You'd swallow me up," Amy had said. He hadn't understood a word she'd said that night, but now he did. He could see her in this glass-and-chrome room, with its designer tree and the well-designed people, and he could almost feel her misery.

"Other children," David had said. "Other children."

Maybe he couldn't have Max or Amy, but maybe he could do something in life rather than make money.

"Other children," he said aloud.

Instantly, Dawne was at his side, and Jason looked at her as though he'd never seen her before. Reaching into his pocket, he withdrew the ring with the huge sapphire and handed it to her.

"Oh, Jason, darling, I accept. Gladly." Ostentatiously, making sure everyone in the room saw, she reached up to put her arms around his neck, but Jason gently took her wrists and put them down at her sides.

"I'm sorry I've been a bastard. I think you already know that I'm no good for you," he said.

"But, I want you to have this ring. Wear it in good health." He looked away, then looked back at her. "Unfortunately I have to cut this evening short; I've just remembered somewhere I have to be." With that he turned away from her and went into the hallway. Robert, his butler, was right behind him.

"Going out, sir?"

"Yes," Jason answered as the man held up his coat and Jason slipped his arms inside.

"And when shall I say that you'll return?"

Jason looked back at the party. "I don't think I will return. See that everyone is taken care of."

"Very good, sir." Robert then handed Jason his cell phone, something that Jason was never, ever without. Jason took the instrument, then looked at it as though he'd never seen it before.

In the next second he dropped the thing into the trash bin; then he started for the door.

"Sir!" Robert said, for the first time losing his composure. "What if there is an emergency? What if you're needed? Where can you be reached?"

Jason paused for a moment. "I need to talk to somebody who knows what it feels like to lose a child. You know that little church over on Sixty-eighth Street? Try me there."

As his butler's jaw dropped, Jason left the apartment.

CHAPTER SIXTEEN

ONE YEAR LATER

The President of the United States of America would be pleased to attend the grand reopening of the town of Abernathy, Kentucky. He has asked me to convey his particular interest in the *Arabian Nights* mural in the public library as the tales are favorites of his.

JASON READ THE LETTER AGAIN AND WAS ABOUT TO GIVE a whoop of joy and triumph—until he looked at the second paragraph, in which the president's secretary asked that the dates of the reopening ceremony be confirmed. "But that's . . ." He broke off in horror as he looked at his watch to check today's date, then glared at the calendar on his desk to reconfirm his suspicions.

"Doreen!!!" he bellowed at the top of his lungs,

and after about three minutes his secretary came wandering into his office.

"Yeah?" she said, looking at him with big, bored eyes.

Jason had long ago learned that nothing, not any intimidation on earth, could overset Doreen's complacency. Calm down, he told himself. But then he had another look at the presidential seal on the letter and tranquillity be damned.

Silently, he handed her the letter.

"That's good, isn't it? I told you I'd get him here. We got connections, me and Cherry."

Jason put his head in his hands for a moment and tried to count to ten. He made it to eight, which was a new record for him. "Doreen," he said with controlled, exaggerated calm. "Look at the dates. How far from now is the date when the president is due to arrive?"

"You need a new calendar?" Doreen asked in puzzlement. " 'Cause if you do, I can get you one from the store."

Since Doreen had been spending six thousand dollars a month on office supplies, Jason had had to cut off her charge accounts, and he did *not* want to reopen them. "No, I can read one of the ten calendars that are on my desk. Doreen, why is the president coming in a mere six weeks when the opening is planned for six *months* from now? And why does he think the library murals are about the

Arabian Nights when the painter has been commissioned to do nursery rhymes?"

"Nursery rhymes?" Doreen blinked at him.

Jason took a deep breath intended to calm himself, but instead thought of ways to murder his brother. David had, once again, conned his "wiser," older brother into something that was driving Jason insane. Doreen was Cherry Parker's sister, and David had begged and pleaded for Jason to hire her to help him supervise the rebuilding of Abernathy. At the time, Jason had readily agreed because he missed Parker and he'd never found anyone half as efficient as she was.

But Doreen was as inept at business as Parker was adept. Doreen was as inefficient, as disorganized, and as scatterbrained as Parker was perfect. Within three hours of her employment, Jason had wanted to fire her, but Parker was pregnant and she'd started crying, something that had completely disconcerted Jason, since he'd had no idea that Parker could cry.

"Can't you just keep her for a few days?" David had pleaded. "This pregnancy isn't easy for Cherry, and Doreen is her only sibling, and it would mean so much to both of us. After all, you're so good at this that you could do it without a secretary."

Jason had been flattered and, ultimately, persuaded.

That was eight months ago. Parker was still pregnant, still crying at the least thing, and Jason was still trying to work with Doreen as his secretary. If she wasn't misunderstanding everything he said, she was buying things, such as six cases of red paper clips and twelve dozen Rolodexes. "In case we run out," she'd given as an explanation. To make matters worse, she'd also made it a personal mission to help him get over Amy.

"Nursery rhymes," Jason said tiredly. "You know, 'Humpty-Dumpty,' 'Little Miss Muffet,' that sort of thing. We hired a man to paint them, and he's to start on Monday. It's going to take him three *months* to paint the whole library, but the president is coming in six *weeks* to see them. Except that the president expects to see *Arabian Nights*, not nursery rhymes."

Doreen stared blankly at him. Maybe he should call David again and see if his wife had given birth yet, for the minute Parker delivered, Doreen was out of here.

"What about the knights?" she asked at last.

"Nights? As in *Arabian Nights*? Or are you asking whether the painter will work nights?" With Doreen, one never knew.

"No, silly, knights, like in *Robin Hood*."

Jason wanted to scream. "There are no knights in *Robin Hood*." Heaven help him, but he was beginning to understand her!

"Oh," Doreen said, blinking. She was beautiful in a blank sort of way, with enormous eyes that she rimmed in black, which made them seem even larger, and she had about fifty pounds of crinkly blonde hair. The men of Abernathy nearly swooned when they saw her.

"Doreen," Jason said, this time with more urgency. "Where did the president of the United States get the idea that we were doing *Arabian Nights* murals?"

"From that man who discovered the world and rode with the Robin Hood knights," she said.

Unfortunately for him, Jason sometimes almost enjoyed trying to piece together the logic of Doreen's thinking. Now what she'd said rambled about in his head: man who discovered the world, Robin Hood, and knights. It was the name Columbus that gave him a clue. "The Knights of Columbus," he whispered, and when Doreen rolled her eyes as though she was frustrated at his slowness, he knew he was right.

The Knights of Columbus were one of the sponsors of the remodeling of the old Abernathy Library, and for some reason, Doreen had chosen them to fixate on. How she got from Knights of Columbus to *Arabian Nights* intrigued him—as Doreen's brain often did.

"What made you think the library murals were going to be about the *Arabian Nights*?" he asked softly.

Doreen gave a sigh. "Mr. Gables really likes Princess Caroline, and since she's there, of course that's what she would like."

It took Jason a moment to follow her reasoning—if it could be called reasoning. Mr. Gables owned the local pet store, which was next door to the building where the Knights of Columbus met, and Princess Caroline lived in Monaco, which sounded like Morocco, which is part of the Arab world.

"I see," Jason said slowly. "And Mr. Gables's interest in the princess made you think the library was to be painted with *Arabian Nights* stories instead of fairy tales."

"They'd look better than Humpty-Dumpty, and, besides, the president won't come to see Little Bo-peep."

With a glance at the letter, Jason had to admit that she had a point in that. "You see, Doreen," he said patiently, "the problem is that a man is flying in from Seattle to paint the murals and he'll be here tomorrow. The man has spent the last year working on the drawings for the murals, and—"

"Oh, is that what you're worried about? I can fix that," she said, then left the room.

"Here," she said when she returned a moment later. "This came two weeks ago."

At first Jason wanted to bawl her out for leaving a letter lying around for two weeks before showing it to him, but he decided to save his energy and read the letter. It seemed that the mural painter had broken his right arm and would be out of commission for at least four months.

"You aren't going to yell again, are you?" Doreen asked. "I mean, it's just a broken arm. He'll get well."

"Doreen," Jason said as he stood, glad that there was a desk between them or he might be tempted to wrap his hands about her neck and squeeze. "In six weeks the president of the United States is coming here to see a town that is months away from completion, and he wants to see murals in a library that have yet to be painted because I have no painter." At the end, his voice was rising until he was nearly shouting.

"Don't you shout at me," she said calmly. "It's not my job to hire painters." At that she turned and walked out of the room.

Jason sat down so hard the chair nearly collapsed. "Why did I give up business?" he muttered, and, once again, when he looked back on his former life, he remembered it as efficient and organized. When he'd moved everything back to Abernathy, he'd tried to take his key staff with him, but for the most part they'd laughed at him. His butler had laughed heartily. "Leave New York for Kentucky?" the man had said, highly amused. "No, thank you."

And that had been the attitude of everyone else who'd worked for him. So he'd returned to his hometown virtually alone. Or at least that's how it had felt at the time.

Jason looked at the baby pictures of Max that covered the upper right-hand side of his desk. Two years, he thought, and he'd not heard a word about either of them. It was as though the earth had opened its jaws and swallowed them whole. All he had were these photos that he'd begged from Mildred, Amy's mother-in-law, and had framed in sterling silver. Nothing but the best for his Max.

At least he still thought of the child as his. And again in this he was alone, for no one had any sympathy for him when it came to his pining away for Amy and a baby he'd known for only a few days.

"Get over it!" his father had said. "My wife died. She had no choice in leaving me, but that girl you wanted *left* you and she hasn't called since. You should take a hint and get it through your thick skull that she didn't want you and your money, so she hightailed it out of here."

"My money has nothing to do with this," Jason had said quietly.

"Yeah? Then why are you spending a fortune paying a bunch of snoops to try and find her? If she wasn't for sale when she was here, what makes you think you can buy her when she's not?"

Jason had no reply to his father's words, but then his father was the only person on earth who could reduce Jason to a naughty nine-year-old boy.

David was even less sympathetic than their father and his cure for his big brother had been to introduce him to other women. "Kentucky courtship" is what David called it, and Jason had no idea what his brother meant until the food started arriving. Single women, divorced women, women contemplating a divorce, showed up on Jason's doorstep with jars and dishes of food.

"Just thought you might like to taste my bread-and-butter pickles," they'd purr. "I won a blue ribbon at the state fair last year."

Within three weeks of his arrival, Jason had a kitchen full of every kind of pickle, jam, and chutney known to mankind. His refrigerator was always full of cakes and coleslaw.

"Do they think I'm a man or a hog to be fattened for the kill?" Jason asked one night in a bar as he looked at his brother over a glass of beer.

"A little of both. It is Kentucky, you know. Look, big brother, you ought to take one of them out. You ought to get back into life and stop mooning over what you can't have."

"Yeah, I guess so, but . . . You don't think they'll try to pickle me and enter me in the fair, do you?"

David laughed. "Maybe. Just in case, you should

try Doris Millet first. Her specialty is mulberry gin."

Jason gave a bit of a smile. "Okay. I'll try. But . . ."

"I know," David said softly. "You miss Amy and Max. But you need to get on with living. There are lots of women out there. Look at me. I was mad about Amy, but then I met Cherry, and—" He broke off because it was still a sore spot with Jason that he'd lost his magnificent secretary and was now stuck with Doreen.

So Jason had dated one female after another, and without exception, they all fell in love with his money.

"What do you expect?" his sister-in-law had snapped. "You're rich, handsome, heterosexual, and eligible. Of course they want to marry you."

Jason liked Cherry much better as a secretary than he did as a pregnant relative. He didn't need to be reminded that his greatest asset was his bank account.

"What you've done is sanctify her," Cherry said in what had become her usual tone of exasperation. She wasn't handling pregnancy well, as her body was so swollen even her nose was fat. And the doctor had put her on bed rest. "Amy Thompkins is a very nice person but not out of the ordinary. There are lots of Amys out there; you just have to find them."

"But *she* didn't want to marry me," Jason said with a sigh.

Cherry threw up her hands in exasperation. "Are you only interested in women who don't want to marry you? If that's your logic, then you should be madly in love with *me*."

"Ah," Jason said with a smile. "I can guarantee you that that's not the case."

Cherry threw a pillow at him. "Go get me something to drink. And put some ice in it. Lots of ice; then come back here and find the remote control. Oh, Lord, is this child never going to be born?"

Jason practically ran out of the room to obey her.

So now he'd been back in Abernathy for nearly a year, and it seemed to him that he'd been out to dinner with every female in the state of Kentucky, several from Tennessee, and a couple from Mississippi. But none of them interested him. He still thought of Amy, still thought of Max, at least twice an hour. Where were they? What did Max look like now?

"Amy probably has six men fighting over her," Mildred Thompkins had said just last month. "She has that endearing quality that makes men want to do things for her. I mean, look at you. You gave up everything to help her."

"I didn't give up anything, I . . ." In the eyes of a great many people his efforts to save his hometown were great and noble, but to his relatives and almost-relatives in Abernathy, Kentucky, he was simply "moonin' over a girl."

Whatever the truth was, it wasn't an attractive picture, and many times he'd vowed to remove Max's photos from his desk and do his best to get serious about one of the many females he'd dated. As his brother had pointed out, he wasn't getting any younger and if he did want a family, he should get busy with it.

But now he had other problems. In a very short time, the president of the United States was coming to Abernathy to see some *Arabian Nights* murals, and Jason didn't so much as have a painter. Out of habit, he picked up the phone and started to tell Doreen to get Mildred on the line, but he knew where that would lead. Doreen would want to know which Mildred he wanted, as though he didn't call Max's grandmother three times a week.

Jason dialed the number that he knew by heart, and when she answered, he didn't bother identifying himself. "You know some local who can paint *Arabian Nights* murals in the library and do it real fast?"

"Oh? You're asking me? You're asking someone from little old Abernathy? What happened to your fancy big city painter?"

Jason gave a sigh. The rest of the world acted like he was a saint, but the people of his hometown thought that he was doing what he should have done a long time ago, and they thought he should be doing more of it. "You know that the man was considered the best in this country and one of the top painters in the world. I wanted the best for this town, and—" He paused to calm himself. "Look, I don't need an argument this morning."

"So what's Doreen done this time?"

"Invited the president six months early and changed the murals from nursery rhymes to *Arabian Nights.*"

Mildred gave a whistle. "Is this her best yet?"

"No. She'll never top the one where she had the food delivered on the day after the three hundred guests arrived. Or when she sent the new furniture to South America. Or when she—"

"Cherry deliver yet?"

"No," Jason said, his jaw clenched. "The kid is eleven days late now, but David says maybe the dates are wrong, and—"

"What's this about the murals?" she asked, cutting him off.

Quickly, he told her the problem. In the past year in Abernathy, Mildred had been invaluable to him. She knew everyone and everything. No one in the town could so much as bat an eyelash without Mildred knowing about it. "Don't put those two men on the same committee," she'd say. "Their wives are sleeping together and the men hate each other."

"Their wives . . . ?" Jason had said. "In Kentucky?"

She just raised her eyebrows. "Don't get uppity with me, city slicker."

"But *wives?*" Jason felt that he was losing his innocence.

"You think that because we speak slowly that we're some sort of living Pat Boone movie? But then, even ol' Pat's changed his image, hasn't he?"

So now when Jason had a problem, he knew to call Mildred. "Do you know someone or not?"

"Maybe," Mildred said finally. "Maybe I do, but I don't know if this person will be . . . available."

"I'll pay double," Jason said quickly.

"Jason, honey, when will you learn that money can't solve every problem in the world?"

"Then what does he want? Prestige? The president will view his work. And considering how often Abernathy changes things, two hundred years from now, the murals will still be there. Whatever he wants, I'll pay it."

"I'll try," Mildred said softly. "I'll give it my best shot and let you know as soon as I know."

After Mildred hung up the phone, she stood still for several minutes, thinking. Despite her retort about money, she knew in her heart that the Jason who had come home to Abernathy a year ago was not the same man he was today. He had returned to his hometown with the thought that he was going to play Santa Claus and everyone in town was going to fall down and kiss his feet in gratitude. But instead he had encountered one problem after another, and as a result, he had become *involved*. He'd started out wanting to remain aloof, distant, apart from the townspeople, but he hadn't been allowed to, and she believed if the truth were told that now he wouldn't have it any other way.

Now, still staring at the phone, she smiled in memory of all the women in Abernathy who had done their best to win his hand in marriage. Or just plain, old-fashioned, win him in bed. But as far as Mildred knew Jason hadn't touched a hometown girl. What he did on his frequent trips back to New York, she had no idea, but he had been nothing but a gentleman to the women of Abernathy.

Much to their fury, Mildred thought with amusement. There wasn't a sewing circle, book club, or church meeting in three counties that didn't discuss what was going to be the outcome of Mr. Jason Wilding's moving back to Abernathy, Kentucky.

But, Mildred thought, with a smile that was growing bigger by the minute, Jason still had the photos of Max on his desk and he still talked about Amy as though he'd seen her just last week.

Mildred put her hand on the phone. Wasn't it a coincidence that Jason desperately needed a mural painter and she just happened to know someone who could paint murals?

"Humph!" she said, picking up the phone. About as much a coincidence as it was that she'd easily conned Doreen into giving her the mural painter's address in Seattle; then Mildred had written him a note saying he was no longer needed. Then Mildred had sent a letter to Jason saying the painter had broken his arm. That Doreen had taken weeks to give the letter to Jason just added to Mildred's beautifully planned scheme.

She dialed a number that was burned into her memory, then held her breath before the phone was answered, her mind full of doubt. What if she didn't need a job right now? What if she refused? What if she was still angry at Jason and David and everyone else in Abernathy for playing a trick on her? What if she had a boyfriend?

When the phone was answered, Mildred took a deep breath, then said, "Amy?"

CHAPTER SEVENTEEN

AMY LEANED BACK AGAINST THE HIGH SEAT OF THE plane, pulled her cashmere coat tighter about her, and closed her eyes for a moment. Max had finally dozed off, and it was a rare time of quiet for her.

But in spite of the quiet, or at least the roar of the plane, she couldn't sleep. Inside she was excited and nervous and jumpy. She was going to see Jason again.

Closing her eyes, she thought back to that horrible night when she'd "escaped." How noble she'd been that night! How full of telling a man that she didn't need him or his money. How full of romance she'd been, basing her life on the way she thought a movie should have ended—or would have if it had been real life.

Amy pulled the blanket back over Max, since he'd squirmed about in the airline baby cot and uncovered himself. She and Max were flying business class, so she didn't have to hold a heavy, struggling two-year-old on her lap for the whole flight.

Settling back, Amy closed her eyes again and tried to sleep, but she still saw Jason's face. Reaching down, she pulled the thick portfolio from inside her carry-on bag, opened it, and looked at the articles again. Over the past two years she'd collected everything that had been written about Jason Wilding.

He'd sold most of his businesses and become what *Forbes* magazine called America's Youngest Philanthropist. And most of his philanthropy dealt with the town of Abernathy, Kentucky.

Amy again read an article about how Jason Wilding had transformed the small, poor, run-down, dying town of Abernathy into something healthy and prosperous. The first thing he'd done was to invest heavily in the struggling baby food company, Charles and Co.

With amusement, the article told how Wilding had handed four million dollars to a tiny advertising company in Abernathy and told them to promote the new baby food on a national level. Until Jason Wilding appeared, the company had done nothing more than draw ads for local businesses for the local newspaper. But to the surprise and no doubt delight of everyone, the article said, the tiny advertising company did a good job. "Who will ever forget the TV ad of the baby with the 'yucky' face?" the article said. "Or the one with the society hostess emptying jars of Charles and Co. baby food on crackers to serve as canapés?"

The advertising campaign was a great success that year, and Charles and Co. was named as one of the fastest growing companies in the country. "And now they're going international, both in sales and in content. Who would have thought of serving beef Stroganoff to a baby?"

And all the food was made and bottled in Abernathy, Kentucky, giving thousands of jobs to a town that had once had a fifty-two percent unemployment rate. "And the few who did have jobs had them outside the town," the article said. "But Jason Wilding changed that."

There were other articles that dealt less with facts than with the philosophy of why Wilding had done what he had. "What's in it for him?" was the question that everyone wanted answered. Why would a man give up so much to gain so little? It was even rumored that Jason Wilding didn't own so much as a single share in Charles and Co. baby food, but no one believed that.

Amy put the articles down and closed her eyes. How would she react when she saw him again? Had the last two years changed him? There had been next to nothing written about his personal life, so all she knew was that he dated a lot, but still wasn't married.

"Sleep," she whispered out loud, as though she could command her mind to be still, but when it didn't work, she took out her sketch pad and began to draw. It was cold on the plane, and she'd read that the airlines kept their cabins that way to keep the passengers quiet and in their seats. Warm the cabins and the travelers would wake up and start talking and walking about. "Rather like we're lizards," Amy had thought at the time.

Mildred had told her that Jason wanted something from the *Arabian Nights,* so Amy had spent quite a bit of time looking at previous illustrations to get some ideas of what to do. Since all the stories seemed to be either about sex or extreme violence, she wondered how she was going to illustrate them for a public library.

"You can do it," Mildred had said. "And you can stand to see Jason again. He's still in love with you and Max."

"Sure he is," Amy said. "That's why he's dated nearly every woman in Abernathy, at least that's what one article said. And he didn't spend a lot of time trying to find me, did he?"

"Amy, he—" Mildred began, but Amy cut her off.

"Look, there was nothing between us back then except that he thought I was a charity case. He had such a good time playing Santa Claus to me that he decided to do it with an entire town. Have they erected a statue to him yet?"

"Amy, it's not like that. He doesn't have an easy time here. You should meet Doreen."

"Ah. Right. Remember, I only plan to be in Abernathy for six weeks. I may not be able to meet all the women he's involved with in that time."

"All right," Mildred said. "Have it your way. All I ask is that you come back here with my grandson and let me see him. Please, I beg you. You can't be so cruel as to deny a grandmother—"

"All right!" Amy acquiesced. "I'll do it. Does he know that it's me who's coming?"

"No. He has no idea that anyone knows where you are. Not that *I've* known for very long. So, tell me, did my grandson ever learn to crawl?"

"No. He went from sitting to running. Mildred, could you please let up on the guilt?"

"No. I think I'm rather good at it, don't you?"

In spite of herself, Amy smiled. "The best," she said softly. "You're the best."

So now Amy was on the plane, Max sleeping beside her. She was going back to Abernathy and she was going to see the man who had haunted her every thought for two years. But for all her thoughts, all that she'd read and been told by

Mildred, she knew that she had done the right thing in leaving Jason two years before. Maybe he hadn't changed, maybe he was still trying to buy his way into whatever he wanted, but she had certainly changed. She was no longer the innocent little Amy who was waiting for a man to come along and take care of her. Now, when she looked back on it, she thought maybe that was what she was doing when she met Jason.

But, somehow, on that early Christmas morning, she had found the courage to walk away. Now, two years later, she still marveled at the courage she'd had that night, a courage born out of fear, because she foresaw a future without freedom. She had seen a future in which she and Max and any other children she'd have would be swallowed up in the machine that was Jason Wilding.

So she'd left Abernathy on a bus and gone to New York, where she called a girl she'd gone to high school with. They'd kept in touch over the years, and she was delighted when Amy showed up. And it was this friend who'd helped Amy get into a publishing house to show her drawings to an editor, and when Amy got a job illustrating children's books, her friend helped her get an apartment and a baby-sitter for Max. Of course the pearls that David had given Amy had helped. She'd been astonished when she realized that they were real, and the money she received from the sale of them had furnished the apartment and paid four months' rent.

She'd done well, she thought as she looked down at her sketch pad. She wasn't wealthy, wasn't famous, but she was self-supporting. And Max was happy. He went to a play group three days a week, and every minute that Amy wasn't working, she spent with him.

As for men, Amy hadn't found much time for them. Between work and Max, there weren't enough hours in the day. Quite often on the weekends she and Max went out with her editor and the editor's husband, Alec, and their daughter, and Alec tossed Max around in that particularly male way and that seemed to be enough for the boy. Someday soon, Amy thought, she was going to start thinking about men again, but not yet.

Hurriedly, she began to sketch some of her ideas for the murals, and she wasn't surprised to see that every man in the pictures looked like Jason.

When the plane landed, Amy's heart was in her throat. Gently, she woke Max, who started to complain because he hadn't finished his nap, but when he saw that they were in a new place, curiosity overrode the grumpies. Once in the terminal it was difficult to hold Max, as he was determined to ride on the luggage carousel.

As promised, Mildred had a car and driver waiting for her, and his instructions were to take Amy and Max directly to her house.

But Amy had her own ideas. "We'll get out here," she said to the driver as he turned onto the main street of Abernathy. "Please tell my mother-in-law that we'll be there in an hour or so." She wanted to see the changes that she'd read about. Holding Max's hand, she walked slowly down the street and looked at each shop.

She thought she had an idea of what Jason would have done to the town, but she was wrong. She thought he'd make it into a tiny New York, with Versace boutiques and a zillion art galleries. But he hadn't. Instead, he'd merely repaired and painted what was there. And he'd removed the modernization from many of the stores. In a way, walking through town was like a step back in time—except that it wasn't quaint. It wasn't like a stage set or one of those re-creation towns they had in amusement parks.

No, Abernathy looked like what it had become: a healthy, prosperous farm town, with people bustling about and businesses doing well. Amy walked slowly, Max twisting and turning to look at everything, as he liked to see new people and new things.

Suddenly Max halted in front of a shop window, and Amy nearly tripped as he pulled her up short. In the window was a display of pinwheels, and a fan was blowing them about, round and round. Amy's first thought was that they were only pinwheels, nothing special, but she realized that to a child used to complicated, noisy toys, they were wonderful.

"Come on then," she said, and Max's face lit up with a grin.

Minutes later they emerged from the store with Max holding a shiny blue pinwheel in one hand and a candy wrapper in the other. His mouth was distorted around a huge chocolate-coated piece of dried fruit, and Amy was smiling. Home, she thought, was where the store owner gave away a free piece of candy to a bright-eyed child.

At the end of the street was the Abernathy Library. The front door was open, and there were several pickup trucks outside and workmen moving in and out of the door.

Amy took a deep breath. She was going to see Jason soon; she could feel it. Even though she'd spent little time with him, it was as though all of the town was now filled with him. Everywhere she looked reminded her of him. This is where we bought Max a pair of shoes, she thought. And this is where Jason made me laugh. And this is where—

"Shall we go in?" she asked Max, looking down at him as he sucked on his candy. "This is where Mommie is going to work."

Max gave her a nod, then looked at his pinwheel as a breeze made it twirl around.

Taking another deep breath, Amy walked up the stairs, Max beside her. At first it was too dark in the room to see anything, but as her eyes adjusted, she saw that the workmen were nearly finished. They were removing scaffolding and leaving behind clean white plaster walls ready for her murals. She could see that she was to paint across the front of the checkout desk, then up the side of the wall, over and down again. There was a great blank wall in the reading area, and she assumed that this was where the main mural was to go.

As she was looking at the walls, thinking how what she'd planned to paint would fit, out of the back came a man, a pretty blonde woman following him. As soon as she realized it was Jason, Amy stepped back into the shadows and stayed quiet. He was looking at a set of plans, the woman seeming to be content to stand beside him silently.

Now Amy stood where he couldn't see her and watched him. He looked a bit older; the creases that ran down the side of his mouth seemed to be deeper. Or maybe it was just a trick of the light. His hair was the same though: a great thick gray mane of it that grazed the back of his collar.

Damn! He was more handsome than she remembered. Damn, damn, and double damn!

When the curvy blonde leaned over him, Amy wanted to snatch the woman bald. "But I have no right," she whispered to herself, causing Max to look up at her in question. Smoothing back her son's hair, she smiled down at him, and he turned away to stare at the man standing a few yards in front of them.

Amy tried to give herself a pep talk. She was here to do a job and nothing more. A job that she needed very much. A job that . . .

Okay, she told herself. Get over it. Get over Jason. Remind yourself of what a trick he played on you. Remember every photo you've ever seen of him with a gorgeous woman draped across his arm.

She took a deep breath, tightened her grip on Max's hand, and stepped forward. Before he turned to see her, she said, "Jason, what a pleasure to see you again."

As he turned around, she held out her hand to shake. "You haven't changed at all," she said, nodding toward Doreen, who stood close beside him. "Still the ladies' man, I see." She gave a wink at Doreen as though they were bosom buddies in on some secret.

Amy was afraid to stop talking for fear that she might collapse. Jason's eyes on hers were almost more than she could bear. She wanted to throw her arms around him, and—

"Where have you been?" he demanded, sound-

ing as though she'd gone to the grocery and hadn't
come back for five hours.

"Oh, here and there. And where have you been?
As if I needed to ask." She knew she was making a
fool of herself, but the blonde was everything she
wasn't and it bothered her. Of course it couldn't be
jealousy. But Amy did wish she had a boyfriend
whose name she could drop.

"It looks as though you've done all right," he
said, nodding toward her cashmere coat with the
paisley scarf about the neck. Under it she wore a
cashmere sweater, trousers of fine wool, and boots
of the softest kid leather. Gold glowed warmly
from her ears, neck, wrists, and belt buckle.

"Oh, quite well. But as . . ." Frantically, she
looked about, then saw a bag of Arnold potato
chips. "As Arnie says, I take well to nice things."

Jason was scowling and, inside, Amy was
smiling. Her heart was racing at her lie, but then
she looked at Doreen and couldn't seem to pre-
vent herself from continuing. "Max, come here
and say hello to an old friend of mine. And
yours."

She picked up Max, who was staring at Jason
with intense eyes as though he was trying to place
him. Jason wanted to take the boy in his arms, but
instead his pride took over. What had he expected?
That Amy would someday come back into his life,
sobbing, telling him that she needed him, that the

world was a cold, cruel place and that she must have his arms to protect her? Is that what he'd hoped for? Instead, it was just as everyone had said; she'd gone on with her life while Jason had stood still and waited.

So now was he to tell her that she meant everything to him? That while she was having a mad affair with some guy named "Arnie," he had thought of her every minute of every day? Like hell he would!

Suddenly, just as he was formulating an appropriate response to Amy's introduction, Doreen flung her arm around his waist and grabbed him in a shockingly intimate way.

"Oh, honey, isn't Max just the cutest little thing?" Doreen gushed, ignoring Jason's murderously bewildered glare. "I just can't wait until we have one of our very own."

"Honey?" Amy said, and Jason was amazed to see that she looked a tiny bit shocked.

Again, the overly helpful Doreen jumped in. "Oh, that. Well, Jason doesn't like it when I call him 'honey' in public, but I keep telling him that it's okay—engaged people call each other silly names all the time."

"Engaged?" Amy barely whispered the word.

Jason started to remove Doreen's arm from his waist, but she caught his fingers in hers, then leaned against him as though they were Siamese twins joined at the hip.

"Oh, yes," Doreen purred. "We're to be married in just six weeks' time, and we have sooooo many things yet to buy for the house. In fact, we haven't even bought the house yet."

Jason had to stop himself from staring at Doreen in flabbergasted awe. He supposed Doreen thought she was helping his cause by concocting this story, but this time she'd truly gone too far. How in heaven was he going to explain his way out of this? And would Amy even believe him?

"I'm sure that Jason can afford any house you want," Amy said softly.

"Oh, yes, and I know just the house I want, but he won't agree. Don't you think that's mean of him?" She poked Jason in the arm and ignored his furious gaze.

"Dreadfully," Amy said, her voice low.

"But then I guess your Arnie would buy you the best house in town," Doreen said.

Amy straightened her spine. "Of course he would." She flipped the wool challis scarf about her coat collar. "The biggest and best. All I'd have to do is hint and it would be mine. And I'm sure Jason will do the same for you."

"Well, when I do get him to agree, *you* must help me pick out all the furniture."

"Me?" Amy asked dumbly.

"You are the artist, aren't you?"

For a moment both Jason and Amy stared at her.

"I am, actually, but how did you know?" Amy asked.

"You look like an artist. Everything on you matches. Now me, I have trouble matching black and white. Isn't that so, sweetheart? But Jasey loves me just the way I am, don't you, honey bunch?"

Jason tried again to move out of Doreen's grip, but she was holding on tighter than a set of lug nuts to a wheel rim. It did occur to him to hit her over the head with a lunch box that was sitting nearby, but he decided it would be best to explain to Amy once they were alone.

"You, ah, you're to paint the murals?" Jason asked while his hand slipped behind his back so he could try to peel Doreen away from his side.

"Yes," Amy said solemnly, no longer effervescent. "Mildred said there was a mix-up about dates and what was to be painted, so she asked me if I could help out. I brought some sketches that maybe you'd—" She broke off because Jason had given a muffled grunt as though something had hurt him. "Are you all right?"

"Sure," he said, his free hand rubbing his side as though he were in pain. "I'd like to see your sketches. Maybe we could get together tonight and—"

"Now, honey, you promised me that tonight

we'd pick out china and silver. We're getting Nori-
take and real silver," she said to Amy. "Jason,
darling, is so very generous, aren't you, my dearest? At least about everything except a house, that
is."

"Perhaps there are limits to every man's generos-
ity," he said pointedly, glaring down at Doreen
with murder in his eyes.

"Gee, I bet Arnie is generous, isn't he? I mean,
look at that coat you're wearing. He is generous,
isn't he?"

"Yes, of course," Amy answered, looking into
Jason's eyes for a moment and wishing that she'd
never made up this man Arnie, wishing she'd told
him the truth. Wishing . . .

"When would you like to see the sketches?"
Amy asked. "I think you should approve them
before I start painting. And I'm going to need some
assistants, people who can do fill work."

"Sure, anything you need," Jason said as he at
last managed to get Doreen's hands and arms off
his body.

But the moment he was free, Doreen stepped
between the two of them. "That's just what he says
to me all the time. Anything you need, Doreen.
Anything at any time. So it's odd that he won't buy
me a house, don't you think? Maybe you could persuade him."

"Maybe," Amy said, then looked at her watch.

"Oh, my, but I have to go. My mother-in-law will—"

"Oh, then you're married," Doreen said.

"Widowed."

"That's too bad. I am sorry. When did Arnie die?"

"He didn't. He . . . I really must go. Jason, it was good to see you again. I'll be staying at Mildred's, so if you need to talk to me about . . . about work, you know the number." With that she grabbed Max's hand and practically ran from the building.

Outside the car and driver that Mildred had sent to meet her at the airport were waiting for her.

"I hope you don't mind, miss," the driver said as she and Max got in, "but Mrs. Thompkins sent me back to get you and the boy to take you home to her."

"No, no," Amy said hurriedly. "I don't mind. Just go fast!"

Before I start crying, she could have added.

But she managed to hold back her tears until she got to Mildred's, where she found that her mother-in-law had engaged a professional nanny to help with Max. Within minutes Max had decided he liked the woman, and they went into the kitchen to have cocoa.

"Everything," Mildred said. "I want to know everything that's wrong with you."

"I've ruined my life, that's all," Amy said, sobbing into the pile of tissues Mildred handed her.

"It won't be the first time."

"What?" Amy looked up with red eyes.

"Amy, dear, you married a man who was an alcoholic and on drugs, which, may God rest his soul and even if he was my only child, was a disastrous thing to do. Then a rich, handsome man fell madly in love with you and you ran off with just the clothes on your back. And a baby to support. So I'd say that you'd already ruined your life several times."

Amy started to cry harder.

"So what have you done this time?"

"I told Jason I was in love with another man because she was so pretty and they were standing so close and it was like I left yesterday and I think I'm still in love with him, but nothing has changed. He's still the same man I ran away from. He still buys and sells whole towns, and all those women of his are so beautiful and—"

"Wait a minute. Slow down. You act as though I know anything about why you left and where you've been with my grandson for these last two years. And if that makes you feel guilty, it was meant to. Now, slow down and tell me why you agreed to return if you didn't think you were still in love with Jason."

"My editor wants me to get this job so we can use a quote from the president on my next book."

"How did you get started in the book business?"

Amy dried her eyes a bit. "I got a job in New York illustrating children's books. I've done quite well actually and there have been some really successful illustrators who—"

Mildred waved her hand. "You can tell me all that later. So what happened with Jason this morning?"

"He's engaged to be married."

"He's what?"

"He's going to get married. But what did I expect? That he'd been pining away for *me* all these years? In all these two years I've had only two dates, and I only went on those because they were for lunch, so I could take Max. But Max didn't like either man. In fact, with one of the men, Max— well, it was really very funny, although the man didn't think so. Max and I met him in Central Park and—" She stopped because Mildred was giving her a look. "Okay, I'll try to stick to the point."

"Yes, and right now the point is Jason. Just who is he engaged to?"

"Her name is Doreen and you even tried to warn me about her."

Mildred's jaw dropped so far down her chin almost hit her knees.

Amy didn't seem to notice. "She's beautiful: tall, blonde, curvy. I can see why he's fallen for her. Why are you laughing? Is my misery funny to you?"

"I'm sorry. But, Doreen! You have to tell me everything. Every word that was spoken, every gesture, everything."

"I don't think I want to if you're going to laugh at me. In fact, I think maybe Max and I should stay somewhere else."

"Jason is not engaged to Doreen. She is his secretary and she's the sweetest thing but, unfortunately, the worst secretary in the world."

"You don't have to be efficient for someone to love you. I've always been—"

"Jason told Doreen to order duck à l'orange for a dinner for backers for the new municipal pool. Doreen thought he wanted orange ducks, so she had the pool filled with two hundred pounds of orange Jell-O, then had a farmer unload four hundred chickens in the building because she couldn't find a duck farm."

Amy stared at Mildred. "You made that up."

"When Jason was furious, she thought it was because she'd ordered chickens instead of ducks."

Mildred paused a moment to let that sink in. "Doreen files everything by what color the paper feels like. Not what color anything is, just what color it feels like. The problem comes when she tries to retrieve anything because she only knows what it feels like when she's touching it."

"I see," Amy said, her tears drying. "And if she can't find the paper, how can she feel it so she can find it?"

"Exactly. Doreen ordered all new signs for every business in town. They all came back with Abernathy spelled Abernutty."

Amy laughed.

"Doreen collects red paper clips. Ask her about them. She can talk for hours about her collection. She has red paper clips from every office supply store within a hundred and fifty miles, and she will tell you that the amazing fact is that they *all come from the same company*."

Amy started to laugh in earnest. "And Jason wants to *marry* her?"

"Jason wants to kill her. He calls me every few days and tells me the latest method he's come up with to kill her. He can be quite ingenious. I liked the one where he crushed her under a mountain of red paper clips, but I said it might give her too much pleasure."

"If she's so inept, why did he hire her? Or keep her? Why was he hugging her?"

"Doreen may be horrible at her job, but it wasn't exactly her idea to be a secretary in the first place," Mildred said with an arched brow. "You see, she's Jason's former secretary's sister, you know, the formidable Parker."

"Yes, of course. Parker did everything for him. She helped him do all those things to me."

"Yes, yes, Jason was vile. He bought your kid clothes, arranged for you to have a fabulous night out, made Christmas a dream come true, and—

Okay, I'll stop. Anyway, Parker married David and—"

"David? Dr. David? Jason's brother?"

"The very one. Parker was staying at David's house while Jason was with you, and they got to know each other, and, well . . . Anyway, Jason could never replace Parker, so when she begged him to hire her sister, Jason jumped at the chance. He wanted to fire Doreen the first day because she sold his car for a dollar—no, that's another story—but he found out that day that Parker was pregnant and David said it would make his wife miscarry if he fired her sister."

"My husband died while I was pregnant, but I didn't miscarry," Amy said.

"Ssssh. Let's not tell our little secrets, all right? I'm sure David just wanted peace, so once again he conned his big brother." Mildred paused to chuckle. "Jason constantly says that he wants to go back to New York, where the people are less conniving, underhanded, and devious than they are here in Abernathy.

"Anyway, Jason agreed to keep Doreen on until Parker had her baby, and at last count that baby was nearly two weeks late. However, my guess is that once the baby is born, David will figure out another reason his brother should keep Doreen on. But if he doesn't fire her soon, I really do think Jason will murder her."

"Or marry her," Amy said heavily.

"I want you to tell me about that," Mildred said seriously. "What exactly did Doreen say?"

"Something about houses and silver . . . I don't know. I was pretty miserable and Max likes him."

"How do you know?"

"Because she said so. She told me that they were picking out china patterns and—"

"No, I mean, how do you know about Max liking Jason?"

"Because he was more interested in Jason than he was in pulling books off the shelves or seeing what was in the paint cans. And he stood by me and didn't climb on anything. But then Max always did like him."

Mildred listened to all of this without saying a word; then she narrowed her eyes at Amy. "My grandson needs a father. And you need a husband. I've had all I can take of you living in secret somewhere else and my not being able to see my only grandson whenever I want and—"

"Please, Mildred. I feel bad enough as it is."

"You don't feel bad enough that you can make up to me for missing two years of my grandson's life," Mildred snapped.

At that, Amy stood. "I think I should go."

"Yes," Mildred said quietly. "You should go. You should run away, just as you did when Jason wanted you to be his wife." Her voice lowered. "And just as you did when you married Billy."

"I did no such thing!" Amy protested, but she sat down again. "Billy was always good to me. He—"

"He gave you a reason to hide. He gave you a reason to stay away from everything in life. You could have a baby and stay in that old house, and no one expected any more from the wife of the town drunk, did they? Did you think that I didn't know what was going on? I loved Billy with all my heart, but I knew what he was like and I saw what was going on. And after Billy died, you were afraid of stepping outside of that house.

"So tell me, Amy, what did you do when you ran away from Jason? Hide some more? Did you stay in an apartment somewhere and draw your little pictures and only go out with your son?"

"Yes," Amy said softly as tears began to form in her eyes again. Great big drops were spilling over and running down her cheeks, but she made no move to wipe them away.

"Okay, Amy, I'm going to tell you some hard truths. You've hurt Jason Wilding to the point where I don't know if he'll ever recover. He's had a difficult life, and he's learned not to give his love easily. But he offered his love to you and Max, and you spit in his eye and walked away from him. You really, really hurt him."

Amy took a deep breath. "So how do I get him back? I was horrible this morning. I lied and said dreadful things. Should I go to him and tell him the truth?"

"You mean tell him that you've learned your lesson and that you want him so much that you ache inside?"

"Yes, oh, yes. I didn't know how much I wanted him until I saw him again."

"Honey, if you go to a man and tell him you were wrong, you'll spend the rest of your life apologizing to him."

"What? But you just said that I'd hurt him. Shouldn't I tell him that I'm sorry I hurt him?"

"You do and you'll regret it."

Amy stuck her finger in her ear and wiggled it as she tried to open the passage. "Forgive me, but I seem to have gone deaf. Would you go over this again?"

"Look, if you want a man, you have to make him come to you. You know you're sorry you ran out, but you can't let him know it. You see, to a man, conquest is everything. He has to win you."

"But he did already. He went to a lot of effort for Max and me before, but I had some weird idea that I wanted—"

Mildred cut her off. "Who cares about the past?"

"But you just said that I run away and hide and—"

"You do. Now, listen, I've just come up with a plan. That's 'Plan' with a capital *P*. By the time we get through with Jason Wilding, he won't know what hit him."

"I think I'm jet-lagged, because I'm not hearing things properly. I thought your sympathy was with him. I thought he was the wronged person."

"True, but what has right got to do with it? Look, you can't win a man with apologies and truth. No, you win them with lies and tricks and subterfuge. And sexy underwear helps."

Amy could only blink at this woman with her fantastic hairdo. Mildred Thompkins didn't look like the type of woman to use subterfuge on a man. No, she looked more as though she were the type to rope and brand a man. "Underwear?" Amy managed to say.

"Did you ever get that body of yours in shape?"

"I, ah . . ."

"Thought so. Well, I'll get my hairdresser Lars to do something with you. In front of Jason, of course. And maybe we'll even get Doreen her house. Why not? Jason can afford it, and Doreen will probably marry some gorgeous man who knocks her around, so she'll need a house. And you're going to need a lot of help with those murals of yours. And— Why are you looking at me like that?"

"I don't think I've ever seen you like this before."

"Honey, you ain't seen nothing yet. Now, let's go see my grandson."

CHAPTER EIGHTEEN

WHEN AMY AWOKE TWO MORNINGS LATER, SHE KNEW exactly where she was. She was in what had once been her own bedroom in the Salma house. Quietly, she threw back the comforter and padded into the next room to check on Max. He was sound asleep, on his stomach, looking as though he hadn't moved all night.

Poor little thing, she thought, he'll probably sleep another couple of hours.

After tucking the cover about him and smoothing his hair back, she went into the kitchen. But this kitchen bore no resemblance to the old kitchen she'd once tried to cook in. There were no more rusty, broken appliances, no more cracked and peeling linoleum.

Amy wasn't surprised to see freshly brewed coffee in an automatic maker and muffins, still hot, on the counter. "With love, Charles," the card beside the pot read. On a hunch, she opened the refrigerator door and wasn't surprised to see that it was fully stocked. There was a breakfast meal of crepes and strawberries for Max, a red bow tied around the top of the little basket. That Charles somehow knew that Amy and Max were now staying in the house where Max had spent his first seven months didn't surprise her. No one kept a secret in Abernathy.

With coffee, two muffins, and a warm hard-boiled egg in her hand, she went into the living room, and smiled when she saw a fire in the fireplace—a fire that didn't smoke. It would be heavenly to sit and drink and eat and to be able to think in peace about how she got here in a mere twenty-four hours.

It had all started because Max wouldn't stay with Mildred and the new nanny, she thought with a smile. But then, didn't everything start with Max?

Yesterday, as Amy had entered the library, she could feel the heat of Max's body as he lay against her, his head down on her shoulder as he did when he was hurt or, as now, exhausted. Nine-thirty, she'd thought. She'd wanted to have two drawings transferred onto the walls by now, but instead she was just arriving at the library.

Jason had greeted her with a face full of fury.

"How do you expect us to get this done in just six weeks?" he said angrily. "Are you unaware of the time pressure we're under? The opening of the library is six weeks away. The president of the United States is coming. Maybe that doesn't mean much to you, but it means a lot to the people of Abernathy."

"Be quiet, will you?" Amy said, not in the least intimidated by him. "And stop looking at me like that. I've had all I can take of bad-tempered men this morning."

"Men?" Jason said, his face darkening. "I guess your . . . your . . ."

She knew that he was trying to say "fiancé," but the word wouldn't pass his rigid lips. Maybe it would eventually be fun to play the little game that Mildred had concocted, but not now. Now she was too tired.

It was as though Jason suddenly read Amy's mind. "Max," he said softly. "You mean Max."

"Yes, of course I mean Max. He was awake most of the night. I think that being in a new place frightened him, and after a few hours he didn't like being pawned off on the nanny Mildred hired. Max has never liked staying with strangers. He's very selective about the people he likes."

Jason gave her a raised-eyebrow look that said, *That's how we got into all this in the first place*, but he didn't say anything. Instead, with an ease that was as though he'd been doing it every day for years, Jason took the tall, heavy, sleeping toddler from Amy and settled him on his shoulder, where Max lay bonelessly. "He's exhausted," Jason said, frowning.

"He's exhausted? What about me?"

"As long as I've known you, you've never had any sleep," Jason said quietly, his lips playing with a smile.

"True," she said, smiling back.

"Come on," Jason said as he walked toward double doors at the end of the room. When he opened one, Amy drew in her breath.

"Beautiful, huh?" Jason said over his shoulder, his voice quiet so he didn't wake Max. "This was the room the Abernathys built so if they wanted to go to the library, they didn't have to sit with the hoi polloi."

The room was indeed nice, but not because there was anything unusual in it, no carved moldings, no imported tile work. What made the room so beautiful was the proportion of it, with windows all along one side of the room, looking out over the little garden at the back of the library. Going to the windows, Amy looked out and realized that the garden was walled off from the larger play area behind the main part of the building.

"Oh, my," she said. "Is that a private garden?"

"Of course. You don't think the Abernathys were going to play with the town's kids, do you?"

"They sound lonely," she said, then turned back to Jason and held up her arms to take Max. "Here, let me have him. He gets heavy."

Jason didn't bother to answer her, but carefully put Max down on a couple of cushions that were piled on the floor, then pulled a Humpty-Dumpty quilt over him.

"Looks like you're prepared for children's naps," she said, turning her head away so she didn't have to watch him with her son. Sometimes Max stared at men as though they were creatures from another planet, and it made Amy feel bad to think of his growing up without a father.

"Yes," Jason said as he held the door open, waiting for her to leave before him. He didn't shut the door but left it open so they could hear Max if he awoke. "I'm making that into a children's reading room," he said. "We'll have storytellers and as many children's books as the room will hold." He didn't ask, but his eyes were begging her to say that she liked the idea.

"The children of Abernathy are very lucky," she said.

"Mmmmm, well," he said, embarrassed but pleased, she could tell.

"So where do I begin?"

"What?" he asked, staring into her eyes.

"The murals? Remember? The ones that can't wait."

"Oh, yes," Jason said. "The murals. I don't know. What do you think?"

"I need an overhead projector and some assistants and—"

"There's just me."

"I beg your pardon," Amy said.

"Me. I'm your assistant."

"Look, I'm sure you're good at completely renovating a whole town, but I don't think that you can paint camels. Besides, you must have lots to do. After all, you are getting ready for your wedding, aren't you?"

"Wedding? Oh, yeah, that. Look, Amy, I really have to explain."

Part of her wanted to keep her mouth shut and listen, but part of her was scared to death to hear what he had to say. She liked to tell people that she'd been happy when she was married but the truth was that the whole idea of marriage, maybe even the idea of a relationship, scared her to death.

"Could it wait?" she asked nervously. "I mean, whatever you have to tell me, could it wait? I really need to . . . to call Arnie. He'll be worried about me."

"Sure," Jason said as he turned his back to her. "Use the phone in the office."

"It's a long distance call."

"I think I can afford it," Jason said as he went back into the room where Max was sleeping.

"It's awful between Jason and me," Amy said to Mildred over the phone. "Really awful. And I don't know how long I can keep this farce going."

She paused to listen. "No, he hasn't asked me to marry him. He's going to marry Doreen, remember? Stop laughing at me! This is serious.

"No, Max is fine. He's sleeping in the Abernathy Room. Jason is going to make that into a reading room for children.

"No! I am *not* going soft on you. It's just that *I* have never been good at being devious, underhanded, and deceitful." Pause. "Well, if the shoe fits . . . Wait. You'll never guess who just walked in. That's right, but how did you know? You sent her? And *you* bought her *that* dress? Mildred! What kind of friend are you? Hello? Hello?"

Frowning because Mildred had hung up on her, Amy put the phone down and found that her anger at her mother-in-law had put some starch in her spine. Also the sight of Doreen in a teeny, tiny blue dress that looked to be made of angora, a dress that she'd just found out her mother-in-law had bought for the woman, had sent more anger through her. Whose side *was* Mildred on?

"Doreen, don't you look lovely?" Amy said as

she left the office, then gritted her teeth as she saw the blonde wiggle up to Jason. But when Amy saw Jason watching her and not Doreen, Amy gave a big smile. "So when do we start looking for a house for you two, and buying furniture?"

"I think that we need to get these murals done first," Jason said sternly. "Every second counts."

"We have to eat dinner," Amy said brightly. "So why not have take-out in the car on the way to a furniture store? Or, better yet, how about antiques?"

"Used furniture?" Doreen said, sounding disappointed in Amy. "I want new things."

"True antiques go up in value should you ever need to sell them," Amy said, her eyes boring into Doreen's. "Not that you ever would want to sell, but if you buy new furniture, six weeks later you won't be able to get what you paid for them. Antiques increase in value. You can sell them and make a profit."

With great solemnity, Doreen nodded. "Antiques," she said softly, then nodded again.

And in that moment Amy and Doreen formed a bond. Amy wasn't sure how Doreen knew or for that matter how she herself knew what was going on, but both women knew everything. There was a look exchanged between them that said, You help me and I'll help you. Doreen couldn't be so dumb as not to know that within a very few days she was going to lose her job for gross incompetence, so why not get what she could while she had the opportunity?

"Oh, Jason has *no* idea how long these wedding plans take. He won't even take time to look at all the goodies I've registered for over at the mall." Doreen frowned and shook her head disappointedly.

"I bet you've chosen Waterford and sterling, haven't you?"

Doreen's smile broadened. "I knew you were a good person. Isn't she, Jason, darling?"

"Look," Jason said, peeling Doreen's hands off his arm. "I think we should get something straight here and now. I am not—"

"Oh, my goodness, look at the time," Amy said. "Hadn't we better get to work? And, Jason, I would like it very much if you helped me paint. I can use the time to tell you all about Arnie."

Jason's face darkened. "Give me a list of what and who you'll need and I'll see that you get everything." With that he turned and walked out of the library.

For a moment Amy and Doreen stared at each other; then Doreen took a breath. "Tonight?" she asked. "You'll go shopping with me tonight?"

Amy nodded, and Doreen broke into a grin.

And that, Amy thought now as she sipped her coffee and ate her muffin, had been the beginning of one of the most extraordinary days of her life. Looking back at that long day now, she couldn't decide who had been the strangest: Max or Doreen or Jason.

Smiling, Amy settled back on the cushions and tried to sort out her thoughts. First there was Max. She could understand his fit when she'd tried to leave him with his grandmother and the nanny; after all, both women were strangers to him. And, besides, she and Max hadn't spent more than three hours apart since he'd been born, so to suddenly spend a whole day apart would have been traumatic for both of them.

But in the end, Max had hurt her feelings by the way he'd attached himself to both Jason and Doreen. I'm glad he likes other people, she told herself, but still she felt some jealousy.

It had started at the art supply store, where Jason had driven them so she could buy whatever she needed for the job. As usual, Max started getting into everything, and out of habit, Amy told him no, to leave that alone and don't break that and don't climb on that and get down from there and—

"Does he talk?" Jason asked.

"When he wants to," Amy said, pulling Max down from where he was trying to climb onto a big wooden easel.

"Does he understand complex sentences?"

Amy pushed the hair out of her eyes and looked up at Jason. "Are you asking me if my son is intelligent?" She was ready to do battle if he was insinuating that because Max's father was a drunkard that maybe Max wasn't as bright as he should be.

"I am asking about what a two-year-old can and cannot do, and I— Oh, the hell with it. Max, come here."

This last was said with authority, and it annoyed Amy that Max obeyed at once. Even when she used her fiercest tone with her son, all he did was smile at her and keep on doing whatever she'd told him not to do.

Jason knelt down so he was at eye level with the tall toddler. "Max, how'd you like to paint like your mother does?"

"Don't tell him that!" Amy said. "He'll get paint all over everything and make such a mess that—" She broke off because Jason had given her a look that told her her comments weren't wanted.

Jason straightened Max's shirt collar, and the boy seemed to stand up straighter. "Would you like to paint something?"

Max nodded, but he was cautious; he wasn't usually allowed to touch his mother's paints.

"All right, Max, ol' man, how'd you like to paint the room you slept in this morning?"

At that Max's eyes widened; then he turned to look up at his mother.

"Don't look at me; I've been told to keep my mouth shut," Amy said, her arms crossed over her chest.

Jason put his hand on Max's cheek and turned the boy to face him. "This is between you and me. Man to man. No women."

At that Max had such a look of ecstasy on his face that Amy wanted to scream. Her darling little boy could not have turned into a man already!

"So, Max," Jason said, "do you want to paint that room or not?"

This time Max didn't look up at his mother but nodded vigorously.

"All right, now the first thing you need to do is plan what you're going to paint, right?"

Max nodded again, his little face absolutely serious.

"Do you know what you want to paint?"

Max nodded.

Jason waited, but when the child said nothing, he looked up at Amy.

"This wasn't my idea," she said. "*You* are going to clean him up after this."

Jason looked back at the boy and smiled. "Tell me what you want to paint."

At that, Max shouted "Monkeys" so loud that Jason rocked back on his heels.

"All right," Jason said, laughing, "monkeys it is. Do you know how to paint monkeys?"

Max nodded so vigorously that his whole body shook.

Jason took the boy's shoulders in his hands and said, "Now, I want you to listen to me, all right?"

When Max's attention was fully on Jason, he said, "I want you to go with this lady, her name is Doreen, and I want you to pick out everything you need to paint your monkeys. Big monkeys, little monkeys. A whole room full of monkeys. Understand?"

Max nodded.

"Any questions?"

Max shook his head no.

"Good. I like a man who can take orders. Now go with Doreen while I work with your mother. Okay?"

Again Max nodded; then Jason stood and looked at Doreen. She held out her hand to Max; he took it, and the two of them disappeared down the aisles of the art store.

"You have no idea what you've done," Amy said. "You can't let a two-year-old have carte blanche in a store. Heaven only knows what he'll buy and—"

Taking Amy's arm, Jason pulled her in the opposite direction. "Come on, let's get what you need and get out of here. At this rate the president will be here before the murals are started."

"Then maybe you should have ordered the supplies before I arrived. I did send a list to Mildred so everything would be ready."

"And the supplies were purchased," Jason said under his breath.

Amy stopped walking. "Well, then, why are we here buying more?"

Jason gave a sigh. "You wanted watercolors, so Doreen ordered sets with those tiny squares of watercolors in them."

"But I ordered gallons . . . Oh, my. How many of those sets did she order?"

"Let's just say that every schoolchild in Kentucky now has a brand-new set of watercolors."

"Oh," Amy said, smiling; then she couldn't help but laugh. "I hate to ask about the overhead projector."

"Did you know that when you turn a slide projector upside down all the slides fall out?"

"No, I've never tried it. How do *you* know that that's what happens?"

"Because Doreen bought thirteen different brands of them and couldn't find one that could be used 'overhead.' "

"I see," Amy said, trying unsuccessfully not to laugh out loud. "It's a good thing you're marrying her, or you'd be broke in another couple of weeks."

"Amy, I need to talk to you about that."

"Really?" she said. "I hope you aren't going to tell me anything bad, as it puts my work off when I hear bad news. And Arnie— Ow! What was that for?"

"Sorry, didn't mean to hurt you," he said as he released her arm. "You want to get what you need so we can get out of here?"

For the next hour and a half Amy concentrated on what she needed to buy for the huge art project ahead of her, and she couldn't help thinking how wonderful it was to be told that money was no object. It was luxurious in the ultimate to be able to buy the best brands of paint, the best brushes, the best . . . "This is going to cost a lot," she said, looking up at Jason, but he just shrugged.

"What else do you need?" He was looking at his watch, obviously bored and wanting to leave the store.

"Men," she said, which made him look back at her. "Or women." She gave him her most innocent smile. "I need at least three of whichever to help me paint."

"Taken care of."

"That was fast."

"You may have heard that I used to run a business and I often did things quickly."

"Oh? I do believe I heard something about that. So why did you—? Oh, no," she said, without finishing her thought.

Down the aisle, coming toward the cash register, was Max, Doreen following him. Only Max looked liked a young prince leading his elephant, for Doreen was laden with three carry baskets of goods and a paintbrush in her mouth. Only she wasn't carrying the brush across her teeth as anyone else would have done it. No, Doreen had stuck the brush into her mouth so it was sticking out about eighteen inches.

She went past Jason and Amy, spit the brush out onto the counter, then dumped the three big baskets by the register. Only then did she turn to Amy and say, "Your kid is weird"; then she walked away.

"Max, what have you done?" Amy asked, but Max put his hands in his front pockets and tightened his mouth in an expression that Amy didn't recognize as being just like one of hers.

But Jason recognized it and laughed.

"Do you want to buy all of this or not?" the bored clerk said.

"Sure," Jason said, just as Amy said, "No!"

"So which is it?"

"We'll take it," Jason answered, getting out his wallet to hand the young man a platinum American Express card.

But Amy was going through what her son had chosen to purchase, and she was beginning to agree with Doreen that, if not the child, the child's purchases were indeed strange. "Max, honey, did you buy one of every brush the store has?" she asked her son.

Max gave a nod.

"But what about your colors?" she asked. "What colors are you going to paint your monkeys? And what about the jungle? Are you going to make them live in a jungle?"

Before Max could answer, Doreen reappeared with four one-gallon cans of black acrylic paint and a stepladder. "Don't look at me," she said. "He only wants black."

When Max stood there with his hands in his pockets, his face defiant, Jason laughed more.

"Don't encourage him," Amy snapped. "Max, sweetheart, I think you should get another color besides black, don't you?"

"Nope," Jason said. "He wants black and he's going to get black. Now, come on, let's go. We have to get out of here before—"

"The president comes," Amy and Doreen said in unison, then laughed at Jason's scowl. Fifteen minutes later the back of Jason's Range Rover was filled and they were on their way back to the library.

And that's where Amy first met Raphael. He was about seventeen years old, and he had the anger of the world in his eyes, along with an unhealed knife wound on his face.

She took one look at the young man, then grabbed her son's hand and started out the door, but Jason blocked her way.

"Don't look at me like that," he said. "He was all I could get on such short notice. The other painter was bringing his assistants, and this boy needs to do community service."

"Needs?" she said in a high-pitched voice. "Needs? Or do you mean 'sentenced to'?"

When Jason shrugged guiltily, Amy pulled Max to one side.

"You can't leave me," Jason said. "Just because the boy happens to look a little rough—"

"Rough? He looks like something off a Wanted poster. How could you think of letting Max around him?"

"I won't leave you alone with him. I'll be here every minute. I'll carry a gun."

"Oh, now, *that's* reassuring," she said sarcastically. She didn't say any more because Raphael pushed past her and started down the library steps. When Jason grabbed the boy's arm, he said something in a language Amy couldn't understand; then, to her surprise, Jason answered him in the same language.

"Look, Amy, you've hurt his feelings, and now he wants to leave. But if he does leave, he'll have to spend several months in jail. Do you want that on your conscience?"

Amy could have burst into tears, for she knew when she was defeated. "No, of course not."

To her consternation Raphael gave a big grin, then walked back into the library.

"He never meant to leave," Amy said under her breath. "He was manipulating me."

At that Jason laughed, picked Max up, and took him back into the library.

* * *

And that was just the beginning, Amy thought as she ate the last of her muffin and stared at the fire. After that things were too hectic to pay much attention to any one thing. Once she got started with transferring her drawings onto the walls, she was too busy to think about being afraid of Raphael. All day long a steady stream of girls in ridiculously tiny bits of clothing trooped in and out of the library, all of them posing so Raphael could see them. But Amy had to give it to the young man: he kept his mind on his work and never once did his concentration falter.

Not so Amy, as her son seemed to have turned into someone she didn't know. He marched into the room Jason had said was his, Doreen trailing behind him, her arms full of bags of brushes, and closed the door.

And Amy hadn't seen him the rest of the day. Here she'd been worried that her son would fall into a traumatic fit if he was away from his mother for more than three hours, but now Amy was thinking that he'd been wanting to get away from her for his whole little life.

"Don't be jealous," Jason said from behind her. "Max probably recognizes that Doreen is his intellectual equal."

"I am not jealous!" she snapped. "And stop saying bad things about the woman you love."

Then, to add to Amy's annoyance, Jason didn't

make his usual disclaimer about Doreen, but instead, said, "There are other things to recommend her," just so Amy could hear him. As he said this, Doreen was walking into the anteroom, and every male in the library stopped to watch her.

"Drop dead!" Amy said, then stuck her nose in the air and walked away, Jason chuckling behind her.

But Max didn't seem to miss Amy at all. In fact, they didn't see each other all day because Max used Doreen as his emissary.

"He wants to know what monkeys eat," Doreen said on her first trip out of the Land of Secrecy, as Amy had immediately dubbed it after Max had told Doreen not to allow anyone, including his mother, inside the room.

"What do I know?" Amy said over her shoulder. "I'm only his mother."

"Vegetation," Jason said. "Tree leaves."

Doreen went back into the room, but she came out again almost immediately. "He wants pictures of what monkeys eat."

When Amy opened her mouth to speak, Jason said, "Let me"; then he went into the stacks and came back with some books on monkeys and their habitat. One of the books was Japanese.

Doreen took the books into the room, but she was soon out again, one of the books in her hand.

"He says he wants more books like this one. I don't know what he means, 'cause it looks like all the others to me."

"Japanese art," Jason said as he disappeared into the stacks again, returning with his arms laden.

As Doreen took them, she said, "He's a weird kid."

At four o'clock, Mildred showed up with three baskets full of food and told Amy she was taking her out to "lunch."

"Lunch was hours ago," Amy said as she studied the color of the face of one of the horses she was trying to paint.

"And did you have any?" Mildred asked.

Amy didn't answer, so Mildred took her arm and pulled her toward the entrance door. "But I—"

"They're men. They're not going to work if there's food around, so we have about thirty-seven minutes all to ourselves."

"But Max—"

"Seems to be in love with Doreen from what I've seen."

Amy grimaced. "How long were you watching us?"

Mildred didn't answer until they were seated in a booth in a coffee shop across the road, their orders placed, and drinks put in front of them. "I was only there for minutes, but Lisa Holding was in the library earlier to check out a book on abnormal psychology—actually she's engaged to the banker's boy, but she's got the hots for Raphael, so she went to see him—and she told her cousin, who told my hairdresser, who told me that—"

"Told you everything that's going on," Amy finished for her.

"Of course. We're all dying to know what's going on between you and Jason."

"Nothing is going on, really nothing. All the men in there are so hot for Doreen that all work stops every time she slinks in and out of that room. Even my own son—" Amy paused to take a breath.

"Jealous," Mildred said, nodding. "I know the feeling."

"I am *not* jealous. Will all of you stop saying that?"

"Jason told you you were jealous?"

Amy took a drink of her Coke and swallowed, refusing to answer her mother-in-law.

"When Billy was a baby, we were never apart for the first year of his life; then my sister kept him one afternoon and that night Billy refused to let *me* put him to bed."

When Amy didn't answer, Mildred said, "So how are you and Jason getting along? Has he proposed yet?"

Amy didn't say anything but looked down at the club sandwich that had just been set before her. "I know this is a game to you, but I don't want to make a mistake like I made last time."

"You want to talk to me?" Mildred said softly. "I'm a good listener."

"I want to get to know Jason. I want to spend time with him. I made a big mistake the first time I got married, and I don't want to do it again."

She looked up at Mildred with pleading eyes. She wanted to talk to someone, but she was well aware that this woman had been Billy's mother. "I don't want to think what my life would have been like if I were still married to Billy. And one of the few things I know about Jason is that he lies well. He lied to me about being gay, about why he wanted to move in with me, and about why he needed a home. In fact, everything I knew about him was a lie."

She took a breath. "So now I've been told that he's been searching for me for two years, but what does he really know about me, about my son? And what kind of man is he really? Can he take a joke as well as play one?"

Mildred smiled at Amy and said, "With the kind of money Jason has, who cares what kind of sense of humor he has?"

"Me. I care and your grandson cares."

"You're a hard woman to please."

"No, I just want to get it right this time. This time I have to think about a man who will be a *good* father to my son. I don't want Max to get attached to a man, then have the man leave when the going gets rough."

"Or put something in a needle and get out that way," Mildred said softly.

"Exactly."

Mildred smiled. "You've grown up, haven't you?"

"Maybe. During the last two years I think I was able to find out who I am and what I'm capable of. I can take care of myself and my son if I need to. In fact, I can make quite a nice life for the two of us. And I'm proud and happy to have found that out."

Mildred reached for Amy's hand. "And I'm glad you aren't after a man for his money. So tell me all about Jason and Doreen. Tell me everything."

It was nearly six when Amy got back to the library to find a furious Jason.

"Are you going to take a two-hour lunch *every* day?" he said to her.

"If I feel like it," Amy said without blinking an eye.

"She was on the phone to her beloved fiancé," Mildred said. "Love like theirs takes time. I think he might come to see her next week."

Jason's scowl deepened. "In the future, please conduct your personal life on your own time. Now, could we get back to work?"

Amy looked at her mother-in-law and couldn't decide whether to be pleased by her comment or exasperated.

Mildred felt no ambiguity about the situation. "Don't worry," she said, "you can thank me later." With that she turned on her heel and left the library.

So Amy went back to work, even working through the delicious dinner that Charles showed up with. "I owe everything to your son, who has the taste buds of a gourmet," he said over Amy's shoulder.

She glanced around to see everyone eating, Max ensconced in the middle, a plate full of food before him. He didn't so much as look up at his mother.

At nine o'clock, Amy decided that Max had to get to bed, whether he wanted to or not, and that's when she found out that the Abernathy Room door had been locked against her and other intruders. Annoyed, she tapped on the door, and Doreen answered.

"It's time he went home and went to bed," Amy said. "This is too late for him to stay up."

"All right, I'll ask him," Doreen said; then to Amy's further annoyance, she shut the door against her.

Seconds later Max came out, rubbing his eyes from sleepiness, and Amy felt guilty that she had allowed him to stay up so late. Outside, she strapped him in the car seat in the car Mildred had lent her and drove Max home.

And that's when the trouble started, for Max

would not go to sleep. He was usually a good-natured child, but that night he was a demon. He screamed at the top of his lungs, and when Amy picked him up, he straightened out his arms and legs so rigidly that she couldn't get him into the bed.

At eleven he was still fighting, and Amy could not figure out what was wrong with him—and Max only screamed, "No!"

"I'm going to call Jason," Mildred shouted over Max's screams as she picked up the telephone.

"What good would that do?" Amy shouted back. "Please, please, Max, tell Mommie what's wrong," she said for the thousandth time, but Max just yelled and cried, his little face red, his nose stuffed.

"Anything, anything," Amy said as Mildred dialed the phone.

Within minutes Jason was there, and from the look of him he had still been working. He hadn't showered and his clothes had paint on them.

But Jason's presence had no effect on Max. "Poor ol' man," he said as he tried to take him from an exhausted Amy, but Max wanted nothing to do with him.

"I have an idea," he said at last. "Let's take him home."

"Home?" Amy said. "You mean we get on a plane at this time of night?"

"No, I mean his *real* home." Jason didn't give Amy time to say more as he took Max from her, the boy fighting him, carried him outside, and strapped Max into a car seat. By this time the child was too tired to fight, but he still cried.

Amy got into the passenger seat and watched in amazement as Jason drove them through town to . . . At first she couldn't believe her eyes. He pulled into the driveway of what had once been the derelict old house that she and Billy had owned. When she left, she knew that the property would revert to Mildred because she had co-signed on the mortgage, so Amy hadn't concerned herself about the house. She'd assumed that Mildred had sold it, maybe for the building materials, as it wasn't worth much else.

But now the house stood before her in perfect repair. It was what it should have been, beautiful beyond anything Amy could have imagined. Jason had clearly made it his home.

Inside, she didn't have time to look at much as Jason carried a tired, but still whimpering Max through the marble-floored foyer, through the living room, then down the corridor into the room that had once been Max's nursery. It was preserved intact, just as it had been two years ago, everything clean and tidy, as though the baby who used it would be back any minute.

All in all, Amy thought, it was rather creepy.

Jason put Max down, the child looked about for a second, then he relaxed, and finally, at long last, he went to sleep.

"He can*not* remember this place," Amy said. "He was just a baby when he left."

"No one ever forgets love, and he loved this house," Jason said.

And he loved you, Amy wanted to say but didn't.

For a moment Jason waited, as though expecting her to say something, but when she was silent, he said, "You know where your room is," then turned away and went to what Amy knew was the same room where he'd stayed when it was her house.

When she was alone, she went into what had been her bedroom. It was a far cry from what it had been when she lived in the house, and she knew that only a professional decorator could have made the room so beautiful. Even down to the fresh flowers, it was heavenly. Exhausted from her struggles with Max, she did little more than visit the bathroom, then fell onto the bed.

So now it was morning, Max was still asleep, and she guessed that Jason was still sleeping in the spare bedroom.

"And we forgot Doreen's furniture," she said as she finished her tea, then she stood and stretched. She needed to get dressed so she could get to work.

The murals needed to be done before the president's visit, she thought, smiling.

In her bedroom she wasn't surprised to find clean clothes, just her size, in the closet. And when Max woke up, she wasn't surprised to find that Jason had already left the house.

CHAPTER NINETEEN

❦❦❦

"DAMN IT TO HELL AND BACK," JASON SAID AS HE banged his fist on the steering wheel of the car. Just what did Amy think he was made of? He hadn't slept ten minutes last night for thinking that she was in the next room. But his presence didn't seem to have bothered her, for she slept heavily. Quietly, so he wouldn't disturb her of course, he'd checked on her and Max four times during the night.

So now he was driving to the library, it wasn't even daylight yet, and he faced days of working side by side with her. Yet every time he tried to tell her that he wasn't engaged, that he still loved her, she cut him off. Why in the world hadn't he tried harder to explain?

He'd better stop that or he'd go crazy. Sometimes it seemed that since he'd met Amy, all he did was regret his actions. Already he regretted hiring a juvenile delinquent to help paint the library. When Amy saw him and Jason saw her fear, he'd instantly regretted what he'd done. But then Raphael had tricked her, and . . .

"Oh, the hell with it," he said as he swung the car into the library parking lot. Maybe he should do what his brother advised him to do and forget about Amy. Maybe he should find someone else, a woman who would love him back. A woman who didn't run away rather than have to spend time with him.

When Jason entered the library, his jaw was set and he was determined that he was going to stay away from Amy and her son. Maybe it would be better if he went to the Bahamas for a while. He could return just in time for the opening of the library and—

No, he told himself, he was going to stay and fight like a man. Maybe what everyone said was right and he didn't know Amy at all. She certainly didn't *look* the same as when he'd known her before. Two years ago she'd been thin and tired-looking, and she had an air about her of helplessness that had appealed to him.

But this new Amy was altogether different. There was now an air of confidence about her. Yesterday she'd been quite clear about what she needed to paint the murals and who she needed and what was to be done.

"Mildred's probably right, and I only like helpless people," Jason muttered. "I'm sure that after I spend six weeks near her I'll realize that I never even knew her and that the woman I thought she was is a fantasy."

Smiling, he began to feel better. Yes, that was it. Before he'd spent just a few days with her and Max, and of course he'd liked them. As David pointed out they were in need of "fixing," like one of the little companies Jason used to buy then reorganize and sell for a fortune. Amy and Max were like Abernathy. And the fixer inside him wanted to sort them out and do something with them.

Now that he had that solved, he felt much better. But then he looked at his watch and wondered when the hell Amy was going to get there, because, damn it, he missed her.

No, he told himself. Discipline! That's all he needed. He needed the discipline of an iron statue. He was *not* going to make a fool of himself over Amy again. He wasn't going to pursue her, lie to her, trick her, or in any way try to make her like him. Instead, he was going to be all business. They had a job ahead of them, and he was going to do it, and that's all.

Right, he told himself, then looked at his watch again. What in the world was she doing?

When he heard her car pull into the parking lot, he smiled, then went into the office. He wasn't going to let her think that he'd been waiting for her.

"Doreen, dear," Amy said, as she handed half her sandwich to Max, "we forgot all about your furniture last night."

"Yeah, I know," she said, looking down at her sandwich as though it were as appetizing as paper. "I didn't think it would happen."

"And why not, honey bun?" Jason asked.

Both Amy and Doreen looked up at him with startled eyes.

"Are you losing confidence in me already?" Jason asked. "Even before we're married?"

Both women stared at him with their mouths hanging open.

"I was thinking, darlin', that since I don't have a lot of time . . ." Jason shifted the sandwich to his other hand and opened a newspaper that someone had left lying on the table. They were, after all, in a library. "How about this one?" he asked as he pointed to a photo of a big white farmhouse with a deep porch all around the front of the house. It was two stories with a full attic and three dormer windows across the front. Even in the grainy black and white photo the house looked cool and serene under the big trees that were at the sides and back of the house.

"You like it?" Jason asked as he took another bite.

"Me?" Doreen asked.

"Of course. You're the one I'm marrying, aren't I? Unless you've changed your mind, that is." With that he winked at Amy, who still hadn't closed her mouth. "You like the house or not?"

"It's beautiful," Doreen whispered, her eyes as big as the giant cookies Charles had brought in on a porcelain platter.

"Not too little? Too big? Maybe you'd like something more modern."

Doreen looked at Amy as though for advice.

Amy cleared her throat. "If that house is in good condition, it'll hold its value better than a new house," she said softly.

"So what will it be, love?" Jason asked.

It was Doreen's turn to swallow hard. "I . . . Uh . . . I, ah." Suddenly she blinked hard, as though she'd made a decision. "I'll take it," she said enthusiastically.

In the next moment, Jason picked up his cell phone and called the realtor's number. Amy and Doreen sat in silence while they heard him tell the man that he wanted to buy the house pictured in today's newspaper.

Jason paused. "No, I don't have time to see it. No, I don't care what it costs. You do all that, just bring me the papers and I'll give you a check." He paused again. "Thank you," Jason said, then turned the phone off.

"You can't buy a house just like that," Amy said.

"Sure I can. I just did. Now, shall we get on with the painting? What color are these saddles supposed to be?"

"Purple," Amy said, and she had no idea why she was annoyed, but she was.

Twenty minutes later a hot, sweaty man appeared with papers, saying that there had to be a title search and it was all going to take time.

"Anyone living in the house now?" Jason asked.

"No . . ."

"For how long did the previous owners own it?"

"Four years. He was transferred to California and—"

"Then I'm sure the title is fine." Jason picked up a pen and paper, wrote down a number, then handed it to the agent. "Okay, then how about this figure to sell it and forget the title search?"

"Let me make a phone call," the agent said, and five minutes later he returned. "You got yourself a house," he said as he pulled a set of keys out of his pocket. "I think that under the circumstances you should have these."

Jason handed the keys to Doreen. "Now, what else do you need?"

As Doreen clutched the keys to her breast, she looked as though she was going to faint.

Of course no one had done any work while this was going on. And even Amy gave a bit of a smile.

At last I did something to please her, Jason thought, even if it did cost me six figures. And if it took giving a gift to Doreen to get a smile from Amy, then Jason was going to buy Doreen the whole state of Kentucky.

"I hate him," Amy said to her mother-in-law.

"Calm down and tell me again what he's doing."

They were in the library, it was late, and Max was asleep on the little bed that Jason had purchased for him and set up so he could sleep while his mother worked at night. Amy was sanding as she talked, taking the rough edges off a fresco of an elephant draped in gold.

Amy took a deep breath. "I have been here one whole week, we live in the same house, work together all day long, but he pays *no* attention to me. None whatever."

"I'm sure he's just trying to proceed slowly. He probably—"

"No," Amy whined. "The man doesn't *like* me. If you knew what I've done in these last few days . . ."

"Out with it. Tell me all." Mildred glanced over at her grandson and had the sneaking suspicion that he was awake. "I want to know everything that Jason has said to you."

"That's just it. He never says or does anything."

"Is that elephant supposed to be red?"

"Now look what he's made me do." Amy grabbed a rag and began rubbing, which did no good, so she painted over the red with gray; it was going to be a very dark elephant. Taking a deep breath, she tried to calm herself. "I thought he wanted . . . Well, that he was . . . You said . . ."

"That he was in love with you and wanted to marry you," Mildred said quietly. "He was. Is. I'd stake my hairdresser on it."

Amy laughed. "Okay, so I'm being overly emotional. It's just that, well, he's a good-looking man, and I . . ." She glanced at Max, who had his eyes suspiciously tightly closed. "You know that red peignoir set they had in Chambers's window?"

"The tiny one with all the lace?"

"Yes. I bought it, then made sure that Jason saw me in it. I acted embarrassed, but I could have been wearing my old chenille bathrobe for all he noticed."

Mildred raised one eyebrow. "What did he do?"

"Nothing. He drank some milk, then said good night and went to bed. He didn't so much as look at me. But then I'm no Doreen. She has curves that—"

"—are going to turn to fat in about three years' time," Mildred said, waving her hand in dismissal.

"Don't say anything against Doreen," Amy snapped. "I like her. And Max adores her."

Again Mildred looked at the child and thought

she saw his eyelashes flicker, and there seemed to be a crease forming between his brows. "So tell me what my grandson is painting in that room."

Amy rolled her eyes. "I have no idea what's in there, since he won't let me see. Top secret. Secret from his own mother! And he won't sleep at home even if Doreen stays with him because he's afraid that if I'm here in the library alone, I'll snoop."

"And would you?"

"Of course," Amy said as though that were a given. "I gave birth to him, so why shouldn't I see his painting? It couldn't be worse than what I saw inside his diaper after he ate the abacus. And, no, don't ask."

Mildred laughed, especially since she saw that the crease was gone from Max's forehead and there was a tiny curve to his lips. Obviously, the child knew his mother well. "So what are we going to do about you and Jason?"

"Nothing. When this is finished, Max and I go home to . . ."

"To what?" Mildred asked.

"Don't say it," Amy said softly. "We go home to nothing, and no one knows that better than I do."

"Then stay here," Mildred said, and her voice was a plea from her heart.

"And see Jason every day?"

"See *me* with *my* grandchild!" Mildred snapped at her.

"Be quiet; you'll wake Max."

"You don't think taking him away from his only living relative besides his mother will wake him? Amy, please—"

"Hand me that can of green, will you, and let's talk about something else. I'm not running away this time; I'll just be going home."

But right now an apartment in New York City didn't seem like home. With every day that she was in Abernathy, she was remembering things that she'd always liked about the small town. At lunch she made Max quit work and the two of them took a stroll through town so they could eat their sandwiches under the big oak tree at the edge of town. And as they walked, people called out to them to ask how the library was going and they teased Max about his secret room.

"Home" was taking on a new meaning.

CHAPTER TWENTY

AMY DIDN'T TALK TO MILDRED AGAIN FOR A WHILE because for the next ten days she was so busy that she had no time to think about anything whatever. She was existing on little more than four hours of sleep a night, and she was glad that, somehow, gradually, Doreen had taken over the daily care of Max. Amy didn't know whether to be grateful or sad that her son took so well to being bathed by someone other than his mother, dressed by someone else and read to sleep by another woman. And she hadn't had time to sit down with Max and hear what he had to say about spending so much time away from his mother.

Somehow, Amy wasn't sure when or exactly how, Doreen had moved into the Salma house. And why not? Amy thought. It wasn't as though anything private was going on between her and Jason.

After Amy had been in town only two days, Cherry Parker gave birth to a baby girl, and within two weeks Cherry had organized her whole household so well that she had her baby waking for only one feeding during the night (which David took care of) and Cherry was helping Jason to sort out the town of Abernathy in preparation for the library's opening.

"I love you," Jason said once after Cherry rattled off a list of things that had been done and were being done.

"Hmph!" Cherry said, but they could all see that she was pleased by his compliment. She was wearing a white Chanel suit, but strapped across her chest was a huge scarf that had to have been made in Africa, and inside, her newborn daughter was sleeping peacefully.

After Cherry returned to work, Doreen moved into the house with Amy, Jason, and Max and began to look after the little boy. By that time Amy had overcome her jealousy and was just grateful. Every morning Doreen saw that Max was fed whatever Charles had cooked especially for him; then she took the boy to the library. And each morning Max would take the key out of his pocket and make a ceremony of opening the door to the Abernathy Room, then disappear inside for the whole day.

Amy did, however, have a fit of pique once when Charles showed up and Max invited the chef into the "secret" room. Thirty minutes later Charles came out, his eyes wide in wonder, but his lips were sealed.

"Did the boy's father paint too?"

"I don't know," Amy said. "Why?"

"That boy got a double dose of talent, and I just wondered where it came from. Can I be here when the president sees that room?"

"Did you forget that you're catering for him?" Jason shouted from the scaffolding, where he was on his back painting the ceiling.

"Right," Charles said, then leaned forward to Amy to whisper, "How long has he been in this bad mood?"

"Since 1972," she said without hesitation.

Nodding, Charles left the library.

It was well into the third week that Amy began to see what was happening between her and Jason. It took her that long to get over her annoyance that he was paying no attention to her, and she was so busy with the painting that she hadn't had time to look and listen.

But by the third week they were all into a routine, and she began to see things. She wasn't the only one who had changed. Jason had changed too, but she didn't think he knew it. As the days passed, one by one, her objections to him were destroyed.

The first time it happened she hadn't paid much attention. A little boy, about eight, tiptoed into the library and silently handed Jason a piece of paper. Jason made a few marks on the paper, said a few words to the boy, then the child had left the library with a big grin on his face.

The next day the same thing happened, then the next. Each time it was a different child, sometimes two children; sometimes as many as three inter-rupted Jason as he painted.

One afternoon a tall boy of about sixteen came in, shoved a paper under Jason's nose and stood there with a look of defiance on his face. Jason wiped off his paintbrush, then went into the office with the boy and stayed in there with him for over an hour.

If Amy hadn't been up to her neck in painting, she would have been quite curious as to what was going on, but she had too much to do to think of anything but getting the murals on the walls.

It was after the sketches were up and all that was needed was days of fill-in work that she was sitting with Doreen and Max, eating the pasta salad and crab cakes Charles had made for lunch, when two lit-tle girls came in with papers and handed them to Jason.

"What is he doing?" Amy asked.

"Homework," Doreen said.

"What do you mean, homework?"

Doreen waited until she'd finished chewing. "He's Mr. Homework. He helps the kids out with their schoolwork."

"Doreen, so help me, if you make me beg you for every piece of information . . ."

"I think it started as a joke. At the pet store. No, at the barbershop. Yeah, that's it. The men had nothing to do on a Saturday, so they started complaining that they didn't understand their kids' homework, so somebody said that if Jason really wanted to help Abernathy, he'd make the kids smart."

"So?" Amy asked, narrowing her eyes at Doreen. "How could Jason make the kids smarter?"

"I don't know, but the board of education says that our kids are a lot smarter now."

Amy wanted to ask more questions, since she didn't understand anything from what Doreen had said, but she had a feeling she wasn't going to get much more information from this conversation. Amy turned to her son. "So how are you doing in there? Can I see what you're painting?"

Max had his mouth full, but he gave a smile and shook his head no.

"Please," Amy said. "Can't I just have a peek?"

Nearly giggling, Max kept shaking his head no. This was a daily conversation, and Amy went to great lengths to think up persuasions and promises to try to get Max to let her inside the room. But he never came close to relenting.

It was the next day, when David came to the library to view the progress of the murals, that Amy managed to get David off into a corner. "What is this Mr. Homework stuff I've heard about?"

"Mildred didn't tell you?" David asked. "I would have thought she'd have told you everything and then some."

"Actually, I'm beginning to think that no one has told me anything."

"I know the feeling well. My brother has an open door to any child in Abernathy who needs help with his homework."

When Amy just looked at him, David continued. "It started as a joke. People in Abernathy were suspicious of Jason's motives for helping rebuild the town, and—"

"Why? He's a hometown boy."

David took a moment before he answered. "I think you should ask Jason about that one. Let's just say that they were a little concerned that he had some devious, underlying reason for what he was doing. So one day some men were talking and—"

"Gossiping in the barbershop."

David smiled. "Exactly. They said that if Jason wanted to do some good, he could help the kids with their homework."

"And?"

"And he did."

Amy looked at David. "What is it that you're holding back?"

"Would you believe, love for my brother? Jason had Cherry look into the test scores of Abernathy's children, and I can tell you that they were appalling. A town that's had as many out-of-work people as Abernathy has, has depression for dinner each night. Jason knew that it would do no good to give a pep talk to the people that they *should* help the kids with their schoolwork, so he hired tutors."

Turning, David looked at his brother's broad back as he helped Raphael with a painting. "My brother didn't hire dry, scholarly professors. No, he hired out-of-work actors and dancers and writers and retired sea captains and doctors and—" Pausing, he grinned at Amy. "Jason hired a lot of people with a lot of knowledge who wanted to share that knowledge. They came here and worked at the schools for three months. And afterward, quite a few of those people decided to stay here."

Amy was silent for a moment as she digested this information. "And he helps the children with their homework?"

"Yes. Jason said that I'd given him the idea. I'd said that there were 'other children.'" David's voice lowered. "I was talking to him about there being children other than Max."

"I see," Amy said, but she wasn't sure that she did see.

It was after that conversation that she began to watch Jason more closely. Over the past two years, when she'd been in New York trying to make her own way, she'd built up an image of this man in her head. She'd read all the articles about his philanthropy and she'd applied that to her own situation in which Jason had spent a lot of money on her and her child. She had concluded that Jason and his money were one and the same.

But giving of money and giving of yourself to help children understand long division were two different things.

It was after her talk with David that Amy quit trying to entice Jason. Instead, she tried to see him as he really was and not as she'd thought he was based on a few press articles and what she assumed he was like. As secretly as she could, she began to watch him.

For one thing, he complained all the time about how much everything was costing him, but she never once saw him turn down any bill. By snooping through some papers he left lying about, she found out that he owned the local mortgage company and that he had given low-interest loans to most of the businesses and several farms in the surrounding area.

Amy also saw that the formidable Cherry Parker seemed to have changed toward him.

As nonchalantly as she could manage, as though it meant nothing to her, Amy said to Cherry, "Is it just me or has he changed?"

"From black to white," Cherry said, then walked away.

One Saturday morning, Jason wasn't in the library and Amy found him at the school grounds playing basketball with half a dozen boys who made Raphael look like an upstanding citizen. "So how many boys like you has Jason taken on?" she asked Raphael later that day.

Raphael grinned at her. "Lots. We used to have a gang, but . . ." He trailed off, then went back to painting. "He thinks he can get me some more work like this," Raphael said softly. "He thinks I have talent."

"You do," Amy said, then wondered if Jason planned to paint the inside of every building he owned just to give these gangsters a job.

When Jason returned from playing basketball, Amy looked up at him. He was wearing gray sweatpants that were dirty, sweat-soaked, and torn. And she'd never seen any human sexier than he was at that moment.

For a moment Jason looked at her, and Amy turned away in embarrassment, but not before Jason gave her a knowing grin.

"Hey!" Raphael yelled because Amy had just drawn a camel's face on a princess's body.

"Sorry," Amy murmured and refused to turn back around to look at Jason.

Just a few more days, she thought, and a thrill of excitement went through her.

CHAPTER TWENTY-ONE

THE NIGHT BEFORE THE OPENING OF THE LIBRARY, ALL of them except Doreen and Max were working in the library until three A.M.

"That's it," Jason said, and looked up at the others. "Tell me, do I look as bad as the lot of you?" he asked, his voice hoarse from talking so much in an attempt to answer the thousands of questions fired at him that day.

They all looked around. The library was as finished as it was ever going to be.

"You look worse than we do," Amy said, deadpan. "What do you think, Raphael?" After six weeks of daily contact, they had come to know each other well, and Amy marveled that she had ever been afraid of him. And Raphael had proven to be quite talented, both in art and in organization.

"Worse than me," Raphael said, "but then old men always look bad."

"Old?" Jason said. "I'll give you old," he said, then made a leap for the young man, but Raphael sidestepped, and Jason went down hard on the oak floor, and he cried out in pain.

Instantly, all of them were hanging over him. "Jason! Jason!" Amy cried as she put her hands on the side of his head.

Jason kept his eyes closed and a little groan escaped his lips.

"Call a doctor," Amy ordered, but in the next second Jason's hand shot up, grabbed the back of Amy's head, and pulled her mouth down to his for a long, hard kiss.

After a long moment she pulled away, although she didn't want to. And the instant they broke contact, Jason was up and after Raphael. Tackling him, Jason soon brought the younger and much smaller man down to the floor.

"Just didn't want to hurt you," Raphael said when Jason finally let him up.

Amy was standing in the shadows, her back to the group. She was still shaking from Jason's kiss, a kiss that hadn't seemed to mean anything to him.

As he always did, Jason drove Amy home and tried not to think about how lonely his house would be once Amy and Max were gone.

"One more day," Jason said. "And then it's over. You'll be glad, won't you?"

"Oh, yes, very."

Jason didn't say anything, but her words hurt. "Max will be glad to get back, I'm sure," Jason said. "He must miss his own room, one that isn't as babyish as the one he has here."

"Yes, of course," she said.

"And that man . . ."

"Arnie," she supplied.

"Yeah. No doubt he'll be glad to see you."

"Madly," she said, trying to sound lighthearted and happy.

"Amy—"

"Oh, my, look at the time," she said as Jason pulled into the driveway. "I bet Doreen is waiting up for us."

"Sure," he said. "I'm sure she is. Look, about tonight . . ."

"Oh, that," she said, knowing that he was talking about the kiss. "I won't tell Arnie if you won't. I'll just say good night here, and I'll see you in the morning," she said as she made her way up the porch steps. Minutes later she tiptoed in to see Max, to make sure that he was all right. He was sleeping so soundly that he didn't stir when she pulled the covers over him.

"I think maybe your grandmother is crazy," she whispered to the sleeping baby. Amy had promised Mildred that she'd let Jason make the first move.

"Until he tells you that he's not going to marry Doreen, you're to keep on telling him about Varney."

"Arnie," Amy had said.

Max rolled over in his sleep, and for a moment he opened his eyes, saw his mother; then a sweet smile appeared and he closed his eyes again.

To melt the heart, she thought as she looked at him. He had a smile to melt a heart. "And I am blessed at knowing you," she whispered as she kissed her fingertip, then touched it to Max's lips. Standing back, she yawned. Time to go to bed because tomorrow the president of the United States was coming to visit.

"Here's the first of them," Amy said as she put her hand on the paper rolling out of the fax machine; then as she read it, her eyes opened wide, first in horror, then in disbelief.

"Tell us!" Raphael shouted. "What does it say?"

With a face full of disbelief, Amy handed the fax to the boy. His knife wound had healed in the last weeks, and he looked less like a murderer looking for a victim.

Raphael scanned the paper, then let out a hoot of laughter and handed the fax to Jason.

Everyone who had worked on the murals was in

the library huddled around the fax machine as though they were freezing and it was a fire. This morning the president had visited Abernathy, and now they were waiting for the clipping service to send through any reviews of what the president had seen. What was in these reviews could make or break Amy's career.

"A cross between Japanese art and Javanese shadow puppets, with a bit of Art Deco thrown in," Jason read aloud. "Stunning, individual." He looked up at Amy in disbelief.

"Go on," she said, "read the rest of it."

When Jason said nothing else, Amy took the paper from him. "Basically, the article dismisses my murals as 'well executed' and 'appropriate,' but Max's work was . . ." She looked down to quote exactly. " 'Art with a capital *A*.' " Amy looked at her son sitting on a red bean bag chair and smiled at him. "And they are," she said. "They are magnificent."

They were in the Abernathy Room, the room that for six weeks had been locked against Amy as her son created in privacy. When Amy looked back on it, she knew that she had been prepared to console Max when no one was impressed with the black shapes that a two-and-a-half-year-old called monkeys. But when she'd finally seen the room, she was walking behind the president and she had been too stunned by the art on the walls to remember whom she was with.

"Holy Toledo," she'd murmured as she looked around the room, and her words seemed to speak for all of them, as no one else could make a sound. All the walls, the ceiling, and spreading onto the wooden floor was a shadow jungle. Huge, towering bamboo plants seemed to move about in a breeze that wasn't in the room but was in the pictures. Monkeys peeped out from the branches and stems, some eating bananas, some just staring, their eyes looking at you until you stepped back, afraid of being too close to these untamed animals.

"I've never seen anything like it," a short man in the back whispered, and Amy had already been told that he was an art critic for *The Washington Post.* "Marvelous," he said under his breath as he craned his neck this way and that. "And you painted them?" He managed to look down his nose at Amy even though they were the same height.

"No, my son did," Amy said quietly.

The little man turned surprised eyes toward Raphael, who was standing behind her. "This is your son?"

"My son is over there," Amy said, pointing to where Max stood near Jason.

For a moment the art critic and the president as well looked confused. She couldn't mean that Jason was her son, could she?

"Max, sweetheart, come here," Amy said,

holding out her hand. "I want you to meet the president."

After that, all hell broke loose. The president's visit to Abernathy had been undertaken half for the sake of creating some good publicity, as he was on his way to another meeting about the Middle East, and half to pass out scholarly awards to the schoolchildren of Abernathy. Because of his ultimate destination, he was surrounded by journalists. And now, when they saw that this extraordinary room had been created by a very little boy, they started firing questions. "Young man, where did you get the idea for this room?" "Come on, now, tell the truth, your mother painted this room for you, didn't she?" "I think you'd better tell the truth about these monkeys, don't you?" "Just tell us the truth: who painted these pictures?"

Jason picked up Max and glared at the photographers. "If you'll excuse us, it's the artist's nap time. If you must badger someone with your questions, ask one of the adults." At that, he nodded toward Amy and Doreen; then he left the building, Max held protectively to him.

The journalists started shooting questions at Amy, since they knew that she'd painted the murals in the other room, but Amy directed them toward Doreen. "She knows everything. I wasn't even allowed inside the room to see what was going on."

Turning, Amy expected Doreen to be shy with the

press or at the very least reticent, but she wasn't. Instead, she took to being interviewed and photographed as though she'd always lived in front of a camera.

So now, hours later, they were reading about what a triumph of achievement the "Shadow Monkeys" were, and Max was being hailed as a newly discovered genius.

"I always knew he was brilliant; it's just nice to have the world's verification," Amy said proudly, and they all laughed.

"Here it is," Jason said as the door opened and Charles entered carrying three magnums of champagne. Behind him trailed four young chefs carrying great trays of food.

"Who is all this for?" Amy murmured, and Jason turned to her with a broad grin.

"I invited a few people to celebrate," he said. "I knew you'd be a triumph, so I planned ahead."

It didn't matter to Amy that her work had been dismissed and that in her heart she knew that she'd probably never be a great artist or achieve great success, but Max had accomplished both and would continue to do so—and that was enough for her. To have produced a child with the talent that Max obviously had was all that she could ask of life. Except, she thought as she looked Jason up and down, maybe she might like to have a father for her child.

"To us!" Jason said as he raised a glass in a

salute; then his eye caught Amy's and his smile changed to one of intimacy, as though he could read her mind.

Behind the chefs came the man who owned the general store in Abernathy, and behind him came his wife and three children. They were followed by the hardware store family and the elementary school principal, then the four teachers at the school, then—

"Did you invite the whole town?" Amy asked.

"Every one of them," he said. "And their kids."

Amy laughed and knew that she'd never been happier in her life than she was at that moment. It's too good to last, she heard a little voice say, but she took another sip of champagne and thought no more as music came from the outside garden and, to her astonishment, she found that a band had set up there and was playing dance music.

Smiling, she turned to Jason, who was watching her, and from the look on his face, he wanted her approval. She lifted her glass to him in a toast.

At one A.M. a fleet of cars arrived in front of the library to take everyone home. Jason had even given lists of addresses to the drivers so no one who'd had too much champagne had to worry about remembering where he lived. Doreen carried a sleeping Max out to one of the cars. She had already told Amy that she would put Max to bed and stay with him until Jason and Amy got home.

In an astonishingly short time, Amy and Jason were left alone in the library, and after the frivolity of the party the library seemed huge and empty. Amy sat down on one of the hard oak chairs by a reading table and looked up at Jason. The triumph of her son was still running through her veins, and it would for the rest of her life.

"Happy?" Jason said, standing in front of her, looking down at her with an odd expression on his face. He had a glass of champagne in his hand.

"Very," she murmured, looking up at him boldly. Maybe it was the soft light in the room, all those reading table lamps, but he looked better than he ever had before.

"You aren't a bit envious of Max stealing the show?"

"What a sense of humor you have," she said, smiling. "I have given birth to the greatest artist this century has known. Let's see my son top *that* one."

Jason laughed, and, before he thought, said, "I have always loved you."

"Me and every other female in this hemisphere," she said before she could stop herself.

At that Jason threw his glass against the wall, where it shattered into thousands of tiny shards. In one strong swoop, he grabbed Amy to him, pulling her out of the chair and up into his arms. Then he kissed her hard. But the kiss soon softened, and the moment his tongue touched hers, Amy's body went limp in surrender.

"So long," she murmured. "It's been so very, very long."

Jason held her to him, caressing her back, his fingers entangled in her hair. "So long since me or since . . . him?"

"There is no 'him,' " she said, her face pressed into his neck.

At that Jason pulled her away from him and held her at arm's length. "There is no Arnie?"

"Only the man who owns the potato chip factory."

It took Jason a moment to understand; then he pulled her back into his arms. "Me. I bought the factory and named it after my great uncle."

"What about Doreen?" Amy wanted to say more, but she couldn't think with Jason's hands on her body.

Jason grabbed her with all the pent-up passion he'd been holding back and kissed her with all his body. "I love you, Amy," he whispered against her lips. "I've loved you forever and will always love you. Doreen made up our engagement . . . she thought she was doing me a favor. I tried to explain."

Amy's sigh of relief said it all. She believed.

Jason pulled Amy even closer and looked deeply into her eyes. "Don't go, Amy. Please don't go away. Stay here with me forever."

What could she say but yes? "Yes," she whispered, "yes."

After that there was no more breath for words as they tore at each other's clothing, pulling and tearing, tugging, then giving great sighs of pleasure as each new bit of skin was exposed. When they were naked, they fell down on the mattress that Max had used for his afternoon naps, and when Jason entered her, Amy gasped in pleasure and disbelief—how could she ever have left this man? How could she—?

"Amy, Amy," Jason kept whispering. "I love you. I love you."

And all Amy could answer was, "Yes."

It was an hour later when they lay still on the mattress, exhausted, their arms wrapped tightly about each other. "Tell me everything," she said, sounding like her mother-in-law. "I want to know about all the women, about everything. What I see and what I feel coming from you are two different things. I want to understand, to know you, but I can't. I need words," she said.

At first Jason was reluctant to talk; after all, what man wants to tell a woman how much he needs her? But once Jason began to talk, he couldn't stop. Loneliness is a great tongue loosener. And it hadn't been until he'd met Amy and Max that he'd known how empty his life was.

"I'm sorry," she said, and the words were from her heart. "I'm sorry for your pain."

He told her how difficult it had been in Abernathy, how the townspeople had fought him. "I thought they'd be grateful, but they resented a New Yorker coming in here and trying to tell them what to do."

"But you were born and raised here," Amy said.

When Jason said nothing, she pulled away so she could look at him. "What is between you and this town? And your father?" she asked softly. "Not even Mildred would tell me what happened."

It was a while before Jason spoke. "Sometimes a person has to face his worst fears, and . . ." He took a deep breath. "You know that my mother died when David was just a baby."

"Yes. And I know that your father had to raise you two boys alone."

"That's his version of it," Jason said angrily, then stopped himself. "My father didn't have much time for kids, so after my mother died, he left us alone to fend for ourselves."

"Ah. I guess that means he left you to take care of David by yourself."

"Yes."

"But I don't think that's what you're angry at Abernathy about, is it?"

Again Jason took his time, as though he had to

calm himself down before he could speak. "My mother was a saint. She had to be to be married to a cold bastard like my father. When she learned that she was dying, she told no one. She didn't want to be a burden to anyone, so she went to the doctor alone, kept the news to herself, and we kept on living like nothing was wrong."

As he paused, Amy could feel the tension in his body. "But one of the Abernathy gossips saw her in a café in a motel about thirty miles from here, then went home to spread the word that Mrs. Wilding was having an out-of-town affair."

"And your father believed the gossip," Amy said softly.

"Oh, yeah. He believed it so much that he got her back by jumping into bed with some hot little number from—" He cut himself off until he was calm again.

"I was the one who found out the truth. I cut school and hid in the backseat of my mother's car. I was in the waiting room of the doctor's when she came out. She made me promise not to tell my father. She said that life was to be lived, not mourned."

"I would have liked to have met her," Amy said.

"She was wonderful, but she got a raw deal."

"She had two children who loved her, and it seems that her husband was mad about her."

"What?!" Jason gasped.

"How did he take it when he found out that his wife was dying?"

"He never said a word about it, but after her death he locked himself in a room for three days. When he came out, he took on extra work so he was never home, and as far as I know, he's never spoken her name again."

"And you doubt that he loved her?"

For a moment, Amy held her breath. Maybe she'd gone too far. People liked to hold on to their beliefs and didn't like to have them contradicted.

"I guess he did," Jason said at last. "But I wish he'd loved us more. Sometimes I got sick of being my kid brother's mother and father. Sometimes I wanted to . . . to play football like the other kids."

Amy didn't say anything, but she could see the pattern in Jason's life. His father had taught him that making money was everything and that if you worked enough, you could block out pain and loneliness and all sorts of unpleasant emotions.

She snuggled against him, her flesh touching his, and she could feel that he was beginning to become aroused again. But he held back. "And what of your life? You seem to have done well."

It was on the tip of her tongue to tell him that she had done very well, that she'd gone off and made herself a fortune, that she didn't need any man. But the words wouldn't come out of her mouth. It was time to tell the truth.

She took a deep breath to calm her pounding heart. "Yes, I've done well, but at first I was afraid that Max and I would starve," she said at last. "I did a very stupid thing when I ran away."

"Why didn't you call me?" he demanded. "I would have helped. I would have—"

"Pride. I've always had too much pride. When I found out what Billy really was, I should have left him, but I couldn't bear to hear people saying that I gave up just because I found some flaws in the man."

"Flaws?" he said in astonishment.

Turning on her side, Amy put her hand on his face. "My marriage to Billy was awful," she said. "I was miserable. I hated the drinking and the drugs, but I also hated that he was weak, and that he could sacrifice everything just so he could feel good."

"When you met him—" Jason said softly.

"He was in one of his sober periods. But I should have known. He made all sorts of remarks that later I remembered and knew that they had been clues to what and who he was. And when you came along, you seemed so perfect, but then I found out that you, like Billy, had a secret life, and I couldn't handle it. I ran. I just picked up my son and ran as fast and as far as I could. Can you understand that?"

"Yes," he said as he ran his hand up her bare arm. "It makes sense. You're here now and—"

"But it was so awful! I was so frightened and alone and—"

Jason turned her in his arms until her face was buried in his shoulder. "Shh, it's all over now. I'm going to take care of you and Max, and—"

"But everyone will think I've married you for your money. They'll say that I learned my lesson with Billy, so this time I went after a man with money."

Jason smiled into her hair. "I think it's more likely they'll say that I went after you. Did Mildred tell you that I had private detectives looking for you for over a year? They could find nothing. Yet all the time Mildred knew where you were." There was a touch of bitterness in his voice.

"But she didn't. She just found us a few months ago, and that was by accident."

Jason pulled away to look at her. "How did she find you?"

"She bought Max some Christmas presents because she said that she never gave up hope of seeing him again, and one of them was a children's book. She saw my photo in the back of a book I had illustrated."

"That simple," Jason said, then smiled as he remembered all the agony he'd gone through with the private detectives. "And what is your pen name?"

"My real name is Amelia Rudkin. Using Billy's

name was just a courtesy to him, but I never bothered to change it legally. I was listed in the New York phone directory. I guess I never gave up hope that you would look for me and find me."

Jason tightened his arms around her. "I'm glad it happened. If you hadn't run away, I would have continued as I was. I'm sure I would have kept on working without stop just to prove to you that I could support you and—"

"But why would you need to prove anything to *me?*"

"Because you're the woman I love, the only one I've ever loved."

Turning, she looked at him. "But if Mildred is to be believed, the people of Abernathy have given you such a hard time that by all rights you should want the first plane out of here."

"I agree. They are an ungrateful, complaining lot, but, on the other hand, they treat me as a person. Mr. William, who owns the hardware store, told me that I'd always been hardheaded and I hadn't changed. Maybe it was that I was at last surrounded by people who weren't toadies that kept me here. If I raised an eyebrow at my employees in New York, they backtracked and said what they thought I wanted to hear. But here . . ." He smiled.

"Here they tell you what they think of you," Amy finished for him.

"Yes. Mildred told me day after day that I was

the reason you'd left. She said that David and I had played such a nasty trick that any woman in her right mind—"

"Don't hint that *I* was in my right mind, to run off with a baby and no way to support him."

"Ah," Jason said, smiling, "but it's all come out in the end. At last Max will have a father. If you'll have me, that is."

"I'll take you if you want us," Amy said softly. "But I . . ."

"What?"

"Today has been a revelation to me, for today I've found out that my two-and-a-half-year-old son is not only a better painter than I am, he's smarter than I am. I'm afraid that I'm like so many other people and I couldn't see *you* for your money. But Max always saw what was inside you."

"Real smart kid," Jason said, making Amy laugh. "You think you'd like to have more of them?"

At that, Amy groaned. "Morning sickness, exhaustion, and, oh, no, not breast-feeding again!" When she saw Jason's face, she laughed. "Yes, of course I'd like to have more of them. Half a dozen at least. Think they'll have gray hair?"

But before Jason could answer, they were hit by a solid projectile that landed smack on Jason.

"What in—" he began as he tried to sort out arms and legs that seemed to be everywhere.

"You little devil," Amy said, laughing as she started to tickle her son. "You made Doreen bring you back, didn't you?"

For a moment Jason was a bit horrified at the thought of what the child might have seen and heard, and he was also shocked at the lack of privacy. Little did he know that such adult things were gone forever.

But he didn't have time to contemplate his fate and the blessings of it because Max stood up and shot himself forward. Amy knew what was coming and protected her face with her arms, but Jason caught the full weight of the boy on his face.

"Monkeys!" Max squealed, then started bouncing on his new father's stomach.

LOSE YOUR HEART TO THESE
ROMANTIC SERIES FROM

Jude Deveraux

The Montgomery Annals
HIGHLAND VELVET
VELVET ANGEL
THE VELVET PROMISE
VELVET SONG

The James River Trilogy
COUNTERFEIT LADY
LOST LADY
RIVER LADY

The Chandler Twins
TWIN OF FIRE
TWIN OF ICE

POCKET BOOKS
A VIACOM COMPANY